EMMALENA L. ELLIS

Ginsterpigs

Cover Photography Design by Paul Cocken © 2012

https://www.paulcockenpvr.com/

Image edits and website tweaks by Nick Koriagin, who dedicated many hours of his time labouring over seemingly endless files and documents to help create the author's website and the final dust jacket.

The author gives her sincerest thanks and gratitude.

https://www.koriaginn.com/

First edition

ISBN: 978-1-8384845-8-3

This book was professionally typeset on Reedsy.
Find out more at reedsy.com

This book is dedicated to the memories of my grandparents Patrick and Patricia, who always inspired me to write from the heart.

To my dearest mother Louisa, who has been my biggest supporter, from my first tentative manuscript at the age of 3, to my new chapter.

To those who brought me cups of laughter and inspiration; sweet milk with two sugar teas.

And thanks to all the selfless members of the NHS who have bravely put themselves on the front line during the Covid-19 pandemic of 2020-2022.

Prologue: Frank the Ignorant

I 'm sat here drinking a cheap lager with a lesbian from Dover. The two of us are sitting on the cobbled wall made of rambling brick that slopes down at a jagged angle beside the flaking green paint of the bus shelter. She, with a cigarette perched between two tightly pinched fingers, held up to overtly red crimson lips. I, with a bouquet of cheap chips in greasy newspaper, which seemed a good idea at the time.

If I were to try and ask where the lady was headed, the current short absent-minded bursts of cigarette stream would probably erupt, diluting into vulgar terms. That much I understand, reading between the lines from the tattoo on her upper left shoulder.

I can glimpse it just at the cap of where the sleeve of her top would be, were she not wearing a strapless black mini dress. Or, if she were not dangling a faux leather jacket with leopard spot lining across her forearm. Regardless, the tattoo is visible, even from the furthest side of the bench, as I purposefully distance myself away from her.

The tattoo is a thick black ink capital letter inscription, which is simple, unpoetic and to the point -

BITE ME.

The air is crisp, the chips soggy.

"Wanker!"

Her words come across as a shock. Shattering my delirium and a fair few of the chips as if whip-lashed from the oral spray now emanating. In my panic, they drop neglected onto the floor.

Instinctively, I turn towards her as if to confront this abuse, albeit silently.

1

I am mulling over the moment in my mind. It is safer that way.

Wanker? But you haven't even met me yet. While, indeed, I know I'm not perfect, you don't even know me.

God, I'm sweating, and that damn twitch is back again. The one behind my left ear.

"Fool!" That would have been more apt; had her comment been aimed at me at all.

Madam is not even talking to me, and as I scratch the hairs along my eardrum in embarrassment, her short-snipped tone verbalises rapidly into her mobile phone.

The device in question is a metallic red thing that matches her choice of accessories. A hefty red handbag and ruby painted nails. Her phone barely conceals what appears to be a wart or, more likely neglected makeup on her cheek. Nor does it conceal the vicious puffing of her cigarette. She holds both things to her mouth at increasingly short intervals as she vents and screams into it.

In the meantime, she has hunched up her jacket so that it is hastily slung over her arm, and it hangs like a noose against her humerus, leaving her free to multitask more efficiently.

There's something almost comical about these situations. The way she's *talking*, no, screeching down the line suggests that if she weren't a lesbian before now, she soon would be - perhaps swearing off men for good after this conversation.

Not that I truly know what is being reciprocated on the other side.

Logically I suppose, of course, from my limited understanding of the call, the recipient of said conversation has either been drowned out or obstinately deafened by her continuous outburst.

Her frustration building, she starts swinging her handbag.

It's a large, bulging thing with crocodile style patterning - I don't think I've ever seen a red crocodile. Perhaps they're found in America -somewhere I've never been.

The bag darts about in continuously wide circles that narrowly manage to miss the shelter wall.

Then the lady stops, momentarily calm as she heaves in frustration, before yelling: "PIG!"

If I had a girlfriend, the first thing I'd possibly tell her is that the term *pig* does nothing. It only boosts male self-esteem. Pigs are an intelligent species; at least guinea pigs are. But then I'm obsessed with many things, guinea pigs being one of them.

Perhaps, that's why I'm single; that's what my sister tells me. Still, I'm okay with that.

I have always preferred people watching - dependent on the company, but this woman - she frightens me.

Self-consciously my mind begins to fog away from her. I choose to let the words become indistinct, and whilst I can watch her lips form each term, should I choose, in this instance, I no longer have the desire or patience to listen.

I take up the lager once more. It has been resting on the wall; a nice clean slab, relatively speaking, I have kept it away from the moss and smouldering pile of cigarette butts and chips at my feet. I'm surrounded by rubbish, continuously blown up from the road to the bricks by the rush of cars that come with the daily traffic.

My companion still brandishes her bag here and there, hunching her coat further up her forearm to avoid it slipping onto the floor. I suppose it is too warm to wear.

As for me, I begin to feel the onset of pins and needles shooting up my leg and the uncomfortable feeling of the sharp pricks of stone in the wall. Almost as though I instinctively know I am being watched, I turn back again.

Sure enough, the lady's noticed me, and she's rounding on me with scrunched up frustrated eyes.

"Fan-bloody –tastic! Is the bus not comin'?"

"Of course, it is," I hear myself reply, shuffling further away from her. "It always comes; it's Tuesday, so it will come. It always comes Tuesdays." My words, as always, were somewhat clumsy and disorganised - the reproduction of a hazy sunny day and a weekday afternoon.

So here we are, the flat lager, the lesbian, the empty wrapper paper from

the chippy, the greasy after-smell of fried chips. Dover is 5 miles north.
  This is my life.

Chapter 1: Bus Ride Slumbers

My name is Frank Samuel Davis. I live in Cocklescanslanky, Kent, a small, isolated place which very few people talk about and even fewer ask. The town's population is mainly the odd thirty and fifty-year-old fogies. Then there are the cluster of kids and their tired, worn out, tracksuit bottomed mothers, and the socialites - who flock around the coast, with their sunflower strewn hats, with plastic palm footed lawns and me.

Cocklescanslanky, a town which the BBC once recalled, albeit fleetingly, in a documentary as an *"indispensable part of Kent, which crawls out of Britain's rich garden unseen and insignificant."* - Whatever that means. Still, it was deemed impressive enough for the town council. They quickly pasted the phrase on the town's advertisements and billboards before, in time, recovered in overtly shiny glue and metaphorical journalist's whitewash.

Statements like this were notably grand and overstated, in the kind of way that they would make someone influential sit up and notice if indeed they chose to come this way - they never did.

Cocklescanslanky, my mother could never stand the place. Soon after my little sister turned 12, and I was 15, Mum insisted that my father vacate his job and move the family to Dover. Schools were better there, she argued, and there was more choice in the shops.

Despite all this, it wasn't an immediate concern to my sister and me. Back then, our thoughts were somewhat more simplistic. Childlike. *Why* should we care how many clothes were in our mother's wardrobe when ours were filled with hand-me-downs from our extended family, and budgeted charity shop finds? Or *how* such situations made us appear to other members of dignified society.

Our attention was moot, otherwise distracted, as our eyes flicked back and forth from their discussion to the television with disinterest. All the while, my lips were glued shut with liquorice and gobstoppers.

Dad said nothing in those days, merely peering at her from the paper neatly folded open over his knee, occasionally grunting in disinterest. Jack Davis would not *"bore his children with politics,"* he told her. After all, I was *supposed* to be thinking about girls: teenage issues, cartoons and video games.

At that time, and to a lesser extent now, there were two girls in my life. One was the prettiest girl on the planet and my first love. She had brown eyes and black and white tresses of hair in a slight wispy parting. In contrast, the second girl was quite plain. She had a fringe that was drab and ordinary, almost mousy. The first girl was called Mol; she was three years old, my first guinea pig. The other? That was Hanny, my sister.

At 45, I wasn't bad looking, certainly not evil - I had a bulging oblong of a face which was slightly squat at the corners; perhaps they thought I might grow into it later. Greyish eyes framed by my round cheaply produced prescription glasses and a gradual, receding hairline of strait-laced schoolboy brown hair. I had no particular build, I had never been good at sports, but my clothes fitted where they touched.

Clothing wise, I favoured day in and day out the same faded grey anorak, with a matching jumper – which was currently lightweight for the summer. I offset this with a pair of brown corduroy trousers with shoes to match and a slightly off colour white shirt - a habit I suppose I picked up from work; and a sort of eggplant one at the back of the wardrobe, which I saved for when I went out on special occasions.

Not that today was not going to be one of them.

My childhood was quiet in my way, not academically studious, but I enjoyed reading and observing world affairs through my various notations in notebooks. My favourite hobby was, of course, sitting by the edge of Mol's cage in quiet conversation and following the routes of buses using an ordinance survey I had found at the back of my grandfather's desk.

As I grew older, my mother – guilt-ridden (however momentarily), had once more set me up with a few blind dates. She had previously neglected my sister and me in favour of her geraniums. Although, of course, this was merely another of her short-lived aurora cleansing.

Mum was determined if blind-sided when it came to pairing me off with girls. She had a habit of picking those dressed up to the nines, though they all seemed to be lacking the mindset I wanted. She seemed drawn to those with supposedly *perfect* model looks and slender forms. All of them were so skinny. I sometimes imagined that they might snap like pretzel sticks. Trouble was these were the sort of girls that Mum hoped would produce *"only pretty grandchildren!"*- like her side of the family - or so she said. But they were also the type of girls that Dad had occasionally pointed out to Hanny on the television; and told her that was *perfection*, but only when he thought he was out of earshot of my rather argumentative, two-faced mother. I can only suppose she is the one he had *settled* with, for convenience sake, or perhaps to avoid a headache at the time.

Now - aged 75, with fewer pipes and higher cholesterol - Television remains for him as it did then: a necessary form of entertainment and escapism from her enforced domestication.

I prefer buses and guinea pigs.

* * *

Bus spotting is an art. Others might say it is less refined than train spotting. But when it comes to transport, buses alone give me that trembling satisfaction. Watching the vehicle's cushions deflate one by one as the bus pulls to a stop, it's almost as if they are mattresses protecting their cold, painted metallic structure from the black concrete slabs of pavement and muddy B-Roads.—A safety net in a bleak, uneventful world.

Take the Alexander Dennis Enviro 200, which is as ever an impressive beast, even with its previous iteration of the TransBus Enviro 200. Whenever it braked, it would envelop the pathways with a steamy-like belch, like

7

a group of drunks in a choir. The doors always judder open, emitting yet another repeated mechanical sigh, swinging and hitting the stops in an asthmatic fashion.

Thus, when the number 35 came to a stop beside the crumbling shack of the bus shelter, I inhaled, in much the same way a smoker might – long and deep. I was subconsciously letting the smell of faintly burning rubber and diesel flood through my fuel-sensitive nostrils. With each gust of air, it makes me wonder and sometimes worry if the old wreck has met its final stop, a retiree in his prime, choosing never to move again. Thankfully, she continues to both my delight and relief.

In my strange, nonsensical way, I marvel at this bus, of blue and mushroom accents, its moniker reading **DONALD'S** and the miles travelled to get here. I'm somewhat fascinated by the routes on the sides of the bus signs, tracing the thin grey line with multicoloured squiggles, thinking about the delays, the passengers and of course - the driver.

This driver was irritable. He had one of those babyish faces about him; it was all puffed up and red, inflated like a balloon. It must *be one of those days,* I *suppose.*

There was a badge - pinned on his shirt that would have read his name, but I have decided, given his mood, not to look. It's one of those things you don't or at least pretend not to notice. It's like a code, a secret ritual: he was just T*he Driver.*

In my youth, I had proudly known all the drivers' names. Although this young, fresh-faced man seemed relatively new to the process. I made a mental note to look it up later on the *DONALD'S* website. There I could update my notes accordingly - It pays to have updated records.

As for the rest, I imagine his mood was down to his coffee. Coffee will make anyone miserable, especially on a Tuesday at 3:30 in the afternoon.

Thankfully, I felt refreshed, the beer was still lining my stomach, and the little digitalised clock above the mirror blinked in red numerals; noon - unchanged and disconnected, like the town, from the rest of the world and civilisation.

Miss "fan-bloody-tastic," glared at me, perhaps mistaking me for the mysterious former recipient of her phone call. Because although she had initially gone on ahead, she slightly bustled in her walk with self-importance, although madam somehow seemed to lack it once she boarded the bus.

I watched as she played for time by stuffing the smouldering remnants of her cigarette into the flaking trough at the side of what I presume might have become a bin. It might have at one time contained advertising, brochures, fledglings of dying tourism. But it seemed the billboards were proving an unsuccessful venture for the council after all.

So, I proceeded towards the glass partition. Unlike my companion, I did not want to delay the journey further. As always, I remembered the well ingrained, well-versed routine of boarding a bus. It's something I have done many times before.

After a simple exchange of nods between the driver and me, I now sat comfortably. I had positioned myself in the middle of the bus and slipped the bus pass back into my wallet.

In contrast, however, she continued to stall. I watched as the lady remained rooted in her former position; as her face pressed close to the glass separator glowering, she was determined to gain her exact change from a fiver.

All the while, the silver key in the ignition knew my secret. It, too, wanted to travel, grunting impatiently at the lady's negligence as she stormed past the driver and was finally aboard.

Doing a quick count, I surmised about three, no seven of us, if you included the driver, who had embarked today. Still, her ladyship had decided on the front of the bus, squishing past an uncomfortable looking, square-faced man, who coughed timidly. The other occupant, who was standing in the bay area, was a mother pushing a pram - whose pale arms were filled with fading red welts from her large, overstuffed plastic shopping bags she had drooped towards the floor. On the pram, she had rested a cake tin, unknown to the sleeping occupant within. Back and forth, she pushed the buggy in small, measured rocks with her left hand, as her right remained gripping onto an impatient toddler with a few spare tingling fingers.

You may be wondering why I chose the middle of the bus. You will question this and perhaps think that a bus spotter like myself would surely wish for the front of the bus. After all, as I had just explained, the bus was not busy.

Rooky mistake - I'll help you by observing the art of seating.

Should you choose to sit in the front of the bus, you'll always be unable to obtain an accurate view of all of the occupants within. As such, one might miss some key fragment of character, something I pride myself in finding, sourcing out unique specimens, which in idle hours I notate later in a small leather notebook kept in my side pocket.

I advise against the back of the bus because this end prevents ease of travel. You are both squished and prodded by an array of arms, shoulders, and God help me, legs belonging to somewhat glue-faced teens. Their bodies will be pressing and heaving in lustful bouts of Adrenalin and raging hormones.

So quite naturally, the middle is my preference. In the middle, one might have a good view of passengers and landscape, and there is a comforting motion as the bus ascends or descends across the roads and cliffs of Dover.

I had been dozing, half closing my eyes, lulled by the equilibrium of bus hum. My now muted former companion, after a silent reproach from the worn-out mother's glare, had returned her phone to her ruby waxy handbag, giving us all a temporal revive from her sharp, acidic tone.

We were going slowly, but not unbearably so. The driver had unwound his window, and a gentle breeze wafted over my sticky brow. I smiled softly to myself in quiet satisfaction. Outside, a white Peugeot whimpered in protest as the bus swept past it, letting the icy unfeeling box-shaped vehicle get a repainting in a thin layer of mud. Karma perhaps for being in the way or on the road. I was happy.

Yet, it seemed I was doomed to be rudely awoken. Naively upon boarding, I had believed I had built some form of rapport with my fellow travellers, and yet now the silence was broken by the shrill, piercing interjection of the now hysterical toddler.

The child must have sensed my frustration as my eyes opened because his face turned to me before he began crying again. Sudden, sharp foghorn-like sounds began erupting from his tiny lungs. One day perhaps, I'll experiment with how this commotion could be achieved. If that is, I ever manage to find a specimen ready to scream at me; without the mother frantically searching for her mobile to call the police. Seemingly to remove the madman from being near her precious child. However, it is probably the mother who would be traumatised. After all, wouldn't she rather the child be silent than draw attention to her nervous disposition and her ever-growing desire to disappear at that precise moment?

As on cue, the mother's face crumbled. She began vainly attempting to quell the child. "Willy, you'll wake the baby!" She bemoaned and awkwardly hunched to his level on the ground as best she could. As she did, I watched as all the shopping bags dropped to the floor like bars of lead piping. Her gaze was intense and almost squirrel-like as she began subconsciously looking over her shoulder, anxiously aware of everyone else, before returning her gaze to her child again. "Willy, please, people are starting to stare!"

Isn't it ironic? She can square off another woman with a dark look, but she cannot confront her offspring. Perhaps, it is because she worries; she's too harsh, or maybe too soft. Or is it the fact that no matter what she does, 'people will talk,' at least in her mind? With such pressure, she cannot understand whether she has failed and whether it is through her duty of motherhood or to be a part of what is deemed *acceptable* in society.

The boy, however, doesn't seem to care. Oblivious to her inner turmoil and battle with her insecurities, his wails ascend into a medley of sobs. He *feels* sick; he *feels* hungry. He is *starved* of attention. Perhaps particularly resentful of this luxury his presumably newborn sibling receives over him. Or it is because he *must* stand on the bus, *like a big boy?* The pram takes up the seat space along with his mother. The toddler would have been unwittingly ignored throughout the day while the baby is fussed and cooed at by his mother's fawning friends and relatives.

I have to deal with people like this all the time. I work in a "how can I help you today?" customer-care call centre. Day in, day out, Monday to Friday, sometimes Saturday, never Sunday. There is nothing more confining than those four by four, square walls of box cubical and desk where I sit with computer and phone with a pointless pin badge on my chest, declaring to

11

an absent audience: *My Name is Frank.*

I don't understand the badge. Why do you even need one? When your only form of contact, except for a brief lunch break, or occasion team-building meetings, is with faceless individuals on the phone.

Even so, I am stuck with the badge with little else to do. At several points in my day, I have found myself attempting to extract it from my shirt, only to be repeatedly stabbed by the thin needle-like pin at different, distantly tender spots on my thumb.

Now though, I was going *home.* My mother had demanded in her overbearing and obvious way that she wanted us back for her birthday. I stress the word home since I had long ago fled the house. Keen to place a sage green sofa in some ex-council flat that my late grandmother had left me in her will.

I could already taste the sickly-sweet supermarket bought and off-brand birthday cake, with the fluorescent iced lettering that she always insisted she had made. It always tasted of nothing except a washing-up sponge.

The problem is I dislike family birthdays almost immensely.

There is always a fake charm.

Overall, procedure dictates your smile throughout your forced attendance. Usually, unwillingly, with the biggest and the best present compared to your family and peers. And yet, come your birthday, all you will receive likely is a tatty, moth-eaten, hastily written greetings card and a pair of socks. I had chosen to attend early if only to appease her wrath from my usual paltry offerings and find a somewhat adequate gift.

I saw the old, still familiar, comforting roofs of the houses and shops of my boyhood as the bus hauled itself with effort round the cliff-faced landscape. The bus was old now, one of only three left in the town. Nevertheless, it rode well and braved the oncoming drizzle and sea breeze and the whimpers of the now stalling child. He had grown sleepy himself against the crook of his mother's arm and overhanging raincoat.

The brakes squealed and hissed as the bus stopped on the corner of the curb. I dismounted before it swiftly withdrew towards the town centre. Departing with a slight snort of disapproval, the bus left, disgruntled that I would leave it so soon.

Instead, karma reproached me as I ran to cross the road, stepping prematurely from the raised kerb, only to be splashed by the passing cars, including the aforesaid white Peugeot.

Chapter 2: A Bazil Most Faulty

The bell of an antique shop always sounds refined. It chimes like an old Grandfather's clock as I enter under the gap of the frayed awning to the door. The sound lacks the artificial buzz observed in other boutique shops; or the sharp intake of breath and shunting that often occurs with impersonal, automatic doors.

There is, however, the doomed smell of wet dog.

Musk permeates my snout, throwing my mind back to previous visits. I am somewhat aware of how my body odour and the contribution of my damp jacket from the rain and shoes only made more of the scent.

The building is itself dull, horrid and airless. If I were impolite, I might gag or leave the shop altogether. But I have come here with a purpose, a purpose that dictates both decorum and restraint—looking for a birthday present for Mother.

Somehow oblivious to the smell is the old master who runs the store. It is a term that seems to fit the small balding, ageing man with a tuft of a colonial moustache. He chooses a cologne that matches everything else in his shop; that's been dead or left unmoved for years. His eyes appear closed or so tightly squinted together that I often wonder *how* he can see me so clearly. *How* can he move with such energy, *especially* for a man who would have since chosen to retire in other professions?

Yet in an instant, here he was in front of me and grasping my hand, a token gesture of old formality he does with all his customers – at least, or so he's told me, the one's he likes. "Young Davis," he says, smiling. "Back so soon?"

14

"Yes, sir," I nod nervously, privately acknowledging to myself that it is *not soon at all.* Nevertheless, I keep this thought to myself; it always pays to be polite.

Bazil Weatherspoon was a veteran of *The Kings Own Lancers.* An impressive legacy on paper for a man that had boasted of seeing a fair share of action in 15 years. However, the reality, much like his shop, was far less glamorous.

A few years back, a segment on the History Channel detailed the squad in question. I hadn't planned to watch it, as I was not so interested in history, but the programme seemed to reflect on an anniversary or other relating to one of the many world wars. One fellow officer named the squadrons' sole responsibility had been to guard an empty shed on Salisbury Plain.

But Bazil was not one for facts.

Bazil's narrative was that he had arrived in Dover after being accused of cowardice. He had chosen to run away, "somewhere only *pussyfooting failures* hide" to what he billed as his Uncle's second-hand store.

Still, such a claim could never be successfully verified or even disputed locally. As far as anyone knew, the shop had always existed. It was as long as anyone could remember. They also said the same of the somewhat withering yet sharply imposing dominance of Bazil. It was a claim that was passed down like legend by the second oldest man in the town. Second to Bazil himself.

Despite his rather strange disposition, two things seemingly only two things riled Bazil's character:- Tourists and spelling. The latter was understandable since he prided himself on his name as the unique choice of a dyslexic mother; the former was most odd. While the other shops in the area, being a relatively small town, were most keen to welcome the non-natives, Bazil would become infuriated with them. On the door of his shop, alongside the plaque containing his Uncle's name: *J. B. Weatherspoon's Antique Emporium,* Bazil decorated the sides with pieces of wooden planking upon other wooden boards, sign upon sign. Each, detailing his threat:

THIS BUILDING IS NOT A FREE HOUSE (All Prices Final).

Before another sign in even more hostile letters:

STOP ASKING FOR A PINT!

Thankfully, since I was an ally, one of the natives, Bazil, did not gather anything from his growing artillery.

He had a well-stocked collection of pistols and shotguns that he kept in an easily accessible netted mesh against the ceiling, which he *insisted* were for security.

I recalled the time when questioned once by my overly sceptical mother. An attitude that, much like his appearance, remained much the same. At the time, Hanny and I were younger, and we peered down over an oddly shaped arrangement of bottles and vases, trying to see if we could spot any spiders. Despite the bravado, which was mostly for show, somehow we felt safe. Bazil had affirmed this when he replied. "Not worth shooting them, got enough taxidermy at the back."

Thus he had gestured, with an almost grandfatherly twinkle in his eye, suggesting that we should come and look for ourselves. Here beyond the sweeping of the back curtain, which was caught in the slightly humid 1980's breeze, I glimpsed within what us children believed could be the *hints of exotic intrigue and magic.*

But the moment wouldn't last. I would soon be pulled sharply on the arm, along with my sister. My mother, whose taste sated, bustled us out of the shop and *out of trouble* - so we might hurry along to visit my Aunt Bess.

I had been many more times to the shop since that day as I grew up, but never again did I witness the golden nuggets of distant lands. Since then, the mysteries and antiques had been gradually overwhelmed by cheaper, charity shop memorabilia. A jumble sale that others failed to donate or sell. Such was a sign of the times, and as Bazil put it, "*blooming* budget cuts!"

On this occasion, Bazil preferred to return to his shabby, rickety stool by the counter in the corner. From here, he maintained constant vigilance over his only recently discarded tankard and a self-matched game of drafts. Nevertheless, it's always been impossible to know whether Bazil was winning or losing. Both he and the game pieces had remained untouched, save for the odd grunts and mutterings when he had decided on his supposed line of strategy.

Bazil's sales technique had resulted in the odd purchase of a dozen or so brazen figurines of *Lindt* confectionery. Ones' he had left in a spider's web before he extracted them *"from the furnaces of Luxor"*. There was also a box of old modelling paints muddled together with makeup. These, he so told me, "*Belonged to the Great wives of Rome themselves!*" To this day, Bazil would encourage his visitors with long-winded but incredibly detailed tales of their questionable origins, finishing only with the words: "The customer is **always right**".

I passed the shelves of tackily assembled macaroni-cheese cards. Ones' that had no doubt been a salvaged school display by the local 3-11-year old's at *St Thomas and Martin's Parish Academy*. I had been made aware of these on a previous visit, so I paid little notice to my surroundings until I came to a slight upward ramp leading to the larger back end room.

Hither the shelves grew larger, long winding rows of oddities. A "legless" jack-in-the-box, a disfigured crystal, a green felt rag that had been fused onto tuppence for *appearance sake*.

Here was my stop. Sat at the foot of one of these racks, I stumbled against a wooden frame containing a hastily drawn sketch of a vase of flowers. They were large, gold, bold and tasteless:

The kind of thing my mother likes.

Not quite a *Picasso van Gogh* or equivalent.

She is, after all, a relatively simple person to cater for. Her attention is usually as sharp as a toothpick unless someone or something provokes her.

Not to say I was any means of an expert on the matter either, and I did not expect to find one in the emporium. So I placed it down to see what else I could find, barely registering the moth-eaten selection of vintage bed linens when the geriatric but ever attentive man had returned to my side. He was appraising both the supposed 'find' and his potential customer- keen as ever for a sale.

I could not blame him, of course. Visiting *J.B. Weatherspoon's* had been a last-minute, last resort, despairing decision. Whilst I didn't mind popping in on occasion to see him and his wares, I usually tried to find my mother something 'quickly' wherever possible, whatever the event or the experience might be. Such opportunities made it seem as though I had been able to present the best possible gift. Detailing some 'thought' and 'care' might go into choosing something rather than the frantic dash I almost always fell into.

Today, however, only Bazil could save me.

It was also the timing of a match day for our seldom victorious local football team. Unfortunately, such an event usually meant that at least a cluster of the already slim pickings of boutiques and gift shops in the area were closed. Their curtains flickering with the faint light of a television screen and the audible groans as yet again the *Cockleside Rovers* failed to score. We hadn't made championship or regional level in years.

Still, team pride was pride; and I hoped that should I manage to make my getaway from the farce of it all. Maybe for a moment, I might join the fans in solidarity as they drown the dregs of their sorrows in a pint of Guinness at the pub. The painting, genuine or not, would have to do.

Now Bazil was hovering, his hands stroking the faded walnut frame with intense interest. "You would like to know more, Mr Davis?" he asked, his voice displaying an almost operatic wobble all the while.

I didn't even bother to nod, knowing full well that Bazil would begin to detail the piece's origins to me no matter what I said or did. From what I understand of it, though, the canvas was sketched on in 1902—designed in a collection of oils and wax pastels by a young village girl named Suzie for an art competition – though Bazil couldn't recollect entirely whether she had won. *Though, her art had made all the papers* – local ones anyway.

As ever keen to validate his point, Bazil began rummaging around in a box nearby, filled with what I could only guess were some local newspaper clippings, mumbling to himself all the while:

"It's no doubt," he said, waving his arm here and there with a theatrical flourish, "This is a real find Mr Davis, a real find!"

Perhaps it was the slight scepticism I had inherited from my parents, but precaution and common sense quickly occupied my mind. The price wasn't steep, and mother would be happy, though it would still be a good idea to check if his intentions were honourable. I'm not one to get 'had'. Sometimes you have to sell an item to me exactly as it is. That is, without any embellished bells or whistles. For me, a banana is a banana; a guinea pig is a guinea pig. The use of wrapping paper is an accessory, whereas bubble wrap is a must.

Bazil continued all the while. Noting my stance, he asked the dreaded question of one who knew me seemingly so well. "For your mother, I presume?"

In the absence of any perceived objections, Bazil had taken away the picture. He was oblivious to my hedged attempts to browse the rest of the store. His hands toyed with the painting on the counter, casually rearranging its place several times. The trouble was he never truly allowed me to look again, save for the occasional teasingly flashes of the picture from different angles as he twisted and turned it this way and that. *No doubt worried I might change my mind.*

After, he walked to the register just as quickly, having decided that this was my item.

"Yes, she should *like* this," He smiled, a broad, slightly toothless smile. Measuring the painting against a bag, he ushered me to follow him while continuing the conversation with himself. *"Of course, you would like it wrapped."*

I had not quite settled myself with an answer when the store's phone rang. This event somewhat broke Bazil out of his routine, and his face fell, grunting impatiently. Quickly, he excused himself, running to another concealed door in the shop. This personal office, he kept locked with a simple old army sign captioned with his familiar lettering. Albeit it had been written with more pride and care:

THE TANK

I was now alone on the public side of the shop, with a half-packaged painting leaning against the till.

I thought carefully, looking once more to the picture, noticing now that the entire painting was upside-down; the frame tinged with lacquer, no doubt to save it from rot and woodworm.

19

Mum would *indeed* like it. She was going through a mass artistic phase, not to paint, but as a pursuer and critique of the subject matter. Dad had humoured her by presenting her a box of 'replica' prints the previous year, wherein she had seemingly developed 'taste'. A subject on which Hanny and I remained on the fence. Personally, I wasn't very design-savvy.

As it was, I preferred to buy presents or treats for Mol. Guinea pigs are rarely ungrateful as a species; I only ever acknowledged gratitude and happiness as I gazed into the sweet jet black eyes of my little companion.

Mol would scurry up the walls of her cage to greet me with a happy squeak. She often joined me in one of many meals together, whether it be takeaway scraps (which we shared when vegetarian) or my ready meal kits for one, bingeing together in front of the television at night.

Such sensations were always a sharp contrast to Mother's praise. She usually overlooked positives by choosing carefully selected and often petty flaws she noticed about my character.

There was a hole in my jumper I had still to fix.

I was not eating correctly, or I *was eating too* **much** *or too* **little**.

I needed to get a girlfriend; I needed to find a better job.

The list went on.

I took the time in Bazil's absence to evaluate the birthday card I had picked up earlier based on my sister's suggestions and prompts. It was a simple one. Pink; Mum's favourite colour, with splashes of glitter and ribbons in a somewhat pretentious design with a poem inside - A saving grace for people like me who never quite had the words to say. Not that Mum would notice anyway. It was best to scribble in our names at the bottom of the card. Hanny and I simulated Mum's impersonal tone that she wrote in all personal correspondence from herself and my father. *From Maureen and Jack*, which was followed by a single 'X' kiss.

Please don't mistake this as Mum not loving us, which she did in her way -but she was continually chasing dreams of a better lifestyle and hobbies. She had always aspired to be *"more than your average housewife"* and start a musical career. Her idols when we were small were Cilla Black and Engelbert Humperdinck. Then, when she realised such a reference aged her, she switched her sources to a more modern "artiste," quoting Madonna or Prince.

The problem was, Mum couldn't hold a note, and Dad always needed his pants ironing both before and after retirement.

She was stuck in a marital rut and bitter.

Taking a ballpoint pen from my pocket, I pressed down on the card and envelope, slowly but gently scrawling out my name so that it might vaguely resemble the word 'Frank'- without coating my hand in glitter. I had just slid both hastily into my coat, feeling like a cheeky schoolboy, when Bazil returned with his usual wheezing and coughing, smoke permeating the already dusty room from a neglected cigar.

Readily he assumed the role of the shopkeeper, and I watched, somewhat fascinated as he began wrapping the painting with wads of thick grease-proof brown paper over a bubble-wrapped shell, which was topped with 'celebratory' golden ribbon. His elderly fingers danced and spun elegant bows into the fabric, no doubt practising some precision and skill he insisted he had gained during the war.

When his task was completed, to Bazil's satisfaction, I withdrew the last crumpled twenty-pound note from my wallet and passed it to him. As always, the money barely remained in my palm. Moments after I extracted it, it effortlessly drifted into the cash drawer, thus exchanged for two solitary pence change 'for the car park', each coin had become antiquated themselves, covered in a layer of evident grime.

I gave another nod to Bazil and took my packaged painting which rested snugly in the crook of my left arm as I made my exit. Heading out through the all too narrow door and back into the crisp summer breeze, I was somewhat relieved as the air returned to my lungs.

Now, I was heading back to the sloping hill that led me back out of town. I was genuinely grateful for the slight reprieve before what would yet again become an all too long a day—birthday lunch with mother.

Chapter 3: Familial Formalities

Mum had taken up knitting. As I opened the front door, using the key that had been hidden not so secretly under the welcome mat, old memories flooded through me unwelcomingly.

Even though I had a house key, my parents, most likely Mother, still insisted on such entrances if only to impose their status above me. Mine was to be used only in emergencies and hung redundantly back in a corner cupboard at mine.

Shaking these impending concerns away, I forced a smile and crossed the hallway to the front room, where the living room doorway unfolded into a carpet of patchwork.

Her latest project was *"practical,"* or so Mum insisted, telling me almost proudly how the intricately tangled bundle of threads and yarns was being used to construct a scarf for cousin Daisy. Aunt Bess's daughter was of those many relatives you unwittingly meet sparingly. Usually, this is at obligatory events such as weddings and funerals or the occasional Christmas. Albeit, she had been spared the fuss of attending on Mum's birthday. Daisy lived in Surrey, and it was *way too far to drive.* "Daisy *shouldn't trouble herself".*

Despite this, you are always guilted when you do attend, as you are forced to sit with people you have next to nothing in common with and can't quite work out how you're connected beyond the proverbial - "B*ecause the family tree says so".*

That said, making a scarf might have seemed an odd choice since I vaguely recall that a number of our family had an allergic reaction to wool. Hanny later told me Mum wanted revenge on Daisy for wearing the same dress at cousin Flora's wedding. Such is the mentality of my family.

As I entered the front room, I could hear Dad in his muted regional dialect; mumbling a few words here and there. Mum had placed herself in her usual threadbare armchair and had turned it awkwardly and strategically, thus blocking my father from the telly and the football. Something she had already muted.

"Maureen, we're never on the telly!" He moaned, hoping to make some vague point to her. Mum issued him a stern look – one I could only imagine might cut through glass, after which he was silent instantly, save the occasional tilt of his head to try and work out the latest score.

Settling back into the cushions, Mum decided to gather us together amongst the selection of gifts and sickly coloured birthday cake.

"Jelly, Frank?" She asked and gestured for me to sit on the sofa opposite her.

I parked myself next to my nervous wreck of a sister.

For the second time that day, I was left unable to answer. Barely registering as a plate of toxic green gloop oozed and wobbled onto my lap and a pointy pink party hat attached itself onto my head.

"Umm ...thanks," I replied uncertainly, sharing a brief look with my little sister. Despite our mother turning sixty-eight, my sister distinctly looked the more worn out of the two. Subtle streaks of dark circles rimmed her pale hazel eyes, enhanced by the thick bifocal glasses she had worn like a bug since we were children. Her hair was tied up loosely in a frizzy plait at the side. Hanny smiled weakly, tugging nervously at the edges of her already frayed traffic cone coloured orange jumper and smoothing a drab plastic apron she wore to protect her skirt.

Sad as this might sound, this dowdy appearance was quite the norm for my sister. This girl had grown up with prescription glasses and hand-me-down dresses and jumpers. She would shy away from asking for anything more than a new pair of slippers one previously bitter winter.

It didn't help that Hanny lived under my mother's thumb, much like our father in his later years. Something I had been keen to avoid as early as I could and had been quick (or sensible depending on your perspective) to leave our domestic dwelling aged 25. It had not been long after I joined the call centre. Henrietta "Hanny" Davis had remained firmly rooted where our mother wanted her – *at home.*

"It made *sense,*" as Mum had reasoned back then, "the room is already made up, and it would *save* on the journey into work,"

This much was right, I grant her, but Hanny's fledgling career as a primary school teacher had been usurped, in part, by Mum's not such subtle pleadings for cups of tea, or a helping hand up the stairs – since she and Dad were *"getting on a bit".*

For six years, Hanny had been diligent. She had even gained a first-class honours degree and qualified to be a teacher. She was the smart one in our family, working diligently to look after the younger generation. Formally Hanny was always in her element, singing and dancing with the three-year-olds as they learned to tell the time and their ABC's, playing to a backdrop of her guitar.

Her smile was genuine then, *even* as Hanny came home to our parents and helped make their evening meal. She *always* brought through at half six *precisely,* into the front room, where Mum and Dad ate next to the television from plastic trays on synthetic fold-down tables.

But slowly and all too sadly, her smile began to fade. Soon her energy for the job wore away little by little.

It broke her heart when she handed in her notice.

That day Mum destroyed her spirit.

For a brief moment, I felt clammy. My legs had grown wetter through my trousers, though that could have been the jelly seeping through the cheap paper plate.

How much I longed to return home to Mol, who would indeed be waiting for me. I had defrosted a leg of lamb for the evening, laying it carefully on the draining board in the kitchen to pair it with a medley of nicely seasoned potatoes and carrots. While I was by no means a master chef, I was very fond of cooking when I had the chance. I was self-taught from the school of trial and error, not my mother's varying efforts, usually on Sunday or every compulsory family Christmas dinner.

Hastily, I collected myself and handed Mum the now bent yellow envelope inscribed with her name and the painting from where I had placed it against the leg of the sofa.

As expected, both the painting and card took pride in Mum's heart for all of two seconds. Comprising of thirty occasional glances each up and down, front and back before residing now neglected, behind the back of the chair, she had given her answer as expected "That's *lovely* Frank."

Mum's following announcement brought an end and beginning to the proceedings. "Sherry?" she asked. There was no need to say *Now* because even if she had, the word would have been lost in a flurry of scrambling arms reaching for the coffee table and the mass-produced, chunky drinking glasses which were infused with its sickly pale brown liquid.

My Uncle George once reminisced - "alcohol bonded our family together." - Although he had been drunk when he said it, there was very much truth in the matter as we clinked glasses and downed the slightly burning drink whole.

Next, Hanny shuffled a tray next to the table of half-consumed chocolates in a greasy paper foiled box. As siblings instinctively know, there was a plan here; something silently plotted by our father, in a vain attempt to keep our mother liquidated and satisfied by the dark hazelnut liquors.

Systematically, it would go like this:

Mum would take an overly generous handful of chocolates, stuffing them 'gracefully' into her mouth until her head would loll gently on her shoulder, a sure sign that she had fallen asleep. This method was how our father could gently nudge Mum out of the way and resume watching the football. However, he would have to catch up on the match in its entirety later via the evening news or the kitchen radio. Even if the football wasn't being broadcast that day, chocolate still provided Dad with some escape, away from the drones of complaints that usually issued from Mum's lips.

Mum had a habit of wittering on about "what my family give me after all I've done!" Or some other depressed variation of such.

"Here was the secret," Dad insisted, "on maintaining a happy and lasting marriage,"

Seemingly oblivious, Mum reached into the centre of the box for her prized 'caramels' and 'coffee liquors'. The rest lay forgotten in the pile of knitting needles, magazines and black and white trash.

Through half-consumed mouthfuls, Mum reprimanded me about how I really should visit home more often.

For my part, I merely smiled and nodded where appropriate to do so, knowing it would not be long before she stopped. We were all waiting with some fond nostalgia as she fell asleep. Mum's hand half flung the chocolate box onto the carpet as she flopped into the chair now mid-snore.

Hanny smiled apologetically at me as we both stood, she to retrieve the fallen package and place it back on the table, mouthing audibly, "You might as well go!" Her eyes, tinged with a slight whimsy, knowing that she had never truly made her escape.

I nodded back, semi-gratefully, thinking to myself how escape could never come soon enough, despite how many times we had practised this routine.

I carefully lifted the party hat from my head, trying to ignore the still sharp ping from wearing tight-fitting elastic. Despite her snores, Mum could sometimes become a selectively light sleeper, stirring as it suited her, to beg or guilt me into staying longer.

Being careful as I could to avoid the coffee table and the maze of items that had jumbled on the floor, I headed to the doorway, making sure to glance over at my father to confirm my departure, but he wasn't looking. Dad had his whole body turned away, just as he always liked it. He was focusing his worn out, grey eyes back on the television, over Mum's slumped head and torso toward the sport.

Whereas Hanny crouched beside him at the table, gathering the few odds and ends of wrapping paper; into a black bin bag, struggling slightly, as they tangled and writhed together with tattered plastic tape and decorative streamers.

Behind her, the parted door to the kitchen revealed a medley of still unconsumed sausage rolls and paper plates; no doubt for the number of people Mum had *invited* who had chosen not to come.

My mother always insisted she was popular and liked by everybody.

She always knew what the neighbours were doing, what the grandchildren were called and the number of roses growing in somebody's garden.

Sadly this was only knowledge she had gained from casual 'eavesdropping' through the thin brick wall of their crumbling mid-terrace home. Or, waving all too cheerily at the other occupants of the road as she hung up the washing or pottered around the garden in her fleecy eggshell slippers and dressing gown. It all felt relatively flat; and fake as the icing that remained mostly untouched and sickly on the birthday cake.

Although every part of my body yearned to leave, my conscience returned. So, I draped my coat on the edge of the sofa and kneeled beside my sister; I fetched a second bin bag with a well-meant smile.

Two heads were better than one.

After a few minutes, both bags were filled. I tucked each under the crook of my arm and joined Hanny in the kitchen. As always, I carefully shut the adjoining door, where I could still see the ghosted-out figures of my parents and hear the dull mumbling of the television. Hanny took the bags from me, tipping each into the small recycling box we had by the front door, ready for collection day later that week. Then she strolled over, back into the kitchen until she could rest herself against the stove. She pressed her knuckles into the cold plastic counter-tops of the units, breathing in relief.

As I leant casually against the room's single radiator, relishing the warmth that filled the sodden ends of my trouser legs, my sister stared into space. It almost looked like she was distracted or deep in thought because her large innocent cow-like eyes were slightly focused away from me. I guessed she could have been looking at the kitchen clock, positioned on the wall just above my head. The fridge buzzed against the silence.

Finally, she spoke: "Frank," she murmured in a soft voice that lacked confidence. "I think I'm in love."

My composure left me, and I blinked, gaping like a fish, hoping to string some form of complete sentence out.

Instead, all I could muster at that moment was a primitive, sharply exhaled question. It was one, no doubt that Hanny had been asked a million times before. "What?"

Chapter 4: Work Time Blues

Call me naïve, if you will, but I didn't know what to say. For the briefest of moments, the world was utterly obsolete. Temporarily my surroundings had been replaced with a camera obscurer playing back some hazy, pixilated version of my life. Situations that were so familiar in places and yet in others; I couldn't recognise them at all. The pictures and facts themselves felt distorted and upside down as I tried to process what Hanny had just told me. The word *love* playing over and over, repeating without any clarity in my mind.

I must have been out of it as it took me a while because I only registered the kitchen again as Hanny's hand moved before my eyes like a window washer's sodden rag.

Nervous and flummoxed, I stepped back and yelped slightly as my leg touched the now consciously warmer radiator.

"Frank," Hanny asked gently, then she paused. "Frank? Did you hear me?"

"In love?" a voice asked, not entirely my own. My idle tongue possessed it. I hoped that I sounded almost human again.

My sister smiled back to the comfort of a one-word answer. "Yes."

Of course, I was happy for her, but still, it came as some shock – a thought I reasoned was *best* kept to myself.

The trouble was that I had always assumed rightly or wrongly that I would find my significant other first. Justly, I had believed such because I was older and left the house a lot more than my sister. Hanny had a habit of mainly retreating into herself like a mouse does a paper bag.

Whilst, to an extent, I had found my forever after with Mol, I knew that this was different: that Hanny was speaking of a living, breathing human being; at least, I presumed so.

My sister had never been a pet owner, and Mol had always been my pet, having been a rare treat on my seventh birthday.

This isn't to say that Hanny didn't like animals. It was more about Mum, who had always insisted we didn't need more than the guinea pig. She told us this since "too many animals breed all kinds of mess!" –And I had been so keen to leave, even if I never kept more than the one presently in my flat.

In a needlessly dramatic voice, almost rivalling that of a stage whisper, I resumed the role of the older brother and asked. "Do Mum and Dad know?"

Hanny smiled in a rare display of confidence.

No doubt she had time to prepare this and nodded again. "Yes, Frank."

I frowned a little, still not entirely satisfied.

Coughing a little to clear my throat, I poised my next question. I was burning with curiosity, knowing I should have asked this from the start. "Who?"

Searching my brain for a moment, I thought of all the men around my sister's age who would share a mutual interest with her. Flipping through my memory's yellow pages and phone books, I distantly recalled several men in the area who were about Hanny's age or had previously appeared in some form in her life until now – but most of them were faces I hadn't seen or thought of since school. I didn't even remember her having a partner beyond my chaperoning at the prom.

As it turned out, it was the milkman.

"His name's Steve," she said, as though justifying her newfound romance.

Steve was just one of *three* milkmen who came to the road though it was of little surprise that Steve had been appointed my parents regular.

I could envision the scene even as Hanny began to explain herself. They would have met by chance as my sister carefully unlatched the front door on what would have been a cold, dreary early morning. Her hair would have been a mess of hastily rinsed curls, which resulted from the always cold shower. She would be dressed in her brushed cotton stripey dressing gown and discoloured pink slippers, now turned a drab mushroom with overuse and age. Her body reaching for the clean white milk bottles that perched against the brickwork of the house. Somehow she would catch her dressing gown cord as it unwound itself against the sea breeze, daringly exposing a flash of soft pink nylon nightie. Giggling slightly, though nervously, a flush of red would gather on her pale cheeks highlighting the row of peppery brown freckles at the end of her nose, and their eyes would meet for the first time.

She would seem beautiful to him, swept in the innocence of former teenage puppy love. As she painted her rosy-tinted view of the world, to me, Hanny's very nature was sweet, like a freshly opened bar of soap or a solitary yacht cruising along the bay. I smiled inwardly; she deserved something for her.

After this, we talked about work; and my job, making occasional references to Mol and my news – or rather the lack of. We continued until we heard the short bursts of snorting grunts from our mother rousing herself from her nap. Soon she was calling out to us from the living room – woken by a mixture of boredom and television feedback.

The kitchen clock read a little after quarter past four.

It was time to go home.

I made my goodbyes and promised to visit again soon, then strolled, coat in hand, down the road to the bus shelter. There was nothing to do but wait for the bus. Stretching my legs had been necessary to arrive at Mum's on time, but now all I had was a sudden urge to go back to bed.

Although I didn't feel exhausted, I felt mentally drained, answering my mother on and off about the likelihood of me bringing back a girlfriend.

Before I left, Mum had thrust a hastily wrapped piece of birthday cake into my hands, insisting that I needed to eat correctly. Still, alongside the half-hearted attempt at jelly and bloated sausage rolls, I had all but lost my appetite.

Work loomed on the horizon like a pimple eclipsing my moon of visions, shadowing me from the fading light. I was silent, still and alone, returning to my bachelor pad with my pet guinea pig and a two-by-five inch stain on my trousers from muddy puddles and half-hearted birthday celebrations.

It had been a long afternoon.

* * *

Coming through the door to the doting eyes of a pet is one of the best feelings in the world. As I walked in and switched on the light, Mol greeted me with a soft whinny of pleasure, making her way to the first corner of the pen to welcome me with unwavering loyalty.

Perhaps, this was why subconsciously, I never had looked for a girlfriend. Reaching between the bars of her cage, I smiled to myself as Mol chattered away happily, ready to receive the raw piece of broccoli I had saved her from my lunch. Her little face gently beamed as she took the florets from my hand, eagerly munching and all the while nuzzling my palm.

Mol didn't mind that I was home slightly late or smelt of gelatine and sponge cake. Mol didn't care that I wore the same coloured clothes for convenience sake most mornings, knowing that I worked hard at my job instead. There was always a pile of unfinished crosswords left on my kitchen table that occupied our breakfast routine. Mol was just Mol, and I was I.

Relaxing, I peeled off my wet trousers, placing them in the laundry pile I had started to collect since the night before. I would wash it all shortly, but I was content to sit with my pet discussing Hanny and Steve for now. Also, all that had happened at the bus shelter with that leopard print wearing lady. Through it all, Mol listened, blinking her sweet black and gold-rimmed eyes at me with sincerity. All in all, I was happy. And given my line of work, that was very good indeed.

The thought of finding a companion was temporarily pushed back and suppressed into the corners of my mind.

A problem for another day.

* * *

I work in a fishbowl office with slit window pane walls. Inside there is row upon row of glistening white corridors of partition screens, made to match

31

in faded thick foam. There is a cork-board on one side, a desk calendar, a computer and an old hard-wired telephone. The cubicle was a *beautiful*, clinical environment to inspire the masses; gleaming and clean as a hospital, where the staff were friendly, approachable and healthy.

Four people were outside the office smoking.

They hung around the railing gate like scavengers. Banter and occasional insults were exchanged, their secret meeting adjourned, and I entered the tank with its square walls and square unfeeling windows. The building was filled with cold calling representatives and unmerited good Samaritans – the volunteers who still felt perky enough to work for free.

Welcome to the *First Response Against Nuisance Callers*, or FRANC for short. A company whose mission statement promises to provide its "customers" the freedom to avoid nuisance calls. Calls like PPI or dodgy car insurance, bogus accident claim lines, or discuss medical problems and ailments liable for a claim. It sounds fancy, but in essence, it is simply another one of a long list of irritating contact centres that should – 9 times out of 10 be blocked from your telephone for their simplistic, robotic sales pitch.

I worked in the customer service department, which you can reach by pressing three on your keypad or bashing five or more combinations of buttons together. At that point, you will make contact with a real person after ten minutes of painful, tinny stock-library trimmed Classical music tracks.

My headset always feels like rubber. I'm not too fond of it for various reasons, most notably that it slips, so the microphone is still ten inches too close to my face. What's so wrong with just using the phone? Not that I imagine most of them work any more. Mind you; it's a welcome distraction from the illness that confronts me 9-5. "Good Morning, *FRANC*,"

"FRANC speaking," *me, is it me?* No, it couldn't possibly be.

"Yes, this is *FRANC*," An ensemble of FRANC'S echoing through the room – none are me. Slowly, reluctantly I take a call:

"You have reached Frank. How may I help you today?" The voice on the other end is unsurprisingly sour as grapes. I slowly swallow as I adjust myself to the measured, gravelly tone that is listed on the chart of recommendations for every employee right next to monotone and flat.

"Ahh Feck, I've reached the answerphone!" comes the voice cutting through my premeditated waffle, which has permeated the line with stony silence. "Why can't I talk to a real person?!" I clear my throat, louder this time or at least audibly ready to respond but am left with the dull click and drawn-out disconnected tone. That's another one gone. Not that it matters much, as I was never destined to be an employee of the month.

There is a sad but true fact about this place, but I am not one of the eldest at the company; on the contrary, I am the 14th youngest. Not that I know that many of my colleagues by name.

We've been replaced by the routine and semblance of caller ID. Don't get me wrong, there are a few young saps amongst us, but they're in between work. Me? I'm between the centre and the dole queue every Monday making up the hours where I can. It's all peanuts for pay on the frugal minimum wage.

Five people sit near my desk, at opposite corners, so we are cushioned together like squares with our cubicles never quite touching; parallel like rails.

Andy is directly in front of me, and then Poppy, who nurses a hangover, sits at an angle to my left some 45 degrees. Dave is opposite her, eagerly brushing himself once over – he's perky and getting married. Then, to my right is plain - never entirely left Wonderland- Alice, and the boss' son: Mike Jr.

Mike is edgy. For the past twenty minutes, he's been straightening his tie more times than Dave; perhaps between them, they could smoothly run some form of in-office supply and dry-cleaners - if they weren't stuck here.

As it is, with their faint mutterings and Alice's chair rocking, Poppy's moaning and my idle groaning, we could even form a quintet. Not that anyone would listen, this is a call centre, as we are so often reminded and not someone's life story. But I digress.

"I want coffee," Poppy murmurs, forcing herself up onto her desk where she has slumped her head into her hands. She barely props her body up like some tragically abandoned marionette. "Alice, get me some, will ya?" her voice is slurring so much I cannot help but envisage it becoming the coffee she so desires, sloshing against her mind, which nearly hits the keyboard.

Alice turns her head to respond, says nothing and returns to her dream-world with a small "Oh,"

There's nothing for it but to take another call.

"*FRANC*," *Pause for effect.* "*You've* reached Frank," Dutifully waiting for the onslaught of abuse or anguish that will surely follow. Not that I'm ever entirely sure I can help them. We're all only human, in the end, armed with a cup of steaming depression and a half updated computer.

Always the same, Monday to Friday, sometimes Saturday, never Sunday. It's 9-5, and we know it, counting silently within ourselves the moments and minutes before lunch. As for me and my immediate friends cum colleagues Andy and Dave.

We were going to finish the week's proceedings at the pub.

Chapter 5: Confrontations & Concussions

Despite this, my feelings of loneliness would soon return.

"You must be so *pissed!*" Andy slurs, slamming his hand on Dave's back in an off-hand but well-meant pounding. This forces Dave to choke back his drink a little, but we bear it no mind. We're in our self-proclaimed local, squeezed into our usual four-by-four booth away from the large cluster of shrieking bachelorettes, out on a hen-night who have set up camp for their pub crawl in our usually quiet bar.

It is Friday night. Dave smiles mutedly; his face is red from Snakebite and the odd shot.

Andy continues to protest, "Come on, it's *not that much* to ask for. One night in with the guys for the match every Sunday!"

"But Yvonne wants to spend it with her family!" Dave manages to squeak out, looking at me through his now tired blue eyes, pleadingly seeking back-up.

Behind him at the adjoining booth, one of the girls is making herself look *beautiful.* She systematically puffs out her chest as if she were wrestling a pair of ferrets down her top to enhance her figure, but I think she looks like a bloated balloon. Judging by the makeup, however, and the sequins adorning her bodice, she's ready to hit the town. Such activity is much the same as in the animal kingdom, in the dark neon lighting.

Unfortunately for Dave, I don't know what to say. Football - though my father was determined to believe otherwise - is not remotely my thing.

"I just don't get it; what's so great about watching a couple of overgrown man-children in little white shorts chasing after a small white ball?!" I had asked him once to no answer.

To me, guinea pig racing - that's a real sport!

I try, as I always have to relay this information, in lesser words, to my friends, but coherence is not entirely the easiest thing to convey. I am not always a wordsmith, even when drunk. I manage a few choice words here and there about my feelings on the subject. But each time, I was interrupted by Andy again. He swings his drunken upper body towards me, "Oh, lay off it, Frank!" He says with mock seriousness as he clinks our glasses together in a self-serving toast, "Go join them piglets in Guinea!"

I attempt reasoning: "Andy, that is a common misconception, the *Cavia Porcellus* doesn't belong to the pig family, nor come from Guinea at all it. They're from the Andes."

Briefly, Andy was silent, as though this sudden burst of knowledge had paralysed him with respect. But then Dave sniggers, having found his comeback, points his finger out in what he presumes is a straight line towards us and replies: "Hey, you're Andy!"

It was a joke that had been said many times, lame and awkwardly relayed, and I leaned back with some dejection while the pair laughed in the same way I remembered a hyena in the zoo.

I was to be late home again, something I knew I had to apologise for to Mol later. For now, though, I was downing a pint or two of weak, last of the season cider, trying to distance myself from my thoughts once more.

I would have, given a choice, ordered a pint of beer, but Andy bought the round, and you don't deviate from the group's order if the drunkard is not ready to become sober. Andy was already faced daily with a cluster of hangover queens and the bog bowl.

Getting up, I obliged; it was my turn, and we had another round.

Returning, I eased myself back into the booth, just as a lizard green catsuit dressed lady with fish eyes began latching herself to Andy's shoulder. I presumed she had come over when I had been at the bar.

"Hiya, honey! Wanna kiss?" she asked, her voice unnaturally husky. I guessed she smoked.

If only for politeness to call her that, one could argue that the woman was already falling to bits. She was like a big plastic Barbie doll pasted with tangerine and bronze fake tan. Andy smiled, his own glistening, cigarette stained smile toward the thick gaudy lips now pouting at him. "Sure, sweetheart, pucker up!"

I shuddered and edged towards Dave as the woman began to straddle Andy's leg, dangling her ample assets closer to his black and white striped polo shirt with a conveniently relaxed, open-button collar. Now, Andy had begun to groom her hair, and the two shared an unnatural drunken giggle; as he brought her closer to him. She was escaping from her life for the night. With an intoxicated grin and wave towards her friends, she acknowledged those who had stayed together at a larger table, groaning into a plate of nachos. It might have been a dare, but then the hen herself, who was idly waving a tiara, determined that someone would get lucky tonight.

Fed up by their display of pheromones, I chose to exit the little 'show and tell' and went to the men's room to think.

Morses', where we three had set ourselves up for the evening, as we did most 'Lad's Nights', was unique, in its way, that its owner – more likely its contractor chose to furnish the bathrooms.

It was filled with squat stainless-steel cubicles and green avocado sinks. This was hardly picturesque and bleakly presented after surprisingly winning *Free House of the Year* in 1973 - a feat that was not repeated. Here in this small squalor, I was able to wash my face and run a comb over my hair, hoping, hope, against hope, I might be noticed by someone normal.

Although it is hard to find a number one in a series of dots, dashes and hard-core flashes, I am not too impressed by women who would instead peel themselves out of their latex. Their efforts simply a desperate measure to beat their fiance's no doubt equally intoxicating bachelor party.

It was unlikely, at least tonight, that I would find someone here.

My heart sank, and the bile and drink that lined my stomach went flat as I acknowledged Dave with a nod and walked back into the bar. It would be useless to try an alternative venue. Half the town was filled with drunken idiots like this one; the others had stopped selling food.

So, the night dragged slowly.

I considered dancing for a moment but thought better of it as the Hen-Do, Andy, and a half hearted Dave made their way onto the floor. The group's bodies were weaving and bobbing, and their hips and gyrating on one and other to the whoops and wails of approval from their fellow spectators.

All of them were better looking and younger than me. I guessed the others were aged between 22-35. Thus, I sank back down on the solitary barstool I found vacant in a corner, watching the world pass me by in a wall of bottles and the pulsating modern synth-induced din and grabbed a napkin and a pen from my pocket, jotting down my thoughts towards love.

It was half one in the morning when the pub closed that I was finally able to walk home. A jeep beeped in the road, starling me out of my drunken reprieve. "Fancy a kiss?" asked one of the two moon-faced, cider foamed faces from the half-open window at the front before being replaced by artificial canned laughter as the kiss blowing Barbie doll and Andy drove away in the obnoxiously large car.

Dave had crossed the street, probably on his mobile phone for a taxi; I couldn't expect to join him; we lived on opposite ends of the town, and taxis charge double the rate of the buses here.

When there are no buses in these few silent hours, and only the London coaches prowl the streets I walk, it would provide me with a bit of room to think, or at least an outdoor outlet to similar effect.

The lights of the moon bathed and danced before my sleepy eyes and lulled me like a surrogate mother over the forthcoming arrival of my hangover. The few cars that strolled by me glowed like fruit pastels glistening from their newly opened bag. But with my jotted notes, which I had scrawled into the thin budget serviettes, I resolved to myself that I had big plans. I would either join an internet dating website or clean the guinea pig cage.

* * *

Antonia' Toni' Roberta Greta Jones lived an interesting life. Every week she would try some new cocktail of life's flavours and attack the hints of humour they might spring.

To her life, seemed sour, as though a lemon had been drawn through a straw whole without the ice. Relief was her subject, and she painted a dozen or so in this vein before tearing them from the easel and frowning. Her sense of relief was yet to be achieved and had so far not been received.

Toni had long ago found her Prince Charming, in the way of a doll, but had quickly tired of his plastic smiles and deposited his tiny head in the garden some 50 feet from the impractical, plastic body.

No, Toni didn't believe in love; she believed in experimentation. Like the ice-cream coloured paper windmills with which she adorned the lawn. But this story is not about Toni, at least not yet.

* * *

The weekend had passed, slow and uneventful, and I had moved no further forward than the chalky grey landscape that formed the Dover hills and the small mist-clad town where I had lived all my life.

Whilst I had planned to begin my quest for my significant other, I did not understand my drunken thoughts half scurried, half scrawled in my pocket. As such, I remained at a loss at how to start, my plans somewhat scattered on crumpled, cheap disposable tissue and drenched with beer.

One suggestion that Dave had made to me was to go online. He had met Yvonne that way, so perhaps it worked.

Most sites, though insisted on some form of photograph or two, to progress steadily up the popularity ladder, and I had none I liked immediately to hand. I had none with exciting photos and poses, like high-fiving the Dalai Lama or snowboarding in the Swiss Mountains. I considered whether I could use a tiger makeup filter that had been doing the rounds on social media, but Poppy and Alice had insisted that it was cheating; and that I needed to have something about myself to say. Something more than 'Please message me.'

"This, to a woman, sounds like a cry for help," Andy had contributed knowingly. – And I suppose, in its way it is.

Life had been simple once. Reflecting on my days spent at aged 19, where I had envisioned my perfect year without any hesitation or panic over the state of my future.

I had decided I would look randomly at various bus routes by placing my finger on a spot I fancied before proceeding along said route 'til I arrived at a pub. Once at my destination, I would reward myself by ordering a pasty and a beer and document my observations in my notebook to later compare them. A few of the maps and timetables remained in the back of my black bus notebook. They were now simply a memento of the past.

These dreams had never fully happened.

My nervousness had got in the way, and I had never got much further than the Northern square of Dover. But t I told myself that the pasties were nice and added some comfort to my somewhat lightweight persona etched over these musings with a drunken scrawl: 'Guinea Pigs Rule!'

It was Monday afternoon, and now, as I strolled down the hill, wiping the last of the crumbs from a shop-made sandwich from my shirt, I glanced at the building to my left, *J.B. Weatherspoon's. Antique Emporium.*

It had not been so long since I was last here, but now I was determined to refocus my efforts, reminded of my past failures and my sister's small victories. Perhaps I might ask Bazil for his thoughts on romance.

Ever knowingly Bazil who appeared silently at the entrance under the awning.

"Mr Davis," He smiled, beaming at me; "Just the man..." the rest of his words appeared to jumble together as he pulled me inside, "I found some more of those paintings you liked."

I supposed it could even have been considered comical, how, despite the lack of attention, he remembered the painting I had bought for my mother. Or at the very least, he had seen the flash of ID badge from my lanyard, which was outwardly displayed between the lapels of my blazer and on my chest, suggesting I had earlier been at work - I had.

Once inside, I noticed four paintings on his counter-top, each peculiarly angled away from the frame, and he told me there were "A few more at the back," and I only had to ask, and he would fetch them.

My mind was not entirely focused, but each painting seemed more or less the same; the only difference was slight and did not matter to me – the observer. One might argue Bazil's sale technique was perhaps possessive, but addictions are forgivable as vices when they don't harm anyone else.

The trouble is I am a Romantic: dead to the world 'till roused like a guinea pig curling itself in a ball during winter and a cynic the rest of the time, so I don't get tired of waiting.

Outside slight shadows wafted over me briefly as the clouds gathered around our small picturesque town. There was little worth noting, except for the seagull I noticed out of the corner of my eye. It had perched on a lamppost only to release himself a pitiful white droplet of boredom.

After sating Bazil's whims, I decided to buy some chips to take home and share with Mol, turning to the right towards the bus shelter as a sharp, bright red handbag thrust itself against me, yelling the words: *"Bloody bus is late again!".*

Maybe it was the pending concussion as the bag retreated, but this was the start of something *different.*

✻ ✻ ✻

I'm not entirely sure even now what brought me too. The young lady before me in a black leather jacket was bent over me while fumbling with a token bottle of brandy and had dressed me in some thick, gaudy wine-coloured scarf, which draped around my head.

There may have been a slight look of concern on her face, but it was difficult to tell, for as quickly as my groan of consciousness roused her, she pursed her lips and thrust the bottle awkwardly into my hands. "Goose!" she said somewhat heavily, looking at me with some reproach, and I recognised the same vicious lipstick from before.

"Pardon me?" I asked, scratching my head only to wince slightly; there was a bump there I hadn't felt before or at least bothered searching for.

"Goose!" the lady repeated. "If you don't want to get hit – goose!"

"Oh..." I replied, "You mean duck, don't you?"

"No..." she paused, looking at me like I might have had two heads and grabbing the brand bottle from me; she took a swig with determined vigour. "Goose!"

I nodded, dazed and sat up, the blood rushing to my head.

As I did, the scarf untangled itself from my neck and fell in my lap, and she retrieved it, although she seemed in no hurry to refasten it around her neck.

Who was she?

My mind tried to piece things together as it acknowledged her presence. The girl was wearing an ill-fitting miniskirt, a loud strappy t-shirt and mismatched stockings, making her look like a punk rocker. Her hair stood out in bright bubble gum that spoke volumes about her lifestyle. I recognised her now as the leopard printed lesbian I'd seen once before, at the bus stop.

We didn't speak for a while. It was like before; the brandy bottle had replaced the lager, though I would get nowhere being melodramatic and asking my attacker cum rescuer to buy me some.

"Listen..." she declared, at last, looking at me rather sharply with what I suspected were the deepest purple eyes I had ever seen, or at least the latest coloured lenses. "I don't date men with eyebrows."

"Oh. Umm..."

If I had tried to say anything, her words would quickly overcome mine, merging it into her speech patterns with emotional fervour. "So, don't try any funny business; I don't care if you think I'm the one that I'm your saviour- if you try-" her finger lifted and pointed threateningly on my nose. "I'll set Reaper on you!"

My mouth gaped. I was clueless.

Seemingly satisfied with my now stunned silence, she smiled and offered her hand. "I'm Toni, pleased to meet you."

"Fra...Frank," I mumbled shakily as her hand-controlled mine in a meeting's embrace before managing a wavering quivering smile. "Nice to meet you,"

"Good," She replied, wrapping her hand around mine and pulled me up to

42

stand beside her. She had surprising strength. I noticed that Toni was a good five inches taller than me and her eyes peered down at me in a snakelike manner. "Now. Tea,"

* * *

As the day whirred on, I began to feel like a hamster on a wheel. I had no concept of what was really happening but reassured myself that the afternoon would have to get better because my phone had not broken from my gall, and I had received Hanny had text and said Mum had given up the knitting thing.

Despite this, however, I was now sitting in a stranger's house, waiting for a cup of tea.

Things were stranger indeed.

There were two beanbags, each a bright cherry-red colour, on the floor that Toni had hastily slumped down for us to sit in her small, four by four apartment. She lived in one of those ground floor places, by the old railway line with lots of nouveau art that she had done herself in pop-tart colours. I later learnt she had been studying in London, but the long drawn out summers of idealising after her muse, this phase all but evaporated when he had been found in bed with a student in photography.

Still, she had a garden of ample size and an extensive collection of ashtrays and plaster cast cats made with squashed up noses and button faces. "I'm not bitter!" She told me as I contemplated my fate, next to a small doll covered in voodoo pins, "I just think he could have done better than a Daddy's girl who listens to the wireless on alternate weekends,"

"Oh," I had said. She seemed to like the way I didn't question her logic, and I liked the way the matter was dropped without sealing me in a vat of icy cold daggers or an ominous glare. There was a small scruffy white Yorkshire terrier in the corner of the room in a quaint basket hastily made up, and a sign scribbled out which formerly read Tibbles.

"That's Reaper," she stated, noticing how I looked at the dog. Beaming at it, as she reached over me to pour the tea. "He's too soft to kill!"

I thought better than to ask whether she meant an act she might have to engage in herself or the dog's temperament as she passed me a cup of tea in what resembled a small beige egg cup. "So what can I do you for?" she asked, sitting in front of me balancing the tankard of her tea on one of her striped rainbow stockings.

"Pardon me?" yet again, overwhelmed by surprise, I sought clarity in the combination of warming unfamiliar liquid and her question. Thus, unfazed, she continued.

"Well, not just anyone bumps into Toni Bobby Greta Jones without wanting something, so what is it?" She had this look about her, like a Japanese cult cartoon figure, though I was somewhat relieved her skirt was not flapping – it would have spilt her drink.

"Erm,…" I mused. My mind was blank, like a room fresh with whitewash but not yet set with wallpaper. *What could she help with? What possibly?* Thoughts and words jumbled themselves together like yarn so that a string of them appeared to unwind into speech. Awkwardly I found myself mumbling something, anything, hoping that this would be my escape. I settled somewhat haphazardly on the name "Susie," Perhaps in some desperate bid to recall any woman's name if only to make my excuses and politely leave. I didn't know what she'd put in the suspiciously green looking tea.

For yet another moment, she stared at me, smiled and leaned back in the chair again, so she could soothingly scratch her pet's ear. "Well, my Nana's called Susie,"

And that, Toni decided, was that.

Chapter 6: Dating Profiles and Quinoa

A half-hearted attempt at a dating profile blinked unwavering on the screen as Toni bashed together letters and numbers in erratic chaos despite my apparent protests.

We had only been acquainted a few hours before she decided she already knew my life story and was determined to help me – a 45-year-old man get my life on track.

Photos were first, and Toni forced me to wear one of her many hats of questionable origin as I sat uncomfortably in front of her blankest looking wall, feeling altogether confused and disorientated. This scenario was not unlike a meeting at the passport office identifying my right to live in this country and visit others should I choose to. I focused my best efforts on trying to smile, watching as the pink bolt of energy whizzed around her home with frenzied and zealous action.

Why she was doing this, I wasn't altogether sure. But Toni insisted to me with her usual firmness that we were *now* friends. Something I had still to come to terms with as her long fingernails had raked over my thinning hair, placing the cap on my head at different angles – to help the camera decide my *better* side.

Now and again, Toni would ask me questions - some of which I acknowledged were a little personal. I noted with some discomfort the reality of my answers being made public on the internet. Others seemed to be blindingly obvious, and I thought to myself that it might be little more than a test to see if I existed.

Dazed from the impromptu portrait session and quiz show, I shuffled over to where Toni now sat cross-legged on a moon-shaped chair, precariously balancing her laptop on her left knee while her tea rested on the other; and peered down at the screen.

In these past minutes, Toni had contended three or four photos she deemed "net worthy". Each one hastily cropped like Polaroids, featuring a blob of pale peach flesh and obtuse novelty headgear that barely concealed my supposedly bald patches – not that I had ever noticed them in the mirror.

The profile read:

About Me:

Frank, 45, Kent.

Height: -

Weight: -

Hair: Yes.

Eyes: I have two.

Sex: Serious Relationship Wanted.

Headline: Looking for that special guinea pig.

The rest of the page was blank, and I watched as the cursor flashed a blinking 'I' across the screen.

Initially, I had tried in vain to explain to Toni that I *already* had my special guinea pig in my life and what I hoped to find was my soulmate. It did little good. Instead, she began to type the small factoids she had squeezed out of me, probing me further where necessary for clarification with her hypnotic violet eyes. Suppressing a sigh of exhaustion, I resigned to my previous position on one of the bean bags. Undeterred, Toni continued, pausing only momentarily to sip from her tea. Meanwhile, Reaper plodded over to me wearing a sad, dormant expression as he nestled against my idle hand for a scratch.

Welcoming the distraction, I buried my hand nervously into the seemingly thick wool hair that coated his head, settling on his ears, knowing well my sensitive spots from years of my mother and selective barbers and pointy plastic combs. The dog said nothing, merely closing his eyes as he flopped down on the floor. I presumed he was satisfied – not that I was fluent in speaking dog. I resisted the urge to doze alongside him.

It was the clapping of Toni's hands above her head that roused me from my thoughts. As she did, I noticed the unusual way in which she had stretched her arms with unrivalled flexibility, narrowly missing embedding her talon-like fingernails into her open palms. "Right," she continued pragmatically. "Suppertime."

For the first time, I would discover the horrors of quinoa.

* * *

Sitting in a bowl of what I can only describe as a facial cream sauce, Toni had sprinkled a handful of tomatoes and choice granules of half-cooked rice-like grit. At least I hoped they were tomatoes, as they quickly became obscured by the gloopy white substance, which Toni had assured me was sour cream, and a stick of celery she had added last-minute – no doubt to add a touch of colour to this less than paltry offering. My stomach lurched uncomfortably at the thought.

Perhaps my mistake had been in declaring that I ate everything. However, I was still uncomfortable and unfamiliar with this exotic creature who danced barefoot and sang off-key in Toni's kitchen while stirring a sticky sludge-like substance in a pot on the stove. So, I smiled and said nothing, making a mental note to visit the chippy or order a Chinese later – when I was safely back in the comfort of my home.

"It's quinoa," Toni called out, oblivious to my displeasure, as she whirled the spoon around with a gentle flick of her wrist. "*Very healthy* and *good* for you."

I looked at her blankly; whatever quinoa was, I was already *unkeen*, dipping the spoon slowly into the sinking abyss, noticing how the dish had an earthy smell not quite unlike compost.

Desperate to calm my stomach, which was roaring like the depths of a furnace, I tentatively lifted the spoon to my lips with as little of the texture as I dared. A mixture of surprise and nausea swept over me, and I gulped it down with the same pleasure a child might when confronted with cough syrup. Even Mum's poor attempts at cooking seemed more palatable than

47

this, or the grease infested scrapings that congealed at the bottom of a pan after one of Andy's 'cheeky' fry-ups.

It was *inedible*.

Luckily, I had a pack of slightly crusty tissues in my pocket and taking one; I stuffed the snow-white paper with the remainder of the meal; I was subconsciously watching as Toni continued to swing herself back and forth next to the stove.

She hadn't seen me.

Forcing back relief, I asked in a slightly meek voice: "May I have a glass of water?"- Still ignoring as best I could the sickly textured disaster that was stuffed from my hand into my trouser pocket.

Still oblivious, Toni gestured me off towards a shabby chic cabinet out of eye-sight and toward what I hoped was a bathroom. My legs felt slightly numb from the bean chair I had been sitting in, and my tongue was raw from the barely washed tomatoes.

Ignoring the shakiness from what I could only hope might be the resulting concussion, I swiftly pushed open the nearest pastel-coloured door. Then fumbled in the slightly dark and narrow space for a tap or at least a bin where I hoped I might be able to conceal somewhat my awkwardly wrapped, quinoa filled tissue. Peeling the soiled tissue all too readily from my possession, I flushed it down the loo and rested wearily against the door. Making a desperate attempt to relax my already shot nerves as I listened to the nasal singing from my new companion with both intrigue and steadily mounting constipation.

Why was I still here?

Something I reasoned was growing on me. That or I had terrible taste in music.

But as Toni's voice rang out like finely cut glass from the other half the hallway, requesting my presence to her latest 'culinary masterpiece' and I dashed back into the room – given my circumstances, it could have been either.

That, or concussion, is a hell of a drug.

Chapter 7: Troubles with Triage

Mol was angry with me.

Even though there was only a smile on my face, her beady eyes only met mine for a moment before turning away. There was no greeting - instead, she scurried to the furthest part of her hutch in the corner. She felt betrayed. I knew she had questions about the evening, but I couldn't answer them. Not when to be honest, I couldn't figure them out myself.

It had been extremely late when Toni and I had parted ways, and despite the lump that was growing on the back of my head, I felt strangely stable on my feet, though as she had almost gently kissed my cheek to say goodbye, the giddiness had returned. I felt drunk and light on my feet at the same time, and I slumped woozily onto my sofa, trying to avoid the glare from Mol. We would both be kidding ourselves if we said it was because she was due a feeding. We both felt unfulfilled, and my mind had become fixated on Toni.

Earlier that day, I had by no means been enamoured by Toni's cooking. But thankfully, due to a combination of the amount of time we had spent in her house; and the hefty blow her handbag had dealt my head, I had been able to coax her into ordering a takeaway. It would help me retain some sugars, salts, and other vital minerals to ensure my recovery. Given that it was my main meal of the day, I was insistent and all too happy to pay.

As such, that evening, we had sat talking, discussing life and her lifestyle choices as we consumed pots of warm strings of egg fried noodles and king prawn sushi.

In other parts of the world, people will often obsess with long periods over different characteristics regarding potential partners. For some, it might be height, hair colour, blood type, eyes or body shape. But in truth, this would not offer any reprieve for my current plight. One that I couldn't entirely put into words or fathomable reasoning.

Love or whatever this was, confused me.

I had no photos of Toni, nor could I describe what or how I felt for her. Whereas with Mol – though photos aplenty was a different species. I also doubt the blood type of a guinea pig would be of interest to most, though you never know there's probably some strange seedy website somewhere with indecent guinea pig behaviour.

Subconsciously visions began etching into my mind as I thought of this crazy pixie pink artisan, with deep purple eyes and the still faint smudge of bold crimson lipstick left on my cheek from her final farewell.

So when I finally got home to Mol, it took me half the night to face her properly. I made a point of almost making sure Mol could not see me until I had washed the imprinted lips from my cheek, trembling against the cold water as I squinted into my small shaving mirror. Subconsciously I traced the line of it for a moment with my forefinger. I reasoned that I was confused and wondered *what* if anything had come over me.

But I determined quickly enough I must still make peace with the one lady already in my life. Mainly since Mol and I lived together and I had not spent as much time as I should with her, even admittedly not for the most part on purpose.

So, I crept from the bed down the stairs with a packet of apple slices that I'd been saving for our anniversary and the new bowl I had bought her for her birthday. I determined that now would perhaps be the best time to present them to her in a bid to make amends. Then I pressed my nose to the wire of the cage. The metal stung like an inserted tennis racket, though I reminded myself I deserved it. "Mol," I whispered softly.

Two black eyes stared at me in the darkness. Mol was listening. At least I hoped so. I didn't want to sound desperate, but I needed her to understand. "Mol," even as I repeated her name, my voice seemed to crack with nerves and anticipation. "Even though I'm just a man, you're a guinea pig. No -" I quickly corrected myself. "You're *my guinea pig*, and you deserve respect!"

Before this incident, Mol and I could converse in-depth and freely. Although I admit, it was easier in the daylight, rather than these twilight hours where we both usually tucked ourselves away. That said, the occasional squeaks and whisker twitches obscured any abuse she might choose to give me.

Needless to say, the damage was done. Mol cried. I cried. She screamed; I sobbed. However, after two hours sinking back in the corner and with freshly developing backache, we made leeway whilst I rocked myself two and through and Mol, ever concerned for me, gently nuzzled my cheek.

We were to remain friends, not just for our sanity but for the lack of Kleenex, which had diminished throughout our angst. However, that being said, it still took some time for me to coax her into remaining at our house.

We'd been through so much together, I didn't want to push her away, and I even promised her that she needn't worry about the rent. I would provide her with the freshest water and food, and she promised me an ear should I need it for the company. That was Mol, always unselfish and caring and a good listener.

Still, I couldn't help but feel a tad egoistic for how I might still be using her. The truth was I needed her, as Mol only too quickly reminded me I was still in what others would consider *crushing on Toni. I* was undoubtedly terrified about being crushed by someone who had been an enigma within my socially-backwards lifestyle for so long.

In a single day, Toni had brought me both happiness and fear and a rush of adrenaline that I might doubt as being legal had I been at work, or that could have been the still lingering taste of quinoa at the back of my throat. I was tired and confused and not sure I could place any of it, wondering to myself:

Is this what it felt like to fall in love?

However, the words Toni had told me about her taste in men clouded my thoughts. To me, she struck me as a sincere person and forthright with her demands and her interests without compromise. Still, on the other hand, she had named her dog Reaper, which suggested a sarcastic sense of humour was lurking in the background of her psyche, not that I had known her long enough to tell.

All of this made me slightly uncertain, based alone on these two sides to Toni's character where I stood. *Was I starting to fall for her?* Could I even tell after a single day? - One where she had both successfully knocked me out and attempted to poison me with her hostess skills and immediately helped me to set up my dating website profile. Not least, I asked myself if I was too old for her? Did she even tell me her age? She certainly seemed younger, although she was certainly more ambitious, if mature, than Andy's type being a university drop-out.

Now I began to ask myself about potentially taking the risk and inviting her on a date, or if I would need to shave my eyebrows off now, or wait till the dust had settled, in the same way, that Mol's early mornings were spent burying deep into her bundle of straw. If there was one thing that our discussion had just taught me, break-ups and people's feelings could quickly get messy, and that was one piece of guinea pig droppings even I couldn't clean.

With each question, my head throbbed uncomfortably.

I knew I should probably get it checked. It was likely I would in the morning.

Still, for now, I was sat on my living room floor, staring up at the ceiling into my hands through the dark at the piece of torn notepaper inscribed with the name and number that was etched in scratchy black Biro by the bubblegum coloured angel I barely knew known as Toni.

Sleep would be best.

But I had pins and needles from sitting too long, so I kept staring up at the paper committing the details to memory until, at last, I fell into a somewhat peaceful reverie.

* * *

At half six, the sound of my alarm clock wailing from my bedroom jolted me awake. No doubt it was protesting about my lack of usual promptness where I effortlessly silenced its quaking silver body against the palm of my hand. Mol frowned at her premature awakening. Unlike me, she was not a morning creature; and it was not long before she had furrowed away back under the covers of her bed. I, on the other hand, grimaced and forced myself to stand, taking a moment to straighten my glasses which had left slight pink welts from where they had pinched the bridge of my nose.

It would be too early to go to the doctor. So instead, I contemplated options for my breakfast, careful to adjust my stride whilst the blood flow slowly returned to my legs and bottom.

Outside from my kitchen window, I could see the hints of smeary grey rain clouds. Hanging above the cluster of flats in which I called home, feeling grateful that I lived on the ground floor alongside the flint slate paths and half mossy window frames, in the conscious fear that I might develop vertigo.

The other residents were mostly quiet, though this was not solely due to the time of day; the majority of them had moved out years ago for something new and better. Perhaps Dover has that effect on people.

I decided to have a slice of toast, plain with a hint of butter, and then since I was awake and motivated, I would clean the toilet before I caught a bus to the hospital for a once over, Toni's number clinging loosely in my hand.

* * *

A lot of people don't seem to like hospitals. I suppose I'm one of them, except there is always the opportunity for subtle voyeurism. Once again, I was observing others from the corner of my notebook. I pondered the precise number of ailments and afflictions that have encouraged them to venture beyond the local surgery. Some I already know are cautious mothers, the first-timers – the self-conscious fussers and doters. Others are the elderly, once with stories to tell, now lost in a collective of furrowed brows and wrinkles. Finally, there's me, huddled quietly in the corner where I am altogether insignificant to everyone else. I am nursing a pack of peas and a

53

tea towel, which I had hastily gathered from the freezer before venturing out. A woman is repeatedly coughing to my left, jerking her head back and forth in quick succession into her hands. I can neither tell if she is dying of pneumonia or has not had enough to drink today, though the small plastic cup left trembling in her hands suggests that she is doomed to wait here in triage like everyone else.

After a few hours wait, I was finally assigned a moment with the doctor, a young chap who barely looked up from the clipboard of hastily stabled papers the nurse or receptionist had provided him earlier. The customary ticks and crosses and scribbles where I had noted my knowledge of any histories, allergies, and operations to date as best I could. I studied his face, in turn, noting the slightly rounded way his head resembled a hard-boiled egg with a mat of slightly yellow straw-like hair – wondering if indeed his yolk had cracked. "Alright, Mr Davis," he said flatly, his eyes finally meeting mine as he pushed forward on his desk so that he was facing me directly. "You appear to have a minor discolouration on the back of your head. However, I'm confident that should you have no signs of nausea or confusion that, you should be fully recovered before long!"

Waiting for me to confirm I understood him, I took his cue and nodded. I am dimly aware that now would not be the appropriate time to mention the experimental dish I had tasted the day before, grateful that I would not require further tests or treatments. The idea of a brain scan was not one I had ranked highly on my list of activities, although tempting as a lobotomy had sometimes felt. Usually, when I was with my mother or sitting with Dave and Andy spectating on another formulaic tedium that was the weekly televised football match, I was happy to have my instincts and vitals as normal as they usually were.

Now the doctor was standing, his body at an angle turned slightly from me, his long spindly fingers lifting a crisp document from the printer drawer. Handing it to me, he smiled confidently. "Have a fact sheet, Mr Davis!" He explained, gesturing his hands slightly as I stared almost blankly at the two-column document filled with illustrations and boxes of all the set text. "It should provide you with all the warning signs of concussion and where necessary," Here, he paused, seemingly for dramatic effect, "What you can and can't do, and when to come back and see me *should* there be an emergency."

I noticed the subtle way he stressed the last part. Taking this as a sign to leave, I studied the document once more before folding it firmly into four corners like a pocket square. I placed it safely into my coat, where it fitted itself snugly against my handkerchief and favoured bus pass. Following procedure and politeness, I shook the doctor's hand and strode out, happy to return to the fresh sea breeze and the chalky cry of seagulls screaming overhead.

* * *

Perhaps I should have had the lobotomy.

"GOAAAAAAAAAAAAAAAAAAAAL!" roars Andy flopping back on his seat as he grins ear to ear with the same enthusiasm as a Cheshire cat, the local team's colours barely wrapped around the tips of his broad shoulders from his scarf. On my other side, his partner in crime high-fives him keenly whilst I attempt to avoid spilling my pint of apple juice.

Perhaps my mistake had been falsely believing my friends when I ordered my drink that the pub would be quiet, forgetting that it was time for another televised match due to my day's longevity. But now, the loud eruptions of the civilised hoodlums and the high-pitched pings from the arcade machines by the door are grating on me more than ever, especially since they lack the cushion of alcoholic padding that I usually comfort myself with against such deafening stupor.

I had decided to go out with my friends this evening, but now I wonder if I am finally getting old. My stomach twists horribly. I distance myself from Andy and company for a moment, allowing myself to slip away to the gents' toilets, unmissed and unnoticed, ensuring to duck at appropriate intervals to avoid blocking the screen. Undeterred, my booth erupts again, this time into a moan of disapproval and petty anger. Someone has been issued a card.

55

Just as I returned from the bathroom, shaking the last bits of moisture from my hands, an outburst of laughter over-cut the room. The sound was pure and carefree as a schoolgirl but as wicked and crude as a jackal. I turned my head instinctively drawn to the sound, noticing her immediately, my pink-haired enigma: Toni.

Chapter 8: Slot Machines and Hitting the Jackpot

Even from a distance, there was no mistaking the striking bubble-gum coloured hair as it danced to-and-throw next to the slot machine, in a somewhat hypnotic manner, the combination of a monumental victory or rain dance. Nervously adjusting my ear to avoid the inadvertent twitch, I cleared my throat and called after Toni in greeting. She twirled towards me like an unnatural ballerina and smiled widely. "Hey, Frank," she said, waving warmly. It was then I realised she was not alone.

Crouching next to the machine, desperately attempting to scoop up the odd penny or two was a tall, thin young man, no doubt Toni's age or a tad older, with long blonde hair, a straggly mat of beard fluff, and a leather trench coat that could have rivalled that of a vampire. He certainly had the right expression: fixed and lifeless. His eyes ringed with creases of exhaustion and makeup. Toni nudged him, prodding him slightly but forcibly in the ribs encouraging him to stand. Startled, he suppressed a low moan and looked at me with bored eyes, acknowledging me with a simple "Yo" before returning to his previous task. This was a man of few words. Somewhat satisfied, I turned my attention back to Toni.

"Winning anything tonight?" I asked gently. Toni tittered, breaking into that smile I had started to grow so fond of. The one that made her eyes sparkle.

"Ten quid," she told me proudly. "But that one was at the Bingo!"

"Ah," I nodded. "What about your friend?"

"What, Billy?" she asked, her tone and brows changing slightly to a mixture of amusement and bemusement simultaneously. In the neon reddish light that surrounded this side of the pub, she looked almost smug. I nodded.

"Ain't got a leg to stand on," She replied calmly. "He only wants shiny ones!" Then as if it were an afterthought or not entirely meaningful, she introduced us. "My brother."

"Ah," I acknowledged. This time, it was seemingly my turn to be stuck for conversation. It surely wouldn't be long before Toni walked away.

At a loss and hoping to keep her there a while longer, I thought desperately about what we might be able to discuss, struggling with the combination of pulsating low budget wall speakers and the presence of her present if not altogether interested *brother*. But I had always sucked at small talk. Fighting another wave of nervousness, I hoped to relay a somewhat plausible reason for seeking her out; rather than returning to my friends. It would not be entirely long before the match finished. I had to say something, anything.

"I don't have a concussion," I told her hurriedly, although I wasn't entirely sure she had heard me.

"Oh," she answered flatly. Beside us, the slot machine made a generic squeal, flashing its row of amber and blue lights, emphasising her thick mascara tinted eyes.

I found myself gulping inwardly, not quite like a fish.

"Umm, Toni," I murmured, trying to gauge the moment as best I could. "Do you think we could have a word?" The silence was beginning to unnerve me; I felt small and insignificant as I had during my school days. Perhaps I should have shaved my eyebrows after all.

Toni, however, nodded, her eyes skimming above me towards the row of television sets and bustling booths. No doubt trying to work out where. Around us, each space was filled with football enthusiasts like Andy and my somewhat abandoned apple juice, and then there was Billy, who was now shuffling slightly toward the vacant ATM. There was no privacy to be found here, at least not on match night.

It was time for the lesser of two evils.

"Come on," She suggested, "Let's go outside!" And with a surprising display of strength, she tugged my somewhat stammering self out through the doors into the bar garden patio.

Its regular patrons knew the place as 'Smokers' Den'.

* * *

We stood together on the porch, slightly apart from one and another, as Toni huddled into herself to light a cigarette, fumbling somewhat with her cold fingers with her lighter. I was silent, too, as I sought clarity in my mind, listening to the faint clicking sound, and then acknowledged the now-familiar thick nicotine smell. I watched as it mingled with the cool sea breeze and drifted amongst the inky black clouds that still hung above.

For a split second, there was nothing else around us, like two floodlights on the otherwise darkened stage of a theatre. Two players embroiled in some deep and meaningful dialogue, an exchange of conflict or love; only I had not quite found the words to speak.

Here I could see clearly the lines of her face. How, the soft waves of pink that clung to her shoulders in candyfloss strands, the hidden gentleness of her eyes; which pierced outwards against the fading light; like a mystical beauty—hiding away from the world in a gauze of cigarette smoke. So unlike the shabby, plain man I knew only too well I was.

It was now or never.

"Toni, do you fancy getting a drink sometime?"

She blinked.

My words had no doubt been clumsy, hastily strung together in a bid to break the ice and avoid meaningless small talk. No doubt Toni already thought I was stupid asking such a question here, right next to the pub.

"Or a bite to eat, perhaps?"

"That's only if you'd like to, of course, no pressure."

Why was I still talking? I scolded myself again inwardly, feeling the first signs of ill-pleasure in my ear. Nervously I moved my hair away from it and forced out a smile as though attempting to validate my foolishness.

Again she blinked.

I thought to go, half hovering my hand over the door, ignoring the apparent thumping in my chest – a combination of what I perceived as heartache and frazzled nerves. I barely registered that Toni's hand was now on top of mine, cold and delicately pale, save for the darkened ruby hues of her nail varnish; and smudges of half-dried acrylic paint.

I turned, hesitantly, not quite sure how to meet her gaze, certain of the rejection that was sure to come, noticing the way parts of the tobacco rods and filter crumbled away into the ground; no more than meaningless pieces of litter – like me.

Into the silence, my heart continued to thud obnoxiously; until finally, Toni answered. Her voice was soft and husky as she brushed my trembling face with smooth claret lips, engaged in a game of Chinese Whispers only we two could hear.

"I'd like that, Frank."

Then she was gone. Back into the world of the slot machines and the footie fans. Back to Billy and the cheap pints of local beer. She left only the thin imprints of a kiss on my cheek and the rich aroma of a smoker's forbidden perfume.

* * *

On reflection, I believe now that it must have been the approaching cold that swept over my shoes rather than the wailing of my companions that drew me back inside. Still, I only stood outside in the garden for a few minutes before I retreated into the warmth of the pub, my eyes taking a few minutes to adjust to the harsh amber glow of the lighting.

Approximately ten minutes had passed in real time since we had ventured out, the football still booming from the black brick speakers plugged at jarring angles against the walls. I was tempted to look for Toni, consciously aware of the contrast offered by my two friends. Dave and Andy were joined in the ritualistic celebration, weaving the local team coloured scarves proudly around their necks as they saluted the on-screen pixilated players with bottled beer.

I made my way to our booth, tentatively sniffing my half discarded drink as I shuffled down as best I could between my friends. Andy clapped his arms around me firmly. "You took a while, mate!" He chirped, nudging me clumsily in a brotherly fashion – one of the many signs he had had one too many. "Stuck in the queues for the bog?"

I chose not to reply, smiling sheepishly, choosing instead to feign as much interest as I could as I carefully redirected his drunken mindset towards the football. "What's the score?"

"2-1. Carlisle's gone for it in the thirty-eighth minute!" Andy grinned confidently.

"Oh?"

Glad my trick had worked, I offered to buy them each a fresh round, grateful that I was not the centre of attention, and I could take in – as best I could, the feelings surrounding my first kiss.

Andy's eyes were glued to the screen; I watched the glazed euphoria return and stood confidently, ready to approach the bar as the match continued; when I realised Dave was pointing at me.

"Hey, what's that on your cheek?" He asked loudly.

Shit.

Nervously I reached for my apple juice and took a long drink, then peered down into the neck, certain that Dave's brazen manner would attract Andy or other punters to our booth to probe me with unwanted questions. My ear twitched horribly.

Dave continued obliviously. "Is that lipstick on your cheek?"

I feigned a smile, trying to shrug him off. "Come on; I'll get you a refill," I said with as much confidence as I could muster.

But, powered by alcoholic filled endorphins, Dave's determination was growing.

"Look!" he relayed animatedly, tugging Andy's sleeve. "Frank's got a kiss!"

"Eh?" Andy replied, still engrossed in the game.

Undeterred, Dave tried again.

"Frank's got lucky!"

For a moment, no one was quite sure that Andy was heard. Initially, he said nothing, preferring to tug his sleeve away from Dave's hands; but then, with a solemn look, he stared at me dead on, almost in disbelief.

It was hopeless. Desperately I tried to ignore the angst in the pit of my stomach and quickly grabbed my handkerchief from my pocket, rubbing the lipstick from my cheek, which stained my face like a tramp stamp. It was still there.

So, still, without explaining anything, I dashed off from the booth, seeking the welcome relief of the bathroom. Instantly I locked the door and began peering into the mirror at the deep crimson stain that hogged the circumference of my left cheek. Briefly, I wondered whether or not this was how she preferred to mark her territory, not that I would in any way call Toni a dog.

Outside I could hear the hammering and catcalls of my Dave and Andy, who had snapped out of his reprieve to holler, "Frank's in love, Frank's in love!" with the same grace and charm as a pair of schoolgirls caterwauling.

It would be best to ignore them. Both would tire of the matter soon, or else they would be approached by a member of bar staff who no doubt would *encourage* them to move on. So I used the time to remove my glasses and splash my face with warm water, dabbing at the remaining lipstick with a wad of disposable towels.

Now alone, I couldn't help but smile. In that instance, I knew two things. The first – that I should have ordered myself a burger, one with extra pickle and cheese, relishing the way the meat seemingly slid between two halves of bread. The other -albeit rather rapidly that I was smitten with this candy floss haired goddess.

Chapter 9: Impromptu Plumbing & Cliff Based Sandwiches

I knew today was going to be one of those days. The toilet was broken. The whole thing was blocked in several arteries of its small porcelain bowl, no doubt from the curry which I had eaten the night before. Takeaway boxes still streamed across the living room floor like confetti with bold red letters on their crisp white paper packaging from where I had discarded them—a casual mess brought on the haze of alcohol and peer pressure.

When I had finally faced my friends, there had been heavy thuds on my back in congratulations and owl sounds ushered in my ear the same repeated empty syllables chorusing "Who?, Who? Who?" And at that moment, the perspective refill of apple juice no longer seemed an option, and my usual pint of larger became my evening's prescription.

Toni and I had made plans to meet up later, a suggestion I had made before bed through a brief exchange of texts. I would send a quick message momentarily, suggesting that she come in the afternoon, giving me enough time to rectify any last-minute plumbing job. My phone blinked at me, a casual reminder that it needed a charge. I rooted around in my drawer for the suitable cable, grateful I had got a multipack of them at the local discount store for such occasions.

Now, I stood on my hands and knees hastily covered by bold yellow rubber gloves and clutching a squeaky duck. I'd never understood it, but the term *Toilet Duck* had been a recommendation by my mother or my wayward, drunken imagination. Even though I lived alone, the whole process still felt foreign to me; lifting the top of the tank and tugging on the handle; in the vain hope that it would flush. Even the duck appeared to mock me, bobbing unhelpfully in the thin body of water. I would need some outside help, a plumber and an aspirin.

* * *

Mol seemed amused as I moved despairingly downstairs into the front room and began rummaging around in the front cupboard for the Yellow Pages, wondering in some distant way whether the name had come from years of mocking pets relieving themselves on the sturdy, brick-like books. Not that this would ever include guinea pigs, which were usually quite well behaved and did not need a barrage of endless treats to perform tricks and fawn after their owners in false displays of love and affection.

With a playful but firm grunt, she caught my attention, pressing against the cage looking towards my computer desk. "Go online," she quipped impatiently. No doubt, unaware of the twists and turns, I always found myself unravelling when I trawled the web. Still undeterred, she blinked up at me with unwavering loyalty.

I hesitated a little as I weighed up my options and recalled relevant conversation snippets here and there. *Had* Andy once turned his hand to DIY? *Was* Bazil likely to have a toolbox I could purchase? Or would it be best asking my father for his opinion? – Assuming I could reach him in the unlikely chance, he was not engrossed in the television or having his ear chewed off by Mum as she twittered and chattered away about various family activities or how he should better spend his pension. My brain ached at the thought.

Having retrieved the phone book, I leafed through the battered pages to the relevant section of speculative 'professionals'. Cocklescanslanky is not by any means a large town; however, I was still hopeful that I might find some person of local interest. I was comparing them to the bold square box advertisements of Dover and the South East Coast's most sufficient water workers.

Mol tutted in disapproval. The clock had just passed two.

Even if I had hoped otherwise, the thought of the vile smell that would erupt from the toilet would not long cloud any view toward furthering my fledgling romance.

I sighed and considered whether it would be best to go back upstairs to retrieve my mobile or to the kitchen, where I maintained a permanent link to reality with the mismatched canary coloured landline when the doorbell rang.

Flustered, I scrambled up from the floor, barely avoiding knocking my head on the lowest shelf, hastily slinging the disused marigolds into my back pocket and peered through the meshed curtain on the door. Internally my heart skipped and sighed. It was Toni.

* * *

Bold or ignorant. That is how Toni presented herself as she smiled brightly, her eyes twinkling with youth and mischief. "Hi Frank, aren't you gonna invite me in?" she asked warmly, moving forward to the open door frame, which I nervously attempted to close behind me as I stepped over the threshold.

She was wearing a red leather mini skirt over leggings with a semi low-cut top that had strategically placed slits in the shoulders adorned with kitschy golden and silver sequins and black thigh-high leather boots.

Through the gaps in her top, I caught the hint of her ever-ominous tattoo, reminding me of that day I had observed her as little more than a fellow passenger on the bus. I resisted the opportunity to stare and gulped inwardly whilst the moisture from the gloves dribbled down my leg.

"Err," I replied, worried both about my relatively personal predicament and my somewhat unkempt appearance. It had been made even more apparent by my somewhat crooked glasses, from where I had attempted to discover some form of plumbing solution – however haphazardly.

As ever, Toni's gleaming purple eyes swallowed me whole. *Why had I invited her here? Dates didn't happen on doorsteps.*

I *had* to let her in.

Without so much as a step, Toni glided past me effortlessly like a butterfly. Her body slid past me in the same way as a librarian would turn the pages of a book. She was no doubt used to my umming and ahhing, which had recently become synonymous with my character, much like the more nuanced mechanics of a fridge.

"So, what's going on?" She asked as she seated herself on my bottle green sofa, acknowledging somewhat silently the takeaway cartons and disposable plastic drinking cups. This was another question I couldn't quite find the reply to, even though I partly knew the answer this time.

Toni's room, in contrast, in our initial meeting, had appeared a haven of 'organised chaos', making me feel more awkward and slovenly. In her corner, Mol had hidden away. I only hoped she had decided to give Toni and me some privacy, though subconsciously, I knew it was a deep-rooted shame at my shortcomings.

I had been alone, too long.

But Toni smiled, a slight grin twitching on the edges of her waxy red lips as she guided the conversation on my behalf. "Must have been a late-night then?" I later supposed this was normal for the younger generation. Perhaps she had seen it all before in some grungy student dormitory or the no doubt musky sleeping quarters of Billy. I laughed awkwardly, again raking my hair with one slightly damp hand. I shouldn't have asked her to come.

But then again, silence wouldn't help.

I forced myself to speak, my throat seemingly raw from the previous evening and the panic I had found myself in. "Yeah," Everything felt uncomfortable and formal, something that usually offered me some relief, now adding distance between us.

I sighed silently.

And now she was repeating herself. "Well, what's going on?" Toni asked, her words casually cutting through the silence. She had noticed the flash of yellow in my trouser pocket, protruding awkwardly like a rubber chicken. "What's that smell? You're not cooking, are you?"

66

I coughed weakly, watching as her nose wrinkled. Resigned as I currently was, I would have to tell her.

"My toilet,"

In the space of five seconds, my imagination managed to conjure up fifty or so scenarios for how Toni would react. However, none prepared me for the eruption of laughter that echoed from my companion as she chuckled haughtily, in the same way, a teenager might. I blinked, confused.

Despite being an older brother, I still didn't understand women.

Yet for a moment, her laughter felt comforting, and I listened to it attentively like birdsong as it danced off my eardrums.

Finally, choking back some composure, Toni looked somewhat solemn for a moment as she asked her next question. "Plumbing problems?"

I nodded sheepishly, tugging the gloves from my pocket with a slight pang of guilt and plastic. "I haven't called the plumber yet," I mumbled, "Perhaps you'd prefer to rearrange our date?"

Standing, I made towards the front door, but Toni stooped me. Whilst she had also got to her feet, she was striding away from my living room door towards the hallway, to the staircase, tracking the source of the offending smell in the same way that the police might employ a tracker dog.

"Where is it?" She asked in what must have been more a formality as I vaguely motioned awkwardly to the bathroom door as my faster, younger companion headed over. My heart was hammering after her as she crossed the hallway, knowing with some flutter of suppressed primal urgency that she was close to my bedroom.

Clearing my throat, I reached her and pointed to the middle door on the left, the foremost one before the airing cupboard. "In there."

"Right," Toni acknowledged, pushing the door open first. Subconsciously I pinched my nose as I joined her.

In the time that I had unwillingly dithered around the subject, a pool of tepid pond-like water had seemingly oozed from the toilet. It had overflowed itself onto the accompanying avocado and beige striped bath mat, and Toni was on her hands and knees looking deeply into the bowl, where she seemed strangely determined or disgusted.

Instinctively I wanted to apologise.

"Toni I-"

"Do you have a plunger?" She requested.

"Pardon?"

Again, she cut me off, this time somewhat impatiently. "Do you have a plunger? And a bucket?"

I had to think quickly, going over the inventory of items I had got when I had first purchased my home, grateful that a few things slowly seemed to click. "Yes," I affirmed at first shyly, then more confidently a second time. "Yes, I do."

"Good!" Toni's words were assertive. I heard Mol's voice in the back of my head. *"Maybe she knows what she's doing!"*

I could only hope.

Forcing myself to move, I raced down to the kitchen, my feet pattering nervously across the vinyl floor, once again rooting around the lower cupboards that now followed under the sink.

In the bathroom, Toni called after me. "Fill the bucket with water Frank,"

"Got it," I shouted back, keen not to hit my head again as I retrieved the bucket from where it hung on a thin gold-plated hook at the back wall, snugly resting under the tap. Placing the bowl in the deeper of the two kitchen basins, I added as much warm water as I dared. Just shy of half full. I reasoned that it would soon become quite heavy, hoping to avoid any "unnecessary accidents". This term had been described hypothetically during a health and safety talk at work.

When I returned, Toni had opened up the tank.

"Good," she declared as she stood again, reaching for the bucket which I handed her bemused.

"What are we doing?" I asked my first question of the day, watching fascinated as she lifted the seat's lid away and began to pour the water down into the bowl.

"Flushing!" Declared Toni, proud of herself as she continued with her work until the bucket was empty. I was secretly glad I had removed the toilet duck before she had arrived, acknowledging it with a silent nod as it sat once more on the metallic rack above the bath.

With a swift and forceful tug, Toni yanked the handle on the toilet, watching satisfied as the blockage, whatever it had been, was beginning to wash away into the abyss. Then clapping her hands satisfied, she smiled as though nothing had happened.

"Let's go out for lunch."

* * *

A short time later, the two of us sat side by side overlooking the water and the white cliffs we knew so well. I was glad to be out in the fresh air after the bathroom incident, watching as the seagulls dived and glided amongst the rock faces, as I enjoyed the relish of my beef sandwich. We had both considered going to one of the cafes in town, but I was happy to avoid the possibility of Toni being confronted with her less than subtle smoking habit. Instead, I purchased us both a meal deal from the local supermarket, glad that one of her many 'vices' – as Toni called them - was being a strict vegetarian. So, she had picked out an egg and cress on wholemeal, which littered a thin trail of crumbs on her skirt, which temporarily doubled as an apron.

"So, how long have you been able to plumb then?" I asked, genuinely interested, while Toni took a drag from her cigarette,

"Hmm?" she replied, exhaling slowly before turning to me. "Able to plumb?"

I smiled. "Yes. You fixed my toilet in no time, saved me having to call the plumber."

"Oh, that!" She replied, grinning now, "Learned a few bits when I was studying. And Billy helped,"

"Billy?" I asked, somewhat surprised.

Toni noticed my tone and nodded eagerly. "Yeah, he has his uses, sometimes,"

"That's good," I smiled inwardly, noticing the faint blush on her cheeks. "Probably not what you were expecting on a first date, though," I joked with a hint of temporal boldness.

"No," She admitted, "But at least you bought me dinner,"

"Dinner?" Now, it was my time to be puzzled. I wondered if more time had passed by than I thought, or if indeed, this was all a hallucination brought about by my still lightly bruised head.

Toni laughed again, a sincere chuckle that I couldn't help but note how much it suited her. "Sure, for the *plumb job,*" she said, referencing my earlier attempts at communication in haphazard pigeon English.

Had I not been so distracted, I might have noticed she was teasing me, but I was temporarily distracted by her smile and the fraying piece of cress that dangled out of her upper lip like a piercing.

"What do you fancy?" I asked, shuffling sideways on the wall a little, careful not to spike myself on the occasional bits of broken flint and brickwork so that Toni could stand with dignity to shake the crumbs from her skirt. I forced my attention towards the water, glad for the sight of the dingy pulling away from the harbour so I could avoid being construed as disrespectful. Heeding the advice Mum had installed into me at a young age, it was not 'nice' to look up girls' skirts. Or, at least following Dad's amendment later in life, *not* without their permission.

With wild abandon Toni shook the crumbs free from her skirt, shimming her hips back and forth like a go-go dancer, laughing freely as a faint wisp of cress drifted along with the breeze. Even out of the corner of my eye, I couldn't help but admire the way her mane of pink hair flew and darted about with her dance. Nor the rich purple galaxy of her eyes crinkled in mirth. Impulsively I stood and danced alongside her as the audience of seagulls chorused down from the sky, thanking us for their breakfast as we whooped and cheered in unison.

Finally, I felt free.

Chapter 10: Italian Food & French Kissing

Sadly the euphoria wouldn't stay.

Growing up, I had always been led to believe that dinner was a formal affair. A romantic view, I had learnt from my Mother. It was merely "Too difficult to host such events!" Mostly this was true when there were children around. "Even if one knew everybody!" Mum would always tell us with a sigh as she put away her prized and seldom seen fine-china after Christmas.

But now Toni and I were sitting in an Italian restaurant on the high street. After several hours outside by the water, my stomach had rumbled uncomfortably, and Toni insisted that we ate something - for real.

The venue? Toni had selected it randomly, based on the font's colour and style on the sample menu. It was a somewhat gaudy and overtly decorative thing, plastered in a metallic gold frame at the front of the building. There were not many places to choose from Cocklescanslanky does not have many dining locations for the average Joe Blogs. Most of our attractions and eateries were further South and along the coast, out towards Dover. A number were overlooking the pier and private jetty of yachts and party cruisers. Each embellished with five-star ratings and white-billboard teeth. So based on familiarity and budget, we chose Italian.

Self-consciously, I hoped somewhat to impress my date even if my initial feelings were somewhat conjured from intrigue and lust.

Inside we were greeted by a waiter. We were asked to wait a moment at the front desk - A small cramped space, made all the more uncomfortable, by a large, plastic-looking potted palm tree. While he looked to find us a table, no doubt given our clothing, something 'quiet' and 'near the back'. Finally, he placed us in a 'private booth', near the toilets. To make up for it, we were presented with a rose and a candle on the table. Toni hastily moved these to the side, murmuring something about Feng Shuai. A somewhat ironic move on her part - as she seemed unaware of the red and white gingham squared tablecloth. Even though this somewhat clashed with her skirt.

I glanced over to her from the folds of my extensive, burgundy coloured menu. I found myself wondering out loud if she were any better than I at deciphering the food selection. All the dishes were written in unfamiliar, slightly cursive Italian. At this, Toni suggested in a bold whisper that we should try squinting. Perhaps, then the "words might somewhat blend together". As she played 'Guess the Dish', I hoped that none of the dishes Toni chose to eat would contain meat.

Still, at least one of us was entertained.

"You sure this is a good idea?" I asked cautiously as Toni ran her finger over the mains looking for familiar phrases. Catching my gaze, she beamed up at me.

"Course Frank," Her voice was cheerful and carefree.

Something I suspected this restaurant wasn't.

My knowledge of Italian had rarely ventured beyond the frozen pizza selection at the supermarket. That, and on occasion, a tin of watered down, tomato-infused spaghetti hoops.

As a child, Mother had always offered us dishes comprising of English staples. Years later, I remain reminiscent of cremated or half-charred sausages that had been cooked both too high and too long. Until the day might come, we lost our taste buds; since, as my father had long since learned, *not to be fussy*.

I didn't immediately notice the waiter had arrived by our table. That was until he offered a somewhat 'polite' and almost dignified cough. "Are you ready to order?" he asked, his voice practically dripping with disdain.

Quickly, I looked down at the selection. I hoped to buy some time. Toni was lost in her thoughts, absent-mindedly playing with the tassel at the end of her menu. Her lilac eyes were staring towards the far corners of the room at the slightly lowered ceiling. Glazed and unfocused, I reckoned she was not on Earth absent-mindedly. How I wished I could join her.

"Well..." I began.

"Sir?" he prompted. I recognised that tone from work.

He was Bored.

"Hmm," I tried again. As I scanned over prices and descriptions as fervently as possible, I inwardly cursed my lack of speed reading skills.

"We'll have the Fettuccine Alfredo," interjected Toni. "And the Marinara,"

The waiter paused. Then slowly bowing his head, he replied. "Very good, *Ma'am*," Before he retreated towards the kitchen, but I stared, shocked and open-mouthed, at my suddenly bilingual companion.

The words, "How did you?" seemed to etch themselves from my lips. Followed by a less-incredulous, "I thought you said you couldn't speak Italian?"

Toni chuckled. "I don't."

"Then, how?" I asked, once more finding myself confused.

Toni only shrugged. "My mother's name is Marina,"

I daren't ask her if this would make me a cannibal. I suspected I would not understand the answer.

So instead, I tried a new tack. "How's the feta cheese?" I asked, praying I had understood the nature of her dish.

Toni snorted in delight. "It's Parmesan,"

No wonder I had always stuck to the supermarket. Restaurant food is complicated.

* * *

Dessert was more straightforward - an overpriced but creamy gelato – which was the same taste and texture for all its flavour, if not the pronunciation of ice cream. Toni had burbled away happily as she sipped on her glass of wine, tittering here and there about the other guests who scuttled uncomfortably past our table towards the toilets. She had gathered the rose from its rather square vase, and pressed its wet and crimson petals onto the lapel of her jacket, and packed a 'doggy bag' in her handbag for Reaper for when she went home.

I had paid. It seemed like the gentlemanly thing to do. I only hoped that my paling face was noticeable as I swallowed and returned to escort my lady from the building. Even I didn't ask for the alternative. Toni's fingernails, I imagined, were more dangerous than my bank balance.

We stepped out onto the high street. I was conscious of the cool breeze that wafted from the sea as I thought over my day. I seldom took any extended time off from work. The last time I had done so was to deep clean Mol's pen – a typically weekend based ritual in which my furry companion and I discussed work colleagues, crosswords and grass. Perhaps I should be cleaning it now. I knew where things went then.

I turned to Toni. Choosing where I could, my words carefully. Sure, however, that she would understand. We were both pet owners, after all. I would use an anecdote to guide the conversation. But just as I had composed my thoughts, in a convincing attempt of sentence structure, Toni's lips crashed onto mine. Slipping in between my nervous and parted lips, a rough but silken tongue.

I was speechless.

At the tender age of forty-five, I had my first kiss.

I didn't count the hasty childlike pecks that had been forced on me at school by idly playing classmates during kiss-chase. Nor did I count the brandy rich pecks from overly familiar relatives at weddings or my male colleagues' lady-friends at the bar.

The kiss was soft and gentle and deliciously wet. Instinctively I pulled Toni closer to me, breathing in as I did the hypnotic scent of her flowery perfume and the taste of cherry liquor from her lips. Toni nestled into me. Having seen her without her shoes in my house, I realised she was actually shorter than me and was instead heightened by her sharp thigh-length boots, so I could cradle her into my arms and listen to the pounding of her heart, as it rhythmically answered to the thud, thud, thudding of my own. Despite her exterior, Toni was deliciously woman. Something I had never dared to notice before. Had I been blind?

I was certainly in awe. Toni was beautiful.

For a moment, I closed my eyes. Listening to the sound of her breath as she moaned into me. And the distant sounds of the seagull chorus above like a choir of seaside angels.

Then, just as suddenly, Toni moved away.

Confused, I staggered nervously, opened my eyes and cleared my throat. I was not sure whether I had done something wrong. Or simply whether Toni needed to breathe. Nevertheless, my stomach lurched somewhat at the thought.

Cautiously I met her gaze. I was once more caught by the ripple of violet lights in her eyes that danced against the summer sun. I wasn't quite sure how to speak. I shuffled over the moments in mind in the same way a card may begin to part the deck. I was drawing blanks. "Toni, uh, guinea pigs um."

She smiled, her voice patient. "Yes?"

"Mol probably needs feeding," I uttered weakly. *Was this how love-struck teenagers felt?* My brain felt woolly, fuelled by hormones.

I was certainly acting like one.

Once more, I found myself tripping on my words. Until Toni answered for me, kissing me gently on the cheek in the same delicate manner that enthralled me the first time.

And then, pinning the flower she had salvaged earlier, she gingerly placed it into my shaking hands and whispered: "Come back with me, Frank."

Her smile was genuine and glittering against the golden and apricot sunset and her candyfloss peony hair.

* * *

If making love is a dance, I have two left feet. We arrived at Toni's, somewhat giggly and stumbling, whilst Toni retrieved her key from her skirt's back pocket with surprising ease. I was not foolish enough to think she hadn't done this before, recalling momentarily the venom she had spouted during our first meeting.

Still, there was slight tenderness in the way her body swayed toward the door, holding a single finger to her lips as she mouthed to be quiet in case of any unsuspecting neighbours.

I, however, was a virgin. Middle-aged and nervous. As Toni unlocked the door, my left ear started to twitch again, uncomfortable with panic and the warm summer breeze.

I took a breath, looking to the road that adjoined hers, desperate to distract myself. Row upon row of uneven flint worked its way asymmetrically at the top of the wall, and a mint green bicycle propped itself against the gate of one of the houses, casting shadows from the slowly setting sun. A ginger cat walked lazily along with the stones, gnawing at the strands of grass that poked through, browning from the lack of rain.

Behind me, I heard the scraping and clicking of the metal key in the lock and felt the warmth of Toni's hand as she padded her nails along my arm like a kitten, whispering huskily. "Let's go in."

I gulped and swallowed. Then without saying a word -

I ran.

Chapter 11: Going Cold Turkey

I was never athletic at school.

Running as best I could, I determined to focus on the sounds of my chocolate brown shoes as they padded harshly on the pavement rather than my already erratic and sharp wheezing; the resulting repercussions of a panic attack and unsolicited exercise. I daren't even for a moment turn to face the confusion and hurt in Toni's eyes or the sharp flecks of her silky rosy hair as it waved forlornly in the wind. Only dimly aware as she called after me. Her outcry stung.

Replaying bus routes in my head, I made a left turn near a post box before immediately doubling over to catch my breath while I acknowledged to my hammering heart. I felt nauseous, and the back of my neck was sweaty with fresh perspiration as my inner thoughts whirred in panic:

I couldn't go back.

I had to get home.

Just had to get home.

Now.

Awkwardly I fumbled with my jacket to check I had my essentials with me.

Phone – Wallet – Keys.

I had everything.

Toni hadn't followed.

This was just as well as I had uncomfortable feeling spreading inside my trousers, which I knew wasn't entirely sweat. I cursed privately. *"Shit!"*

What had I done?

Although it was unlikely anyone would look down at my trousers at that moment, I had left myself painfully aroused and had fled the scene aware of my incompetence pulsing between my legs.

Closing my eyes, I counted down from 10 inside my head until the sensation started to fade, something I felt unreserved relief for, given the occasional nightlife that frequented the area. It was time to go home.

I wasn't ready.

I willed myself to believe I was sensible. That I *was* unprepared, and neither of us had, had protection.

It would be better to tell myself it was lust. It had to be.

However, such thoughts would do me no good.

Toni had entered my heart.

* * *

I didn't call or text Toni for several days. That wasn't to assume I didn't want to. But I wasn't sure what to say. Even from my limited understanding of the dating scene, I knew that chasing someone only worked in movies; I didn't even recall her favourite flowers or even if she ate chocolate. My knowledge of vegan brands extended to the courtesy information on the sides of sweet wrappers I occasionally indulged in. Toni and I hadn't discussed these things - yet.

In truth, I knew very little about her – only that her dog was Reaper and her brother Billy - that her flat was on the end terrace of an estate with a faint patch of the sea just visible from beyond the wall. The penmanship of her tattoo was in some variation of *Cinzel Black,* and her ruby red lipstick tasted slightly of strawberries, half-bitten paintbrushes and tobacco.

Moreover, she tormented me, like a phantom I had barely glimpsed, save for the bittersweet tone she approached life in neon pink battles and leopard print stares.

So, a week went by, long and by choice uneventful, with the semblance of work adding a welcome monotony to my blackened mind.

* * *

"Of course, you won't get her, Frank!" said Andy bluntly. "It's 'cos you suffer from *low* self-esteem,"

We were in Morses', for what Andy called *'Therapy'*, going out after work to *"pick up chicks"* on a Friday evening. I hadn't wanted to, of course, but Andy had insisted I should be his wingman since Dave was *"being conditioned to stay home by Yvonne like a lost cause!"* Besides, Andy remained determined that I would at least remain his disciple in learning how to find some form of romantic if temporary endeavour.

"First mistake you can make, bud, is getting henpecked!" Andy iterated proudly. "You gotta keep 'em *keen*; you know what I mean?"

I didn't.

Instead of replying, I smiled as best I could, hoping that my pint would soon evaporate the sense and clarity of this and similar conversations. I wanted nothing more than to return home to the sympathetic smiles of Mol; and the comfort of my bed.

The problem there was I was a much slower drinker or talker, whereas Andy seemed oblivious and in full animation, as he directed his attention towards one of the girls in one of the opposite booths who had caught his eye.

He would no doubt make his way over there soon, while I guarded our booth against the odd patron who would be interested in getting a discounted family meal and "use it for its *proper* purpose".

Since there were only two of us here tonight, it didn't even seem like we needed more than a table for two. But logic was wasted on Andy. Now was not the time. So, as usual, I bit my tongue and said nothing.

Andy liked to lounge nonchalantly at his leisure would always make a beeline for the booths as soon as we arrived, as to best to encourage his latest female entourage of groupies. It was the same way that a rock star's voice might caress his adoring fans across the stage. When such matters usually transpired, I would sit on the end and nod and engage in relevant fact feedings to bolster Andy's claims that he was the *best thing since sliced bread.* Something I didn't believe but was grateful to play for time until I was asked to get us all another round in or could use an excuse to break away from the throng to go home or stretch my legs, whichever came sooner that evening.

I must have been staring into the void that was my pint for a while because I didn't immediately notice when someone called my name.

Not at least until a ruby red handbag was thrust on the table in front of me, and I was met face to face with a pair of googly purple eyes, enhanced by the foamy depths of my tankard.

"Frank," she repeated. Toni's voice was firmer this time as I blinked and lifted my head to her in a somewhat drunken haze. "We need to talk."

I knew I shouldn't have come.

The harsh splash of cold water temporarily stunned me as I confronted myself in the bathroom mirror. As quickly as Toni had arrived, I had retreated, mumbling some apology about my bladder and used the time to rinse my face.

It had been hard to tell in the somewhat off yellow lighting, but her eyes had seemed slightly redder. *Had she been crying? I* wasn't sure how to broach the subject, so I flattened my hair in the mirror and straightened the collar of my pale white shirt against my neck so that it sat more comfortably against the 'V' of my bottle green jumper and less against my jugular. I was nervous.

Sweating.

Now once again, tongue-tied.

It was somewhat gratifying to know that for a moment, I had some security within the darkened walls of the cubicles, knowing with absolute certainty that Toni couldn't enter here. *It was common decency, after all.* Although, as my mind twisted back to me, *I couldn't leave either.*

I considered whether to text Andy and ask him to accompany me, my fingers half dialling out my digital SOS but thought better of it. By now, if he hadn't already, Andy would be on the dance floor with one or two girls, showing off his *moves.* I could hear the thud, thud, thudding of the bass from the speakers now. *Or was that my heart?*

Maybe I shouldn't have drunk so much.

Pushing the door as little as I dared, I used the tight slither of space to peer out at Toni, whose waterfall of candyfloss hair was still visible from her prior position at the booth. She was waiting for me.

My body trembled a little.

Although we hadn't known each other long, I knew she was not a wallflower when it came to speaking her mind and remembered her verbal onslaught that fateful day at the bus stop.

It was time to face the music.

So, although with none of the grace or charisma of a cowboy entering a salon, I made my way back, walking towards her. Keeping my voice as level as I dared, I sat down opposite her and replied.

"Hello, Toni."

* * *

As it turned out, she *had* been crying.

We both had a lot to say, but despite the strong feelings we shared, all Toni did was sit quietly, her lilac eyes filled with unasked questions. *"Why?"* She hissed, her voice barely audible over the room.

I frowned inwardly. Was there a correct answer here? I was almost confident there was none.

Around us, the world seemed to continue obliviously.

I could hear the whirring and cheeping of the slot's machines and the popular music that shuddered through the speakers. And here still, the incomprehensible chatter between friends at other tables and in clusters around the bar and the interspersed bursts of laughter from Andy and his temporary new love interests went on.

Guilt weighed down on me as though even the pockets of my coat and trousers were filled with sand. Toni deserved an answer, but I couldn't give one. *Not here.*

So, I said the only thing I could think of: "I'm sorry, Toni,"

We both paused.

However, life sped up.

I barely realised as a fist headed straight towards my face. My eyes had hardly adjusted in the ambient surroundings, let alone the foreign sight of outstretched hairy knuckles. Knuckles of a hand I didn't recognise. How could I? Certainly not before the sickly aftertaste and smell of blood.

My blood.

Then pain.

And black.

Chapter 12: Toni Nose Best

One thing I've decided about pub rugs is they always taste of stale alcohol and chip fat. Fat that's been accumulated for many years, from overly zealous youngsters who lose their grip on their cutlery or a meager morsel of their budgeted dinner, with smudgings of peas, fish fingers and carpet fluff.

It was all this that brought me too, followed by a distinct, sharp pain in my nose. Instantly, I reached, albeit almost blindly, for my handkerchief but was instead greeted with the crisp cheap paper of a serviette and a loud shout for ice amidst the din of music and murmuring punters and bystanders. My vision was blurred without my glasses. I made a note to gather them back onto my face, praying they weren't broken. They weren't. So, I pushed them back onto my face and forced myself to sit, adjusting my vision as much as I dared against the growing throbbing in my nose and temples.

Bent in front of me was Toni, who had crouched low onto the floor. She was kneeling up to my level with a bundle of napkins in her hands. Each complimented the mismatched collection of slightly red blotted serviettes that fell from my torso as I sat. I mused to myself that she might well have been temporarily concerned about me, although right now she was screeching, reprimanding at someone else in the bar, demanding they fetch some ice.

I wasn't sure what to say even now, consumed by a feeling of both carpet fat grogginess and guilt. My voice was slightly hoarse as I murmured a small, almost inaudible "Hi."

It was loud enough. Toni turned almost immediately, her long pink hair almost whipping against her shoulders, as the anger faded from her eyes. Now, a small smile allowed itself to form on her deep red lips for a moment before she recognised the blood and frowned, moving a hand closer towards me. "Frank, I'm so sorry," she said emphatically. "So sorry,"

She sounded sincere, but in this hazy state, I noticed her nails resembled talons of a bird of prey: long, thick and acrylic, a combination of cheap nail polish and painting supplies. Unwittingly I flinched, watching in dismay as her frown deepened further. Frowning didn't suit her.

"Billy shouldn't have-" Toni was still talking, but I cut across her. Even though I knew it was rude, determination over-rid the throbbing in my nostrils.

"No, I am."

At this, Toni stopped. For a moment, I thought she might have turned to stone. I looked into the indigo pools of her eyes, trying to read her, as another napkin slowly drifted from her hands. It drifted down and away from my face, free-falling temporarily. Then it landed onto the floor between us, like an icy, white snowflake that had been swallowed into a momentous vacuum. Now it was her turn to whisper, the words almost sticking in her throat. "Why?"

At that moment, she seemed so vulnerable. So, unlike that girl, I had observed at the bus stop.

How had it been that this was the woman who had spat with sheer venom into her phone with a frightening warning tattooed on her arm? Not that I gave it much attention.

But right now, in that somewhat ambient lighting, she seemed softer, kinder. Furthermore, while I was the one with blood trickling occasionally from my nostrils, it was *she* who looked delicate, knowing that my very words could shape or break her.

"I was scared that night," I admitted, releasing my words and emotions together.

This was my truth.

"Scared that *I* couldn't give *you* what *you* wanted."

At this, Toni's eyes seemed dimmer, downcast in thought.

"And what do I want from you, Frank?" She asked, enunciating every word with considered emphasis.

In a way, it seemed strangely beautiful.

"Sex?" interjected Andy. It seemed at long last; he had decided to join us alongside one of the girls that had caught his fancy from the booth, slinging his hand nonchalantly against her waist.

As quickly as it had come, the moment had gone, and her tenderness was replaced with cold cynicism, the chip fat and the squealing chimes of slot machines.

Toni glared at them, silently rebuking their unsolicited contribution.

Instead, I busied myself on my predicament - My nose was throbbing and possibly, although hopefully not broken – something that seemed more likely after the initial shock began to wear away.

Andy wisely retreated.

As he did, Toni's gaze met mine again, asking and exposing her heart with some painful urgency. "Is that really what you *think*, Frank?"

I shook my head as much as I dared anyway. The pain was throbbing against my temples. I kept my gaze down. "No."

"Well," She announced emphatically as she reassessed the room, briefly meeting Andy again with a cold demeanour as she spoke: "I want to be *happy*," Her voice almost fixed itself with a stark finality. "Happy with *you!*"

"Oh," I replied slowly and smiled somewhat nervously. "Me?"

"Yes," she affirmed, placing her pale, pointed hand on mine. It was ice cold. Thus I drew breath sharply through the bloodied rag, focusing instead on her words. "Blood, guts and all!" Her eyes seemed to dance with laughter in a way that made me want to kiss her.

In retrospect, it sounded like the name of a band.

And my nose was definitely broken.

* * *

After this *almost* declaration of love, the trip to the hospital was mostly in silence.

Despite Toni's protests, I had refused the offer of a motorcycle ride or ringing for an ambulance, opting instead for the shuttle bus from town. This bus would take me most of the way towards one of Kent's prestigious medical facilities, or at least to Dover Priory, where I could get a connection to the A&E Unit at Buckland Hospital. I had hoped to use this time to process everything, but Toni insisted on going with me.

So, *we* sandwiched in together amongst a group of elderly shoppers. A group of marvellous older women had gathered with their trolleys and brollies and carpetbag styled handbags. Each of them waited with trembling hands and fierce independence at the front of the queue.

Toni had shuffled almost into my lap as I held a makeshift ice-pack she had retrieved for me at the bar, made of bar cut ice cubes and salted peanut wrappers. The fact that I could smell them, Toni assured me, was a good sign, even if my nostrils were in evident disagreement.

Billy hadn't joined us, nor Andy, which was probably a good thing since Toni had given them both a frosty berth as we exited the pub. She kept her arm in mine as I busied myself by holding onto my nose like a mismatched married couple.

So sat side by side, she had lain her head slightly balanced on the cold glass window, while I watched the world go by through a frame of somewhat sweet, bubble-gum pink hair.

Later, it seemed that we would have a lot to talk about; and there would be a long wait within triage.

* * *

After a despairing look from the receptionist, I could tell the night might get even longer still. "Bar fight?" she asked, in a formal metered tone that was so clipped and rehearsed—the precursor of a Friday night.

I don't think either of us answered because she systematically gestured in a vaguely apparent direction.

Her fingers waved to a waiting room filled with three rows of seemingly never-ending plastic chairs. Each wall was filled with apparently stuck or half-broken looping screens; that detailed the necessary help numbers, procedures and reminders.

Boredom must have overtaken me, and I spent a few minutes briefly attempting to read a few of them. I quickly found they varied largely - between speaking to staff, turning off our mobile phones, an average of 25 minutes for non-urgent matters, or going to the pharmacist for more minor such issues as a suspected case of the flu. But none of the bulletins could immediately help me. The room was quiet, save faint tinny elevator-style music and the odd cough or splutter from other patients who sat at least two chairs apart for fear of unwanted infection or interaction with one another.

Thankfully, Toni had brought us both a cup of water, holding one to my lips so that I could maintain the compress I had balanced on my already bruised nose. I could sense the impatience in her eyes, those rich violet orbs blazing with indigence as name after name was called. None of them were my own. Her foot tapped with that same annoyance I had just observed from her in a slightly rhythmic refrain.

Despite this, I smiled inwardly to myself and mulled over the situation from all angles of my mind. I mused how Mol would react to my newly formed nasal passage. Or indeed how work would change, now, they had unwittingly gained a wheezy, dull sounding colleague, who made his living solely from their brash, impersonal call centre strictly from the power and monotony of my voice. Such voices were not suitable for customer retention.

Perhaps it might be time to consider another job. Or at least a vacation.

I considered telling Toni, but the joke didn't seem appropriate for now. So, I kept quiet, listening instead to the humming of the music looping miserably over the set of knackered and beaten box speakers. I distracted myself where I could from the sound of my nose whistling by revising my knowledge of famous guinea pig racers.

The beautiful marquee that pitched up every year. That was where my mind longed to be.

Instead, I was here, in triage, still waiting to be seen by a doctor about a potentially broken nose and frozen solid, ice-pack coated fingers.

* * *

It would be past half three in the morning when I finally returned home.

Swallowing my pride, I had accepted a taxi back. My nose was wrapped up in a temporary cast to stem the bleeding of my largely artificial wound.

There are few buses at this twilight hour, save for the overnight ferry coaches that rest peacefully along the shoreline, overlooking the water, their mirrors glistening like crystals by the sea.

Toni had fallen asleep early on, once more using my shoulder as an armrest. It had tickled at first, but the soft pink mane of hair now felt soothing as I listened to the rain from the taxi window – a welcome relief from the monotonous, tinny music from the hospital speakers; I had almost memorised their songs for hours on end.

There had been little point in ringing my family; sure, they would see for themselves when I attended Mother's weekly Roast Luncheon on Sunday. Besides, ringing them was much like ringing work, an unwanted kerfuffle and chatter. I had the weekend and a stubborn self-professed artist- cum-nursemaid to help me recover.

One, who had determined herself, my girlfriend, in the course of a night and affirmed to her brother that we were "back on". Although I was not entirely clear on what we were "on" in the first place, I resolved to clarify things when she was awake and whether this meant I would need to introduce her to my family.

But for now, I needed sleep; a clearer nasal passage – rather than one stuffed slightly with cotton padding and sticky-back plaster; and to feed Mol.

* * *

It was Sunday morning.

Toni was already making herself at home, and on Saturday, she had delighted in restocking my fridge with fruit, vegetables and overtly large tubs of yoghurt. I watched her, trying not to crane my neck in the process as she scraped the plastic lid against the top of the shelf, mindful not to spill the 4-pint carton of semi-skinned milk against the block of cheese that had remained from my smaller, bachelor style shop the week before.

I couldn't deny her skill, if not her sanity.

I was to lay back and rest.

So I focused instead on my latest issue of *Guinea Pig Racing* and the upcoming training that Mol and I might enlist in toward the summer.

After Friday's excitement, Saturday had gone relatively smoothly.

Toni had periodically popped in and out of my room to check up on me. After much insistence on her behalf, she bustled back and forth, in an hourly fashion, from the kitchen to the bedroom or other rooms of the flat, with cups of tea and warming tomato soup and promising at 9 pm that evening that she would return the following day. I became accustomed to the loud pitter-patter of Toni's combat boots in my house.

Now it was 8 am, Sunday, and the phone had rung.

Only two people called my landline, Hanny and my parents – that is to say that Dad would pay the bill for her, while Mother would yell out in her usual fashion the latest verbal contortion.

I counted five rings, mentally preparing myself, before lifting the receiver, grateful for the voice of my sister on the other side.

At least here, things would be calmer; I could put her on speaker. Guilt-free.

After exchanging pleasantries, I told Hanny what had happened—explaining in brief about Toni's existence, about the 'bar fight', Andy's latest conquests, my almost broken nose, asking what we were expecting for lunch and that Toni was a vegetarian.

"She is coming to lunch, isn't she, Frank?" Hanny asked, her voice expectant and hopeful.

I looked up at my girlfriend, the slightly disorganised cloud of pink wool and leathers which had just stacking Tupperware boxes and singing along out of tune to the mismatched melody on the radio and considered my answer. Not ready to relive her experimental cooking again. "I'll bring a nut roast."

Chapter 13: Tasteless Luncheons

P erhaps *I should have brought a duck.*
We arrived early, per my instruction, to take the bus to the faint
smell of burning and banging coming from the kitchen; and the
exasperation of my long-suffering sister.

"Please, come in," Hanny said, unlatching the door and pulling it open only
fractionally if only to hide the ensuing chaos. I nodded dutifully and entered
the foyer, careful to mind the mangled balls of wool and sheets of kitchen
roll and sponges that had no doubt been bought in some hasty, last-minute
purchase. While Toni followed, leather coat and bootlaces trailing behind
her, carrying a foil clad pastry offering. The three of us paused to sit on
the sofa. It was still positioned opposite the armchair where my father was
waiting for us. He had been attempting to doze or catch a few minutes of
the television on the sly while Mum was cooking.

Something she insisted on for her *own independence* every Sunday.

"Hi Mr Davis, Mrs Davis," Toni chirped, greeting my father and my
mother, who had briefly popped her head out, nosily.

Hanny stood and nudged Dad subtly, whispering in a more audible
whisper as much for his benefit as our own.

"Dad, this is Toni,"

"Toni?" asked Dad, somewhat confused from his impromptu awakening.
"I thought you were with that boy Stephen – "

"Toni is Frank's *girlfriend*," Hanny replied, sending us both an apologetic
and well-rehearsed smile. "They're joining us for dinner."

"Oh, of course," Affirmed my father, sitting up and smiling. No doubt, he was cheered by the thought of a new female company, and he greeted Toni with enthusiasm. "It's a pleasure to have you join us,"

"Even though no one told *me!*"Argued my mother coldly from the doorway. "No, if they had told me there was another mouth to feed, I'd have put out my *best* china!"

Toni stood. "Please," she defended calmly, keeping her voice polite and cheerful as I had hoped. Somewhat still rehearsed from my notes earlier. "I brought a nut roast for myself."

Mum sniffed dismissively. "Needn't have *troubled* yourself!" She answered flatly, returning to her pots and pans in the kitchen with newfound percussion and overarching passive aggression. No doubt, the appearance of a foreign and unplanned item insulted her pride.

Undeterred, Toni joined her, carrying in her dish to plate up. I daren't help. Instead, I sat down on the sofa and sighed, rubbing my temples as Dad turned up the volume on the television.

Hanny offered another brave smile, tugging as she always did when she was upset or nervous at the fraying edges of her cardigan. "She seems nice."

I nodded. I was hoping that by the end of the meal, Mum too would see it. *She didn't.*

* * *

Lunch and the table were a balancing act, in which we all squished into the square dining room area, trying not to clash knees, elbows and personalities as Mum served up the turkey.

The table was old and clunky, which is why it was usually kept in the attic - save the festive season or when my parents had 'people' over. The facade was evident in the hasty application of polish on the faded lacquer; still, sticky under the lace table cloth. This had been kept pristine and preserved from the day my parents were married, stiff from bleaching, pressing and a solemn iron.

Now and then, the whole table wobbled, a sign of ageing and imbalance from hoisting it hastily down the attic stairs. I wondered if it too was afraid of Mum, who was sawing deeply into the meat. As she cut ample portions of poultry to serve with the veg, I could see the veins throbbing in her neck and temple, and we quietly passed our plates to her in the usual way. One at a time, murmuring only a thank you, regardless of the portion control.

We would *eat* on her terms: When she *was* ready. And in *silence*.

At the same time, she sized up the competition.

My father, however, had other ideas.

"So, Toni," he asked warmly, "What is it you do?"

I gave Toni's leg a gentle, reassuring squeeze.

"I'm an artist," Toni declared.

"And *does* that make a living?" Mum asked, in a mood that could melt butter.

"Sometimes," Toni replied, "It's more about the expression involved."

Mum snorted.

Dad remained oblivious, reaching over my mother for the salt shaker. "*Expression*, eh? What's that pet?"

Perhaps, I mused to myself; this was how goldfish felt in their bowls, being ogled at by a multitude of individuals over and over. Still, at least *they* could forget the faces each time, blurring them together with the menagerie of time, algae and seaweed. My mother's disapproval was burning into my mind.

"Well, it's all about the process of finding a subject and discovering it," Toni explained to the table, although her answer was almost as vague as before. "The art, the form and colours."

"Right!" Snipped Mum. "And does it *make* a living?"

From my slightly raised position at the table, I could see Hanny folding her napkin nervously over and over again. It was a wonder – for all her nervous twitches, my sister hadn't mastered origami.

I attempted to eat, aware of my mother's increased scrutiny forcing down a Brussels sprout, which slid like a lump in my throat.

The tension in the room was palpable.

"At times," Toni voiced earnestly.

I could see now the flash of friction in her eyes as she raised a slice of her nut roast to her lips.

Her voice was eerily calm.

"But it helps me to meet people,"

"Like Frank?" asked my mother, sliding her knife sharply into a piece of turkey with a jagged clatter.

"No," I interjected, hastily swallowing a bit of both, in a bid to keep the peace between them. "We met on the bus."

My mother's answer was curt as she cut into her meat again. "*Oh,*"

I attempted another sprout. Again, feeling its existence, bulky, green and agonisingly slow.

"Did you?" asked Hanny, her voice squeaking with curiosity despite my mother's rebuttal.

All eyes shifted on me. It was a strange sensation, where everyone was either very big, or I had decreased in size—a bit like a bug in a very tiny jar. So, I forced myself to swallow, pushing away, somewhat awkwardly, from my chair with a scrape and a thud.

"I'll wash up then,"

* * *

Escaping into the kitchen had always been meant as some form of reprieve for my sister and me. So, releasing my stack of plates into an organised clutter from where I had gathered them from the table against the draining board, I leaned back against the sink and sighed.

In the other room, I could hear the sounds, or rather the lack thereof, of awkward silence once more, save for the loud, abrasive ticking of the clock from the hallway, counting the seconds before Hanny would join me.

Sure enough, the familiar excuse came from the other side of the wall. Barely audible, trimmed and rehearsed, but still well-meant, "I'll help Frank with the dishes,"

I remembered our older, more exclusive hiding places in moments like this. When Mum had done the hoovering, there was a small crack left between our parents' bed, the far bush in the garden overlooking the neighbours' lawn where we could be drowned out by Mr Simms mowing his lawn and rose petals. The brick wall opposite the school near the corner shop, where we could avoid lessons and detentions, exchanging unwanted parts of our lunches with the pigeons as we tore the crusts off our sandwiches.

Instead, here I was within the kitchen yet again seeking answers. "What should I do?" I murmured quietly.

Hanny patted my arm sympathetically. "Pass the marigolds,"

Life remained unresolved. But for now, we would tackle something else: dishes.

The warmth of the water was somewhat soothing as my fingers rubbed in repetitive motions through the tea towel, drying off each plate as my sister passed them to me, dripping from the draining rack small pools of bubbly, foamy soap suds. Mum and Dad's house was small and lacked the luxury and space for a dishwasher, but I was grateful for the chance to talk, primarily uninterrupted, so long as we kept our voices low from the other side of the wall. Still paper-thin and crumbling – just as it had always been.

It was one of the many 'charms' of the house, along with the creaky floorboard that adjoined the two rooms, which ran parallel to the doorway. However, this fact came in useful since we could always predict when someone was about to enter, allowing us to tune the conversation accordingly. So I could speak freely, the jargon in my mind flowing more naturally, save at a quieter volume.

"Mum hates her, doesn't she?" I asked as Hanny scrapped at the remnants of gravy left on one of the plates, using one of those thick iron-wool based scouring pads.

Hanny's reply was as forthright and honest as ever. "Yes," keeping her eyes down on the pile of still unwashed dishes.

"How did she *like* Steve?" I asked in vain, hoping that Mum might also have responded in a similarly dismissive matter of my sister's partner.

"She *likes* him," Hanny answered, blushing a little. "But then, he brings her milk."

My sister's sense of humour, much like my own, was dry, a by-product of our mother's lack of imagination and father's indifference. Thinking about

Toni in the other room, I only hoped Dad would not bring up politics in our temporary absence.

"Is it her age?"

Hanny's brow creased a little. Had she not thought of this? Although I supposed my sister was closer in age to Toni than I, even though living with our parents had long lost her youthful vigour.

"Perhaps you should talk to Mum?" she questioned, at last, tugging off the rubber gloves and passing me the dessert. We had delayed it long enough.

The heaviness in my chest tightened at the thought.

* * *

It was a fruitcake for pudding.

A bowl of tinned peaches had been hastily placed on the side in one of what Mum called her 'crystal collection', no doubt to compensate the dryness that cake might bring after the main meal.

Fruitcake, to me, was usually a tea time treat, sandwiched between lunch and supper around Christmas time. But the arrival of a visitor had warranted this exception, to hastily lift it from the tin that so usually tucked unassumingly below the far-right counter.

My father greeted us with enthusiasm. "Toni was telling us all about the bus," he reiterated warmly.

All heads swivelled to meet me, almost expectantly. "Right?" I asked, smiling nervously, before setting the cake down with a painful thud onto the table, the daunting round globe of sponge and raisins barely resting on my mother's vacant china.

"Yes," continued my father, his warmth somewhat comforting against Mum's emotionless demeanour. "You met on the mainline into town and asked for her number, right?"

"Something like that," I nodded, rubbing my head to avoid my familiar itch spot. My ear already felt burning hot, as though it had been branded with iron and coals. "We didn't speak much, though."

My mother's eyes narrowed. "You didn't meet, *online* did you?" She asked, her words almost crushing. "Such places are rather dangerous for *young girls.*"

"Well," argued Toni, with some objection. "I helped him set up a profile before we started dating."

My mother went pale. "Oh, not one of *those* websites," she moaned, clearly suggesting something more adult in nature.

It was time to put my foot down.

"Actually, I was writing about guinea pigs,"

My mother didn't say another word.

We all drank in the silence, fumbling through brick like slices of fruitcake and cups of lukewarm tea.

Outside it had started raining again. My umbrella was at home in the hall.

* * *

"See, that went well," expressed Toni, towelling off her bubble gum hair with one of my many hand towels from the laundry cupboard.

We had half run, half sprinted across the driveway of my parents' home and down the hill to the bus shelter before realising the extended delay caused by Sunday service and began running again back to mine.

I said nothing, uncertain if she had meant the meal or the journey back.

Deep down, I was praying that the tightly wound bandage around my upper nose would save me from getting a cold.

So, I waited for her direction, asking as vaguely as I dared "Did it?" deflecting my gaze as I wrung out one of my socks against my shoe. Still watching from the corner of my eye, the wet waterfall of pink, bubble-gum and candy-cane slip away under the ragged, faded cotton where it became frizzy and vibrant.

Toni nodded emphatically and relaxed beside me, "Your father seems nice,"

"Yes," I replied, giving her a small smile. "And my sister too,"

"True," she hummed with a slight sigh. "Your mother-"

"Is being overly protective? Assertive? Resentful?" Words tumbled out of my mouth with uncertainty; as I met her gaze. Toni had slunk one slender arm around me, her leather jacket falling on the carpet, still damp from the rain. I gulped, barely maintaining my balance as I placed my foot, still slightly shaky, back to the floor.

"No, She's a feminist," reflected Toni with a wry smile. "Now, let's get you back into bed!"

Her lips were red and glittering in a way that dazzled and meant anything but sleep.

Although I wasn't complaining, I still didn't feel like I understood women.

Chapter 14: Mysteries of the Feminine Kind

"Even women don't understand women," In his usual mixture of blasé meets flippancy, Andy had confirmed the abstract statement with a pair of craft scissors in one hand and a crumpled wad of napkins in the other.

We were sat, cramped and clustered together around a small circular table with Dave and a bunch of other friends and male relatives, tasked with the art of creating hanging garlands and makeshift decorations for Dave and Yvonne's wedding party.

The upcoming nuptials were a week on Saturday. So in the way of a joint bachelor-cum-hen party, the bride and groom had invited all their nearest and dearest to attend in a spot of crafting to *save* costs, or as Andy had muttered only moments earlier, "to *avoid* any funny business."

Across from us at another similarly shaped table, the ladies were hard at work and engrossed in their task resembling a group of confident, domestic Goddesses. They certainly seemed a world away from our corner, where grown men sat cursing and mumbling in a collective panic over glitter and an oversized pot of PVA glue.

From the corner of my eye, I could see Toni. She was happily creating pleats and folds with a piece of sticky green crepe paper.

The marital couple had settled on lime and cream for their wedding colours, something that Yvonne had insisted upon, "to make the salmon terrine entrées pop!" As Toni's gaze momentarily met, I smiled and nodded to her, my hands tied up with my task. "There are *worse* ways to spend a Saturday!" I mused aloud.

I was somewhat glad to be out and about after a week mostly spent at home, recovering from my broken nose and my mother's luncheon.

That said, I had done what I could to keep my mind active, watching documentaries about forgotten bus stops and palliative guinea pig care. While these had both proved attractive options, I was somewhat regretful at agreeing to try Toni's new range of soup yoghurts; it was fortunate at least that I could not quite distinguish their unique textures and smells. It made them *almost* palatable.

Returning to work with a lunch box of corned beef, cheese and tomato sandwiches had been a blessing.

Back in the hall and away from my musings, Andy's face had darkened at my words. "On a Saturday?" He asked me, somewhat incredulously.

"Yes," I replied empathetically, "It could be raining during a guinea pig race."

Andy shook his head in despair, his hands filled with shallow scratches and paper cuts as he thrust down his failed attempt at fine-detail crafts. "God, I need a pint!" he groaned.

Given my circumstances, I was undoubtedly in a more positive mindset than my friend. I would not deny that the hosts token offerings of orange juice with short paper umbrellas were less than desirable, but they were cheap, bought in bulk from the weekly craft market, which Yvonne frequented on a Wednesday afternoon.

I watched as Andy's waning expression gazed into the oblong length of his drink, knowing that at our current pace, this was the closest we would all get to daylight today.

"Excuse me, boys, have you got any spare staples?" came a voice over my shoulder. Turning, we were greeted by Poppy, who had strolled over from the girl's table clutching a pile of organza squares in that very same avocado colour. The more I looked at it, the more I wondered if the fabric had come from someone's old bedroom curtains, knowing it would be certainly cheaper per the metre in an auction.

Andy also turned, his eyes swivelling in the same way that some daredevil might brandish dinner plates. I recognised the look. There had been a few attempts where he would use it with some of the girl's at *Morses'*, usually when he had had a few, and he had allowed his bravado to create the aesthetically "pleasing" ladies man.

But this was different.

Poppy, who often sat at work, head bowed down to the desk from nightly drinking, was stood before us completely sober, her soft blonde hair cascading down her back in soft ringlets from a recent haircut.

She looked good, and Andy knew it.

"Staples?" Poppy repeated, placing the organza pile onto our table, squeezing it onto the spartan amount of space that separated the table from our laps.

"Ah, yes, uh," Answered Andy. It seemed like he was sweating, although that could have been the hot air pumping through the lacklustre air-conditioner unit.

He moved his hand quickly across the table to an empty packet on the table and passed it to her nervously. "Here,"

Poppy smiled. Her lips twisted in a faint smile before she walked back with a sincere "Thanks."

Andy's eyes followed; in the way, one might carelessly describe a lovesick puppy.

I considered briefly what had happened in my brief absence from work while my nose recovered.

Had Poppy given up drinking?

Was Andy in love with her?

Yes, women were complicated mammals.

But men are even more so.

* * *

The complication would only get worse.

Poppy was one of Yvonne's bridesmaids. Something she had announced to Alice with some great pride on Monday. The news might have at one point been somewhat exclusive, but it had quickly spread around the office like a game of Chinese whispers, where the latest development reached our group of boys as a rumour before Dave's public acknowledgement.

It was not long before Andy had a smug look on his face.

"Well," he said, placing his hands behind the back of his chair and swinging his seat back and forth cheerfully. "You know what they say about grooms men and bridesmaids?"

"What?" piped up Mike cautiously.

"They get laid," Andy replied with a slight smirk.

Despite my limited knowledge of bridal traditions, I knew he wasn't talking about chickens.

Choosing to say nothing, I sipped my tea from its dirty polythene cup. The cream had unfortunately curdled, but the gamble had seemed plausible when I had seen something unimaginably horrifying issuing out of the milk tap. Still, it was unbearably coagulated and burned in the same way a Vindaloo curry might affect my somewhat fragile digestive system.

Busying myself briefly, I toyed with the idea of pouring the remainder of my drink in the dishevelled potted plant abandoned on the windowsill. It looked like it needed something to pep it up anyway, even though it was no doubt tropical enough with its toxic yellow leaves and sepia tea-stained speckled flowers drooping, half dead, half listless as the office itself.

At least the computer was enjoying itself. It had taken my inactivity as a sign of being granted a break. The screen of spreadsheets and caller IDs had been replaced by a pleasant view of hilltops and clouds in my absence.

Undeterred, I lifted the phone, hoping to busy my mind with another call. But like the corresponding minutes and increasing seconds that would occur in the moments that passed after that, it would feel like every working day – seemingly dragging on forever on and on.

I mulled over Andy's situation, grateful that it was one I had always managed to avoid.

Office romances were often a subject of lengthy taboo, often as long as the rumours themselves, with shared glances and coyly denied blushes much as they had been in school – at least seemingly for the more popular kids.

Andy himself was somewhat branded as a Casanova at *Morses'*, which is why it was unsurprising that female colleagues frequented the bar, no doubt preferring the higher *quality* of establishments found in Dover.

When the matter had been brought up in our Christmas Party one year, one of the girls had briefly recalled a list of men they had banned from kissing her under the mistletoe, placing their indistinguishable tastes of alcopops and nicotine from the year before. I was secretly relieved I was not among them.

Poppy was flicking paper clips and rubber bands across her desk with the same nonchalant attitude we all held as she addressed her caller with simpering sympathy. "We do our very *best* to listen to all complaints and concerns *seriously,"*

I placed down my phone's receiver back into the cradle of the handset and looked back to the computer screen, jerked back into life with an impatient twitch of my mouse. Yes, t*oday would be a very long day indeed.*

* * *

"Do you think a double date would seem less threatening?" Andy posed to me that lunchtime.

I blinked at him, somewhat confused, repeating his words that had so caught me off guard. This was not his standard form, even though I had obtained as his reluctant wingman.

"A *double* date?"

I noticed Andy was somewhat more nervous than usual, sheepish almost. "Yes," he enthused. "How about it? You, me, Toni and Poppy,"

I stared at him in disbelief. Dumbfounded. *"And* Poppy?" I cautioned.

"Why not?" He asked, brushing off my concerns with a shrug of his shoulders. "The girls already know each other."

I nodded slowly; this was true. "Mm, sure."

"Great," he answered warmly, walking away from the kitchen, half-eaten BLT sandwich in his hand. "Thanks for asking her, Frank."

A pit of doubt gnawed away at me in the base of my stomach, fearful of playing matchmaker – someone was going to get burned.

* * *

To succeed, I had to choose my time correctly.

The itch on my ear had flared up in much the same way that it had been when I was around Toni. There were times when I was tempted to scratch it but knew miserably that this was not one of them.

A human ear, red, swollen and ballooning, was never helpful when discussing matters of grave importance; and Andy 'finding' love was one of them.

I cursed silently. *Why couldn't Andy have asked her?* I would relay this to Toni later. Briefly, I wondered if it was because his feelings were much deeper than the girl's he had clinging to his arms at the bar. That might have been the case had it been a meeker man, like Dave or even Mike, but this was Andy: Self-proclaimed "*Casanova of Cocklescanslanky*" or at least that of *Morses'* Bar.

I also hadn't been on a double date before. I had considered attending one with Hanny in the future. So far, I had backtracked on the issue whilst I researched the various or few reciprocal links of conversation between my girlfriend – the vegetarian, selective lactose-based drinker; and Steve, who, apart from his interest in my sister, was known as my parent's regular milkman.

I hoped that this problem would not present itself here.

Poppy and Andy worked together. This fact I half presumed would work in their favour, assuming they enjoyed talking together and not just in an almost non-committal way to our customers. The thought of stone-cold silence was not a comforting one.

But the matter remained.

The plan was to breach the matter over a cup of coffee when there was another lull in the day, and I could pass her a freshly made cup, knowing how sluggish we all felt in the latter half of the afternoon, in that painful 30-

minute interval before home time. The one, which if you are lucky enough to love your job those minutes remain blissfully aware, but otherwise, are waiting anxiously for those seconds to inch into minutes and allow you reprieve from your daily misery.

The coffee machine had boiled steadily for a good five minutes, less instant and noisier than the provisions provided by a kitchen kettle, but with the added convenience of polystyrene and all-in-one dispensing solutions.

I had taken note of the way Poppy had her coffee and noticed the rim of the black elliptical circles left in her wake. Her drink was black, two sugars and a single dash of milk that added neither taste nor colour to the cup. These were another stark reminder of why we should have invested in coasters instead of Espresso machines, not that I was responsible for the company's budget.

Simple, ordinary worker's coffee, painted and unsophisticated water.

I considered whether to forgo the matter or tell Andy to be direct with her, but stubbornness moved me forward. Along with a small fleeting brush of self-confidence from my relationship status, I stepped forwards, ready. I placed down the cup, aware of Alice and the others in the immediate vicinity. Their eyes were watching me with some suspicion, although Poppy smiled.

"Thanks, Frank," she replied gently. "To *what* do I owe the pleasure?"

Taking a deep breath, I attempted the words I had rehearsed a few times over in my head and via email exchange with Andy. Now aloud. "Poppy, would you like to go on a date?"

"Of course, Frank," continued Poppy sincerely.

I smiled back. "Great, I'll-"

The rest of the speech never came. Poppy's mouth was upon mine, swift, unexpected and inviting.

Yes, today was proving to be a very long day indeed.

What was I supposed to do?

Chapter 15: A Prickly Poppy

Although my more intimate encounters with women were somewhat limited, this kiss felt prickly and probing. It lacked somewhat the almost silken touches I had shared with Toni, and quickly as I could, I prized myself from her, mustering as much strength as I could to push her away in an as yet muffled protest. Seconds had passed, yet they grew into minutes as Poppy remained, slightly confused and wobbling, seemingly caught in a daze. Her lips were frozen with a hint of affection, and my feet cemented themselves to the carpet in shock.

I felt like a fish, floundering and then drowning as a sea of our colleagues appeared to wash upon us, Andy amongst them – his eyes filled with concern, confusion and hurt. "It wasn't me," I whispered, half to myself as anyone as Poppy retreated sharply towards the ladies' bathrooms, and I forced myself backwards toward my seat.

Andy's heated stare was probing into my back as I repeated myself anew, like a parrot with some solemn stoic message, wishing he could hear me. But his rage halted all trace of any pittance.

I tried to offer him some visual cue from our limited spaces at the office, my gaze meeting his where we could during the occasional lapse in calls, but he did not acknowledge me. In his mind, I had betrayed him.

Poppy was still in the bathroom. No one was interested in listening to me. Not now.

And in the pit of my stomach, I wondered about Toni.

Should I text her?

Call?

I internalised the dialogue and its repercussions that would surely follow – a reason I never usually focused on my private life at work. My mobile phone, a basic, unglamorous model, usually sat quietly in my desk drawer, motionless. But for now, gripped with uncertainty and my ear twitching uncomfortably hot and sticky, I ran my fingers over its curved and bevelled screen, nervous to look at the photo of my girlfriend that might rescind me further into panic or shame.

Toni's eyes had an almost haunting quality to them, even in picture form, something even the purple glaze of her contact lenses couldn't entirely detract. I would be a fool to ignore it.

She was young.

I was Frank.

It had not been all that long ago since I had changed my computer's wallpaper to one of Toni. I had delayed slightly, having taken some questions and permissions from Mol. After her blessing, Toni flicked through the camera of various upon dozen 'selfies' she had taken of herself on my phone to select one she would deem her most flattering. Flecks of bubble gum and fluorescent pink framed her cheerful round face, her eyes dancing, cheeks creased with laughter lines and faint streaks of paint. I told her she could have been a model. Toni had merely scoffed at me.

What would she think of me now?

My brow furrowed in my internal conflict, focusing where I could, to the clock in the far corner of the room, longing for the lunch break to end. For Poppy to return from her stall and for the world to swallow me whole – whichever came before 5:30.

Poppy was first. Although not immediately – ushered back into the room after a few minutes, by an entourage of supportive female colleagues, about three in total, one - half supporting her in the act of sorority, another rubbing her back in small circles and other carrying an overly large box of tissues. Poppy's eyes were puffy and panda-like, clutching an equally large wad of toilet paper, stained and blotted with mascara. The others faces' were drawn and comforting, their words repetitive and disproving of *all* men.

107

Despite this, Poppy came up to me, stepping away for a moment from her new-formed sisterhood. "I'm sorry," she whispered, a slight hiccup catching on her breath. "I thought maybe you *liked* me."

I smiled apologetically. "I do," I replied, hoping that I might sound calmer than I indeed felt. "But only as a friend."

Poppy nodded sadly, retreating towards her cubicle. At last, Andy ended his silent punishment – his own words hollow and emotionless. "You're *dead*, Frank!"

Now I had three problems.

* * *

"How does one become instantly dead?" Toni asked, swirling her chopsticks in between her second and fourth finger as she sucked on a piece of chilli dip she had stuck into a ball of vegetable wontons.

We were sat half cross-legged against my sofa, surrounded by a small army of half-consumed, lukewarm oriental take-out boxes.

Naturally, I had told her *everything*.

"I don't know," I admitted, scratching my head a little, attempting to process my thoughts, in much the same way one might try to suck a frozen milkshake through a straw.

"Perhaps Andy is just cross?" Toni reasoned, her eyes narrowing for a moment. "After all, *you* kissed *his* girl."

"She kissed me!" I protested, somewhat defensively, as my girlfriend descended into laughter, flopping onto the arm of the sofa with a giggle.

"And they say romance is *dead!*"

The irony felt lost on me, the returning feeling of confusion and the approaching cushion swatting against my head, offering only a further blow to my dented psyche.

There were pins and needles in my legs and Chop Suey noodles on the floor.

So once she opened the bag of prawn crackers, Toni tried to explain to me as best she could about the importance of communication and metaphors. And, after a while, there was no food left, beyond a small patch of unidentifiable but assumed frying fat in one of the cartons, which even Mol refused.

Though her words might have been helpful, I only half-listened.

My mind had betrayed me, whirring like a bus down a B road, trudging along the beaten track resiliently against the elements. I needed more time to consider my options, hobbling with temporarily frozen limbs to retrieve a can of lager from the fridge as she continued. Meanwhile, Mol snuggled down beside us to offer temporal comfort through the bars of her cage.

"Metaphors aren't the problem for me. *Not really!*" I retorted, "I just think people are hard to read,"

Toni snorted. "Remind me why you work for a call centre?"

I guess my girlfriend had a point but could not fathom it entirely. Instead, drowsiness consumed me. I was tired now.

I moved towards her, hoping for the warm embrace of her silken hair, but she held me back, eyes steady. More mature than I could ever expect to be.

"I'll try in the morning," I muttered sleepily to appease her.

"Good," said Toni relaxing a little, the matter seemingly temporarily resolved. "Because the wedding is on Saturday,"

Fuck.

Chapter 16: Severed Communications

S aturday.

A day that usually offered me some reprieve from the monotony of my work. A break from the chorus of broken and complex demands and questions that droned within my ears through the concrete block receiver or painful needle stabbing headsets that work provided its employees.

Saturday.

A day where I could usually discuss with Mol about her progress for the annual guinea pig games: or take a bus to the White Cliffs to take in some fresh air and watch as Toni danced and painted in wild abandon to music that only she could hear.

Saturday.

A day where I could go for a drink at *Morses'* and observe individuals into my notebook, wondering as ever what if anything made them tick. From the ill-fitting tracksuit bottomed teenagers to the occasion of a gaggle of tourists who had strayed too far from Kent's familiar civilisations.

"Yes, Saturday," Toni was staring at me. I wondered if I had been speaking in part aloud - it wouldn't have been the first time, so she said, adjusting her position as I winced in discomfort, my sleepiness departing me sharply as a knife cuts into the flesh of an orange, jagged and sharp.

"*This* Saturday?" I asked back somewhat awkwardly. My mouth felt dry, needing another drink, squawking at her like a parrot.

"Yes," She replied pointedly. "*This* Saturday, Frank. You have got a suit, haven't you?"

"I've got a suit!" I affirmed. I am somewhat grateful that I would not need to visit a tailor shop or go for a round of shopping at such short notice. I remembered having been measured for my school uniform as a boy. The unease of the whole process still led to lengthy discussions and disapproval from my mother.

"May I *see* it?" Toni asked, somewhat oddly curious. I gestured vaguely in the direction of my wardrobe, knowing it should be enough to guide her. Since we first started dating, Miss Jones had been in my bedroom a few times now. I had no doubt she had memorised the simple plan of bed, wardrobe, dresser-come-chest of drawers, side and main window – both overlooking the outer wall of the flat, spare chair, door. There was little in the way of clutter; I had attempted where possible to impress her, save the odd fuzz of grey and black socks that peeped through the almost shut top drawer of the dresser.

I could hear her in the dresser, the familiar gasp of the wood of the door as it creaked open, followed by the scratching clinks of coat and trouser hangers along the rail. I counted along with them to myself. One, two, three work shirts, two missing for the unfinished wash pile and the shirt I was wearing. Six, seven, work-ready trousers in solemn uniform black and grey. Eight, nine two jumpers from Mother at Christmas in bottle green and maroon burgundy red. Ten, the space for my raincoat and a thicker one next to it for snow. Twelve – the suit bag. Zipped up and protected "in case of moths," as Mother had put it, in a cold beige long carrier case. "Found it!" Toni cried.

I modelled my suit with some persuading and not so subtle urging, posing for Toni with shaking hands. This was accompanied by my normal sweating, twitching ear and the jabbing of the metal weighing scales against my sock-clad feet on the bathroom floor. I was left feeling not unlike a dog at Crufts being forced to sit for hours on end against a backdrop of unwanted spectators.

There was no mirror in my bedroom. I had often found such an item unnecessary - especially when, as I reasoned, I could just as easily shave or brush my teeth each morning in front of the reflected doors of the medicine cabinet which overhung the basin in the bathroom. I recalled the time I had dressed for our first date, nervously sliding a comb, over my thinning strands of hair, conscious of how my sister had described my look as 'sharp', though apart from height and girth, I did not resemble a pencil.

My suit was not in any way remarkable. It was void entirely of both colour and personality, which was admittedly why I had initially bought it: A single suit that would go with everything. Birthdays, weddings and funerals. Still, it came to life at opportune moments, with the bolt of avocado green and salmon pink fabric. Toni hastily held up squares with alternating hands, seemingly measuring them against the upper vest pocket. The materials themselves salvaged, I supposed, from the decorating tasks we had all laboured on days previously. "You have to try and match the theme," she replied to my splutterings, "Even *without* a waistcoat."

My stomach clenched awkwardly as I paled in front of her, forcing my following words out like someone who has forgotten how to breathe: "Waistcoat?"

Saturday suddenly felt both too near and too far away.

* * *

Monday and Tuesday at work crept by stolid and mostly routine. Wherein the work cubicles in which I and my fellow beings began feeling more and more like floating shelves stacked without thought or purpose on invisible walls. Each, collectively containing small impersonal shells of ourselves, all boxed up and ornamental. Save for the drone of necessary assistance on the phones, none of us spoke – even to each other.

I longed to reach out to speak to Andy but was not sure of the right words to say. It was almost as though the dictionary of the English language had prized itself out of my reach. The former phrases were tumbling down into my brain like dull, incomprehensible syllables and sounds. Not unlike the phonics used to reach a baby to speak.

Nor could I reach out to Poppy. She had avoided all eye contact wherever possible, seeking solace in the thick-rimmed basin of her coffee mug or the distraction of her incoming calls. I had also decided against emailing either of them, uncertain that a hastily strung collection of sentences would replicate my concern or remorse.

Oblivious to it all was Mike. He was humming a little to himself about Dave's upcoming nuptials with the same spirit as a child might be playing with his favourite guinea pig or dinosaur. The sound felt a little alien to me, off-tune and tasteless as the workplace's filtered water.

And here, in this fishbowl of life, I was drowning in limbo.

Uncertain how to sink or swim.

It was time to change tack.

* * *

I approached Andy's desk cautiously. Aware of the gathering collection of discarded and half crumpled staples that were flung with wild abandon on the surface space. Andy had always been one for littering his area with stationery supplies. No doubt to alleviate some of the boredom and frustration with his job. He had also invested in a stress ball. An awkward squished red sort of thing that reminded me as much of a clown's nose as a means of administering self-therapy. He had his back to me, and his headset was on, but I knew he wasn't on a call. Although genuinely speaking, I preferred the hand-held receiver; I could ascertain this from the absence of any flickering red light on the dashboard. It was apparent. He was ignoring me.

I cleared my throat nervously. "Andy, I-"

Nothing.

I tried once more. "Andy?"

This time Andy swivelled around his chair. His mind seemed to be processing many different emotions, which I observed like a black and white film as they flickered in his eyes. Bitterness, anger, confusion and then finally hurt. "What is it, Frank?" his voice was flat in his reply.

"I was wondering if we could-" He cut me off again.

"Talk?" Andy asked, his voice rising slightly.

113

My own barely cracked. "Please," I asked, sure that even my sweat smelt of desperation. I recalled how Toni had reminded me of the importance of communication. "After all," She had resolved. "Didn't all the years of our friendship and kinship at the office mean nothing?"

Andy looked away. "I've got nothing to say," he recalled sharply.

I felt deflated.

"Poppy kissed me!" I blurted out awkwardly. The words trembled free from my lips with as much panic as there was nervousness.

Andy spun round. For a moment, I thought he was going to hit me and cringed a little at the thought. "Sorry?!" he asked, first accusingly and then dubiously as he repeated my words as though to himself again. "Poppy kissed you?"

I halted. While I had spoken the truth, the scenario seemed phantom to Andy. Mainly, I supposed, not to a man who believed himself more than comfortable and successful with the ladies—an Alpha. As though even such a suggestion was not a remote possibility.

The words that followed were not my own.

"Yes, I did."

Both of us turned wordlessly to where she stood. She was here, previously unannounced or perhaps quietly unnoticed, the third member of our dysfunctional trio – and a single word was uttered out between us both.

"Poppy!"

Chapter 17: Inspiration, Perspiration, Interpretation

I am not sure if it was resolve or resignation that led to Poppy's thought process at that moment. Yet here she stood, unwavering and firm, a far cry from the usual worn out, hunched over, mid-30's self-described train wreck—a mixture of reflection and bravado.

Andy and I drank her appearance in. Poppy's flaxen hair had been pulled tight into an unassuming ponytail, which along with her jet-black kitten heels, had been chosen to add height and subtle dominance. Although I ultimately decided against it, I considered complimenting her, not yet sure if my comments would send out the wrong impression.

For a moment, Andy remained uncharacteristically silent. The colour had all but drained from his face, in the same way one might consume a bottle of milk until all that is left is a slim, ashen column of translucent grey plastic. His words were slugging themselves out with some effort as Poppy waited still within that cold, clinical silence.

"But *why?*"

Sensing that I might no longer be needed, I considered making my exit. Yet despite my intentions, I found myself anchored to the carpet once more, my legs frozen to the spot, as though compelled to understand everything in seemingly morbid curiosity.

Poppy's shoulders shrugged with partial indifference, her words considered, perhaps rehearsed. "Boredom, I guess?" The question seemed like rhetoric masking controlled emotions.

Andy was having none of it. "Boredom?" he asked incredulously.

Again there was silence.

Was it my turn to speak?

This situation required tact. Both parties I believed to be my friends, not just colleagues. With the wedding fast approaching, I worried that I would be forced explicitly to choose a side; in so doing, I might inadvertently offend someone despite being predetermined by the upcoming wedding's seating plan. The silence made me only more aware of the battlefield I found myself in, a stalemate of broken promises and unspoken words.

Andy's anger was palpable, but Poppy's attitude confused me – a far cry from the girl who had run away from me as quickly as she could, her eyes filled with tears and dripping mascara. In truth, how could I say anything?

Feebly, I turned back to my desk, looking for a distraction. I supposed I was hoping to occupy better the silence, which burnt like a black hole between us all.

I attempted to fixate on a polystyrene cup, which I did not remember filling, that was now left cooling on my desk. The cup's contents were filled with lukewarm liquid that I imagined had once been tea.

But the rest of my desk remained plain and ordinary, much like the other occupied cubicles in our block. I knew that each was consumed with soulless, tired individuals that were droning together in a collective monotone. "*This is FRANC. How can I help you?*" Thus, returning me to the dilemma at hand.

The sad fact was, I couldn't detract from what had been said and done - Even if I had been an unwilling participant in all of it.

My ear twitched uncomfortably hot and flustered, and I wished more than ever to sink away, the more time passed in awkward, humid silence—everything seeming insufferable and broken.

Still, at least the computer was enjoying itself. Windows had taken my inactivity as a sign of it being granted a break. In the elapsing minutes, the screensaver replaced the previous screen of spreadsheets and documents. The company chose a default one, which featured a pleasant view of hilltops and clouds. It was ironic at this very moment, and I asked myself how different things might be if only I could be there now.

No, anywhere by here.

If there had been a moment to fix things, it had indeed passed.

I closed my eyes, listening to the thudding of my heart and the ticking of the clock in the far wall and whispered awkwardly. "I have to go!" My statements were as much for myself as for them.

I forced myself to walk back to my desk with some moralistic difficulty, all while feeling deflated and awkward. I couldn't look at either person, choosing instead to repeat the mantra of

INSPIRATION, PERSPIRATION, INTERPRETATION

over and over to myself. Such was a slogan that had been drilled into the company's heads since our induction into call centre life. It meant as little then as did now: empty, woolly weasel words attempting to boost morale for what had initially been taken up as a temp job, a means of making money for a rainy day.

I wondered if it was raining now, for, despite my well-intentions, nothing had been solved.

Nothing that was except for piles of statistics stacking against my spread-sheets and documents, recalling the daily ratio of dwindling optimism.

"Coffee?" chirped Alice.

* * *

By three o'clock, the metaphorical noose I hung my expectations on was slowly starting to untether. I wished I had taken the day or at least half a day off. I spoke with a customer for about half an hour, reciting the script with slight disembodiment and boredom when the boss called me in for a meeting.

Such was not an uncommon occurrence, though perhaps, I mused, given the circumstances, it was almost a welcome one. I stood, stretching my legs a little, as the blood flow returned from where I had sat, somewhat fixed in one position for a few hours. In the fish tank, it was easy to lose track of time.

The manager, Mike's father - Michael Sr., was by no means a sleek and clean-cut individual, baring a monocle, carrying a white Persian cat or a Cuban cigar like the villains of some cliche movie I had watched as a child. Instead, he was a squat, balding man of middling height, who had been hired for his ability to speak in a soft, calming voice that appealed to the faceless entities of head office and his nervous catalogue of 'customers'.

One-to-one meetings were also customary. They had been built up from the company's need to improve staff relations; it was a thin veil of confession made with some expedition that we might advance things for the better. It was something that might appeal to fresh recruits to the company. But I had been there a decade and had yet to see any permanent results. That was except for a new brand of toilet cleaner—another matter offered to the cleaners in a bid to cut costs.

But as it was Wednesday afternoon, I still wondered the cause; a few scenarios played themselves like old black and white movies in my mind as I headed towards his office. Finding it was easy.

Set away from the maze of call-centre style cubicles, he had his own designated space. It was tucked away in a somewhat central square room. The door was opposite the desk at Reception; and adjacent at a forty-degree angle to the entrance of the building.

Here, Mike Senior sat, in half ambient yellow lighting away from the sea of phone calls, focusing instead on his computer and the switchboard of occupied lines. It was a curious contraption, perhaps even a little dated. The system he had devised had been made with cork-board. Once upon this had been complemented by a trim of blue felt. But that was fading now - having aged as well as the rest of the building. Its purpose was to store an interweaving system of lights and naming schemes. These consisted of a distinct round peg and diode, placed in order with swatches of a once-white taped cartridge card with an employee's name and number. As the line engaged, the board would light up in the area corresponding to that person's name for every call undertaken. It was the mission, if not the desire of the accounts department, eyeing up our quart electricity bill that these lit up like a Christmas tree.

My light and name sat vacantly amongst them, temporarily redirected to the switchboard to join the caller or callers as it sometimes was into an impersonal game of bingo as they waited for their number to be selected in the queue of never dwindling airwaves.

"You asked to see me, Sir?" I asked, standing before him. It was customary to wait for him to ask you to sit once he had acknowledged you. Something I supposed was to do with respect towards one's superior.

In reply, the boss nodded, gesturing his hands to the vacant chair as he surveyed his modest empire before turning to me.

"Frank," he said earnestly, leaning forwards so that our eyes were almost level. "I'd like to promote you to senior management," *Like to?* The idea seemed ironic in my mind; how a man seemingly "liking" such statements can take ten years to decide to do it. Still, his term stuck with me, uncomfortably in my throat, an unspoken yet omnipresent *but.* "Tell me, where do you see yourself in five years?"

My mind whirred with uncomfortable questions. Had someone said something, had my earlier unwanted transgressions been observed. Or was I merely overthinking everything?

"Take a minute to think about it," he continued, oblivious to my inner turmoil. "I know it's a big question to take in," His words were polished with repetitiveness, no doubt from earlier conversations he had, had through the years. Squeaky clean and impersonal, like the patterns on his tie.

I frowned inwardly, pondering my answer as he suggested. Had someone asked me if I had seen myself here five years ago or even ten, I would have communicated a simple, "*No!*" The young 35-year-old Frank dreamed of running a guinea pig cafe, a popular idea now in Japan – where eccentricity was more likely excepted. I wondered about it now in my mind. I was picturing it as I always did: A small but comfortable restaurant, carefully selected in town I had called *Ginsterpigs.* It was a name I had chosen about the pasties I would sell to my customers and the guinea pigs who would accompany me in this new venture. And it was here, the dream world, where the sun was always shining – as it always does in dreams. Awash of clear blue skies overlooking the cliffs of Dover to the south. There, Toni would be sitting drawing in a corner wearing dungarees. I noticed how her knees were covered in a matte of hair from both guinea pigs and Reaper, whereas I was behind a counter chopping lettuce and serving up cold refreshing lemonade and beers. Perfection.

Mike Sr cleared his throat impatiently, startling me out of my delirium. "Well?" he asked, his eyes probing mine as though he had been looking at the same dream.

But that was all it was, a hap-hazardous, hazily coloured dream.

Thus, it was 45-year-old Frank who was the one to answer to him - my voice clipping slightly with a mixture of resignation and regret. "I see myself here, Sir, at *FRANC*,"

It was, after all, the only acceptable answer. The correct one on a quiz shows on TV is an integral part of any daily programming. Sure, television networks always try to pad them out for drama, but the formula remains the same.

Thus, I received a promotion and a new name badge, which was identical in every single way to my last, save it being printed on gold paper. I knew I ought to feel proud, but, in truth, I felt empty and deflated once more. "What was the point of a badge, designed entirely for show and office theatre, when none of the clients would know at all of my supposed 'superiority' to my peers. A small voice in my head told me they would distance themselves further from me now, trapped in a job offer I couldn't entirely refuse.

The whole thing felt cheap and a sell-out—a metaphor for my miserable existence. Perhaps, as I willed myself to think, things would be better at home.

* * *

As soon as I dared, I trudged home. My mind was now consumed by thoughts of Toni, hoping that the idea of my promotion might be met with some earnest joy rather than my continuing distress.

A smell of pine forest issued from the living room as I entered, which threatened to turn my face as green as the sofa. Waft over waft over the odour permeated the room like a hookah, though more likely a can of cheap supermarket air purifier. Perhaps, I guessed, Toni was spring-cleaning.

I had reached the spot where the dog basket sat. Reaper greeted me with sympathetic eyes. Was this what aurora cleansing was? I asked myself, trying to recall what she had mentioned to me previously about negative vibes. That said, this cleaning was not sufficient at actually organising the home, and as I glanced around the room again, the usual clutter remained. That was save for that small haven of the sofa, coffee table and television, which remained a square of calm and space. This space, which we always prioritised in our chores remained, for as long as Toni and I wanted to watch television and eat takeaways as a guaranteed safe zone. Reaper agreed, coating his usual spot on the floor with a thin layer of dog hair Reminding me once more of my ever distant daydreams.

I flopped onto the most substantial cushions of the settee, grateful that the day was over, musing a little about which takeaway menu to select from the pile for the evening meal. My mind was too tired to cook.

"Frank?" Toni called. I could tell by her voice coming out of the kitchen, and I half looked up at her. To my surprise, her hands were wrapped up with oven gloves, presumably from cooking something.

"Yeah?" I asked, not rising from my newfound position. By now, my tie was loosely tied and had the top three buttons undone on my shirt. Three truly is a magic number. A single button, you might feel restrained, with two buttons you seem unbothered, but three? With three buttons, you can relax after a hard day, and the tie can be tugged off with minimal effort.

It would be easy to drift off until the food was ready, letting her stroke my hair until I had gathered my mind to talk about my day.

What she said next, however, tugged me uncomfortably awake. The words were almost alien on her tongue. Eerily formal and somewhat awkward.

"My mother's *here* for dinner,"

Chapter 18: Monster-in-Law

Had I been with Andy and Dave at *Morses'* at that moment, or indeed anywhere rather than here, I might yet again repeat that women are a strange species. That was, of course, based on my growing encounters with them. Indeed, drawing weight on the book about *Martians & Venus-fly traps,* or whatever it was that I had once spied on Hanny's bookcase. From her fleeting so dubbed 'feminism' faze. She had told me not to worry about it, so I had slid it back onto the bookcase without another word. Although, in hindsight, it might have been helpful for me now, as I faced this strange apparition before me.

Because in the space of a few working hours, Toni, the seemingly controlled, free-spirited young woman I had fallen, if rapidly, in love with, had utterly transformed. I forced myself upright, the blood rushing to my head as I attempted to re-button my shirt, trying to focus on this strange apparition who bore her name.

Her usually scatty pink hair had been hastily tied into a side ponytail, which hung to the side of her head at an unnaturally tightened angle, showing off more than the usual amount of scalp. However, the most noticeable change was her makeup, which she had toned down significantly. She looked pale, nervous even.

Her dress was different too; I was almost certain this dress was not one I'd ever seen before, although I was not one for understanding fashion. The whole design was relatively straight, with a bit of flair at the boom of the skirt where it came down below the knees. Despite this, she had chosen well, opting for a medley of colours and prints with brown and gold leaf prints and bare black heels – shoes she told me later, she usually reserved solely for job interviews when money was tight.

Overall, everything suited her, but it felt unnatural, and she fumbled awkwardly with the hem of her dress; and as I staggered to my feet, I noticed for the first time since I returned that we were not entirely alone.

A further person had appeared in the kitchen doorway, taking its place behind my girlfriend. The lighting dimmed as if in foreboding as it took the form of a tall, thin, graceful woman with mid-length blonde hair and deep blue eyes. Briefly, I wondered if there had been some mistake, questioningly. In my opinion, at least initially, this woman was too young to be Toni's mother. Still, as I stepped closer to greet her, I could see a thin streak of wrinkles along her forehead and jaw, carefully obscured in blush and concealer. Not that she would ever tell.

"You must be Frank," She the lady, her voice silky, like the purr of a contented cat, her gaze travelled down the length of my appearance in the same way a spider might study a fly, stretching out a hand.

I gulped and smiled nervously, shaking it. My words were betraying my broken syntax slightly. "Yes *Mam*, erm, Mrs Jones, I am,"

The lady's eyes narrowed as she withdrew a little.

Had I done the wrong thing? Had she expected a kiss?

I attempted to look to Toni for a cue, but her mother spoke once more. "Please," she purred, "Call me, Marina; Ms Collins seems *so* formal!" I nodded and offered her a seat on one of the room's spacious armchairs, which had seldom been used. There was less dust on them than usual. Perhaps Toni had prepared.

Once her mother had settled, her daughter joined us and sat with me on the sofa, folding her arms and replied stiffly. "Mother chose to *keep* her maiden name,"

"*Antonia!*" Her mother reproached slightly. Her mood almost darkened yet still maintained the same unnatural singsong tone. "This is a *modern* world; a woman reserves the right to choose! She turned back to me to continue as if unfazed by the interruption. "You'll *forgive* her. Of course, I'm sure my daughter was blessed with her father's quick tongue!"

Toni scowled, eyes narrowing but was silent. I wondered if Toni's approach to fashion and life choices were a bid to escape this woman. After all, she had barely mentioned her before; save the time of our initial pasta dinner date. I knew she had a brother, as my nose would so remind me, and a sister, who Toni had once described as older and *"perfect!"*

But given Toni's introduction to my parents, neither family was usually the topic of our conversations. Except for the odd relevant antidote.

The two women were opposites. Assuming, of course, they did not kill each other. At least to the untrained eye. My mind scurried away with its usual observations, preparing for a new section of my little pocketbook for later.

Marina presented herself as a luxury, trophy wife. A lady who believed in outer beauty lavishly displayed through her husband's success, whereas Toni was bright, spirited, wild and carefree. She had, as she had self-professed to me, her adventures had seen her run away aged 17 to live in a caravan park to be with a boy she liked who had washed the cars. It was there she had dyed her hair for the first time a bright, vivid blue. Her mother similarly appeared to dye her hair, concealing the slightest trace of grey with a salon bottled blonde.

Although there was much tension on either side, both remained silent. Toni's face resembled that of a sucked lemon. Bitterer. Such circumstances made it difficult, as small talk had rarely been my forte, especially with the endless need to mention the weather. Still, as Toni's boyfriend and the nominated host, it was up to me to break the ice. Sliding my arm around Toni, I squeezed her slightly in a bid to comfort her and faced her mother with a smile. "Toni's made dinner, haven't you, darling?" I asked, as much to Toni to the room. Toni followed my lead and nodded numbly. Her apprehension was increasingly evident through her usual fierceness.

"Yes, yes. I was telling mother," she said, gesturing vaguely to the kitchen. Marina merely nodded, smiling that same awkward smile that never quite reached her eyes. It was increasingly alarming.

"What are we having?" I asked, attempting to continue the conversation.

"Casserole," Murmured Toni, standing shakily to her feet and retreating to the kitchen as her mother and I headed over to the dining table. The table was surprisingly clean and free from dust and bus maps I often laid out at weekends; the inner section had been folded out to accommodate the three of us.

Before this meal, I had believed that casserole and other stew-based dishes were typically slow-cooked, left to marinade as possible to provide as much flavour as possible. Despite this, the evening's stew had not - which may have been why it tasted so tough. Thankfully, this warranted more than a single need for a glass of water and presented ample opportunity to move away from the room at select intervals. All the while, the tension continued. It was like a cheaply produced crime drama, sat on either side of an integration table – the suspects and the detective.

Toni timidly played with her food at my side, chasing a pea with her fork like a game of tag.

"The meal is lovely, darling," I said, kissing her cheek and smiling as I dabbed my lips with a napkin, continuing the show.

"Yes, very *nice,* Antonia, though I don't recall *this* particular recipe," Marina's reply was curt. There was no sign of relief.

I swallowed and reached for the water-jug, my facade fading and asked, "A refill?" before I hurried back to the kitchen to recollect my thoughts. As the water filled up the decanter, I placed my hand on the bars of Mol's cage and wondered to her and myself how I might entertain our unwelcome, unexpected guest.

But then there was an uncharacteristically loud clatter of metal on china, instantly forcing me into action. I moved the tap to a standstill and ran back to the dining room, where Toni and her mother had begun to bicker in the same way that one might observe school children.

"Your father's hair would go white if he saw you like this!" Marina Collins spouted, casting her eyes over Toni conspicuously. "What look were you going for, thrift shop bargains?!"

"My father's hair's already white!" Toni spat back. "Once he discovered the hot tub you had commissioned for you and your lover."

"Lover?" Marina chuckled. "My dear girl, why would I need a lover when

I have my Cutsie Pink Bubblegum!"

"Who?" I asked uncertainly, only for another joint glare and a *"My/Her* dog!" from both parties before the argument continued.

I sat back down.

Three rounds of courses and quarrelling took place. With each, an increasing ringing followed, cutlery thrust on plates and bowls being scraped crudely with evident aggression. Dessert seemed soggy like the napkins turned Kleenex with blots of tears.

The night dragged by. I longed for the embrace of cotton, so I could block my ears or sink into the oblivion of sleep. Such could not continue. With Mol's encouragement in the back of my mind, I stood my ground. "I got promoted today!"

A pause.

Then Toni smiled, "That's fantastic, Frank!" she exclaimed, beaming. Throwing her arms around me, I treasured her embrace when her mother's saltiness cut through the room like the remains of an expired crisps packet or Uncle Joe's Fish Pie, dripping in sarcasm.

"You've finally got a man with a job? Well done, Antonia, well done!"

My news was forgotten as quickly as it relayed. The two of them fired verbal shots at each other through pudding and courtesy after-dinner tea. (Ms Collins had insisted on coffee). Rarely I understood the entirety of their discourse as they joined increasingly together as they rapidly forced their opinions on each other.

To some, it might seem musical, but for me, it was neither a harmonious repertoire of melody nor soft, bubbly and clean humoured; as the songs I listened to. Although I was confident, they would need soap once as and when they ceased in their quarrel as they aired their dirty laundry and grievances at each other as many times one might attempt to re-bleach a shirt, which had been washed with a red sock left in the machine.

Finally, having wrung it for all its worth, Toni breached the question; I, too, had been too polite to ask. "Why *did* you want to come tonight, Mother?"

Her mother placed down her latte-mocha-espresso frothy cappuccino like coffee. The point would finally be made. "Because it is customary for a mother to meet *her* son-in-law!"

Toni growled, but Marina stood, prompting me to my feet. An old habit, I suppose.

"It was a pleasure to *meet* you, Frank," she said and smiled again dangerously before moving towards the front door. Here she had left an ornate velvet coat was draped on the seldom-used hooks of the foyer. "I'll *see* myself out!" She enthused loudly, before draping herself with her jacket, as a tailor might dress a mannequin and opening the door, she reproached Toni again with a final blow:

"Antonia, you *must* do something with your hair!"

Thus she was gone, the door slamming with more grace than the falling of Jericho. The silence in the room was returning as Toni watched the doorway, seemingly waiting like an Angel or the wafting apparitions of Death. She was heaving slightly as she caught her breath.

I would have to be strong a while longer.

"I think you look nice," I spoke determinedly.

Toni said nothing as she tugged her hair free from the band and made a beeline toward the sofa. Instead, I pulled her into my arms, holding her for a moment, digesting everything. Finally, she seemed quieter when she spoke, as though seeking verification. I wondered if it was as much for herself as I.

"Why does she think she can decide who I can and can't date?!" She asked as much to me as anyone. "I'm a grown woman!"

"Yes, you are," I replied, agreeing with her. "But maybe something's need to change."

"What?!" Toni asked, forcing her head up to look at me as level as possible, given that she was still my junior in height.

"The locks!" I reasoned, hoping my joke, though crass, was not out of place.

Thankfully, she smiled.

"Yes. Now about that promotion...."

And before I knew it, we were back in bed.

* * *

Heated, angry sex was not one I was usually accustomed to. But, given the added length of the day, it was not unwelcome. Toni's hair fanned out around her shoulders like a mermaid, and I ran my fingers through it comfortingly as she laid her head satisfied on my shoulder. She slept the same way a child might. Curled up in the foetal position, her hands tucked under her chin in prayer, turned in towards me and my chest. I loved to watch her like this, free from her earlier angst which she so often wore to mask her insecurities. In that small moment, I felt like a man, strong enough to protect her.

Over on her side of the bed, I half-watched the alarm clock, soothed by the sounds of her deepening breathing and the gentle ticking. For once, all seemed well, and I almost allowed myself to drift off into the scent of her natural tobacco coated perfume. A smell that, until recently, I had not thought myself to like.

I snapped awake at the thought. Could it be that Marina's presence haunted me, like an unpleasant aftertaste or phantom from my sleep-deprived mind? I could see the disapproval in her mother's eyes burning through into mine, asking over and over.

Why was Toni even with me?

And as much as it pained me, I was not sure.

The questions bubbled away uncomfortably into my self-consciousness as I willed myself to believe that Toni's feelings were as sincere as mine and not a tactic to stir up trouble at home. She had undoubtedly seemed happy hearing about my promotion and defended me clearly to her mother through their head to head. But still, my brain flittered back and forth undecidedly.

Things were going too fast.

Much too fast.

And my feelings for Toni, whilst earnest and well-meaning, had somewhat slipped away. I was treading the boards between love and lust. I had always prided myself in knowing the difference. *Hadn't I?*

It would do no good; I could not, no I corrected myself would not sleep now.

So, I rose quietly and headed downstairs seeking comfort, the type only Mol could give me. The unchallenged bond of man and guinea pig.

Perhaps I was a fool—an unlikely fool in love. Life and Lady Luck had rarely favoured the likes of a call-centre representative like me.

Why then should it start now?

Chapter 19: Reflections on Life and Love

I'm not sure how long I stayed sat with Mol, but somehow as we lost ourselves to our conversation, the dark hollows of the room were bathed in an eggshell, cream sort of colour as the sun attempted to pierce itself through the curtain clad windows. All the while, a painful set of pins and needles had attached in the interim to my legs. Had I slept? I was not sure, my mind still processing the previous night's events as I supposed it was now the beginning of Thursday.

In two days, I would be expected to attend the wedding of my friends, who would be declaring before their closest, nearest and dearest that they were ready to commit to each for eternity. Despite Yvonne's obsession with some questionable, if traditional French hate-cuisine, Dave balanced this with his afternoon pint; and seemed generally contented with his soon-to-be extended family of glamorous foreign beauties.

By contrast, my romance with Toni seemed to increasingly blur in an eclectic mix of missed matched events and incidents. And while it lacked the seemingly lustful underbelly of Andy's usual endeavours, I remained uncertain whether Toni's saw me as an eternal promise or a conquest in her thirst for superiority against the equally domineering force of her mother. While I could acknowledge that my mother's grip on my life was by no means distant, I felt the choices I made in life were entirely mine as I had quickly left the family fold, rather than moving into the house next door as my sister had.

Still, the whirlwind like nature in which we had taken to each other was perhaps somewhat unusual, mostly since she had accepted me as a boyfriend so readily after her last breakup. I still recalled how she had barely acknowledged me on our first meeting beyond the need for a bus's arrival.

I reminded myself, however, that despite this initial impression and her age, Toni was not wholly immature. Instead, she had brought me forward into a new world, foreign from my very own in blotches of colourful, splattered paints and vegetarian cooking.

Oblivious to my inner turmoil, Reaper lay snoring within the corner of the room. I watched fondly as his little legs kicked slightly in the air in the fevered fits of the dream world. It was difficult not to envy him for this, although deep down, I knew my night's insomnia had been self-inflicted by my indecision.

In just over an hour, I would have to return to work - to the fish tank and my new, unwanted position of power.

So, propelling myself from the floor to a standing position, I eased myself upwards and headed to the kitchen with similar automation. Tugging the fridge's handle, I grabbed the bottle of milk from its shelf. Quietly hoping that when it took for me to make tea, I could decide between toast and cereal' weighing up each trivial factor in my mind. It would prove a welcome distraction, today at least.

Breakfast during the week was almost always for one – even after Toni's arrival. Although not generally an early riser, she started her day with coffee – black and a bunch of grapes and figs she had insisted on buying during one of the usual bursts of activity at the weekly farmer's markets in Dover.

Thus, my thoughts returned to her again as I returned to the bedroom to gather my clothes. I had already decided to shower later. My shirt and trousers lay on the floor, strewn in the throes of passion, like a pile of discarded and jumbled up autumn leaves—the name badge etching itself to a sock within the collection with self-imposed importance.

Toni was still asleep in the bed. She had remained in the same position as she had been when I left her earlier, curled up in a flannel nightgown that had long since faded in the edges. Still, She was 'comfortable' when the weather appeared undecided – as it had for the past few nights, as a metaphor for my conflicted life.

It was instinctive that I longed to scoop her in my arms once more. But I chose against it, if partly in fear at the prospect of waking her. Instead, for a second, I considered sliding into the half pocket of the bed that her sprawling mass of hair had not taken up. As she slept, it pooled across her cheeks and shoulders like a mermaid drifting through the sea, alluring and hypnotic. Again, I held back, watching her. I only wished to read her mind from this improved angle, peering at her the same way a seagull above the peer spies the perfect chip. I knew I loved her dearly but was it fully reciprocated? Even Mol had not been able to decipher that one, and there was no one else we could ask. Neither of us spoke dog.

I watched her awhile before returning to the kitchen where the kettle roused me from my mundane musings and poured the hot steamy water into my mug, breathing it in, in a bid to revive myself.

Before Toni had arrived into my life, it had made some form of sense, set by the exact boundaries and routines that I had imposed upon myself. It would not be long before I attended the Guinea Pig Games, a niche competition that a few other enthusiasts and I frequented as per the rural tradition. I wondered whether such a sport would interest her.

My stomach groaned uncomfortably, an unwelcome cocktail of restlessness and hunger, so I finally opted for the toast, sliding a piece of bread into the toaster and tried to distract myself as I foraged in the cupboards for butter and jam. Some decisions, I believe, come naturally, like choosing apricot over Marmite, sweet over bitter, and guinea pigs over ferrets. If only the matters of the heart were less troubling.

For all my internal tossing and turning, the matter remained. I looked over at the bedroom door listlessly and considered scrawling Toni a note to find upon waking. But the idea did not seem practical. It was a gesture I had seen done in the movies that Hanny and my mother liked, in which the lady rose from her chamber to find a lavishly presented breakfast. A long-stemmed rose and a glass of orange juice atop a tray with croissants and grapefruit.

And time was ticking on.

For years, despite what Mother had told me - I believed that love was usually reserved for something or someone special, like a pet guinea pig or otherwise treasured, life-long companion. It was *not:-* pink-haired punky personality sporting cigarettes and combat boots.

But who said love made sense anyway?

I realised more and more observing the antics of my friends and others in my notebook that I knew as little as I ever had; my mind and notes had thrust themselves into the churning depths of romance before I could study what I had.

Thus, in the moments remaining, I wrote a shopping list, willing my mind to focus and seek comfort in the mundane, bread, jam, mushrooms, bacon (though not for Toni), a clove or two of garlic, lettuce and carrots for Mol and some wafer-thin slices of cheese. Small, simple pleasures that reminded me of home. I slipped the paper into my pocket, making a note to take the bus into town after work.

Perhaps the distraction would prove me well.

Lord knows I would not find it at work.

* * *

Life at the fish tank remained drab and unimaginative. Someone had brought a selection of cakes and buns round, a token gesture usually reserved for promotions, bereavements, or birthdays.

Maybe it was the early morning or the persistent feeling of nausea that built my resistance against choosing—heightened by the slight indentation of fingerprints and smudges within the veil of icing from the Danish pastries and chocolate eclairs. My body thudded against my desk chair, glad to be still in the same place if only for the routine that I desperately craved from my rambling imagination.

I made my way to the kitchen and made a cup of tea, knowing that my lack of sleep would be of little use to my new position. As always, the taste was foul and more like curdled cream, the flecks of milk and sugar bobbing unnaturally against the sea of opaque beige liquid.

Upon my return, a thick, double wired, doubly bound binder had been placed on my desk, in an assuming covering the keyboard kind of way. No doubt it contained my new contract, which had made hence signed by Mike Sr and the terms of my new role. I flicked through it, comparing the clauses and vital legislation which were jointly highlighted in the rule book in bold, permanent yellow marker; and amended with post-it notes. There was nothing glorified about it, even though the raise from beyond the minimum wage would give me some comfort.

"Morning all," said Mike chipperly, sliding away from his booth as far as he could, his headset wrapped against his neck and trailing against his ears.

"Morning," I acknowledged in turn, listening to the familiar grunt from Andy's station. I considered greeting him more personally, but I still felt stuck in limbo from our last full conversation.

Poppy was already on the phone, taking her first call of the day. "This is *FRANC; how* may I help you?" she asked in her singsong voice with deep estuary tones.

How indeed?

* * *

At a little after 10, my tea was half-drunk and cold, which played well to the need to stretch my legs. I placed my headset down against my chair, resetting my phone to place any intermediate callers on a temporary redirection trail, which took on the form of a vaguely sympathetic, female voice that offered reassurances that their 'call was important to us. We will answer your inquiry as soon as we can' that did not belong to any of my colleagues; although I doubted it belonged to Head Office in London either. It sounded too polished, too kind—probably robotic or, as Toni put it, 'Stepford Wife' syndrome.

At the same time, Dave arrived, nervous and shaky. I observed his spoon clattering in his mug like a stone might rattle unwantedly in a shoe. His eyes were bleary as though he had been drinking or crying, rimmed pink and red with smudges of exhaustion. Except for Mike, none of the immediate group was particularly 'morning' people, but I could tell something was wrong.

I paused, wondering how to approach him. Should I? - I asked myself to use the newfound knowledge of my employment guide or as a friend? Neither of which, I will admit, I was naturally gifted at – at least when it came to other people's feelings. People are much more complex puzzles than guinea pigs. If, that is to say, not always as smart.

"You okay, Dave?" I asked, trying to time my questioning to when he was not holding a scalding cup of freshly brewed coffee; and had fully acknowledged my presence.

Nothing. Just the same cold blinking,

As such, I made to go; when he plucked up the resolution to speak. His usually timid disposition, even more mouse-like. A tone that somewhat reminded me of my sister.

"I don't think I can marry Yvonne!"

Yes, I knew *nothing* about love.

Perhaps probably even less now.

Chapter 20: Mary

For some people, finding the right words to respond with is easy. Be it the banter-based humour that Andy so often used as armour, or the disinterested grunts of my father who only half-listened, when there was a brief pause in his television viewing. The quiet, patient compassion from Mol, the stern sales patter of Bazil, or the usually brash decisiveness of Toni; each had their style of communication with their peers.

Despite working in a call centre, I was not naturally gifted as an orator, and I sometimes believed that had I not got this job, I might have been better suited to a more distinct role, such as a traffic warden or car park patroller. But cars can be cumbersome when one prefers the freedom of buses.

Without much experience of relationships myself, I was not sure how best to encourage the subject, especially given the delicate nature of our location, the office kitchen frequented by fifty-odd employees at varying parts of the day. It was neither private; nor quiet, a communal watering hole, for drinks, microwave snack lunches, and gossip.

Dave's face was white with fear, all-round trembling with varying undertones of pallor, and into the elapsing silence, he looked confident, only in that he was going to run. Hesitating, I shuffled forward, cursing inwardly my inability to set him at ease in the same way that Andy's outlandish charisma oozed. Awkwardly I addressed him, trying to tread the fine line between colleague and friend. "Let's go to the meeting room," I said quietly, motioning to one of the corner rooms within the western wing of the office.

Dave barely nodded, his expression monotoned and flat, "Okay."

The meeting rooms, of which there were two, had private booths and a larger conference room, typically stood apart from the building's overall glass enclosure. It had been chosen this way because such methods had since the building's construction been touched up with a seemingly luxurious touch of paints and cheaply produced plaster, all to represent the company's 'public face'. But it was still a facade, a rushed fix or bodged job, forced upon Mike Sr from a time many years ago, when a stray football had smashed one of the windows.

Checking the board to see if one of them was free, I was relieved to see the lack of squiggles across the three spaces and entered in my name and the time, noting on the large wall clock across the hallway that it was a quarter past the hour as I handed the board to Dave in turn. For once, though, I felt strangely calm. It was almost as though my brain had been temporarily silenced against my usual insecurities, auto-piloting itself from my earlier lack of sleep.

Given the rare luxury of a choice of rooms, we selected one of the smallest. It was much more inconspicuous than the others, and assuming the door was closed would provide ample privacy. Placing my drink on the table, I lent across from Dave. Nothing that was not too dissimilar a move to that of interviewer and interviewee. Indeed, I could tell Dave felt like one, his knees knocking against the wood of the table with pangs of panic as he looked down towards the floor. Clearing my throat from a mixture of dust and concern, I asked in a neutral tone, "What's happened?"

Dave's gaze stuck in silence, and for a moment, I wondered if I had somewhat imagined the past few minutes, hyperactively seeking a distraction from the drudgery that work so often gave us. But then he spoke, his voice weak from tears and nausea. "I can't marry Yvonne."

"Why?" I asked, repeating my earlier question. "What's happened?" A few scenarios played over in my mind, mostly from what I had observed from films and TV shows. Recalling one from Hanny's collection of so titled chick-flicks. "Do you need a blanket?"

Dave's head snapped up, a slight hiccup and sob left his throat, his eyes blank with confusion. "Sorry?" he rasped.

"A blanket," I continued, "You know for the cold feet?"

A glimmer of a smile peeked through his retched form before the misery resumed. "It's not cold feet, Frank," he told at last. "It's an incompatibility."

"Incompatibility?" I parroted back to him, hoping to encourage him. Dave nodded, processing everything.

"Yes, Yvonne wants to move us to France after the wedding, and I don't," he stated solemnly.

As it had been through the entire conversation, I wasn't sure what to say, barely managing a small "Oh," as he retreated inwardly.

The truth was I somewhat understood him, and the feeling daunted me a little at the remarkable similarity.

For Dave and I, Cocklescanslanky, insignificant and unnoticeable save from the very edge of the cliff faces of Dover was all we had ever known. The small, unassuming town had and never would feature prominently in the headlines of newspapers. That was unless it was promotion day for a sale of some resident's collection of jam or gaudy gnome statues that featured in the more luxurious homes. The community centre's notice board had not been updated in some time, with current affairs in our town long forgotten or still the same as ever. It merely existed, cuddled up in a silent embrace within the English coastline.

But Dave was also younger than I., And I knew, despite his evident panic and often quietly stated mannerisms – there was more of the world he had seen. He had even been abroad, regularly visiting France to see the in-laws on holiday and escape the grey muggy weekends with a quick trip across the sea.

I recalled how he had first described Yvonne to us. A tall, confident lady whose legs towered effortlessly in heels, dressed like a model in a magazine, who had wanted to improve her English for a photo-shoot and accidentally brushed across him at a sandwich bar. Somehow, he had won her over. *This* was a feat, which he described towards the somewhat jealous Andy at the time as having told her a joke.

At 32, he was about to cement a loving relationship of three years. He had previously seemed excited about marrying a woman whose family supported a different football team to his own. The initial fact that he'd said didn't matter anyway.

But now she wanted to move back home. She was thrusting Dave perilously into the unknown and replacing the bubble of soon to be married life with a lurching panic.

"Have you spoken to her?" I asked objectively, almost sure I knew the answer. Dave shook his head, swallowing slightly.

"I can't!"

"*Can't* or *won't?*" I queried.

"Can't," He admitted sheepishly, ducking his head down again.

I frowned a little, chewing my bottom lip in thought. It was, in truth, a difficult decision to make. One I knew I couldn't decide upon – not for Dave nor anybody, including myself. There were too many people involved, not to mention the catering company he had booked for the after-party buffet. Most of all, though, Yvonne would be devastated.

So, patting his shoulder, I replied the only way I could. "You need to tell her how you feel."

"About France?" Dave motioned, his tone mooted.

"About everything!"

Painfully aware of how hard such personal advice was to follow. Especially on a personal level.

I'm not sure how it was in which I made my way to the supermarket that afternoon. My mind had thus been somewhat overwhelmed by thoughts of Dave and the conversation he would be having with Yvonne. I hoped that Dave had mustered up the confidence to speak to her; and not retreat to the pub. Somewhat grateful he had voiced some of his concerns to me and not Andy, who might have suggested 'liquid courage', which would be unlike to help beyond a pending mid-week hangover.

However, I was somewhat grateful that Toni would not be waiting for me at home, valuing the time alone to digest the events of the day while she spent some time in her studio. My shopping basket was scarcely filled, save the staple essentials one accumulates in a solitary bachelor existence. A single existence of ready meals that taste of nothing but convenience placed without much regard into the microwave to heat through. I had also picked up an onion and a bag of frozen peas, reasoning that they were helpful to keep at the back of the freezer for any occasion, be it cooling, sprain or soup. I was mulling primarily about the term supermarket and whether such a thing *could be justified* when I felt the slight jab of metal bars against my leg.

Looking up, I recognised the young boy I had seen some time ago on the bus, who was attempting to push the trolley, with his baby sibling sitting cooing on the enclosed plastic seat. His mother, tired and worn as ever, was instantly by his side and took his hand, scolding him slightly. "Willy, please don't be so reckless! You've got to be careful; you could hurt somebody. Say sorry now," she begged, turning to me, her face flushing red in recognition.

"Sorry," said Willy sullenly before reaching to the aisle opposite, having spotted a selection of sugary sweets and confectioneries.

"It's okay, really," I replied, looking somewhat fondly at the child as I recalled the distant mischief I had, had with my sister.

The lady's eyes brightened a little in relief. "Thank you," she affirmed, trying to take the chocolate bar from her son's grip. "Willy, no."

"But mam," He wailed, puffing out his cheeks stubbornly. "You said I could have *one!*"

"Alright," She sighed. "But then we've got to go home,"

Willy grinned, showing a row of steadily forming baby teeth before thrusting his prized possession in the cart.

I watched them for a while, marvelling at the way the mother balanced it all while taking her two young children and a growing array of shopping bags, disposable and otherwise, back and forth on the bus. I then proceeded to head to the checkout with my Charcuterie selection of meats, a six-pint bottle of milk, a portion of fruit, and vegetables.

Perhaps it was my job as part of a seemingly soulless entity, but I always preferred the work of cashier and conveyor belt. That and there was something somewhat pleasing about watching my food glide seamlessly through the till with a series of rhythmic beeping. After paying £31.29, I gathered my bags and headed out to the carport, where the first spots of rain had begun to fall.

Ducking under the sizeable overhanging awning and brickwork that adorned the complex, my shopping tucked neatly under my arm; I caught sight again of the young family who had also elected to take shelter. Willy was wrestling slightly with his mother, who was attempting, one-handed to zip up his raincoat, no doubt wanting to play in one of the developing puddles.

It was too wet for them to walk home.

Instinctively I adjusted my gait to check my watch, glad I knew the bus route from here without the need to walk further into town; catching the eye of my fore-mentioned companion, I nodded at her and asked. "Do you need some help?"

* * *

Mary, as it transpired as her name was 35 and her two children, Willy and Beth, were five and fourteen months. She had moved to the area relatively recently in a bid to start a new life from her now ex-husband, who was a builder. Having accepted my help, loading her cargo onto the bus, she had insisted I come into her home for a cup of tea; "to take the edge off the cold".

I had gratefully accepted her offer, as one should never refuse a good cup of tea and slipped into her flat, a small cramped bedsit cum studio, which she afforded through child support and a little cleaning job, while her eldest child was at school.

"Please excuse the mess!" Flushed Mary, gesturing vaguely in the direction of the whole front room. Shaking my head, I surveyed the scene—this apartment comprised of thinning beige carpets that a bare-minimum landlord had provided. The floor itself having been strewn with a few toys here and there; a battered old sofa and a child's bouncing buggy seat, for when she wanted a moment to relax or distract Willy with the television; which for now sat silent and off in the corner.

To her left, the open plan living room-cum-kitchen diner featured a small 'L' shaped set of units, hastily bolted bits of wood cupboards, a gas stove, fridge and kettle, which she turned on as I helped her to unload her shopping; leaving my own by the door.

"It's very nice here," I continued tactfully as she bustled about the cupboards to find a seemingly clean or *unchipped* mug, appreciating how difficult it might well have been to allow someone to see her lodgings and glimpse more of her life. Mary was not naive to the dust and flecks of old paint that coated her walls, but she was certainly doing her best to keep smiling, despite the slight bags under her eyes from work and motherhood.

Pouring the tea into two mugs, Mary sat across from me on opposite ends of the small three-person sofa. Balancing her daughter on her knees, she had placed her cup of tea set on the nearby window ledge. A tactful move, just out of reach of prying, curious hands as Willy sprawled on the floor, playing with a set of wooden bricks and a pocket-sized car making slight motor noises to himself.

Outside, the rain batted down, slightly stronger now, although not entirely unusual for the time of year. Again, I inwardly thanked myself for remembering my coat and watched the world awhile, unsure what else to say. "We've met before," recognised Mary quietly.

"Yes," I nodded. "On the bus."

"That's right," Mary remembered, her cheeks reddening, quickly asking. "How's the tea?"

I smiled at her.

"Very nice, thank you,"

We spent the next hour talking about life and its various stages. Finding quickly, we had a few things in common beyond the initial journey. Mary liked guinea pigs and had a pet one as a child, a dark blonde one she had affectionately called Chunky. So, I entertained the family a while divulging the details of the guinea pig games, burrowing into my pockets to retrieve a leaflet, which I often carried with me on the off-chance I might be thrown into a conversation. She accepted it gratefully, asking about Mol and whether she and I were ready to enter this year's proceedings.

Time passed unknowingly, and before I knew it was getting dark and I noticed how Beth had drifted off to sleep in her mum's arms, and Willy's movements were slowing in a mixture of hunger and fatigue. "Perhaps I should go?" I asked.

Mary frowned a little but nodded somewhat guiltily as she scooped her youngest into her arms in a gentle rocking motion. I made towards the door, gathering my shopping from the threshold. "We'll see you again?" she asked in a soft low voice.

I smiled sincerely. *"I'd like that."*

Mary's hand caught the edge of the door, brushing mine as she lent to close it, her smile matching my own. *"Me too."*

My heart fluttered in my chest like an unknowing bubble of intrigue.

Could it be possible I was finding myself inadvertently drawn to her?

Guilt clawed at me as I reached into my pocket for my phone, checking for a call or text from Toni. But there was none.

No doubt she had become engrossed in her work and would catch me up to speed upon her return. For now, though, there was the faint lingering touch of Mary and a half defrosted ready meal for one.

Alone.

Chapter 21: Nagging Loneliness

Returning to my flat, the exterior somewhat shrouded in darkness, I looked around sheepishly around for Toni, as though half expecting and half hoping to explain to her my prolonged absence. But she was not home. Nor was Reaper, the dog's bed lying absent, save a few shed hairs. No doubt Toni had taken her with her earlier for company or inspiration, depending on her muse.

I sighed quietly, setting down the somewhat wet bag of shopping on the kitchen counter and turned to my beloved companion, unlatching the hatched gated entrance to her cage and scratching her gently on the back of her ears and neck, hoping to soothe my thoughts.

I knew Mol would listen to me, although she was hungry, and her eyes - round and black like raisins watched me with mild interest before turning away. A hint perhaps that what I needed most was some semblance of routine. So, I stood once more and grabbed a carrot from the fridge, washing it under the tap and placed it on the plastic chopping board that I usually kept on the draining board along with a sharp knife from the drawer left of the sink and began to slice it into even rounds. It was important in my mind to keep Mol well-fed and happy; my food would not take long, thrust with much less thought into the microwave for a few minutes with a few choice holes pierced into the plastic lid. My appetite had somewhat dwindled from the events of the day, although I knew I had to keep myself nourished if I were to think things through rationally.

My head was swimming with confusion, churning like my ready meal in a sea of lust, love, and nausea as I finished and slipped them circled carrot offerings into Mol's usual bowl, watching her scurry over whistling in delight and approval. "What am I going to do?" I mused quietly.

Someone once said, probably Mike Sr or one of the induction training videos imposed on us, that "a good customer service representative should have all the answers," *Well, I certainly didn't.* It was a question many customers had asked over the phone at work, though this time, there was no script or prompt sheet in which to help me. All I had was a ready meal for one and a bleak, migraine induced existence.

"You should follow your own advice," reasoned Mol, acknowledging me as she finished a piece of carrot and took time to drink from her water bottle.

"What about?" I asked although I knew feigning ignorance would do no good. Mol had an uncanny way of delving deep into my soul. It was both a comforting and unnerving feeling. It was built from the bond of years of simpler times, ones of just us two. Man and guinea pig.

I ought to feel elated like I had when Toni had agreed to go on our first date and shared our first kiss. But that same emotion gave me vertigo, as though I were teetering out at the very cliffs, I had found some inspiring before—a mixture of guilt and confusion and niggling insomnia.

After a chewy but somewhat edible dinner, I headed to bed, doing what I could to clear the gristle from my teeth with my toothbrush and a cheap wooden stick—purposely detaining myself from the looming déjà vu of another sleepless night.

I glanced into the mirror. I noticed how the thin strobe lighting hugged the shadows of my face.

I felt *old.*

Old and tired, the same way my father did in front of the television. A life resigned to the existence of repeats and breaking news, soap operas, political affairs and obscurely named quiz shows.

Climbing into the bed, I rolled almost instinctively to my side. A now familiar habit so that I faced inwardly and away from the wall. Usually, after a period of lovemaking or the rare times I allowed myself a lie-in, typically Sunday's, I would reach over to Toni on the other side and stroke her hair from her cheeks, revelling at the soft breath or sigh that escaped her. The relief of being real, of being touched. Now, however, I marvelled at how vast such space felt with just me lying there. The sheets were still creased slightly where Toni's frame had cocooned itself the night before but now felt cold in her absence.

Sleep would not immediately come. Still, I told myself that I would not detain Mol tonight. Thus, I remained there, gazing up at the ceiling. Here I counted the lines and cracks that had gathered from years of neglect until my mind drifted away from a cocktail of boredom and exhaustion.

* * *

One of the few perks of becoming a more 'senior' member of the FRANC team was the rare opportunity to take the occasional time off on a Friday. Given my exhaustion and confusion, something that was perhaps well-needed, although I decided against it—hoping that the buzzing noise of other people's concerns on the phone might distract me from my own.

I walked into the fish tank, taking my usual place at my booth, gathering my receiver from its cradle in preparation. "Good mornings" and "greetings" were passed around between my immediate group in the conventional fashion. Grunts of early-start disgruntlement from Andy and a brief hello from Mike already on his first call.

I didn't have to wait long. A few minutes had barely crept past when the line burst into life. The caller, a panicked and overly protective mother in her sixties, was despairing of her middle-aged, wayward son.

Despite her efforts to smother him in cotton wool and escape the world from his "terrible ex-wife," who "spitefully" kept him from his daughter, she had found him flittering away money they didn't have on pay-day loans and slot-games and now wanted all the advice she could get. She, herself not willing to accept the hard truth that she might shoulder some of the blame over any part of her account that would see her as a bad mother. She was like any other caller who phoned as an advocate—always wanting quick assurances, not therapy.

None of this had anything to do with PPI.

Still, I smiled a little at the distraction. It would be a long morning.

By half nine, the centre was filled with a song of scripted, impersonal calls. But, amongst this medley of the usual unmelodic hubbub, I noticed, half gazing away from my cubicle, that a member of our dysfunctional orchestra was missing.

Dave.

Setting aside the handset as my call ended, I looked to Andy, who sat sideways on staring innately at his computer screen.

Would he know anything?

We had barely spoken about or with Poppy since the discussion, save the odd necessary pleasantries. The tension had seemed somewhat palpable between us, aided in part by a lack of shared coffee breaks, and I was not one to speak over delicate and private matters in the loos. Apart from the unmistakable smell, they echoed terribly with every possibility of attracting gossip which wafted from the communal vents with the ladies' next door.

So deciding to form an investigation might not have been ideal, especially with a less than willing partner. Still, nevertheless, Andy's cubicle was closest, so I asked him in a half-whisper, "Where's Dave?" Hoping that he would hear me above the usual office thrum and put aside his still ill-fitting anger and bitterness to answer me.

Andy turned and raised an eyebrow. With his headset still slipped around his head, he looked a little like an owl and had concern not dominated my mind I might have laughed. Although the unexplained absence of our colleague and friend was not a trivial matter, and I gestured towards Dave's spot. Thankfully, Andy nodded.

He, too, was happy to have a temporary escape from the mechanical motions that lead so many of us every Friday.

But we didn't have long; there was only a small window of downtime before another call rang through for either of us from the eternally unsatisfied Joe-public.

Rotating his seat a further 90 degrees, Andy carefully removed his headphones and poked his head in between the division that generally separated the two colleagues during the working day with a faint pretence of privacy. Although it was muffled through the fabric partition, I could hear his voice inquiring. "You okay in there, mate?"

Silence greeted him.

The booth was empty, save the usual office furniture. Computer, desk, chair, and phone; a choice selection of post-it-notes and a collection of blue and black pens with varying degrees of ink. But no, Dave.

Still, composure was needed. Accordingly, I willed myself to believe Dave was safely back at home. Perhaps, I mulled over the scenario; he would have spent the evening having a heart to heart with his bride to be. The pair of them perhaps discussing the opportunities and costs that would come either with his moving abroad or Yvonne becoming a British-French citizen once they were wed - thus staying here in our small bubble on the outskirts of Kent's coastal underbelly.

I was about to take another call when Andy called me over, his voice hissing with slight urgency. There was a post-it note in his hand, a crumpled yellow sticky thing tattooed with Dave's familiar scrawny penmanship in impersonal black Biro.

'I can't do it any more. Sorry.' I need to get away from it all.

An alarm vibrated through my temples, created by the unwanted mixture of bubbling panic and the phone's off-the-hook warning, which had begun in the elapsing seconds as I had hastily cradled it into my hands. It had an automated voice, not too dissimilar to a tinny robotic parrot screeching:

"One of your telephone handsets is off-hook. Please replace it immediately."

This repeated over and over fell on my now deaf ears as the receiver slipped from my grip and clattered on the carpeted floor.

By now, Poppy and Mike Jr had noticed, and they joined us also. The four of us standing mismatched together, all of us awkwardly resembling some hastily put together teenagers at school being forced to compile a compulsory, grade changing school project.

"What do we do, Frank?" questioned Mike, his voice warbled a little.

It was my responsibility as team leader.

Trying to project calm, I gulped inwardly. Words from the previous day were replaying themselves as they had done so often in my mind. I guessed with hindsight if our conversation in that small square room had been a case of pre-wedding jitters or a cry for help.

Work was the last thing on my mind.

"I'm going to go look for him," I decided, grabbing my coat and headed away from the mob and out towards the door. Andy nodded, following my queue.

"Where?"

The truth was I didn't know, nor did I have a semblance of a plan, something I would admit to him later. But at that moment, I hoped that I might recall the place that Dave would be. His sacred haven away from work and home; a location he had once joked was his second office on a weekday or match day night. *Morses'*

"The pub."

* * *

We walked quickly in relative silence, the world seeming to blur as we increased pace down the road towards *Morses'* familiar white stucco pebble-dashed facade and entered through the narrow double doors.

The room was dimly lit, the curtains half-open from the cleaners who had come in the early hours, with a slight neon glow from the artificial lights and switches of the slot machine, chirping and whistling its jaunty jingle. I moved towards the bar, acknowledging the hunched over figure sitting on one of the bar stools.

"Dave?"

Dave didn't move, and for a moment, I wondered whether he had fallen asleep; however, he groaned quietly upon our approach. "Leave me," he mumbled, the unmistakable musk of alcohol on his breath as he slumped back onto the counter. His upper body barely supported him.

"What happened?" I asked, taking the seat beside him, trying my best to ignore the smell, while Andy looked on uncomfortably standing to the side. The trouble was Andy had never been good with emotions, and he shuffled slightly from side to side, keeping his hands in his pockets like a sullen schoolboy sent to detention.

Dave sighed, acknowledging us both reluctantly. "Leave it, Frank," he said quietly, his words stilted and slightly slurred. His eyes looked read.

"How much have you had?" I deflected in turn, gesturing vaguely to the somewhat new round circles from a wet tankard that had sunk into the wooden surface from the lack of a coaster. I suspected the cleaners had left these, perhaps deliberately, as Dave slumbered on in drunken stupor.

Dave frowned. The words seemed to bother him. "Why do you *care?*" he asked coldly. His tone was uncharacteristically flat. Even in the dark, I could see dark circles under his eyes, so unlike the friend I knew.

Andy must have noticed, too, as he was prompted into action. Sensing the overall discomfort in the room, he placed his hand slightly on the small of his friend's back. "Yvonne?" he asked, keeping his voice low.

Dave groaned in reply. "She's left me," he whispered solemnly.

Silence washed over the three of us.

It seemed like everything had already been said.

Chapter 22: Bachelor Based Depression

Breakups are hard.

Although we sat in silence for a while, eventually, Dave decided to leave the pub after some subtle insistence from Andy and me to get some fresh air. Although in truth, it was more filtered at best, a mixed-up cocktail of the sea and Andy's newly lit cigarette. We sat on the cobbled wall outside and looked out at the cliffs and the water below.

Dave's body hung like a scarecrow in the newly created nook of his friends' arms as we carried a broken man. His head, albeit metaphorically, was mangled and his spirit crushed at the sight of Calais in the distance, the delicate etchings of building outlines across the 18-mile Dover strait. The country Yvonne called *home*.

"Time to go," I murmured, nudging him upright slightly. The problem was none of us knew for sure if Yvonne was still in the house since she had thrown him out the night before. Initially, setting him up in a Bed & Breakfast seemed like an option, and I spent a few minutes looking up a few on my phone before weighing against it. Such an idea would be expensive right now, especially since Dave had just paid for the final instalment towards his now-cancelled wedding.

Thus, we decided instead upon Andy's sofa, believing that the warm shower and the somewhat short springs from the worn-out futon might help clear his head and help steer him towards his next course of action. At the very least, a change of clothes would help. Clothes that didn't still smell of yesterday's poor choices and cheap, refillable beer.

By now, it was 11 am, an hour had passed by in the absence of any clock watching, and we made our way towards the centre of town, in an odd three-man-four legged ensemble, Andy, Dave and I as we half-carried-half hobbled. Up, past the bus depot, where a line of smugly assembled taxis was waiting parked against the curb. Although my back was killing me a little from the dead weight of my friend, I was not sure if jovial conversations would be appreciated from a man who had skipped breakfast in favour of an early liquid lunch.

Further on we walked, past the rows of trim and artfully arranged gardens and white-washed houses, scattered with tall plants like foxgloves and rose bushes and hideous garden gnomes. These were the houses that Mum had admired long ago in glossy magazines, with a Dover postcode and a market value to match, one I imagined Marina might occupy. Not that I planned on visiting.

Andy lived in one of those awkward box flats above a shop, without a separate entrance except the communal intercom and a flight of stairs beyond the door. I had never seen inside, although we had chatted outside it before, sharing a guilty late-night kebab from the takeaway across the road, on one of those rare occasions he had not headed in with a girl. He had preferred to 'splash out' on his car, telling us that he didn't sleep more than he had to anyway, just enough to escape his office-based misery, a sentiment which the entire department shared.

Upon entry, I saddled Dave on a bean bag chair, looking around at the eclectic collection of figurative art and pots of instant noodles. "It's lived in," I said somewhat distantly, hoping that I might seem cheerful enough to rouse Dave's spirits at his new temporal lodgings. Dave said nothing.

Andy, on the other hand, was all smiles. "Welcome to *the* bachelor pad," he said, spreading his arms wide about the room, like a television presenter on one of those overly recycled formats about house renovations they showed around tea-time.

Again nothing. Dave had reached into his pocket and took out his phone, glumly refreshing the screen every time it started to fade for black, checking for messages from Yvonne.

We would have to guide the conversation a while longer. Reaching over,

I gently took the phone from Dave's grip, noticing the disproportionate number of calls and texts he had left her since the night before. There had been no reply. He barely registered this, letting out a small choked "Hey," before hanging his head in shame.

"Come on; you'll feel better after a shower," I enthused comfortingly before turning to Andy and shaking my head.

"Yeah!" Andy hyped, bouncing over slightly like an overly eager puppy, "Bit of wash, fresh clothes you'll soon have the girls lapping up your every word."

"I don't want girls," Whispered Dave forlornly. "I want Yvonne!"

"Sorry, please excuse me," I replied somewhat guiltily and then stepped outside to the hall. Although there was no real ideal time to do it, there were a few calls I had to make as per the protocol I had engrained into my head.

The first call was a business one—someone needed to let the office know where we were and where Dave had gone. A trivial matter, I knew, given the sheer volume of people who had stared as I marched from the building, an important one, especially given my authoritative role.

It was not normal for me to make a premature departure from the typical structure of the day. But I supposed it was exceptional circumstances like these which we have been told to prepare for, advanced practical training if you will. Not that the receptionist cared promising to pass the message on with the same conviction as one might have to watch paint dry.

Next, I phoned Toni. I wondered whether she was at the studio or she had already heard, though as a bridesmaid, I imagined she might have. While neither Yvonne nor Toni was particularly close friends, I knew that wedding decorum and formalities usually lay with both parties. In the absence of Dave, Yvonne was probably picking up the pieces of her ceremony and her heart.

"Hey," Toni answered, her voice bristling slightly. I could hear someone wailing in the background, confirming my suspicions of female solidarity. "Yes, she's *told* me,"

"Ah, should I pass a message on?"

"Yes," She paused for emphasis. "Go to hell!"

"No need," I stated, sadly ending the call.

In my mind, Dave was already there.

* * *

Stepping back into the main room, I was relieved to hear running water. Dave was in the shower. Andy was in the open plan kitchen, munching on some toast. "Yvonne?" he asked, noticing the phone as I slipped it back into my coat.

I frowned. "Hurt,"

He nodded, wiping a stray crumb from his shirt. "Guess that's to be expected."

"Yep," I affirmed, wondering if I should broach the subject of our friendship. Since the situation with Poppy had ended with the two of them alone, I was not entirely sure how he saw me now.

"Andy-Frank," our words came in unison, tumbling and awkward as we both attempted to bridge the silence, which fell uncomfortably in the room against the backdrop of falling water in the shower.

I gestured to him to proceed. "You go," Not even sure if I knew what to say.

Beyond more vague, impartial sentences.

Andy nodded, "Poppy and me. The thing is. Yeah, we were never going to work," he sighed gravely, his tone uncharacteristically awkward, the combination of pride and acceptance of a past transgression.

I smiled sympathetically. "I'm sure you'll find someone!"

"Yeah, cool," Andy repeated, dropping the subject. Dave would be out soon. Perhaps grateful for the timing of the water stopping from the bathroom.

Andy was happy to return to his routine of cheap chat-up lines and rounds of drinks; it was a bit sleazy, not that his efforts often amounted to much beyond a hangover or a few shaggy dog stories of his exaggerated conquests at the pub. Perhaps Andy had considered trying his luck with one of Yvonne's sisters at the wedding.

The older I got, the more I knew that everyone was different.
And so is love.

* * *

Dave returned from the shower, not entirely refreshed but certainly cleaner, wearing an oddly styled shirt that Andy had grabbed him from his cupboard. It looked like it had been there a relatively long time, with slightly bobbly sleeves and a bit of fraying on the hem, which Andy enthused was style. Not that I ever professed to knowing about fashion. Perhaps it was a 'charity shop vintage', something similar to what Toni favoured. The colour was not quite burgundy or maroon. It was hideous.

But at least it *fit.*

Mostly.

"I think *I* should talk to Yvonne," Dave reasoned, attempting to redo one of the top buttons at Andy's insistence that it was more flattering for the ladies to show a little chest hair.

Andy shook his head, almost wildly in disbelief. "Yvonne? Mate, you can find better at *Morses'* you'll see!" Thus he reached forward to unbutton the shirt once more, the same way a mother might dress her child for school, although with less restraint for revealing a bit of flesh.

"I don't want *better,* though," Dave said dejectedly. "I *want* Yvonne!"

"But," Andy retorted. "She doesn't want you unless you move to France,"

"Well, at least I'd be with her!"

"That's not love. That's control!" Andy continued his lecture on masculinity. Placing his hands on his hips like a portrait of one of our many patriarchs, he turned to me expectantly. "What do you think, Frank?"

I froze as the question hurled towards me. It was usually within my nature to take a neutral stance, but the chance of being impartial might offend one or both. I believed my own opinions to be unnecessary, and thankfully Andy had already returned to his train of thought. "You've just forgotten the fun of being *numero uno!*"

Dave frowned. "Who'll iron my socks?" he asked meekly.

"*No one* irons socks!" Andy replied. "Now, come on!" and without another word, he frogmarched Dave out into the hall. "Let's go!"

It was best not to ask where.

We still hadn't had lunch.

My stomach rumbled at the thought.

* * *

Outside, with a packet of crisps, a shrink-wrapped ham and cheese roll and a can of fizzy drink from the corner shop below, I watched a pair of seagulls hovering on a nearby lamppost, squabbling over space and pickings of discarded rubbish. Andy was still in the shop, purchasing a magazine and a pack or two of cigarettes. Dave had wandered in with him and then wandered out not long after. He had declined to buy anything, and he placed his hands awkwardly in the pockets of his trousers, seemingly deep in thought.

I held out the bag towards him in an automated sort of gesture; the kind one might do directing traffic or passing a bowl of peanuts across the counter of a bar.

"What's the flavour?" asked Dave shyly before shuffling closer, his head drooping toward the ground. The world on his shoulders.

I turned the packet, not entirely sure, having grabbed what was readily available in the meal deal, my mind ruled by the effectiveness of the cost, if not the selection of the store's offerings.

"Pickled onion,"

Dave gave a rare smile and moved to take one when Andy exited and quickly nudged the bag away with a stern look. "No, pickled onion!" he explained sharply.

Dave yelped a little in surprise. "But they're my favourite!" he protested.

Andy looked at him incredulously. "Don't you want the girls to *love* you?" he asked. "Your breath needs to be minty fresh."

It took less than a beat for Dave to bounce back. "But don't you smoke?"

Andy smiled, winking at me knowingly over Dave's shoulder. "This isn't about *me,* Casanova!" Thus still debating the ethics of toothpaste and mouthwash, the three of us headed down towards the town.

Perhaps, slowly but surely, with some delicate conversations and time to reflect, Dave would be okay.

But Andy didn't really do subtlety.

* * *

It would be hours when I finally returned home—the day somewhat blurring from early and sustained drinking brought about at Andy's insistence and Dave's sadness. Although I had been reluctant as the latter, Andy had brought us both to a so-called "gentleman's club" he had found in Dover. he said that he believed that the change of scenery would do our newly single friend some good, albeit for not entirely selfless reasons.

"Happy Hour," Andy purred as we entered through the main entrance as he beckoned us past a neon pink sign saying, 'Poles Open'. I thought to comment on this but decided against it, having made a point where possible to steer clear of politics.

Andy ordered the first round of drinks and some soggy chips "to cushion the system". They had not been soggy when they first arrived but quickly became so once Andy and Dave sloshed them with beer. I had never been a heavy drinker, and all around me, the colours blurred together. At the same time, the drumming inside my head doubled and tripled like some dance from some forgotten tribe. It reminded me of my conscious role in everything. It would not take long for either of us to realise why Andy had brought us here.

Up, on the stage, a group of women appeared scantily dressed, weaving to and through, like snakes caught in the trance of a serpent's dance, all wearing garments of cheap sparkly synthetics: latex and Polyester. Andy and a couple of others in the room were whooping and wolf-whistling, their voices sounding more like animals or the backing track of some of the thumping heavy music I overheard from teenagers' headphones on the bus. The room was hot and suffocating, an uncomfortable wafting fog of body odour. I longed to remove my coat but thought against it, not entirely confident whether I would find it again in the artificially lit booth. Dave sat against me, wearily. "This *could* have been my stag do, He reminded me.

"Yes, it *could*," I returned, lifting my reluctant pint, needing sustenance and hydration. Somehow having an accidental toast as the tankard clinked against his own, Dave let out a small laugh, low and bitter and sealed the opportunity. "Here's to *love!*" he called out, his words falling into the void of the room catering for unsated lusts.

Yvonne's image seemingly still burning like a vigil, praying within the very embers of his breaking heart and mind.

Chapter 23: Mia and the Motorcycle

Friday crawled into Saturday, the same sluggish way a snail might ease itself onto the guttering of a wall, slipping slowly through the hours with cheap shots of liquors and beer.

My head pounded a little as I woke to the sound of dawn's morning traffic. Outside there was buzzing and clattering from the weekend's market traders on the way to and from Dover. Thus, I was somewhat grateful that I was not expected to work. Slowly I rolled from the makeshift bed I had fashioned myself on the floor, which I had made from my coat by bunching it in the corners to make a pillow—at last, acknowledging my blurry, unfamiliar surroundings.

I reached for my glasses, finding them on the coffee table to my left and peered around the room inquisitively as I scrambled to my feet, forcing my eyes to focus.

I was back at Andy's.

Confident of this fact, I looked around for my companions, surmising that we came in together using Andy's key, some point between 12 and 2. It was unlikely in the short time that had elapsed since we had gone on the impromptu pub crawl that Andy would have cut a new key for his new flatmate, so all of us had ended up here. Andy's door was closed, although I presumed he was in his bedroom, perhaps with a young lady. I decided against knocking. For now, I was more interested in Dave.

So, I turned towards the makeshift sofa bed to greet him but was surprised to see the faded yellow sheet that Andy had gathered for him yesterday now crumpled on the floor. Lifeless and creased, it was vacant of any sleeping body. "Dave?" I asked cautiously, staggering closer as I forced the blood flow back into my toes. There was no answer.

Instinctively I reached for my phone from my trouser pocket, praying that it had some battery life left. *32%, 19 notifications.* I scrolled through the lock screen to prioritise where I could, the number of callbacks and messages I would have to answer to at a more socially acceptable hour. His name was not amongst them, and I cursed my inability to text while I nursed the prospect of a likely hangover, certain that his phone would be dead or near it like mine.

Thankfully, the door in the hallway opened. Andy stepped into the room, in his boxers, his arm around a girl I didn't recognise, who had wrapped herself in his duvet cover, giggling somewhat tipsily as she asked in a sugary sweet voice, "What's going on, Andy-bear?"

"Give me a minute, sweetheart," Andy replied calmly, kissing her on the cheek as he unlooped himself from her embrace and headed into the open-plan kitchen-cum-living space and picked up a plain grubby white plastic kettle from the sink. "Anyone for tea? Frank? Mia?"

I didn't answer. Not entirely sure if I even knew the correct words to say and nodded mutely. I looked at my watch, grateful it was still on my wrist and not amongst my small assortment of things on the floor. Perhaps the tea would help me wake up.

It was 5:43. AM.

A few more minutes passed, and cradling a cup of lukewarm tea, I willed myself to believe that the swirling mass of residue on the sides was from the teaspoon of sugar and not limescale built up from the somewhat chalky water. Now 5:45 AM.

In these small interconnecting minutes and seconds, I had sat on the couch feeling like an overly protective mother, watching the door for Dave.

Seemingly uninterested in their surroundings, Andy and Mia canoodled in the kitchen opposite me; the duvet had occasionally slipped from her shoulder as though she was teasing him. And whilst I had, of course, vocalised my concerns about Dave's absence, hoping that Andy might use his phone to call our missing friend, Andy seemed otherwise preoccupied with his new visitor's sweet-nothings and wandering hands.

Over the multitude of kissing and petting within my line of vision, I coughed and asked my less than captive audience. "Has any*one* seen Dave?"

Flushing slightly, Andy looked up. "Dave?" Andy seemed puzzled. Perhaps the lack of oxygen had gone to his head.

Mia prompted him, but she, too, was hesitant. "Your friend, right? I think he popped out."

The venom and last whisper of tea-soaked beer-hops almost burnt my tongue. "When?" I asked incredulously, adopting the stance of an integrator on a televised cop drama, hoping that my desperation might rouse Andy from his lustful stupor.

"About half an hour or so, maybe an hour?" Andy replied half heartedly, scratching his head. Mia nodded, though both admitted neither had been clock watching.

Because, whilst I had given them some grace period to wake up, I had always been a great believer of the importance of time. I found gentle comfort in the regimented lines and grids of bus timetables or the TV listings when I was a boy running home to watch cartoons after school. Fondly remembering the simpler days of sitting cross-legged on the floor with packs of pick and mix and Hanny bundled up on one of the loose sofa cushions. I smiled for a moment before returning to the immediate matter as a calendar reminder flashed from my dying phone.

2:30 PM – The start of the wedding ceremony, a permanent reminder of the events that had previously been set in stone, the presence like an unwanted and ill-thought-out tattoo designed in permanent marker. Although I was not in a hurry to rush home or force myself into the ill-fitting waistcoat that Toni had discovered in the folds of my wardrobe, the sadness over the cancelled affair lingered like stale birthday cake.

We all stared at it, the little self-assuming box lighting up with self-importance in shorthand text. *Dave. Yvonne. Wedding. Day.*

Andy wavered, his eyes flickering with recognition as it prompted him into action.

"Andy, do you have a charger?" I asked. He nodded and fumbled

161

backwards through a medley of kitchen drawers before dangling a slightly bent second-hand cable in his hands. Although it lacked the enthusiasm and precision of a waiter serving soup at one of the more prestigious establishments in Kent, it was a start.

Standing, I passed him back my phone, and we moved like a swarm with bated breath to the nearest plug socket.

Sleep, sex and tea were now the furthest thoughts from my mind.

I was going to call Yvonne.

* * *

With her long spindly fingers and elegant weave of raven hair, it was hard to imagine Yvonne's morning routine beyond the realms of a supernatural drama. However, it was also reasonable that Yvonne would be an early riser given her meticulous attention to detail. She liked plenty of time to prepare herself for the day ahead. Makeup was something to be applied, not slept in.

Yvonne answered her phone on the third ring. She had a densely thick French accent that clipped awkwardly as she acknowledged me as one of her former fiance's friends. Her voice was strained. She had been crying. "Frank?"

How best not to worry her?

I took a deep breath, conscious that my insecurity fogged up the handset, which I would consider cleaning later when I could find a clean handkerchief or some kitchen roll. The others waited.

"Is this about Dave?" Yvonne asked. In the background, I could hear one of her friends; loud, angry and outspoken.

"Tell him to shove it; he's blown it!" And other such expletives I would not wish to repeat nor hear.

Yvonne was quiet. "Frank?" she questioned again, her voice cracking as the tears threatened to overwhelm her further. "Is *he* okay?"

"We don't know-"I was about to tell Yvonne about the previous night and his apparent mood when Andy grabbed the phone from me like a jealous girlfriend might accost her partner in a bar. His words were rapid and barely enunciated, lacking the rehearsed polish he usually carried. I bit my lip, resisting the urge to scratch my burning ear.

"He's nervous, but that's to be expected, getting ready for *your* wedding day, you know. Yes, the wedding is still on! He's sorry he's been *such* a loser. *I know you know what men are like.* Just a little stag doo prank, I'm sorry. Yes, 2:30. Best be getting ready. Okay, see you there. Bye now."

Then he hung up and tossed the phone back to me.

"What did you do that for?!" I asked sceptically, hoping that this wasn't another one of Andy's half-baked plans like taking Dave out clubbing or the spontaneous hook-up from the night before with a girl, who I only knew by name and tea preferences, still dressed in his bedding. I expected to rebuke him, but I needed to be sure I understood him and that it wasn't merely a fever dream brought about by cheap alcohol. "The wedding isn't on, is it?"

Andy flashed a smile.

"Just leave that to me!"

Without any sign of an explanation, he retreated into his bedroom, waving his hands dismissively. "Go get dressed, Frank. There's a wedding to save!"

* * *

When asked, Andy had told me his strategy, if you could call it that. One of those fool-hardy ideas that come from a mixture of drinking and bravado, although it made some form of sense to my not-entirely sober mind.

We had eight hours.

Gathering my phone, belongings, and coat from the floor, I dashed out of the flat and sprinted down the road towards the taxi rink, sure that my journey home would be more productive and ultimately time-saving if I were not bathed in sweat and body odour.

Not that I expected the taxi to be entirely different.

That said, it was relatively early, and Saturday granted me some freedom from tourists, not that I had seen many beyond seagulls visiting from the English Channel. Despite my preferences, there would be no buses at this time, most of our slice of England would be enjoying its slumber whilst I powered through the results of another sleepless night. As anticipated, there was no one there.

I went into their main building in desperation, praying that one might be available within a few minutes, recalling how some used to park a little further into town as I headed to the front desk.

"Taxi, please!" I panted toward the less than impressed teenage faced operating clerk.

She looked bored. "Address?"

I was about to answer when someone patted me on the shoulder. Whirling around, I was greeted by an unexpected driver, dressed head to toe in leather, red plaid, lipstick and a pair of old biker's helmets, swinging by the neck-straps in her left hand.

"Toni?"

"That's right!" Conveyed my girlfriend beaming as she tossed one of the helmets into my trembling arms. "We've got to go!"

I swallowed my looming nausea in the back of my throat, barely scrambling out a "How, where?" as she tugged me out into the road. She had parked a rather rusty looking motorbike that even a Hell's Angel would probably say was unsafe. Not that I could afford to be picky about transportation, even if I had never seen it before.

Momentarily I gaped wordlessly as Toni strapped her helmet back on, tightening the tethers across her head before straddling the motorcycle at the front half of the seat. Sensing my unease, she had turned around. "Come on," she stressed slightly more urgently.

Steering myself, I joined her, calling out over the sound of the engine as it roared into life. "Whose bike?"

"Billy's," I nodded and closed my eyes, nestling my head into the space between her shoulder blades. "Where *are* we going?"

Toni smiled, tapping the side mirror into place, "Relax, Frank, I know about Dave," she said over the howling wind that came from the seafront. No matter how many peanuts and beers I could have had beforehand, my stomach was knotted and lined with stress and wrinkles as we drove towards what I hoped was home.

The still crisp morning air and the scent of early morning nicotine that lingered on Toni's jacket made me want to cough, and I took a moment to collect my equilibrium and my balance, my mind buzzing with questions. We had parked not far from Bazil's shop, and I recognised the rows of older brickwork buildings edging up and down the hill.

"How?" I asked, somewhat relieved to be on Terra Firma. The solid ground was a welcoming sight as the temporal adrenaline faded further from my now aching limbs, and I hastily removed the uncomfortable strap from my neck. Toni said nothing and pointed toward Bazil's. To both my relief and confusion, I recognised the bent-over figure of Dave in the doorway, a small velvet box in his hands. Apart from a five o'clock shadow, he looked unharmed, though I noticed a crumpled up can next to the door's awning to the shop. Had he been drinking?

With a sense of déjà vu, Toni and I approached him. Cautiously.

"You okay there, Dave?" asked Toni, taking the initiative. Dave nodded numbly.

"Going to pawn this," He mumbled unconvincingly. Although shaking, he managed to open the box, which seated two wedding rings on the plush velvet cushion within. No doubt, he hadn't trusted them with his 'best man' after the dangerous cocktail of drinking the night before or merely never handed them over.

"Don't be silly," scolded Toni shaking her head. "Mr Weatherspoon *won't* take it."

Dave puffed out his chest. "They're real gold," he promised earnestly. "Much better than half the stuff in his shop," And he gestured vaguely in an abstract direction.

"Maybe better giving it to Yvonne," I expressed, watching as Toni crunched up the empty beverage can with her foot before pocketing it; perhaps I thought, for recycling later or another art project. She nodded at me, following my lead.

"No point," moaned Dave glumly. "There is *no* wedding!"

"You'll have to tell her that then!" answered Toni emphatically. "Everything's been paid for, and her family's on their way from the port,"

Dave's gaze widened in confusion. "What?"

"Come on, buddy," I said, steeling us both up. *"We've* got a wedding to go to!"

Now we had to make it happen.

Chapter 24: Cold Feet Need Warm Socks

Today was my first wedding—at least one I was actively involved in. Rather than the day existing as a token gesture of attending the church for some cousin or far removed relative whilst my mother busied herself with a ghastly polyester or nylon dress and matching hat. Toni was wearing one now, a bold and flamboyant number that resembled a bird's nest entwined with multicoloured feathers, which she called a fascinator.

"Fascinating," I had replied disinterested, as she preened herself a little in the mirror, and I adjusted the buttons of my waistcoat and suit jacket, attempting to hide the obvious sweat marks.

After picking up Dave, the three of us had taken lightning-quick showers back at my flat so that we could get back to the village hall before 10 am. We needed to assemble everything, decorating and masking the chaos of the limbo in which the ceremony precariously hung. Both a medley of guests and decor and confer with the registrar.

Grateful that everything we were doing had been paid for.

Thankfully, we were not alone, having regained the help of Andy and his new acquaintance. Mia was surprisingly good at cutting and sticking when things started to fall apart. Many of the items had been tangled together like Christmas lights, half-abandoned in the box. Once this slight panic was over, she busied herself further by grabbing plastic cups of orange juice and water from the hall's adjoining kitchen to keep us all hydrated. She looked somewhat more respectable now and had taken her seat at the back of the room. As his newly acquired plus-one, she had dressed in a lilac polka-dot dress, which was undoubtedly more becoming than Andy's creased folds of grubby bed linens.

Before long, the hall was transformed by the garlands and decorative strings of bunting. The wedding party had previously made decorations to make up a whimsical vintage English country garden theme. I supposed such things could have been found in one of the plush wedding magazines I saw aligning the lifestyle shelves of the newsagents. They were always placed more prominently, seemingly preferring my more desired 'Complete Guinea Pig Guide' and 'Bus Enthusiast' periodicals. Not that I knew much about wedding trends. I hadn't bothered to read any.

Our group assembled the guests, Toni taking on the role of calling each of the other bridesmaids to ensure they could help Yvonne into what Toni had described as being a vast meringue of a dress. My stomach rumbled hungrily at the thought, and I regretted not getting breakfast beside a single snack pack of biscuits from the shop across the road. As the guests filled in, the room slowly began to fill up with more over-the-top gaudy fashion pieces, none of them exactly fit the theme or its colour.

In the corner towards the doorway, the PA system hummed and crooned familiar love songs, hastily chosen by Dave and his beloved and their wedding planner in an exotic mixture of Anglo-French fusion. It was no doubt to appeal to attendees from both sides of the English Channel. I caught hints of familiar refrains of 'La Mer' and 'L-O-V-E' by Nat King Cole, a song I always felt was mistakenly attributed to Frank Sinatra – perhaps for the similar crooning 40's/50's Swing sound.

Dave stood at the far end, away from the main body of the congregation. He adjusted his tie with the same panicked pulls and tugs one might perform on their first date or a meeting with the parents. At least one that was consensual before popping the question. I had only experienced similar thus far with job interviews, many moons ago.

I watched as his similarly nervous disposition had dispelled a few fevered glances towards the door, although whether he was planning his escape or waiting for Yvonne, we were not yet sure. For my part, I noted how the polyester-wool suits chosen for the immediate wedding party were uncomfortably hot. Cheap and mass-produced on hire from reputable suit makers. I tugged my collar a final time, away from my neck, which had been brushing against my ear, hoping to hide the ever-present twitch, as we waited for the bride to appear.

Toni had insisted to me that brides were always allowed to be 'fashionably late' - Something that in my mind bordered rudeness and anticipation from all involved. As such, within the lapsing intervals, the venue's music had begun again, looping on the thinly tracked CD without so much as a single pause of staticky silence as the first play through faded away in conclusion. I hummed away as it eased itself into my subconscious.

Minutes passed.

Finally, Yvonne arrived, approaching the beginning of the aisle with her father. Clutching a hastily clustered bouquet of off-white roses and some otherwise indistinguishable green leaves in her hands. I noted how they matched her wedding dress and the netted veil, which hung across her hair and eyes—a seemingly deliberate choice to hide her tired, tear-stained eyes under the guise of wedding traditionalism.

As if on cue, everyone stood, uniformed and to attention as we were made to be *'upstanding'* members of the community. Collectively we were all a strange band of elegant, high-fashioned French citizens and a disorganised rabble of Dave's nearest and dearest who were eyeing up the after-ceremony buffet. I did my best not to think of the spread, watching instead as Yvonne edged nearer.

As the ceremony began, a collective hush overcame the group. The registrar, a tall, plump faced woman with peach coloured cheeks and a navy-blue suit named Janet, turned to face us all, encouraging the bride and groom to face each other and hold hands. Both did so timidly, meeting each other's gaze for the first time in days. The usual pledges of truthfulness and commitment that come with marriage had already been tested, although I hoped they would be stronger for it. Basking in the magic of Janet's voice as she told us about the beautiful moment we were there to witness today.

Despite this, everything seemed more formal and orderly. The registrar spoke in a smooth, gentle voice that reminded me of a lullaby. Gently she guided the couple and their attendees through the process as she first called for the readings.

Initially, it was Andy's turn to stand. He strolled rather brashly towards the pulpit, clearing his throat as he began his assigned comprehension, titled: 'A Poem About Love'. One he insisted he hadn't Googled.

I listened to the poem, enjoying how the vowels rounded and smoothed together in an oddly pleasing way. A few of the others seemed to agree, and select clusters of the room shed a few tears.

A few more readers followed this, and the majority were given from differing friends and family members.

This also included Dave's teenage brother, who was almost certainly younger but definitely equal in looks. Both men were baby faced, though the junior member looked like he had *only* shaved for the first time that morning.

Perhaps he had.

Next was one of Yvonne's tall, elegant sisters, who Yvonne later introduced to us as Nicole. Janet called each at their given moment whilst the photographer snapped and clicked the camera flash. He knelt at selected intervals of sincerity and emotion as he deemed suitable and profit worthy.

Then rings were exchanged between the couple, and the bands retrieved from a flustered Dave a few hours ago shone brightly now. Toni had taken the extra time to buffer each with a borrowed glasses wipe earlier to remove traces of sweat, grime and alcohol from the last two boozy evenings. It was a story Toni suggested Dave only tell later in select company, grateful that they hadn't been pawned off to Bazil.

Following from this was their handwritten vows. Each comprised a collection of short lines on a separate page between them. Dave and Yvonne spoke to the other personally about their nuptials, each voicing apparent delight and love for their partner. It was evident that for now, they would be putting aside the panic, nausea, and the necessary documentation as one should, in silent acknowledgement of the unwavering love for your significant other.

It was no secret that Yvonne would have had to acquire a settlement license after the wedding, as this was required of any foreign national to marry in the UK. The couple had organised it several months before, long before she had hinted she would prefer to move back *home* to France.

Still, even with this formality and slight concern in place, the couple's words were sincere and loving, especially when compared to the scripts given to us at work or the automated replies of tourists at customs who shuffle past the desks of airports marked *nothing to declare.*

The couple and the wedding party were collectively smiling in anticipation. The officiant spoke again, asking if anyone had any objections to the marriage. I was glad that she was seemingly oblivious to the earlier turmoil of the past few days. However, I was almost certain that Dave would be whispering repeated profound apologies later in place of sweet nothings to his beloved.

Janet's voice began booming into the room with finality.

"It is my great pleasure to now pronounce you husband and wife. You may kiss the bride!"

∗ ∗ ∗

"Thank god that's over!" breathed Andy as we sat at the somewhat cramped fifth table at the wedding breakfast in a group of 12. There were Andy, Mia, myself and Toni and several people I didn't recognise, I presumed from Yvonne's side. Such was all part of a "fun" game; I supposed from the newly-weds to encourage mingling and conversation. All of which would be painfully awkward to those unwittingly involved.

In the background, a number of the wedding party, mainly English, were clustering by the bar drinking and dancing in a half-hearted fashion, the same way that teachers shuffle back and forth at a school disco.

Cheap and mass-produced white round plates and bowls were filled with a jumbled assortment of leftovers on the table. Food comprised rocket lettuce, cheese, pineapple chunks and sausage rolls – the usual medley of quick and easy party foods presented by shops and budget caterers. I surmised that half the budget for such accommodations had gone towards the drinks,

171

with an open bar promised later that evening.

Andy rubbed his temples as he lay his head slightly into his hands. The two of us still nursed inner exhaustion and fatigue from the night before. However, this was not something neither could openly display, given the present company and the overall attitudes of the room. So instead, Andy had provided an overstretched and oversaturated smile.

A hollow display that matched the same everyone had given the bride and groom as they passed for some courtesy chat, repeating "thanks for coming" to the *"many* congratulations".

I deeply sympathised.

"That cake better be worth it," Andy muttered lowly.

"Late night, wasn't it?" I rhetorised with some irony. Toni turned to me curiously.

"What happened last night then?" she asked, folding her arms ever so slightly over the narrow rim of the table.

"One hell of a bachelor party!" Covered Andy.

Toni raised a brow.

"We should try to mingle with the other guests," I said awkwardly, feeling myself trip over my words. Thankfully, the chiming of a glass being tapped lightly with a spoon or other available cutlery signalled a change in the proceedings. As Dave and Yvonne had returned to the head table, they were greeted by a chorus of somewhat drunken "speech, speech" from the immediate vicinity of the guests. The sound was not entirely unlike the broadcasting of a Premier League football match with a gang of loyal supporters rousing each other at the pub.

As tradition dictated, Yvonne's father, whom I had noticed earlier, performed the opening speech. Monsieur Leloup – The family name translated from French to English as *Mr Wolf,* was aptly a rather brisk man with a stern gaze that reinforced his overly protective affection towards his pack of beautiful Amazonian styled daughters. At first, he was silent, surveying the room before picking up his glass and beginning his toast, his voice coming in a thick, northern styled accent, in confident though admittedly broken English.

He spoke at length about his daughter and a few antidotes and advice for the married couple and raised his glass again before passing the microphone to his new son in law. Dave nodded, gulping as he drank in the crowd of onlookers and his wife's family. The finality of his actions finally dawned on him.

"Thank you, Monsieur," he began, "Yvonne, sincerely, I do *not* deserve you!" The group awed appropriately. "But I am ever grateful for your patience, your love and your understanding," He paused for a moment before nodding to Andy and me before continuing. "And for *all* of you for sticking by me,"

Such words would for now remain a secret bond between the three of us—this would be a newly created shared memory between friends. We might speak of it at some point, but I was content just to let things lie dormant. I smiled a little as Yvonne nestled into his embrace, relaxing and Andy and Mia slid closer together with some familiarity. Everyone seemed happy.

Life, or perhaps something like it in the past few days, had seemingly been nothing short of a roller coaster, and I was ready to disembark the dizzy heights of others ever-changing love affairs for something less strenuous:

Guinea pig racing.

Chapter 25: Guinea Pig Games

'**G**UINEA PIG GAMES TODAY'
Bright yellow flyers with red scarlet lettering announced as one such document was issued out to me by one of the two smartly dressed, bowler-hatted gentlemen wearing tailcoats, who stood at the front of the thus titled marque.

A week had passed since the wedding. I marked the days on my calendar, ticking each off with a blue highlighter as work dragged endlessly from one day to another. Such dates were slow and mostly uneventful. Dave's seat at work had been left vacant again, although this time it was expected, as he and Yvonne were now on honeymoon. The remainder of the group at *FRANC* sat together, lost in a sea of misery: calls, complaints, and occasional fleeting compliments on our continued service.

This Saturday morning, I had taken the bus away from the central hub of Cocklescanslanky to the Northern Eastside. The cluster of occasional tourists far less commercialised this part of the town. The locals focused more on the upkeep of slowly disappearing folk traditions and the price of fish and pasties rather than keeping postcard kiosks for the White Cliffs of Dover.

This bus was a less frequent one, the number 81 only making journeys at select day intervals. The ride had been a little bumpy, a mixture of the rough, stone strewn track and the sturdy plastic travel case in which Mol wedged herself between my legs. But I was as ever delighted and excited as I caught sight of the splendid jelly shaped tent on the approaching fields, its ruby, burgundy and claret, flagged tops rippling in the breeze.

Every part of me felt alive again as I disembarked from the bus and walked towards the marquee. Still clutching the cage, I lifted the sheet in which Mol had sheltered and walked straight toward the ring of our predestined fantasy, flashing my season ticket pass that hung around my neck like a trophy. With every fibre of my being, I smiled.

Briefly, a slight feeling of sadness pressed at the back of my mind, at the reminder that, yet again, it was just us two. It was a shame, my mind told me that we had come alone, but I readily pushed such thoughts away, reasoning that it had not entirely been Toni's cup of tea. She had seemed happy enough as she waved me off with a smile as I left her earlier that day with Reaper and her paintings.

My mind also justified to itself, if not my conscience, that Mary might be attending with Willy and the baby, assuming she had not simply attempted to be polite for my earlier displays of chivalry.

In all these many years, the atmosphere had not changed. When I was about seven; I had entered for the first time; having wandered off as children do and marvelling at the vast wall of fame; projected with pictures of dozen upon dozen guinea pigs, each with well-formed and proudly bred names of former legends. Names like Augustus, Sampson, Oswald IV, and Chive. "Such remarkable creatures!" I remembered one judge saying as he looked over me with evident pride, "Part of our tradition, there's nothing quite like a guinea pig..."

Repeating this mantra to myself now, I smiled and walked through the throng of the gathering crowd for refreshments and souvenirs with a book of guinea pig statistics and a measuring stick, which matched those held by the various ushers, judges and seasoned race professionals.

"The measuring stick is about a metre long and is used to form precise markings for your lanes; so that unfair leverage can be avoided, you understand?" Asked one of the stewards towards a group of curious spectators, pointing towards another member of staff who was drawing out a rough idea of the racetrack in tailor's chalk.

Impressive? Yes; however, this measure was mostly for show.

Those amongst us, at least who had raced over the years, knew that there weren't any formal rules. Not at least ones that decided the overall shape of the track. Instead, they reflected the distances and spaces between them. I had discovered this fact, like many others in the summers of my youth and bachelorhood, Where I busied myself making tunnels and courses out of disused motorway cones and chequered flags from mothy, hole-filled t-shirts. Always overlooked by my mother, who merely rolled her eyes and hoped in vain, I would grow out of it.

Present-day me surveyed the marquee, which basked in a glow of neon and ambient white and gold street lamps. These gave the whole place a sepia tone, away from the sleepy-eyed town which lay beyond the folds of pre-prepared waterproof plastic tenting. As always, I had dressed my best for the occasion; in my dapper bottle-green suit and black cravat tie; something I still reserved for guinea pig events; since Mol had once told me that the colour of freshly cut grass was relaxing and inspired her to win.

Sitting beside me now in her allocated pen, Mol calmly and patiently acknowledged her fellow racers with a trained discipline that only a real contender knows, whilst the stewards and judges nodded at me in recognition. She had been registered into the first race: entrant number 16, Mol.

Everything is always cordial before a match, and any grunts of disapproval are left unspoken in favour of soft straw and last-minute tactics. Mol had already done me proud, dressed in her sleek golden and auburn gown of fur with the lovely ornate black pattern that reminded me of contrasting nuggets of onyx and amber.

In the adjacent waiting pens, a pair of twin white and orange splattered guinea pigs sat grooming each other; quietly debating which races they each favoured; their names displayed on the rota as Sherbet and George. To their left, a larger Abyssinian pig contented himself with his bowl of water; an old friend of Mol's who had been her fellow racer for four years named Roland; and in the corner, a shy little thing whose blinking little eyes remained dazed in the lead up to her first race.

Spacing in the tent was rather significant, and I had often marvelled at its size, particularly compared to that of circuses which had sometimes come and gone on tour when they needed to fill unfilled quotas of entertainment in Dorset. Here there were souvenir stands, which offered guinea pig shaped balloons, bookmarks, guinea pig shaped chocolates for the younger visitors, guides, maps, and more thoughtful pamphlets for the keen enthusiasts. The fair number of refreshment stalls offered mugs of tea, hot chocolate, and coffee; jacket potatoes, hot dogs and burgers with various sauces and toppings for the people and hay, grass and a few select vegetables for the pets. Outside there were also a few rides for the children, of which a charming carousel tune jauntily wove its way through the tent against the speaker and the distant sound of a foghorn from the Dover ferries seemingly wishing the attendees well.

In the main centre of the tent, all the stalls and beauty like events - such as *Grooming* and *Treats for Tricks* had been sandwiched together. This was to provide enough coverage for the relay track. It had been finished with plastic trees and small miniatures, which gave the whole place an air of elegance that a tiny village collector could be proud of. It was more than tempting as my eyes travelled up the paths and little cottages to lose myself in a world of previous, more straightforward years. But I knew I still had responsibilities, not least to Mol, who was geared to win her first rosette of the day. I needed to do her proud for a while, relishing in the overall mysticism.

* * *

There is something kind of magical about the slight strokes of artificial light as they curve over the valley of the track. The subtle groove of a guinea pig's fur, as it glides seamlessly like a painting; as all, at once, it blurs with movement, as graceful and warming as art. And so, it was as Mol descended upon the track.

The start signal went, and soon, Mol's little feet were dashing in pre-orchestrated rhythm as she made her way along the path. I could have sworn that she was singing out with the desire; and pride that echoed my own affections, our momentum seemingly bound as one. This was her moment, the song from her heart.

I know that people can often say they feel a bond with their pets. Many of them are shown on television, in hyper-realistic, reality disapproval shows with clickbait titles such as *My Moggy, I Can Hear Each Other's Thoughts* and *My budgie the Serial Killer*. Still, the situation was far more sincere and more decisive for Mol and me. It always has been. Mol and I held no secrets. Instead, I have often thought that we were the same beyond the fur and the layers of clothes, the masquerade of languages. Eating, sleeping, seeking close friendships, and finding our way in the burrows of life in which we otherwise sat paled and shaking.

Mol was winning the race; she had already left behind the confused twins who sat bickering amongst themselves; and the young one who had decided not to leave her hutch. Roland kept a solemn pace alongside Mol, aiding her with the noble companionship a true gentleman provides.

Although the spectators had come and gone, guinea pig racing was never fast; never a blood-sport and nearly always predictable; I felt a renewed glow of happiness as I noticed a few families cheering beside me. One had put together a small banner, improvising their craft skills with a crisp white handkerchief. She somehow caught my attention, and as our eyes met, I could not help but smile.

Mary had arrived, with her small brood and her cheeks took on a soft rose colour, caught in the rapture of innocent enjoyment and our shared glance mid-race.

"Enjoying yourself?" I asked, stepping closer to her side of the ring, in part to avoid a collision with a buxom lady who had barraged past me to record some notes of the performance swinging a large black clipboard.

"It's amazing!" Mary replied earnestly; her hair had tumbled free of its formally captured bun; twinkling in the light like a waterfall of pure gold. "Thank you for inviting us, Frank," I nodded, not entirely sure what to say, though grateful as she hoisted Willy up onto her shoulder so he could peek over the fence to watch the race. Beth cooed sleepily in her carrier sling, strapped around her mother's chest. All eyes, save hers, returning to the race.

After a few minutes, Mol continued at her practised, steady pace through the pre-placed obstacles that dotted along the track to emerge victoriously. It had never been about winning for us, although such a sight was always very welcome. Mol puffed out her chest fur in evident pride as they presented her with a small red rosette. I beamed up at her as she stood atop the platform to the followers and supporters of our noble tradition, taking a photo on my phone to print later for our racing scrapbook.

Outdoor photography, however, was usually a rare occurrence at these events. A reporter at our local and county papers might stop by on fleeting occasions. In previous years photographers usually sprinted in and out to take a picture of the marquee at the start of the day. But there was little excitement attached to this now as the follow up was limited to a squished last-minute report, usually into a small section of the Sports page. Or a supplement about resident low budget affairs.

Still, the occasional flash of a phone camera clicked now and then by a select few individuals; whilst the older generation merely grunted and shook hands. Other events would soon follow: The more mundane beauty and obedience tests - which had been pressed on the contenders in more recent years - in a bid of showmanship that we might become more like the 'dog shows' of which the mayor's wife was so fond.

But with Mary looking the happiest I had ever seen her, I encouraged Mol to take part in these also, suggesting they worked together. Soon the pair of them were bonding over fur brushes and ribbons, and I was happy to watch Willy and Beth whilst the youngest slept, and the boy darted back and forth to look at the various attractions.

Though it was never said, there was a strong underlying sense of chemistry in the air. Nods and smiles from my fellow competitors barely suppressed the masks of surprise at Mary's presence in my usually singular booth.

Perhaps, I mused, it was as though they believed her to be my other half. I denied this, of course, but the more I watched her lovingly brush Mol's fur and aided a group of children making paper foil. Tuppence weighted medals, it was becoming increasingly difficult to correct them. My chest tightened at the thought. Again, reeling in the stark contrasts of my relationship with

Toni and my phantom feelings towards the single mother.

Feelings I had thought that coming here, I might forget.

It was a warm day; for the season, and I decided to get some sandwiches from a small chain store across the road in the event's interval that would commence at lunch. If anything, I told myself I should clear my head; and avoid further unvoiced questioning.

Without much more than a small word, I excused myself from the group, handing back the sleeping baby and her son, then stepped outside under the pretence that I needed some air. Suddenly, however temporary it had been, Dave's indecision and panic seemed very appealing.

* * *

Candyfloss clouds draped through the sky as I walked outside the buttercup yellow gazebo in which two teenage girls squatted on the grass to make daisy chains. One was slightly taller and thinner than the other. She had strawberry blonde hair, a pink skirt with red and peach flowers, and a similarly coloured jumper that depicted a smiling kitten. The other; had shorter hair cut into a bob. This girl was dressed in black apart from a pair of long purple and orange striped stockings.

Even from the short distance, of which I stood, her bottom lip seemed disfigured by a piercing that appeared to dwarf the rest of her face, which was hollowed out with its pale skin and deep black eyeliner. They could have been sisters or a couple but were seemingly perfectly content in each other's company - how I envied them such personal unfiltered luxury.

Was I doomed never to be happy?

I had known that dating Toni would never be easy. Our age gap had always raised a few brows, not least from both our families, although I had attempted to laugh it off at the thought of Marina and my own mother ever meeting each other. But it had not been the reason I now found myself confused.

Meeting Toni had been impactful, not least for being hit over the head when we first exchanged pleasantries. Since that day, my life had seemingly rushed around me with the same urgency and flapping as a junior gull, taking its first steps into flight—sprayed into the wind like an abandoned plastic bag. There had been adrenaline, of course, and the attraction I had to her was obvious. But I knew my hair was slowly thinning, both from my age and stress at work. I needed some stability and support rather than a series of happy accidents. – Which from all accounts had happened more steadily since our first encounter.

Perhaps that was why I felt myself drawn to Mary, relishing somewhat the stability and familiarity she offered. Despite the tired lines that sometimes crossed under her eyes when she spoke of her ex-husband, she was also charming. She had looked radiant today, the same way a fresh white sheet covers a newly made bed. Warm and inviting.

The whole thing was very confusing. Raking a hand through my hair, I entered the shop, barely registering the selection of sandwiches that sat in a buzzing old fridge next to plastic cartons of milk pints and this week's newspaper captioned with some vague title of current political affairs. The ones' in my head were immediately more vexing.

"£7.99, please," Said the cashier. A tall, lanky boy with a row of spots on his chin. No doubt a teen whose voice had recently broken and taken a job to pay his way through puberty. I had placed three sandwiches on the counter, plain cheese, ham, and tomato, which I imagined would be a safe choice for a small child. I handed over a tenner and held out my hands in exchange for my receipt and change. Nothing seemed any more straightforward in my mind.

It had been easy when Poppy had kissed me to refuse her, but such lingering possibilities circled my mind at the thought of Mary. She was sweet and genuinely kind with a ready-made family that might otherwise pass me by. I did not expect to have kids with Toni, feeling that my dead-end job would soon grow weary on a self-sufficient artisan floating from canvas to canvas.

"You okay, mister?" asked the boy, snapping me back to reality. My hand was still outstretched, though now containing a few coins, I counted them £2 and a penny. I nodded quickly and dropped the penny in the adjacent charity tin beside him before retreating with my purchase as he called out. "Thank you. Have a nice day,"

His words were neutral if well-meaning, but this innocent prospect seemed impossible now.

Chapter 26: Inappropriate Feelings

"Frank, Frank!" called out Mary in delight as I returned. She was beaming at me, waving something bright and colourful in her hands. As I motioned closer, I realised it was a new rosette that flapped to and through within her fingers. It was a crinkled purple one with a gold centre, which reminded me a little of a crocus or a pansy. Not that I spent much time looking at flowers beyond my mother's somewhat wilted garden.

The ribbon was from the Beauty and Grooming Pageant. Mol and I hadn't entered before, although I recognised the colour from the various other regular attendees of which I spoke to through the years. "She won, she won!" exclaimed Mary emphatically, whilst Willy danced up and down, chanting something resembling Mol's name.

I approached them where my guinea pig sat on an improvised grass podium, preening herself with embarrassment at her newly acquired fan club. "What's happened?" I asked curiously, placing the recently acquired lunches down on an adjoining picnic table opposite the podiums.

"Mol won," Mary repeated, handing the rosette to me. Her grip was, as I remembered, slight but warm to the touch, without the sharp stabbings I often encountered with Toni's longer self-manicured hands. I shuddered at the almost forced comparison, brought by my supposed conscience, but smiled to her, hoping that I appeared pleased. Aware or not, Mary was grateful, and she smiled back.

"I bought us some lunch," I said, nervously deflecting my gaze back to the makeshift meal.

"Sweets?" asked Willy hopefully. His mother shook her head, hoping to avoid a scene.

"Willy, don't be rude!" Mary reproached softly as she turned to look at the table's offerings. "See here, Willy, there's ham and cheese."

"And tomato," I added enthusiastically, attempting to follow Mary's lead. Willy scrunched his face up for a moment but then agreed, laughing.

"You're funny, Mr Frank!" He giggled, taking in each of the sandwiches that had been wrapped in cardboard and plastic packaging; before attempting to tear into one of them with the same eagerness as a beaver building a dam.

Mary reached over to help him as ever, taking the hint before turning back to me and mouthing, "Thank you,"

My heart fluttered once more.

Desperate to distract myself, I diverted my attention back to Mol. She had finished grooming herself and keenly watched our small interaction with apparent interest. "You like her, don't you?" she asked, her eyes questioning. I nodded mutedly, grateful that Mary was somewhat distracted as I acknowledged my feelings. "*More than* Toni?" she asked probingly.

I turned away from her scratching my left ear a little. The performance ring felt uncomfortably hot, and slight nausea washed over me, the same way the tide continuously threatens to approach the sand. "Not *here,*" I hissed pleadingly, afraid of the continued feelings of confusion and doubt and those of my guinea pig.

"Tonight *then,*" motioned Mol firmly.

"Alright," I agreed reluctantly. "Alright,"

The rest of the day continued with some formality; the events would continue after the designated lunch hour as scheduled without drama. Save perhaps the odd disgruntlement of a huddled trio of patrons who mumbled about the dwindling numbers of our sport and its loose-footed politics. In truth, I didn't notice it. My mind was toying with the conflicting interests of head and heart like a love-sick fool.

Other activities had been scrawled on a large piece of laminated card. Written in over the top and flashy typography, each spaced out at even intervals to allow for the go-between of both spectators and participants. I slid my finger over them, explaining their various merits to Willy, whilst Mary excused herself for a moment to feed the baby. Swimming had been cancelled. Yet again, due to a lack of interest. But there were to be three tug-of-war contests and tunnels and ramps for the more athletic pets before the *'Best in Show'* finale.

Willy bounced in excitement, a mixture of anticipation and sugar, asking a series of questions as I briefed him more on the local history of guinea pig gatherings. He had never had a pet before, but Mary would tell me later that she had given him a teddy bear which he sometimes confided in when no one was looking since Ted was shy and didn't talk to strangers.

Hoisting him onto my shoulders, I experienced the tent with new eyes at his urging. The dizzying heights of the pavilion, the whirling sweep and glide of music that faded in and out from the tannoy, and the smells of sugary sweet candyfloss and roasted almonds spilling out from the bags of other enthusiastic young children, running around aimlessly. "Hey, look, Mummy!" Willy squealed delightedly, waving as Mary returned, cradling a contented Beth in her arms.

As I looked at her, my stomach tightened the repercussion of cheap sandwich filling and butterflies. She had a serene smile, one that played within her eyes, making them twinkle a little against the canvas backdrop of the inner side of the tent. I noted her dress, which was a soft shade of cornflower with a cluster of small, stylised, white flowers, probably daisies, in keeping with the little I knew of fashion trends I had observed over the summer in my notebook. Flowing down just above her ankles, she wore comfortable low heel pumps with rounded toes. She had kept her hair down now. A choice that suited her well - the scrunchie now resting on her wrist like some makeshift bracelet.

My cheeks felt heated, and I forced myself to look away as she strolled next to me, greeting her son on my shoulders. Together, our small, renewed group, along with the crowd, watched as two guinea pigs sat calmly next to a temporarily vacant food trough, and the umpire enthusiastically explained the rules.

The premise was simple. Once the proceedings were underway, the umpire would place a generous celery stick, chosen for its length and the rich nutrients it would provide each competitor. The two would pick out this vegetable and begin to chew; before the inevitable playful tussle over who would get the more significant portion and finish it off. Usually, I knew this was a clear-cut finish with the more boisterous and bigger 'pigs taking the lead; but there were equally excitable youngsters on occasion. These were typically thinner but taller youngsters who used their upper paws as leverage. It was always a good comedy to watch—a welcome distraction.

It would be better not to tell Mary my thoughts, as I wallowed in the possibility of being a womaniser - especially since I had prided myself on avoiding Andy's dating tips wherever possible in my previous, bachelor filled days. Finding only questions toward my motives, I wondered whether this was simply a desire to be a family man and settle down? Or merely the joy of finding a human friend who appreciated my strange eccentricities without judgement and partially shared experience. I had longed for a human companion, someone to pass the mantel when I was old, and my albums of rosettes and trophies, a child or wife of my own. Something that Mol, whilst well-meaning, might not fully understand. So, instead, I resolved to speak to my sister, grateful that the weekly luncheon was only a day away.

There would be another sleepless night ahead as I performed the rest of my actions with some autonomy, crushing the growing feelings of yearning that thudded within my heart.

***

"Frank, you look white as a sheet!" Insisted my mother fussing as I entered the living.

"What?" asked Dad, only half listening from his usual television induced livery in the adjoining room.

It was Sunday, and I had come alone, carrying with me a bouquet of hastily chosen flowers that I had picked up as an apology from Toni, who was thankfully engrossed in another daily art project. It was a courtesy more than anything since I doubted my mother cared much for her attendance anyway, after their first doomed meeting.

"I said, he looks white as a sheet, you silly dolt!" Mum repeated, swatting him with a damp tea towel, which only minutes before she had used with her myriad of pots, pans, and somewhat half-peeled vegetables before exiting the kitchen. She was still in her cooking phase.

Dad merely raised his eyebrows, feigning agreement. "Yes, *woman*," he muttered, his gaze returning to the box.

"What's the matter?" Hanny asked, entering the living room from the lobby behind me. She had been rehanging coats in the hall as she always did; it was hoped that such measures ahead of time would provide a quicker getaway, should either of us need it. We were always escaping from unwanted questioning or probing of extraneous matters and opinions from Mum's establishment.

"I didn't sleep," I answered quickly, loud enough for mum to hear, hoping she might acknowledge my secret look, the code we had established as youngsters' years before. Thankfully, she nodded. We would go upstairs once Mum dozed off after the turkey. Heavy, fatty food always affected her; it was our gracing period.

"Where's that *girl* of yours?" asked Mum, her attention drawn to her new flowers with some suspicion.

"Working," I replied non-committally.

"Oh," acknowledged Mum before hurrying Hanny over to fetch a vase. Her fingers were covered in vegetable peelings before reaching for the kitchen timer on the side table in front of her and comparing it to the kitchen clock, which was could only just be seen over her shoulder if she twisted her head a little; the same way an owl might.

"What are we having?" I asked, continuing the charade.

Dad snorted. "Turkey," His eyes were glued to the television. I stepped further into the room and sat across from him on the vacant sofa as white and red-shirt players paraded around the screen across the green. The elapsing time and the score had been etched out in the corner in friendly white numbers. 2|1. I didn't much care for football, but at least it beat forced conversation.

Unlike guinea pig baaed activities, football tended to run long into tedium, with less grace and poise and far less gentlemanly decorum than the likes of my often angry, if faceless-via-proxy customers. I also reasoned that Dad's presence in my life had been shaped mainly by encounters of various sporting matches, especially in his later years. He would more than likely be able to wax lyrical about how England won in 1966; rather than the birth of his son nine years later.

I reasoned that while he had shown some interest in Toni, especially when she first came around, this was more to do with the new introduction to female company, other than his wife and daughter. Rather than Toni, the person. It would be unlikely he could give me any advice on love and lasting happiness, seemingly content to stay his wife out of habit and obligation rather than a vow of everlasting devotion. My mother mostly dominated the conversation; she distracted herself with various pastimes and third-hand gossip from neighbours or those she passed by on the street. The whole thing was rather sad, although I had learnt quickly to accept it, distancing myself where I could from the family dysfunctions, keeping my head down.

By keeping a notebook on people watching, my intent was not to pry into their private lives merely to understand them. This was in part due to my role at work. Despite the onslaught of abuse that often dominated our calls, we were expected to remain impartial and helpful at FRANC. This led me to prefer simpler things and the company of guinea pigs was more sincere than the majority of the two-faced sales reps that dominated the *FRANC* office. Not that by keeping it, I fully understood myself.

Turning back to the television, I watched the ball passing over the green several times.: it was a small, white round blot, which seemingly dotted from one man to another towards the goal, the commentators droned on with piqued debate from their unseen box above the stands—listening to the roar and thaw of the crowd of spectators down below. Dad joined them from time to time, throwing his arms up in frustration or grunting as it suited him. Mum made music clanging down pots and pans and silver trays of roast potatoes and Yorkshire puddings into the already stuffed oven in the kitchen. Something Hanny jokingly called the dysfunctional Davis Musical or a *Comedy of Errors*. As always, I regretted coming back every Sunday, but this was our family's tradition.

It was not yet my place to create my own.

"Turkey's ready!" Declared Mum plopping a large, overly generous bird on the centre of the coffee table with a slight clatter, startling out of my little reverie. I looked to the spread, which was as usual stuffed with bowls of food and condiments that were insisted upon for Mum's *growing boy*, a term which I observed with some irony due to the weekly expanse of my waistline; somewhat relieved that I was not on any diet.

The space was less generous, and I briefly entertained the prospect of dining here, all of us then cramping up together with our knees touching like a school canteen. But just as quickly, Mum swept it up and brought it into the seldom-used and made up dining room. This room was only for show and equally as uncomfortable if only serving to keep our postures all upright.

Forcing my appetite, I ate silently, only half listening as Mum remarked on the activities of absent family members and the antidotes of various cousins. She had a habit of repeating herself and dominated the conversation. If she had been worried about my appearance, I was somewhat relieved she had not seen me the week before. Although, in retrospect, I had not slept properly in weeks, using my increasing periods alone to reflect and ponder, observing the same unimaginative walls.

After what seemed like too long and too heavy a meal, Mum sank into the cushions of the sofa, resting her fluffy, slipper feet on one side and dangling her apron on the other of its two arms, since she wanted a "break from the kitchen" whilst dessert slowly browned in the oven. Although she was upright, it would not be long before she drifted off. Hanny and I took a pew on the vacant armchair and one of the kitchen chairs, which had been dragged with minimal effort across the room. Mum would protest slightly, but we could cater to this. We had rehearsed such a pantomime over and over the years, knowing that such a measure was necessary if only to please her temporarily.

Our father, as always, didn't care.

"Thanks for lunch, Mum," I said.

"Yes," Hanny echoed, "It was *excellent*, thanks!"

The words to a point were sincere, although had been chorused in rotation every week, like the repertoire of two parrots at the zoo; changing who would say it every week if only to keep it somewhat fresh and to boost our mother's ego.

Mum took the bait.

"Honestly, you two, it's not *that* difficult," she told us all proudly. "Perhaps I should teach you how to cook one of these days so you can treat your father and me to a Sunday roast, right Jack?"

As ever, Dad grunted in reply.

We did, however, know how to cook. At least the basics like eggs and pasta, Hanny had even made a more than edible omelette once when I had popped over to hers when the odd occasion aligned our working habits and patterns, although I usually stuck to tea. Still, Mum proceeded with her spiel, and we asked her many laborious but seemingly well-intentioned questions.

How did she prepare the stock?

What was the seasoning she used on her potatoes to get them the right shade of golden brown?

Mum's answers began enthusiastically, but her eyes slipped half-shut in and out of consciousness, and her head nodded towards her chest within minutes. As together, we conducted her makeshift lullaby of commentator's chatter and purposefully, overly complicated, half answered questions with dwarfing enthusiasm as she slowly began to tire of it all.

At last, she drifted away, lulling comfortably against the crook of the couch. My sister and I shared a nod before carefully covering our mother with a blanket and heading up the stairs; Hanny first, and then I followed, shutting the door as I did, muffling the sounds of the television down below. Finally, alone.

"So, what is it?" asked Hanny, looking at me expectantly. "Is Toni *really* working? You haven't had a fight, have you?" Her words were spewing quickly and freely like a parent seeking the reasons for detention, pacing up and down the interceding stretch of intervening carpet.

I shook my head. "That's not it,"

"Okay, so I'm sure the dog's not sick!" She reasoned before pausing, "You've not got her pregnant, have you?"

"God, no!" I blurted out, my pride wincing at the thought. Hanny seemed relieved, determined though to find out my supposed secret.

"So, come on, what is it?"

With a slight tinge of déjà vu from our last intimate conversation, I looked down at my feet, barely resisting the urge to scratch my ear again as I felt the uncomfortable patches of nervous sweat spreading through my body. Thus with a pounding heart, I forced out.

"I'm in *love* with someone else,"

Chapter 27: Growing Apart

"Y ou *love* someone else?" Hanny parroted, uncertain what else to say, perhaps hoping the gravitas of what it meant might dawn on me or spring me into action. Words I was sure I would be doomed to rehear, as and when I levelled with Mol and then finally Toni herself.

"Yes," I replied solemnly.

Hanny moved forwards, and I flinched, half expecting a slap, but she stepped back again, considering her actions, still waiting for me to speak with wide, searching eyes. I wasn't sure what to say, leaving her again to lead the conversation with her obvious but justified sense of judgement.

"Who?" She asked quietly. My heart throbbed, dwarfed by my irrational fear as I left my conscious thoughts exposed. It would do no good to be silent now.

Still, Hanny was already onto her next question, firing them in a disjointed and erratic fashion, like the glitzy but disorganised quiz show hosts I had sometimes seen on television. I took a breath, prepared to answer her. "How?"

"Her name is Mary, and I met her on the bus," Stumped by my lack of rational thought, I closed my eyes for a moment and told her everything. I began to detail the strange series of encounters that had led to our meetings, making sure to reiterate that she was a single mother of two and had previously owned a guinea pig.

My sister, at this time, was silent, sitting cross-legged on the floor, listening to everything like a Dictaphone, only stopping me in places so that she might clarify the odd matter. Reminding me of the time she had told

192

me about her partner, who she was considering introducing to the family fold as more than just the milkman, when, and *only* when she stressed the timing was right. I recollected my premature introduction of Toni, who, previously, I had been so confident of despite my mother's frosty reception, which jarred my opinions. Even though Hanny enthused that she had liked her, my stomach had lurched in despair, further cementing my confusion.

"Have you told her?" Hanny asked, at last, her words somewhat ambiguous, although I knew she was asking about Toni first. I frowned awkwardly, grappling with the question.

"No, do you think I should?"

Hanny nodded, slowly standing as the sounds of my mother's arousing from the sofa were audible from the calls for pudding from the stairs. Still, Hanny pressed on. "You have to be fair to her," She continued levelly. "And to yourself."

I gulped again, believing that my sister was wise beyond her years. "How?"

"Everyone deserves to be truly loved," determined Hanny, and then without a breath or rebuttal, she was gone -descending the landing towards the waiting bowls of slightly burnt, sticky crumble and custard.

I resolved to try.

After pudding.

∗ ∗ ∗

Thus, collecting myself as best I could, I returned to the kitchen where Mum looked slightly frazzled, ushering us all to turn away as she hastily raked a hand through her hair. Perhaps hoping to remove the drool from her afternoon nap without drawing too much attention to herself, we humoured her out of respect even though it usually had the opposite effect.

While it is almost commonplace in hotter countries like Cyprus or Spain to have a siesta, Mum always seemed embarrassed by the idea. She often said that such opportunities were *absurd* and familiar among older generations. She was not frail by any means, but her skewed view of the world was hampered by her makeshift mirror, comprising of one of the silvery lids that came from her collection of saucepans, as ever resisting ageing disgracefully.

Everyone sat silently around the table, spoons scraping the cheap ceramic bowls like a cat at a window leaping for a butterfly aimlessly that flies undeterred on the other side of the glass. I resisted talking, the custard, curdling and burning the edges of my throat in guilt at the task that lay ahead.

Still offering that fake smile to Mum as she burbled about her latest in a string of activities and the sketchy details of the neighbour's holiday she had eavesdropped on through the fence. My head wobbled obediently back and forth like a Bobble-head doll until I said my repeated goodbyes.

Part of me was debating speaking with Mol first, as I had previously promised, but with growing awareness, I knew I should talk with Toni directly. Tossing my thoughts from one side to the other, I decided to walk the long way home. I headed along the cliff face, bracing the cold sea air and salt spray, and lifted my phone from my pocket. Tapping a message rapidly to one of the few numbers I had committed to memory.

Toni, we need to talk.

She didn't reply at first, though that was usual with the delay of cellular service, and she usually divided her attentions between paints and brushes, easels and mannequins that decorated her makeshift studio, or to Reaper before she returned to her phone. That was assuming it was on or hadn't run out of battery, as it often did.

But this time, after a few minutes, my phone jingled back into life with the familiar alert sound.

I know.

A pause.

Where can we meet? Shall I come over?

I paused, wondering if it was easier to talk things through at her place or mine, though the prospect of an argument or heated debate was not going to be more comfortable in a flat with paper-thin walls than it would be at the pub. That said, the idea of an audience of spectators was the last thing I wanted or felt she deserved.

My insecurities and inexperience betrayed me, and now I had taken too long to reply. The phone was already ringing, but I rejected the call, choosing to text a somewhat hurried reply. Usually, I was not fond of typos and took the time to avoid *txt* chatter. For now, though, none of that mattered. I forced out my words on the touchpad.

Yes, I'll be there.

Above my head, the seagulls circled pathetically; occasionally, they descend from the crags of the cliff beyond and out to the sea. This was the prime time to look for scraps and titbits, usually stealing chips from unsuspecting vacationers, who walked unsuspectingly around Dover's Deal Pier, like a makeshift buffet.

I wondered dismally if I would be happier joining them, away from the struggles and pitfalls that seemed to follow falling in love and the complex layers of the affairs of the heart. It was not because I didn't care for Toni. I had been drawn to her in a way that a moth is drawn to a naked flame. But the truth was I felt like I couldn't keep up with her. The whirling, swirling hurricane of her artistic endeavours was a far cry from my simplistic middle-aged existence. Convincing myself that she would tire of me before long.

As I finally reached the threshold of my flat, I could see the familiar form of Toni in the doorway; her hair was loose, and she had turned away from me, unwilling to expose her makeup smudged tears. I approached her gingerly. "Toni?" my words almost whispered under my breath.

She swivelled around, her eyes catching the light in a way that I had always loved—iridescent orbs of glass that always reminded me of the night's sky. If I was not careful, I might get lost in them, but I scolded myself and stepped backwards so as not to lead her into an embrace. Difficult as it was, I determined to keep a cool head and keep a check on my feelings, confused as they were. Toni watched me slowly.

There was a small part of me that had hoped that my first encounter with Toni might show me how to proceed with such a delicate matter. Especially for a usually headstrong and determined young woman. In this precise moment, however, there were no swears or slings of insults, with a growing sense of maturity I had witnessed upon the departure of her mother.

I wondered whether this impromptu encounter had inspired a previously unaddressed maturity, although I could not begin to read her since I was not well-versed in psychology. For all I knew, it was merely the calm before the storm. One that would lull the mood slightly before the barrage of verbatim and angst that lingered unspoken in the air erupted. The elephant in the room, or a hair in the soup of a restaurant where through gritted teeth, you tell the approaching waiter that everything *"is fine,"* After all, you're not an esteemed food critic; chances are you're not even a chef. Why should *your* opinion matter? Save on an anonymous online review board.

Since I was no means an orator, I had attempted to use the short time I had, whilst walking home, with leaden footsteps to try and string together the words that eluded my mind. Hoping to soothe rather than simply add to any immediate distress and keep a rational mind.

Admittedly this was one thing to practice and another to realise. So, taking a deep breath, I cleared my throat and began the best I could. "Toni, I- "

But my sentence was never finished because Toni had already cut across me. Her words were decidedly more awkward than my own. "Frank, I want to go to University,"

Muted, I nodded and issued her into the flat. We sat together on the sofa as she rustled around in her bag for a moment before drawing out a large brown envelope, which contained a neatly typed registration form. The words **UCA Canterbury - University for the Creative Arts** headed the top with an official-looking logo, presumably, I reasoned, the university's crest. She placed these on the table before me.

I blinked at her somewhat awkwardly.

"Surprise!" she said weakly into the silence.

Surprise indeed.

How could I tell her now?

196

Chapter 28: Education And Reflection

Sitting side by side, on the small, cushioned sofa, our knees knocked somewhat awkwardly into the coffee table; I let Toni talk, listening to her newfound enthusiasm for Art and university life. Although I had never been, my understanding from those who had, with the exception perhaps of my sister, was that it was a great cocktail of self-exploration and discovery, a jungle of extroverts with opinions and politics that I had little chance of understanding.

My stomach knotted somewhat guiltily as I thought how to convince her how to pursue it, for not entirely selfless reasons.

I could not begin to predict whether Mary returned my lingering feelings, and much like Toni, I would be taking a risk with my inevitable course of action. I owed it to us both, waiting for the verbal cues that she was ready for me to provide my feedback.

There was a pregnant pause.

Forcing myself upward, if only to give us both space, I switched on the kettle, making myself a cup of tea and her usual coffee – black.

"I think going to University will be good for you," I said earnestly, hoping my words didn't sound scripted, passing Toni her usual mug. A force of now established habit.

"Really?" she asked. Her lips curled into an unnatural ruby red smile.

I nodded again somewhat thoughtfully.

As the gears rotated around my head, Toni seemed to busy herself discussing the various merits and syllabuses that came with the courses on offer. In addition to the registration form, which she had temporarily stuck back in the envelope, she had brought along a prospectus, a stack of highlighter pens, post-it notes, and a smart leopard print coloured ballpoint which had an elegant silver nib. Usually, she preferred to write in green ink, although I reasoned, she was attempting to seem a little more professional, given the subject matter's seriousness.

I nodded along automatically and enthusiastically as it seemed appropriate, as Toni plopped the book down onto the table with a dull thud.

Mol had stuck her head out from her hutch, drawn out by the commotion and watched intently for a moment before returning into her habitat. She had never been fond of loud noises, and Toni's excitable chatter was not well received. Had Mol sensed my frustrations? She would undoubtedly be curious about why we hadn't talked, knowing of my growing attractions to Mary. Still, grateful for the chance to move away from her, I fetched a cardboard tube I had saved from the recycling at work and stuffed it with a fresh batch of hay, to which my guinea pig reciprocated, calming.

Like the elephant in the room, the small voice in my head from my sister persisted. I owed it to Toni, to be honest, since I did not share her dream. Hadn't that been what she supposedly liked about me? My strait laced and unimaginative wording. It had been these nagging thoughts that had kept me awake since meeting her mother, although I could not and would not blame Toni for the impromptu invasion into my home. Such resentment wouldn't be fair.

The process, if there had been one at all, had been more subtle nudges from my self-consciousness, as the concussion of our whirlwind romance faded and I became more acutely aware of the world, small as mine was, around me.

Toni travelling to university cemented this fact. She longed for adventure and creativity, I for stability and my home comforts, niche as the subject matter were. I owed her my honesty. However, the situation required tact and timing.

Giving her room, I sat down on the armchair, resting her drink on a coaster on the side table for when she wanted it. Once she had paused in her efforts, I made her a coffee – her usual strong blend; and looked over her workings. I was somewhat impressed by how she had taken over the table's width and breadth in such a short space of time. I shouldn't have been surprised, though, recalling her home and studio kept in similar disarray.

"Have you made a decision Toni?" I asked.

Toni paused, screwing up the corners of her eyes to think. "Sort-of,"

With both hands, she held out the prospectus, trying in some haphazard way to avoid it falling closed and losing her place. I remembered how similarly my sister had always held her textbooks together with other equally weighty tomes or with her elbow held upright against her head as she read. I often spotted her trying to complete her homework at school during lunch; she had sporty or interested in the latest playground craze.

I allowed myself a small brief smile as I reminisced before focusing on the matter at hand as she waited, hands outstretched with the book.

"Let's see then," I whispered, almost to myself, looking closer at the UCA's official brochure, which was now tucked into the crook of my knees. Toni quickly moved off the sofa and onto the floor. Now she was more level with my view of the pages and began moving her hands here and there to explain the merits of each course and their varying syllabuses and perks.

Her animated gestures were comical in a way, much in the same vein as a weatherman might present the differing outlooks for different parts of the country. The map on the South-East barely recognised our small town. It was usually obscured by the more significant, more important places like Dover and Folkstone, which were labelled in somewhat large, impersonal text in the regional broadcasts and overcome completely by London on the national news.

The courses she had circled read as follows: -

Fine Art, a three-year or four-year course, provided an in-depth approach to both the practical and theoretical subject.

Graphic Design – this also took three years but was more marketing based, at least from the examples of typography and vector graphics shown in the corner.

The campus also offered a curiously titled option named 'creative computing' and a cluster of Industrial and Architectural designer degrees. But whilst Toni might relish the idea of creating some grand-scale art piece with a blowtorch and some scrap metal, she was unlikely to conform to the tight deadlines and budgets that came with such discipline. She also ignored the interior design options; no doubt was burnt out by her mother's desire for domestication and idealistic perfections.

"I can see you doing Fine Art," I mused, tapping the first one gently. "Or is that too similar to your last course?"

Her cheeks puffed slightly, exhaling.

At length, she had told me about her unrequited love for a tutor at the local arts project, a man she described vividly with pencil-like features and a charcoal brush of hair and face fuzz. Her former Adonis wove romantic tapestries of life in France and Italy, studying the craft; whilst ignoring her in turn for a petite but well-figured blonde who clung to his languages of love and wine. The so-called *Pig* was reduced to target practice when she played darts now.

Pausing for a moment, she shook her head.

"Well, this looks more *professional*," she said considerably. "But it's *four years*."

Toni was a far cry from the brazen, sharp-tongued persona I had first met. Something that endeared me to her even as my heart wavered with its conflicting emotions. It was easy to recognise the concern in her voice when she let her guard down with someone she trusted.

I patted her shoulder comfortingly. "You can do it!"

Another pause. Longer this time. Toni was unsure of herself, despite her earlier enthusiasm.

"You think?"

"Yes, I do."

"It's a *long* time," she said with a slight sigh.

"Why not take a tour of the campus?" I mused.

Determined to encourage her this way, I flicked through the pages until I found a section on accommodation and the city and turned it toward her. It was a double-page spread with a glamorous composited photograph of people sitting outside on the terrace of a coffee shop with great, airbrushed smiles and the Cathedral in the background. "This looks nice. *Quaint.*"

Toni seemed renewed by my words, taking the bait. "Quaint?" she asked, squinting at me again, with a slightly furrowed brow as she grabbed the brochure from me. "It's historic, Frank!" Thus launching into a detailed and impassioned speech about the city.

I had been on a geography trip once, but I feigned ignorance, listening to her, confident that this would propel her focus and determination.

For the next few hours, we worked on a list of things she would need to do to enlist and with a sense of fortitude and a continuous duty to Toni, I gave my word to help her.

By the end of the night, she promised me that she would go online, look up the tours and Open Days, and seek the best ways to begin her personal statement and fill in the registration form.

But now, my feet and posterior were numb, and I stretched, forcing a yawn as I stood, reminding her I had work the following morning.

Toni nodded apologetically, grabbing her belongings and her coat; she headed through the door before turning to me expectantly as we kissed cheeks in farewell at the threshold.

"You said you had something to tell me?" she asked.

Her words burned through me, but still, I held firm determined not to be exposed whilst my mind wandered.

"Another time," I replied, forcing a smile, before closing the door. For now, my *fantasies* and fantasies they were, were not what mattered. Nevertheless, I would have to come clean soon, though I lacked the rhetoric and memory for mind games, unlike Andy. However, I hoped this redeemed my twisted character.

With or without me, Toni deserved a *happy ending* and at least one more day of hope.

* * *

I made concise efforts to keep busy at work the following day, answering the incoming calls with impersonal monotony, grateful that my brain was not needed.

Truthfully, the reappearance of Dave smiling with a slight tan and rose-tinted glasses of love as he returned from his mini-honeymoon offered no further relief. Out of politeness, I offered him a brief nod but held my phone like a shield against the idle attempts at chatter, my tongue still robotically reeling off the script that *FRANC* executives had derived all those years before.

There was some comfort to be found in routine, even an otherwise mind-numbing one. If only for a moment, the fish-bowl office seemed welcomingly busy, if only so I could distract myself from my pending resolution.

"How can I block these cold callers?" moaned my client, a seemingly flustered elder woman who occasionally lent her ear away from the phone to update her equally eager husband.

My duty was to explain things to her as best I could, explaining the public register's visibility and how she might have had her details compromised.

"I understand your frustration, mam," I said using my most sincere voice, aware of how other cubicles around me parroted it.

"What?" the lady's husband called within my ear.

"He says he understands!" She clucked back at him. "What can *we* do to get some privacy around here?"

I bit my tongue, aware of the irony of her words.

"Well, mam, the Data Protection Act of 2018-"

"2018?" There was confusion.

Great, a long call. Just what I needed.

After three hours and seven or so calls later, I was waiting patiently for a gentleman who was finding his so-called "handwritten notes" on the number of calls he had been forced to ignore and block over the past few months. "I won't be a minute," He wheezed into his speaker-phone, "Just looking for a pen, sorry!"

Out of the corner of my eye, I noticed Andy was waving at me for attention. I raised my brow in recognition as he mouthed, "Pub lunch?

Balancing the receiver against my head, I looked down and opened the drawer at the base of my desk and glanced at my lunch box, which I had assembled earlier that day; a roughly cut ham sandwich oozed out of the uneven bread, coated with smears of butter and mustard where I had scraped against the bottom of the jar.

Maybe beer and a burger would be better than hastily prepared sandwiches after all.

Chapter 29: Soap Opera Confession

Morses' was uncommonly busy this lunchtime, having been booked for a Women's Institute function. However, we had managed to get a spot together outside on the terrace, under one of the large over-the-top hanging umbrellas which sheltered us from the ever-persistent threat of rain.

As always, it was just the three of us, Andy, Dave and I. Poppy herself had strongly declined. She had been increasing her efforts to stay sober after an embarrassing feat of drunken dancing at the wedding. Mike and Alice had still been on call, not that they really left the office during working hours except for emergencies, fire drills and the odd run to the sandwich van that sometimes turned up mid-morning with sausage rolls, egg baps and pastries.

I enjoyed the jaunty little tune it made as it approached the fish tank office but had often been too busy to go and get something, either held up by the phone or the snake-like line of people queuing outside from all over the building. The miniature jam rolly pollies they sometimes sold were nice, though.

Dave, who was excited to show off his holiday photos, had been nominated to get the first round if only to soften the torment. Andy and I watched with amusement as he squirmed away from the gathering of women who hoarded the overlapping sides of the bar. He was attempting to place an order; something made slightly more challenging by the drones of conversation, and the blasting of music from the speakers hung above him at a 90-degree angle to his left.

It was lucky our lunch break was an hour long.

"Do you want to tell him or should I?" asked Andy with a rogue grin as he held up his phone where there was a newly installed app that allowed us to order from bar to table without much fuss.

I shook my head. "You're cruel, Andy," I murmured, making a note to try and find the app if my older phone supported it on a later date.

"What's our table number?" Andy replied, purposefully ignoring me as he looked at the phone once more. I glanced over the counter conspicuously.

"43,"

Since we had time before the food and drinks arrived, I considered talking to Andy about my conundrum. Whilst he was by no means as loved up as Dave and Yvonne, he had changed his photo on his phone's lock screen to one of the two of them laughing and joking as she smudged an ice cream cone into his face. His usual bravado about girls had changed somewhat since meeting Mia, even addressing her as his girlfriend rather than the familiar pattern of one night stands.

I considered waiting until Dave returned with our drinks, but given that he had only just reached the counter, he might be a little longer.

But how would he respond to my asking for help?

After all, Andy was still the most testosterone-driven out of the group, even if Mia had changed him.

"Andy," I asked, somewhat meekly, as I looked up at home. He was scrolling through his phone and smiling; Mia had messaged him.

"Hmm?" he mused, half listening.

I would have to change tact. Clearing my throat a little, I tried to be more direct. "Do you *like* Toni?"

"She's alright, I suppose, but I wouldn't choose her, too fiery!" responded Andy somewhat automatically before shooting his head up curiously as his brain processed my words. "*Why?*"

"I think I've fallen for someone else."

Andy's response was much like my sister's, somewhat incredulous but peeked with the same expression one might receive from a puppy promised a game of fetch.

It was time to give the dog his bone.

"Yes," "There's someone else I like," I continued, attempting to pace my words.

"Well, this is a first-"Andy replied but was cut off by Dave's re-arrival, sheepishly carrying a small black bar tray with our three drinks.

"What is?" Dave asked curiously as he passed my drink before rejoining us at his seat and sipping his beer.

"Frank's torn between *two* women!" Andy chirped.

Dave's eyes nearly popped out of his head, rounding on me with interest. "What?!"

I sighed a little, looking down into the pint of Guinness he had got me, suddenly wishing for something *stronger*.

But that would be impractical. We had to return to work for the afternoon.

"Yes," I told them both somewhat matter of factly before explaining to them about Mary.

"Wow!" exhaled Dave, slowly reaching for his drink. Andy was silent.

Neither of them had seen it coming.

But then, nor had I.

Attempting to collect myself casually, I asked. "What do I do? *Do* I tell Toni?"

"God, no!" Dave blurted as though I had just signed my own death warrant.

Although very few people had seen the softer, kinder side of Toni, I understood his reaction well, recalling the rough handed manner in which she had spoken on the phone when I first saw her. It seemed like ages ago now. Instead, I allowed myself a small lazy smile nodding. I could at least keep her secrets. It gave her some power.

"So what do I *do*? She wants to go to university," I said, referring back to the latest developments.

To me, this was a deal-breaker.

"And you're not keen on being a sugar daddy?" Joked Andy, ending his silence. His brow twitched a little in jest.

I frowned.

"This is serious!" Dave echoed, sensing my unease.

"Alright, *alright*," Andy cackled, chuckling a little to himself before straightening a bit as the food finally came to the table.

A collective silence formed as we ate. A quick glance at my watch told me we had around twenty minutes until work resumed.

With a chip half-chewed, pursed between his lips, Andy mused. "And how does Mary *feel?*"

Deep down, he had a point.

Was it worth risking everything if she didn't feel the same?

* * *

That evening I found myself back at Mary's door. I had bought some flowers, a small cluster of tulips and daisies I had chosen at the supermarket after work. I had chosen a simple bouquet in yellow shades since the cashier had told me they were "happy colours," whatever that meant. I recalled Mary's lovely daisy dress when we had last spent time together at the marquee.

Before, I had texted her asking if I could pop over, sure she would be home. She had replied later, apologising as she had been caught up with housework.

Pop round, 6:30?

Nervously I knocked on the door listening for the comforting sound of footsteps that came from the somewhat cheapened wood structure.

I could hear a few other sounds in the meantime, including what I could only describe as running water, a slight thud and a high pitched giggle, no doubt Willy was up to no good. "Hello?" I called out cautiously. "Hello?" there was a grunt followed by another giggle and then-

"Just a second!"

Hastily, I hid the flowers behind the door frame's adjoining pillar; it didn't feel entirely appropriate with the kids.

When the door eventually opened, Mary stood slightly frazzled and wet fifteen minutes later. Her hair was tied in a braid, which dripped at the ends and over part of her muted blue top. The other shoulder had been draped with an equally wet peach bath towel. The effect was similar to a toga, albeit with much less effort. She was heaving slightly for breath, but she gave a nervous smile when she saw me. "Sorry," she whispered softly. "Willy *wanted* a bath,"

I nodded despite myself, noticing the slight sarcasm in her words and was about to bend down for the flowers when Willy appeared at his mother's heels, wrapped only in a matching towel and equally wet hair and feet, which dripped onto the threshold.

"Hi Mr Frank, sir," he said impishly, whilst his mother shooed him inside. *He would get cold just standing there; they both would.*

With her back to me once more to ensure her son behaved, I picked up the bouquet and followed, closing the door behind me, the flowers concealed behind my back.

Willy was wriggling slightly as his mother rubbed her former shoulder towel through his hair; it had grown somewhat longer in the short time since I had last seen him, and he squirmed and made his muffled protest, covered by the thicker cotton barrier. "I don't *want* to be dry!" He moaned up at her, his eyes filling with slight crocodile tears.

I could see why they called it the terrible toddler years. But to me, Mary was an excellent mother.

"Come now," she murmured softly, "You'll get a bedtime story soon,"

Once Willy was settled and dried, she sent him to his room to change into his pyjamas and turned to me, flushing a little.

"Sorry, Frank," she said sincerely before ushering me to the sofa. "Please, sit," she continued before dashing around her kitchen, justly animating her thoughts. "I'm sorry, you must be hungry. Can I get you anything?" the words rushing like a hurricane of her scattered suggestions. "Tea? Coffee? Water? Squash?"

"Just water, thank you," Mary nodded, fetched a glass, filled it with tap water, and finally sat beside me. I smiled. I hoped I could help her relax.

The conversation was casual at first and unassuming. I would let Mary lead.

"How was your day?" She asked. I lent back, attempting to seem comfortable, although careful not to flatten the daisies and smiled.

"It's been okay, busy, of course."

Mary nodded again. She could relate.

"Everyone told me it would be *easier* when Willy was able to walk," She told me solemnly. I could tell she was trying to make a joke, but the bags under her eyes showed a ring of truth, and for a moment, I wasn't quite sure what to say."So, what can I do for you?"

With a slight pause, I gathered the flowers from behind me, where I had attempted to hide them under my coat; "These are for you,"

"Oh gosh," she replied, flushing slightly. "Frank, you shouldn't have!"

I brushed the comment aside. "No matter,"

"No, really," She had got up and gone to fetch up a makeshift vase from the cupboard and was once again busying herself. "What's the occasion? Your girlfriend won't get jealous, will she?"

I discretely shook my head, watching as she darted back and forth like a flitting hummingbird against the flowers, my words, which I had repeatedly vocalised to others now awkwardly bursting out of me. "I think I'm falling in love with you."

The words stopped her dead, and the flowers tumbled to the floor.

"Oh."

Oh indeed.

* * *

Forcing myself to move, I reached out to her, attempting to pick the scattered flowers on the floor. Our hands brief brushed for a moment, and she flinched, pulling away but said nothing. An eclipsing silence seemed to surround us, and I longed to reach out and touch her but was not quite sure what to say when the sounds of crying came from the children's room.

"Sorry," she whispered demurely and ran from the room; her cheeks were red and burning.

Shit.

Clearing the rest of the flowers away, I placed them in the vase she had left on the counter, somewhat grateful she had not dropped it at my revelation.

Beth had been roused no doubt by her hyperactive older brother and was hungry. In the other room, I could hear Mary fussing the baby. My own stomach gurgled a little at the thought.

Although I had a somewhat filling lunch, I had come straight to Mary's, stopping only for flowers on the way. Some small part of me had been hoping to take her out for dinner, but in hindsight, I should have asked her first. She was a single mother, after all.

Who would take the kids?

I considered making excuses and leaving.

Mary's slight frostiness had said everything. Hadn't it?

Gathering up my coat, I thought about how to say goodbye when she returned, calling my name gently. "Frank."

I turned, gushing my words in a bid to appease her. "It's fine; I was out of line; you don't see me that way-"

But Mary cut me off with a kiss.

We both revelled at the moment; her lips were rougher than Toni's without the refinement of lipstick or chapstick to soften them against the weather, but the kiss was tender and sweet, and I let her lead us.

As we broke apart, she had found her voice. "Please wait?" she asked. Her words were still quiet, mouse-like and uncertain. No doubt, she was considering her own thoughts and feelings.

"I *like* you too,"

Relief quickly spread over my face in a broad smile, and without another word, I kissed her eagerly again, relishing as, after a brief hesitation, she kissed back, this time more fondly.

Mary liked me back.

We could work out the rest later.

Chapter 30: Chips For Tea

Reality jolted me back with a crash as I felt the bump of a small body against the back of my leg as Willy returned into the room, running in a whirlwind of energy and cheap flannel cotton pyjamas before face planting into my calf.

I grunted slightly, not winded as such but with slight embarrassment as his mother, and I sprung apart. Mary had a slight flush on her cheeks as she turned to greet her son, whose wide eyes stared poised with questions.

"What are you doing?" He asked in a singsong voice, his lips curling into a slight, innocent grin.

"Willy darling, you should be in bed!" Mary reasoned, attempting to brush him off.

Willy shook his head. Undeterred.

"Mr Frank, what are you doing?" he asked me in turn.

I had to give the boy some credit; his curiosity rivalled my own as a boy. I made a note to take him over to Bazil's at some point.

"Willy, it's bedtime!" His mother reproached, although it lacked the panic that usually accompanied her. She was smiling. I liked that.

"But *Mummmmy*," recoiled Willy, protesting slightly as she guided him back towards his bedroom, her hand gently tugging her son out of the room.

"Come now; we don't want to wake Bethy!" She insisted.

Willy frowned, scrunching his eyes as though he might cry. "But, but-"

"No, buts," Mary enforced. "Have you brushed your teeth?"

"No," mumbled Willy dully before quickly recovering himself as he sensed a new opportunity for freedom. Springing from her newly released grip, he ran, giggling back towards the bathroom.

Mary watched him go, making sure he applied a pea-sized amount of toothpaste to the brush before she returned to the living room, her body hanging against the door frame.

A small silence elapsed between us, and for a moment, neither of us spoke—the only sounds coming from the running tap water.

I took my cue. "I should go," I repeated, once more gathering my coat where it had fallen onto the sofa in the moment of Mary's and my brief embrace. But the newly formed frown deterred me. "Unless you'd like something to eat?"

She nodded somewhat nervously, gesturing wordlessly to the bathroom. Still, I understood.

"We could get a chippy."

"That would be lovely."

* * *

Stretching my legs as I walked in the cold air towards the chip shop felt cathartic, and I relished the sight of my breath as it floated against the air. It had made sense for me to collect the food, saving the extra pennies on the delivery charge, and I took a moment to reflect on everything that was happening.

Mary had stayed behind, still attempting to get Willy to settle into bed for the night. A difficult task aided by his seemingly boundless energy and internal alarm clock of curiosity. I chuckled at the thought.

The evening was cool, but not unbearably so, and I hummed slightly along to the sounds of an earworm I had heard earlier in the day from the radio of a passing car. Usually, I was not a fan of pop music; the tinny pips of sound often distorted themselves down the phones at work. All of it seemingly reduced to empty background filters and reproduced on-hold music. But my mood felt lightened, and I could improvise around the tune, melodic in its way rather than the thud, thud, thud of a bass beat that had in more recent years become the norm.

I was happy.

Waltzing into the chip shop, I was pleasantly surprised that I didn't need to queue. I checked my watch, comparing it to the clock on the wall at the waiting bay. It was a little after 7 pm. A place like this shouldn't be this empty this time of day. I felt a bit guilty as one expectant team member eyed me with some fleeting interest from his dock at the fish fryer. But he quickly looked down as I confirmed I had ordered ahead to the woman at the counter wearing what appeared to be a thick white lab coat and a blue hair net. She might have worn a name badge, but as always, I chose not to stare.

The woman handed me a printed, greasy receipt from the till and ushered me to the waiting area. "10 minutes!" She estimated before the automatic bell rang again. An elderly gentleman with thinning ginger hair entered behind me and requested the *OAP special.*

Grabbing a wad of napkins from the dispenser, I smiled and nodded to the man as I took the end chair on a group of slightly raised seats, a row of scuffed moulded blue plastic stools that reminded me a little of school. Although the view was obscured somewhat by the gathering darkness and the store's prominent painted name in gold arching lettering, the seating looked out towards the sea. Something nice for the patrons to look at should they choose to eat in.

There was still a while before my order was ready, and I texted Mary to let her know.

Her answer was brief, a single *'K'* and a kiss. No doubt Willy was keeping her occupied. Still, unlike Toni, she had replied. The moment endeared me further to her.

"Quiet tonight," Mumbled the old man, shuffling towards me carrying a slim rectangular tray with a plate of what I presumed to be cod and chips.

"Yes," I said, standing up to help him. Grunting slightly in thanks, he pushed the tray into my hands and forced himself up onto one of the stools.

"Used to be able to get real peas," he snorted, looking around slightly as I placed the tray back down in front of him. "Now it's just mush from a can!"

As he spoke, he looked over at the canteen staff and then to me, as though he were letting me in on a well-kept secret.

I pacified his unspoken request, listening. "And now?"

"Everything's overpriced and moderated," He continued humourlessly, lifting one of the chips with his finger and jabbing it slightly at me. "Too *little* salt, too *much* vinegar; got to watch your blood pressure and all that political yadda-dada!"

"Come on now, Del," Rebuked the woman from the counter gently. Although her voice was stern, it was softer now; I guessed she was used to his jibes and custom.

Del frowned, popping his chip into his mouth as he watched her with a guarded look. "No privacy these days!"

"Number 93," my server ignored him, holding out a thick brown paper bag. she called, smiling at me as I stood and collected my order. The smile didn't quite reach her eyes.

Hastily I paid and moved towards the door, turning briefly to say farewell to the eccentric octogenarian. "Bye, Del."

My new acquaintance chose not to reply. The moment had passed, and I knew I should hurry along, save the chips got too cold.

* * *

By the time I returned, Mary had laid the table and had filled two plastic cups with wine. Later apologising since she didn't often have guests and only had a simple bottle that was surprisingly icy - both to the touch and the taste. Presumably, it had spent many nights neglected in the fridge, but then Mary only drank on special occasions - like -so she said- tonight.

She had also changed into a jumper, presumably since her top was somewhat soaked through from Willy's bath time antics. It was pastel pink and fluffy with the drawing of a rabbit wearing heart-shaped sunglasses. The playful print suited her.

"Battered sausage, my lady?" I asked as I unwrapped one of the greasy paper bundles from the bag and slid it onto the plate.

214

Mary giggled. Pursing her lips slightly as she adopted a more pronounced manner.

"Why, thank you kindly, Mr Davis," she said, bobbing a slight curtsy before sitting herself down opposite me and reaching for the bottle of tomato ketchup she had brought from the kitchen.

I also took my seat, unfolding the chips package and relishing the warm, greasy fingers of golden potato that flaked so effortlessly against my fork and then lifted my cup. "Here's to us!"

"To us!" Mary chorused, toasting our cups together.

Evening and wine flowed naturally, and we spent a couple of hours talking and giggling, keeping our voices low so as not to wake the children.

Mary had switched off the main lights since tucking Willy into bed. The after-effect gave the room a warm ambience bathed in the kitchen counter strip light's soft yellow glow. Everything seemed so simple, and I watched her fondly as she brushed her hands against mine as she rose from the table to get dessert and crossed through the room, standing on tip-toe to fetch down a tin of biscuits she kept on top of the fridge. "To deter any stray little fingers," She mused at my slight curiosity.

No doubt Willy had a sweet tooth.

I recognised the tin from the day I first saw her, finally seeing inside and the treasures that lay within. The tin was circular in shape with a slightly bevelled edge, and its metallic surface had been painted in duck egg blue and magenta with trims of gold. A procession of carnival animals decorated the sides; in a carousel-like parade.

"What tickles your fancy?" Mary asked, holding the box and lid in each hand.

I paused to look. Attempting to avoid holding my sides a little from the already fulfilling main, somewhat regretting how I had shovelled down an extra portion of chips despite my earlier luncheon. Mary had made an effort; I wanted to do the same.

I selected a slim finger-shaped biscuit that melted a little against my fingers, a mixture of soft buttery chocolate and the pleasant warmness of the room. It felt a little erotic, and I felt my ear twitch a little in familiar nervousness at the thought. It would be too soon. Sheepishly I looked away, attempting to busy my premature expectations focusing away from the increasingly beautiful woman who stood in front of me, stooping slightly to frame her face in the shadows and light like a goddess.

"I recognise the tin," I continued conversationally as she replaced the lid and popped the box down between us on the table. Hoping I didn't sound like a stalker now that we were somewhat more familiar with each other.

"Oh?" Mary seemed curious. She had chosen a Viennese whirl and a shortbread.

I nodded, taking another bite from the finger.

"Yes, I saw you with it once on the bus,"

Mary stared for a moment, reflectively. "Did you?"

I smiled fondly, "Yes," finishing off the cookie in a further bite before retrieving my trusty leather notebook from my coat.

Turning quickly to the correct page didn't require effort since it corresponded so neatly with my mother's birthday. Not that I would tell Mary this straight away. Right now, I didn't want to think of my mother.

Whilst it might seem rather cowardly, I was concerned that thoughts of Mum might also make me think of Toni, whose initial descriptions I had also noted here. I collected myself, covering the paragraph with my thumb, trying to ignore the imprint of the pink-haired artisan who had forced herself back into my mind, with the same bold sharpness as her handbag had collided with my head.

Mary gazed at me quizzically at the silence, like a child might expect a bedtime story.

I cleared my throat and continued attempting to maintain the role of a seasoned orator. "Here we are—March 3rd. I took the shuttle bus service through town on Thursday. I got off at Market Road near the antique shop."

"Ah," Mary replied, in acknowledgement from the date. "There had been a bake sell at Willy's nursery; everyone had to bring a cake."

I chuckled, pausing in my notes. "What was your flavour?"

"Apple."

My lips moistened expectantly.

Yes, being with Mary would be good indeed.

For the next hour or so, I entertained Mary with my studies in people watching and the various musings and habits of my beloved guinea pig. With every murmur of appreciation and the barely suppressed peals of laughter, I found myself warming to her all the more. Placing the book down, I instinctively pulled her closer, leaning my back to the foot of the sofa. Although I wanted nothing more than to kiss her again, I resisted. Instead, I held her in my arms, listening to the sound of her heart.

"Mary," I whispered softly.

"Mmm?" She replied drowsily. It was late now, and she was so close to dropping off.

"When will you tell Willy about us?"

"Soon," she murmured.

I nodded. Despite my nervousness, I understood. If Mary and I became a couple, we would not be alone. I would be taking her on, along with her children, and while Beth was still naive in blissful infancy, Willy would be soon questioning. He had already demonstrated this so far today, and it would be up to his mother to gently transition me from friend to boyfriend and potential step-father – should things develop as I hoped they would.

The trouble was now I had to tell Toni.

Something in my gut told me that it would be tough.

No, very tough indeed.

Chapter 31: Cutting Ties

Although I was resolute in telling Toni the truth about my newfound love with Mary, the thought of her brother made my ear twitch uncomfortably. So, I was grateful that she had agreed to meet me alone as I arrived at her studio. I hadn't been around to the place often, but the smell of paint burnt into my nostrils from the community art project she had propped against the outer brick wall. I glanced at it whilst I waited after knocking on the door. Her makeshift wooden canvas was filled with splishes and splashes and colourful splodges of thick acrylic paint and environmentally-friendly glitter, a concept I didn't fully understand. But I supposed that was the beauty of modern art. All of it was subjective with little to no meaning.

I smiled a little as I recalled my mother's birthday present; the yellow framed painting I had so awkwardly chosen had gone on display in the downstairs cloakroom, where Mum proposed it might be a good alternative for those who might go in there to read.

I had admittedly not told Toni the reason concerning my impromptu visit but knew it was best coming from me rather than through second-hand gossip. Her venomous phone conversation I had partially witnessed on our first meeting still echoed in my mind. Redirecting my thoughts once more, I knocked on the door of a chalky coated entrance and sucked in a breath to steady my nerves.

People can be cruel when upset.

There was no answer.

"Hello, Toni?" I called, knocking a little louder. Perhaps she had music on and couldn't hear me. Not that I knew if such a venue was soundproof. Toni's soundtracks had a habit of bouncing off the walls.

Meeting here had been her suggestion.

Not wanting to fuel unfounded paranoia, I double-checked on my phone, hoping that once inside, I could overcome my nerves with a cup of coffee. I rarely drank it. But tonight, I would need something richer.

Clearing my throat, I tried again. "Toni?"

Nothing.

Where was she?

Scratching my head a little, I considered calling her. I had barely dialled the first few letters of her letter into my contacts when the sight of her familiar pink hair materialised out of the shadows, holding herself in a slightly hunched position from a recently lit cigarette.

"Hi, Frank," She greeted me, rolling her R's with a slight emphasis that suggested she might be drunk. A mixture of drying paint fumes and recreational cider.

"Hi," I replied, awkwardly hoping that I could train my heart to observe her with slight disapproval. Such thoughts didn't come naturally. Was it better this way? I asked myself. To distance myself from the creative artistic rebellion that had once so warmed my heart. But it was not natural for me to be cruel.

She was tilting her head at me quizzically, perhaps noticing my frown as it projected outwardly.

"Frank, is something wrong?"

I gestured to the building. "Can we go in?" I asked. I preferred the quiet anonymity that came from being indoors, away from the chorus of perceived onlookers in the way of the cluster of seagulls who had gathered on a neighbouring roof. Or the noise that swept up from the road.

"Sure," she replied with a slight pause and sidestepped away so that I might enter first. She joined me a moment later, but only after she finished the smouldering remains of her cigarette before crushing it into the already overflowing ashtray that had been left conveniently on one of the two brick pillars that held up the fence—a relic of 20th Century architecture.

The studio was a single wing of a larger community space. It had been lit with an artificial ambience of cheap, eco-friendly lighting, which buzzed every so often in a dull, monotonous sound. Its interior was predominately taken up by a long lab-like table, with a 'round armed stool covered in a faded, soft leather that might have once sat in a modish bar in town, but Toni had found it in a skip and upcycled. Her current project sat crowded by a medley of half washed paintbrushes and fabric scraps, and I eyed a bag of peanuts with some suspicion about whether it was lunch or work. Thankfully the kettle was still there, and I filled it hastily with water from the adjoining kitchen space that Toni shared with the Boy Scouts, ballet classes and other outreach projects who used the main hall.

As the "resident artist," Toni was usually left undisturbed, although I suspected this was more to do with the twilight hours she favoured, woken by the spirits of her muses. I heard her entering the kitchen after me.

I felt some comfort in playing mother.

"Coffee?" I asked.

"Sure. What's this all about?" Toni nodded, reaching into the cupboard beside me and pulling out two mugs and a box of long-life milk.

Several sleepless nights and fervent soul searching had brought me to this place. And whilst resolved in what needed to be done, the way to say it still alluded me. It would be easy to say, "I'm not in love with you any more!" But such a phrase on its own was a cheap cop-out for the underlying reasons. Reasons I was not sure I could not or was not yet ready to divulge to her. Not at least until I could be sure there would be no heavy punches or sharply flung handbag missiles.

Her verbal retorts and bitterness I was prepared for, having witnessed it. But I knew my partner, as she still was at this brief juncture in my life, was in love with me. Whatever I told her would hurt. It would be superficial to say that we weren't on the same page any more, even if that were also true. I knew whilst it was kinder to let her move forwards with her life, it wouldn't stop the temporal pain and anguish, especially in all that she had done toward an awkward, stumbling but generally pure life routine together.

But keeping her in ignorance was not fair either, and neither would be gossip. Something my mother or others like her would be quick to spread indeed.

I cleared my throat into the eclipsing silence.

It was time.

My words slipped out of me. Awkwardly.

"Tony, uhh, we need to break up. Sorry."

God, I needed to work on my tact.

* * *

"That was heartless, Frank," Hanny told me bluntly as I related things to her the following morning stood side by side with our backs toward the kitchen window. "How did Toni take it?"

I had not invited my sister over for her moral compass. Although left alone, my burgeoning guilt was already gnawing away at me, the same way Mol sometimes tackled a bundle of grass clippings.

What I sought were her counsel and her compassion.

Hanny, however, seemed to be on the fence. She had come to my house out of obligation and sisterly duty but viewed my breakup with the same uniform judgement I supposed all women did to rally around one of their own. A brief subconscious conjecture where *all* men are swine.

"She kicked me out," I replied gruffly. I hadn't slept much, which somewhat surprised me. I had assumed that being free to be with Mary would be liberating, but Toni's cold violet eyes had burned into my soul as I fled with shame.

She hadn't said anything.

My sister frowned, pursing her lips. "I'm not surprised!"

I raked a hand through my hair, sighing. But Hanny was not entirely sympathetic. "No one told you this would be easy," Said Hanny but softened a little. "Does anyone else know?"

"About my feelings or the breakup?" I asked rhetorically before continuing.

"Andy and Dave know there's someone else, but Toni doesn't know who. Why?"

"Because," Hanny answered flatly. "You don't want people to get hurt,"

* * *

By *people,* I supposed Hanny meant Toni, but as I was quick to discover, she also meant Mary.

A sea of people had gathered on the bus as I travelled to work the following morning. They were greeting me with cold, harsh stares of indifference that burned into my headrest as I took my place amongst them.

The likelihood that my former girlfriend had incensed the whole town with our breakup was unlikely, but I knew she took the same route when she was not leathered up on the motorbike with Billy. Thankfully, that wasn't frequently – usually only when she was heading to the job centre, a soulless exercise that created a fitting mascarade toward her attempts at adulthood. A somewhat frequent attendee, the dole paid toward for her fare.

I wanted to run into the warm embrace of Mary, but upon Hanny's advice, I had decided to force some space between us. This step was necessary; she told me to create a niche interval of bachelorhood to arouse suspicion about my fidelity or intentions. I had texted her explaining as best I could, hoping she would wait for me.

Mary had yet to reply.

She was by no means the other woman, but I acknowledged that I owed her some protection or privacy. Her heart was still fragile from her divorce, and I was incredibly grateful that she had even registered an interest in my affections.

The problem was, as it had always been. People talk.

Being single had somewhat suited me, a 9-5 rotation of shared existence with Mol. It had undoubtedly been free of complications, save what we wanted for dinner, my mind willingly switching off for the day of seemingly never-ending phone calls and customer service based angst. But, as I reminded myself in this moment of weakness, being single had also been desperately lonely, for as much love as a guinea pig can hold; travelling with them on most buses is frowned upon – with rare, protocol rich exceptions.

Whether it was the bleak misery of early morning or the bleak mid-April showers, the bus was fuller than usual, and it groaned in obvious displeasure as it pulled away from the curb.

Keen to distance myself from the internal monologues of individual judge, jury, and execution from my fellow patrons, I attempted to busy myself by reciting bus operators' names within the post-war period. It was proving a difficult task, and my ears were temporarily buzzing uncomfortably from the static of a nearby phone user.

The young man was not looking at me, but his choice of music could still be heard – at least the bass of which through their large, cumbersome earphones or buds as I was sometimes corrected.

Gone were the days of my understanding of modern music, although my sister would argue I never had. It had been Hanny who had come home clutching a newly prized cassette or vinyl record she had borrowed off a friend or their older siblings. Others of my former contemporaries at school sat creating low-quality mix tapes for their loved ones trying to make a 'clean' copy of love songs on the cheap, distorted by radio disk-jockey commentary or the crowds of fellow adolescents on Top of the Pops. For my part, I had been quite fond of the countdown chart jingle in the late 80s. This synthy, bouncy track reminded me of the neon-coloured jumpsuits with large unnaturally proportioned shoulder pads. The wearers of these were reserved for exercise conscious, health-conscious 30-40 some-things I sometimes saw on early morning television. Or contestants who remained fixed in time on the endless quiz show reruns - shows I had seen in their original airing or multiple times on the disapproval before. It made me sad to think of it.

Instead, I thought about the nearest cluster of bus companies, both the family-owned and those by corporations in Kent. The phrase Arriva, Metrobus, Travelmasters, Stagecoach becoming a small vigil I muttered under my breath to calm my nerves and avoid the look of discontent from an older woman who sat directly opposite me; poised with sharp eyes and knitting needles.

Maybe it was the crucifix around her neck or the way she watched me with hawk-like precision, but I was glad for once to take my stop and head into the fish-bowl office away from her. Religion had never really been a theme in my household, apart from a single incident involving Dad's now long-departed mother. I believed Hanny, and I had only met her once; both of us had been but small children. And our paternal grandmother had been a short, angry woman who bitterly demanded our parents reconsider whether we would be sent to Sunday school.

People in the office were no better.

A number had swarmed around the water tank like flies or wildebeest drawn to a watering hole. A few of them, the younger crowd, usually ignored me, which rarely troubled me. By and large, this was because the office was so grandiose and so impersonal that I assumed I would be forgiven for not remembering many of my colleagues by name. Save, of course, those who were in my immediate vicinity and my friends. It was likely their appearance had been more to do with the coffee machine being on the fritz, as it had an increasing habit of being more recently, and I would have ignored them all together had a shout not caught my attention.

"There he is, there's the letch!" piped up an unfamiliar girl with a bob of short green hair and oversized glasses. I supposed she might be fresh out of college.

I gulped awkwardly, ready to defend myself if needs be, when I noticed through the slight gap in the crowd that she was holding a glossy magazine. Similar, I suppose, to the ones you might find in hairdressers and newsagents.

"See? There's the dick who thinks it's cool to string his wife along with some cheap tart!" she seethed, jabbing the open page to some tabloid headline about the misdemeanours of some celebrity love triangle. The picture was big and 'purposefully revealing' although the people themselves were as relevant to me as watching the football, which I only did out of obligation to my friends.

Paranoia clawed at me as a cat does at a scratching post, leaving it raw and worse for wear. I knew this was normal but still swallowed, forcing myself to retrain my eyes back to my computer and the phone beginning to jangle at my desk. I dreaded to theorise how it would be if anyone knew, grimly imagining the dartboard mugshot of my face that Toni and her brother might use as target practice at the bar. The resulting secret I hoped that saving my sister, no one else knew. Save it be on my terms to redirect the story. Something that was less selfish and would increase self-preservation from my previously bloodied nose.

With a mixture of stress and nervousness, my left ear twitched again. *Work was the last thing on my mind.*

Chapter 32: Manmade Emotions

"That takes some balls!" Cried out Andy incredulously.

His eyes were focused on the large screen that was strategically placed above the bar, vital for any key events of what he had once dubbed the *"Working Man's Sporting Calendar"*.

I had taken my pew at *Morses'* with Andy and Dave whilst sipping on my first pint of the night, hoping to numb my insecurities whilst they debated the evening's match.

I nodded, only half-listening as his words drowned away towards something I presumed Dave had said about sport.

We had just finished our daily shift. For the past seven hours, I had been buried in paperwork and phone calls, drinking from a plastic cup of lukewarm water and brown grit. It was, I supposed, was a mixture of instant coffee and burnt-in grime from a makeshift budget jar that one of the receptionists had rushed to purchase at lunchtime—no doubt attempting to appease the mob.

A phrase Mike Senior liked to call *"maintaining momentum,"*

Although attempting to focus and distance myself from the monotony, I felt the hours crawling. Mary still hadn't replied. It stung slightly. But I consoled myself thinking she was probably still busy, convincing myself that school days often were.

Still, accepting a spur of the moment night out from Andy after work was a welcome distraction. Especially from the alternative – a lonely defrosting tuna and tomato pasta bake that I had hurriedly placed on the draining rack earlier in the day.

Nothingness for a while at least would be welcome.

Dave, however, had news.

"Yvonne wants us to have a baby," He squeaked; somewhat meekly, his cheeks slightly red, a mixture of the bar's cheap misplaced mood lighting and his quickly drained pint, for what our mutual friend called liquid courage. "And I think I'm ready to be a Dad."

Andy looked like he wanted to spit out his drink.

His face drained of colour into the silence. "You're serious?"

The football, however, temporarily, was quickly forgotten.

Dave nodded solemnly, his words holding gravitas. "Deadly."

My interest peaked at the subject and its unfamiliar territory.

If Dave and Yvonne became parents, they would become the first in my immediate circle to do so.

While it could be said that Andy had started to enjoy going steady with Mia, none of my other friends had married or started their little nuclear unit.

I had seen them, of course, assertive parents who tightly held their children's hands as they frog-marshalled them around the supermarket. Or the sweet doting families who went on outings to the park or the museum, breaking for photos and ice cream, recalling, however briefly, the delighted squeals of pleasure when Hanny and I ran away from our mother down to the shoreline to watch the boats and ferries, waving them off to France. Yet of my group, none of them had ventured into parenthood.

The rites of parenthood seemingly passing us all by.

Perhaps then, should they commit to this new life, it might be intuitive to ask for tips.

Willy was already a bundle of energy, and I knew it would not be long before Beth joined him. Mary might even want one or so of our own in the future.

It would be good to have a friendly ear with such thoughts in mind.

The trouble was Dave and Yvonne were somewhat familiar with Toni, and given my facade of bachelorhood, I knew I should avoid trying to raise unwanted suspicions.

"You? Kids?" Andy queried. He was stunned and stumbling over his words.

Again, Dave nodded. Patiently.

"Yes."

This time Andy was silent. I guessed he was processing everything.

I smiled.

"That will be great for you both. Congratulations."

"Yeah, good," Andy replied, somewhat curtly, returning to a state of bravado. His eyes returned to the screen. "The match is on."

It felt like someone had touched a nerve.

For a while, at least, everyone was silent. Save from the occasional grunts of acknowledgement over the ball's proximity on the screen. Andy was quiet and sat with his arms folded.

It wasn't until the food came that he spoke again; keeping his voice somewhat level, he casually observed. *"I don't think I'd want kids."*

Neither Dave nor I answered. The latter fidgeted a little with a bottle of tomato ketchup that seemed stuck within the airless plastic bottle.

Whatever it was, it didn't seem quite the time to talk about it.

* * *

At around 10 pm, the match ended, a convenient interval for the evening news and time to stretch my legs on my walk home. It was a route I somewhat favoured at this time of night as it faced outwards towards the sea with a soft, cool breeze. My small group headed out at the side entrance, which faced onto the pub's car park. Dave left almost immediately, waving to both of us with his gentle but oblivious demeanour, leaving us as just two.

Andy lit up a cigarette.

Now exposed by the aura of the floodlights, I could see him correctly. His face was puffed up and solemn, the same way I recalled a gorilla had looked at me when I was a small boy the time my school had once visited the zoo. He looked tired. I wondered if he even knew I was there.

"You ever feel like a failure Frank?" he asked quietly.

I considered answering him and had barely gathered a string of words together when he continued, seemingly content using me as a springboard instead.

Thus, I listened.

"My mother's sick," He persisted, the casual nature seemingly jarring with his outer expression.

I opted for sincerity.

"I'm sorry,"

"*Don't be,*" said Andy flatly, keeping his gaze forwards, away from me. "It's terminal."

"Oh."

Again he fell silent, and at a loss of what to say, I considered making excuses to depart when Andy laughed. It was a cold, hollow sound.

"She thought I'd be a doctor. you know."

"Really?" I asked quizzically.

It was rare for Andy to open up fully. I must choose my words carefully. "What speciality?"

"Oncology," He replied.

The bitterness was unmistakable.

Reaching out, I patted him gingerly on the back. I had never lost a parent, and my grandmother had died when I was still young - when I was perhaps too young to understand. Her absence had been explained as she had gone away and wasn't going to visit any more. My other three grandparents passed long before I was born.

At first, he stiffened and remained stoic, as though rooted to the spot with his typical masculinity, but then he sighed, looking down towards the floor, his feet idly playing with the sprinkles of ash that gathered on the tarmac.

With slight uncertainty, I repeated myself. "I'm sorry, Andy."

He sighed.

"*Me too,*"

There was a brief pause, and in the absence of conversation, I could hear the sounds from within the pub of the nearby slot machine whirring and gurgling on the wall adjacent to the door. The landlord's voice rang out with authority. "Last orders, please!"

Time was getting on.

Andy cued me back to reality and coughed apologetically as he moved away, pretending to take an interest in the row of shops on the opposite street. They were all dark and closed, save for the kebabery, which was open for orders with a neon red and blue sign that had been purposefully chosen to direct drunken punters.

It was a lonely prospect indeed.

"I'll see you tomorrow," Andy finished cheerlessly, plastering on a smile, which didn't entirely fill me with its usual warmth and sincerity.

I hadn't seen him this dark for a long time.

I nodded. "Want me to call you a cab?" I offered.

"No need," He brushed me off. "Mia will be worrying about me,"

Despite the otherwise bleak situation, I was pleased to hear things were going steady and smiled back, attempting to mask my worry.

The problem was a universal one.

Real men don't cry.

And Andy was unlikely to start now.

Tomorrow he would return to his mask of masculinity, acknowledging the evening the only way he knew how - bragging about the football and Dave's supposed cuckolding from Yvonne. I watched him go, walking into the night and headed off the other way: with the only thoughts I knew, my own.

* * *

It was too late to ring Mary by the time I got home, but I knew I wanted to. I pictured her tucked up in bed with a cotton nightdress with a collection of books by her dresser. One's she always intended but never had time to read. The image effortlessly burned itself into my mind, although I scolded myself a little at not taking a photo when she and I had been together. There would be plenty of time for that, though.

She was getting older now, and I didn't want to wake her unnecessarily. Given the time, I knew I should be in bed too, but my mind buzzed uncomfortably, intruded by the events of the day. My life felt in limbo, balancing precariously between the varying weights of adult responsibilities. The idea of burrowing myself away like Mol did, laying on the warm, safe blanket of hay that doubled as a snack in a moment of carefree whimsy, was an attractive one. But sadly unobtainable.

So instead, I scrolled through my phone, lazily looking at memories and photos of people I had known through my 45 years. The majority were happy and prosperous, many more of them having left Cocklescanslanky years before. Apathy had long replaced my feelings of desiring verification and recognition from these people, most of whom had been little more than acquaintances. Fleeting connections. Childhood dreams.

The log of their lives, for now, seemingly paused as the world continued spinning silently in slumber.

There was only one person online – a single, solitary green circle within a sea of greyed out names. One I was not sure I could reach either.

Toni.

Chapter 33: Offer Of A Lifetime

Thinking little of it, I put down my phone on the night stand and was reaching for the mains charger that I kept, tethered at the foot of my bed, when the screen flickered instantly back into life.

'You have one new message: Toni Jones'.

I paused, still dangling over the edge of the bed, my eyes wavering over the notification. I felt somewhat dumbfounded, and my hands trembled a little as I inserted the cable and sat upright once more, swinging my legs around onto the bed like a monkey. Still confused, I flicked across the lock screen and stared at the now maximised messages tab, which had briefly shown a solitary notification. It was late, and my muddled mind wondered if this was an illusion brought on by stress and insomnia.

"Hi, are you awake?" – Toni had sent the message at **11:49 pm**.

Should I answer?

The vivid memories of how Toni had treated someone before me still burnt into my mind. Although, I had seen how she had softened slightly.

Still, it seemed rather odd to hear from her at all.

Especially given the cold manner in which she and I had parted ways. I had almost expected her to block me and sever all ties. That's how Andy always said things went when women were hurt or broken-hearted. Something he had always done, well, at least before he had got with Mia.

Thus, I asked myself *why then was she reaching out?*

Inwardly I battled a little with my emotions. Part of me felt guilty for leaving her the way I had, but it would have been crueller to string her along. Toni didn't deserve that.

I reasoned that whilst I hadn't missed every aspect of her cooking, there had been some charm in nibbling noodles together.

We had both experienced a greater degree of freedom in how we could debate the merits of modern society. This made a refreshing change of scene to discuss someone whose mind had not been corrupted by the pitfalls of my workplace.

Curiosity won out, and I replied after what felt like a few painful moments. Attempting to, the most neutral way I knew how:

"Hi," – 11:51 pm.

"Hi," – 11:52 pm.

Toni replied, somewhat automatically but in kind. Our former closeness had already reduced to the same painful small-talk one endures at a business lunch.

She was already typing again. She had always been quicker than me when she wanted to be. No doubt, wired up by acrylic paints and caffeine. *"Can't sleep?" -11.52 pm.*

"I must," -11:52 pm.

Each fragmented sentence was drawing us closer to midnight.

Part of me still longed to tell her what was on my mind. Confiding in Toni had always felt much more straightforward than what was shared with the guys at *Morses'.* Those interactions were usually reserved for superficial retorts, debates of football and lad mags. The evening's interlude with Andy had been an exception. It was never the rule.

"But?" 11:54 pm. Toni had queried into my silence, quickly followed by a string of question marks in quick succession.

I had been too vague.

Toni persisted. *"Wanna call?" - 12:01 am.*

It was an olive branch, not that I deserved one - not after I had broken her heart.

"Sorry, I can't right now."12:03 am. I replied lamely. Only too aware of how awkward it sounded.

She was disappointed. *"Oh, okay," - 12:03 am.* There was a pause.

"Is anything going on?" - 12:04 am.

I sighed.

Nothing I said would make a great deal of sense over text. The problem with such a method, especially once a proper exchange began, was that whilst it offered a fast, convenient communication method, texting lacked the critical registers of tone and intonation that came through speech.

My words were clinical and cold to an outsider, and her replies would always come in the same impersonal tone. That was just how messages worked, regardless of whether voiced from boredom or genuine concern. It all sounded the same.

Flat.

But I had already said too much.

Maybe messaging wasn't the best idea.

My insides lurched.

This was a mistake.

"Goodnight, Toni," 12:05 am.

I didn't expect an answer.

Thus, I turned off the phone, setting it down to charge again – another night of insomnia and ceiling watching ahead.

* * *

I wasn't sure the exact time I drifted off, only that I finally awoke to the screeching sound of my alarm clock. A purposefully jangling melody that forced me to move my aching muscles into action.

There were several texts on my phone. One was an automated offer for some takeaway which the rounds every so often to drum up business, a somewhat reluctant goodnight from Toni, and finally one from Mary.

Gratitude and relief flooded my lungs.

Her style was conversational. Friendly like sunshine.

"Hey Frank, all okay here, sorry I've been a bit tied up here," - *6:32 am.*

Mary was an early riser. No doubt part of her fixed routine she had established feeding Beth.

I checked the time. It was a little after 7.

Breakfast time.

"No problem," I replied, keeping my tone light. *"Is everything okay?"- 7:03 am.*

I knew better than to expect an immediate reply.

From the moment she gave birth, Mary's whole world had been her children. Love had brought her to that point, and even when the rose-tinted glasses she had once worn surrounding her former husband had begun to fade, Mary had been propelled through her maternal instinct to provide for them and give them a better life. She would always be a mother first. And I was sure that despite her internal fears, she was a good one.

I loved her even more.

Although I knew not what lay ahead for the day, my spirits lifted, and I sang a little to myself, pocketing the phone into the folds of my dressing gown. Then I fetched a cup of tea from the kitchen and began pouring a portion of cereal into one of the generously sized bowls I had at the back of my cupboard.

I was subconsciously deciding to look after myself.

I was halfway through the meal when within the thinning cotton design of my pyjamas, I felt the familiar buzz against my leg.

My phone was alerting me to its presence with a new notification.

Mary was back.

"Yes, sorry," She continued. *"I've been preparing Willy's costume for the upcoming Easter show at the Nursery."- 7:13 am.*

The explanation made me smile, and for a moment, I wanted to fob off work and join her. The prospect of craft store shopping, whilst by no means my area of expertise, the distraction - for want of a better word, would be a bright and kaleidoscopic relief against the bleak reality that would surely greet me at the *fish tank* office.

My smile faltered a little as I thought of Andy, wondering if he too had spent the night counting the cracks in the ceiling; or whether he had purposefully ignored it using Mia as a comfort or a distraction. That was, of course, if he told her at all.

I could not scold him for this; I was not ready to discuss such heavy topics with Mary. And whilst I was many things, I was not a *hypocrite*.

Dispelling the cobwebs from my mind, I focused instead on Mary.

Picturing her for a moment sat in a field of differing lengths of corrugated card, pompoms, pastel and neon coloured felt squares, and PVA glue, attempting to fix something together, whilst Willy squirmed and wriggled against her.

"It tickles!" he squealed in what seemed to be across between a protest and a giggle.

I wanted to see them.

"Dinner?"- 7:14 am. I asked. Hoping I didn't sound too forward. My hands tingled with nervous energy, the spoon clanging against the sides of the porcelain - like a makeshift percussion instrument.

"Sure, that would be nice," - 7:15 am.

My heart soared, my mood brightening a little.

Today, I would achieve euphoria.

* * *

That confidence was not to last.

The familiar sight of the fish tank returned me to reality with an uncomfortable jolt. Andy was smiling, widely, as he leaned back on his chair. He had resumed his masquerade of confidence and charisma that hid the quiet, pensive despair. "Morning, Frank," he said casually, as though he had forgotten the previous night's revelations.

I sensed deep down he wanted to.

Keeping up the pretence, I nodded back to him as I booted up the computer. "Morning."

Mike Jr. was also smiling. We didn't speak much - beyond pleasantries.

That wasn't to say he wasn't approachable, but the boss's son had a slight air of nervous energy. An eagerness to please that long surpassed his father's position, as though hoping that he might one day escape the shadow of Mike Sr's dominant personality.

"Morning," He chirruped back to us, his tie always looked rather stiff and twice ironed. Perhaps he would have been an accountant or at least an intern at the bank in another life.

We both acknowledged him again, as did Poppy, who had arrived a few minutes later; bustling past us to her desk with a large, slightly damp umbrella; and a cup of coffee shop coffee. One could always tell since her drink of choice always had a somewhat richer smell than the charcoaled sludge provided by our ageing dispenser. Today, she had worn a scarf - some turquoise and purple sausage-like thing, which hung in a stylistic knot over her cardigan.

"The *big boss* is coming today," revealed Mike in a surprise announcement.

As if in slow motion, the room stopped for our small quadrant, each staring at him as we voiced in unrehearsed unison.

"*What?!*"

Such news could never be more universally unwelcome - especially when unplanned.

FRANC HQ was based in London, the brainchild of Saville Row suited, blue-chip executives. Who acted on the desires and whims of supposedly government think tanks and surveys to try and sway the public's favour against the influx of nuisance callers that swung the balance of the national election. It was no secret that the biggest employer in the town was only within our small garden of Kent due to affordability and profits surrounding the building rent. I doubted that to anyone else, Cocklescanslanky was even on the map.

Therefore on the rare occasions that these big-shot corporate types strolled in unannounced, it was usually a sign of number crunching, uncomfortably long meetings and presentations and fake, impersonal smiles.

"Oh, goody," Poppy murmured sarcastically whilst Andy, in his usual show of dark humour, made questionable gestures, purposefully doing so within the younger man's blind spot. Not that it was *entirely* Mike's fault.

"Well, at least there will be pizza," suggested Dave, attempting a smile.

Mike nodded, following his lead and clapping his hands together. "*Yes,* see?"

"It's always cold!" Murmured Alice, who had somehow been following along up until now but had as ever remained silent. Sometimes, I admit I forgot she was even there.

Only students and hungover tricentennials like cold pizza.

The rest of us only take these offers up because it presents an opportunity to save on additional expenditures at lunch, and we cling to the vague hope that someone higher up the corporate chain has shelled out on beer for everyone.

But as usual, they hadn't

Thus, given the topic of today's double block presentations - 'Updating and modernising databases' and 'Recognising and retaining customer information.' would have been better received.

I wish I had taken a rain check and stayed in bed.

After all, who would notice me?

* * *

"Frank, *just the man!*" called out Mike Sr, patting me firmly on the back as I headed to the prepared spread of pizza and sandwiches that the girls on reception had prepared as part of the usual 'set dressing'.

I turned politely.

Beside him stood a taller man, who was long and wide like a rugby player, with a thick coat of gelled black hair and gleaming white teeth that didn't look entirely natural when he smiled. He had a herringbone suit on, the kind that usually reserved itself city life, wearing a claret coloured tie with criss-crossing, alternating diagonal lines of purple and blue on the pattern.

"Clarence Fisher," he conveyed, extending his hand. His voice oozed with a painfully nasal dialect from the city.

No doubt he thought himself charming.

I did not.

I shook it cordially.

"Frank Davis."

"Mike here was just telling me you've been here ten years! You must *feel* part of the furniture?" The grin widened.

It was a joke, I supposed. Still, I had a part to play and nodded, bristling inwardly.

"Yes, sir, I *have.*"

Clarence Fisher was one of those smarmy types; I imagined he played golf during business hours. His eyes glittered dangerously.

"You must *tell* me about it," he declared, leading me away from Mike and the food. My stomach rumbled in discontent.

It would be cold pizza for me, once again.

We walked out to the deck. It was a single elevated platform-cum-balcony usually reserved for big deals and smokers, which was a shame because it had a relatively decent view of the surrounding area - when it wasn't littered in cigarette butts and discarded rolling papers. The green, white, red, silver, pink and liquorice streamers drift like some tobacco user's confetti.

I watched the town around me; as Fisher made small talk about business acumen and projected growth. The seagulls in the car park gathered over a disposed of polystyrene container. The cluster of patrons waiting for the bus as it inched its way along the roads towards them.

Everything seemed so insignificant.

So routine.

I thus told him, as instructed about my life in the company over the past ten years, a bland microscopic view of what I thought he wanted, forgoing my feelings in a bid to seem as impersonal as possible. That was how training had always instructed us back when I was somewhat younger and more hopeful about my prospects.

It wasn't to say I was cynical now, although I longed to venture beyond the means of the fish tank and to progress up the ladder before I was 50. And as my mother so eagerly reminded me - *time was ticking on.*

"You know," Fisher continued obliviously, giving what I could only presume was one of his many rehearsed and polished speeches. "I *admire* you, Frank. You've got gumption."

Gumption. The business way of saying I had balls.

Usually, a statement such as this was used as a blanket term, signalling that the speaker was about to say something earnest, suggesting they had a degree of trust or confidence in the other. I had always associated it better with people like Andy or the staple agents in the team; the one's who bolstered results at the Christmas parties with generous hampers of port, scotch and expensive cuts of deli counter ham.

As such, I did not expect Fisher to invite me to join him anywhere, least of all London.

But for some reason, he did.

"You've been with the team a long time!" the city-slicker enthused, "And we could really use your energy in corporate,"

I stared dubiously.

"Sorry?"

"Mike speaks highly of you," He paused, seemingly for effect, as he rattled off his proposal. "We'd like you to come to London and show *them* how it's done!"

Suddenly, at least in one man's eyes, I was the *hottest* thing in customer service—a poster boy who far too neatly matched and aligned both the company and name.

But in the past few weeks, my mind and motivations had rapidly changed. *And now, I didn't want any of it.*

Chapter 34: Decisions, Decisions

Ambition is a funny thing.

One day we lust for it, grasp at it desperately, wrestling from within the folds of our bed, snatching desperately for our futures, the same way one might cling to fireflies in a jar for the hopes they will bring us light. The next, we are suddenly comfortable, and when we wake, we forget our dreams.

The obvious parallel between myself and my father, vegetating over his television, was a strange one.; although I felt somewhat contended in the looming simplicity of monotony. London was a big and yet vastly crowded space. One I was not sure I entirely fit into, especially in the world of business. I was a fish out of water.

A lot was riding on this. For both myself and the company and I asked myself without closure:

How could I answer?

I thought of my world. The one I *knew*: where, back in my cubical, the phone occasionally rang before being redirected to another available operator. Where the computer dawdled through its loading screen and screensaver, instigated during the impromptu morning of presentations. Or the plastic lunch box I had somehow prepared myself with the tuna and tomato pasta bake I had meant to eat the night before would be waiting until tomorrow and sat dormant in the fridge.

Cocklescanslanky people were by and large simple. Mary would be on *Pinterest* for makeshift costume ideas for the play, whereas Bazil would be sat in his store in *The Tank*, musing over his never-ending game of chess.

Toni would be flinging art on her canvas, and Andy and Dave would rope me into the pub for a drink or two - where we would watch the game or discuss company politics, women or other grievances.

We were not the fancy polished shoe types with tailored silk ties and Oxbridge family airs and graces. None of my world was fancy; all of it was methodical and, to some outsiders, perhaps *boring*.

But I derived comfort from this, knowing where I stood among it all.

Clarence Fisher cleared his throat with thinly veiled impatience, still wearing his all teeth smile, the same way a shark might lure its victim in. His eyes were shining with expectations. And now Mike Sr. had joined us, as though the whole discussion had been planned.

"So what do you say, Frank?" Mike asked. The two senior men reiterating their points the same way overly keen, mischievous schoolboys demand a weaker peer to do their homework. "Great career prospects, good pay, fantastic transport links. A *future*."

The twitch behind my ear was back, as I felt the sweat dripping sickly hot against the back of my neck, hidden only by the collar of my shirt, and I gulped inwardly.

Confrontation had never been my strong point, and my gaze darted away towards the panelled glass door behind them, attempting to lighten the atmosphere with some misdirection about the quality of double glazing.

Neither of them budged.

Wrangling my words and my hands, I forced out an apology. "Thank you for the opportunity; I'd like some time to think about it if *I may?*" I asked. Every part of me felt sick. Nausea threatening to overwhelm me, I looked to Mike, appealing to him silently.

The mood had changed.

My boss nodded.

"Of course, Frank, take all the time *you* need."

Without a moment's hesitation, I propelled myself back towards the main building until I was out of their direct line of sight before darting towards the bathroom, somehow grateful I hadn't consumed a slice of the lukewarm pizza beforehand.

* * *

The men's cubicles at *FRANC* always smelt of strongly squirted, cheap budget cleaning products. Partly because they were cleaned once a day, at closing time when everyone was heading home by a subcontracted, faceless individual, and because whoever occupied it often sat for a longer moment than they might otherwise. The space served as a bunker to avoid the stress and overwhelming sense of antagonism. One that greeted us on the other end of the phone.

I sat cushioned in the middle cubicle, hoping the wooden doors on either side would protect me from the seemingly impossible task of pleasing everyone. I could hear the sound of one of the taps dripping, most likely the corner one, as the stale, cold sound slid against the cheap metallic basin.

Closing my eyes, I took a deep breath pondering the future. Knowing in some ironic way that this was what Mike Sr and Cuthbert wanted me to do, albeit for their skewed reasoning's.

A year from now, I pictured Dave and Yvonne would be proud parents of newborn twins, red-faced and curly-haired boys named in some French style like Philippe and Jean-Paul. Both of whom Dave proudly placed at the fresh-hold of his desk in some slick golden frame, a wedding present from his in-laws, which he polished more vigorously than Mike Jr. knotted and re-knotted his tie. Yvonne would, of course, have wanted girls, perhaps even telling us all how "they ran in her family. In contrast, for all his bravado, Andy is nominated, godfather or guardian. It would not be long before he would be found in the pub discussing at length the ethics of how old they would need to be to start playing football.

Similarly, Mary and I would have moved in together. Both of us would have been nervous at first, but with Willy close to school age and Beth making her first tentative steps, it was the logical way forwards. I had proposed to her, after a few months of dating; surprising her on her birthday with a bouquet of daisies, in honour of the dress she had worn when we went guinea pig racing, a music box I had found at Bazil's and a ring - the sweet silver band filled with small, dainty diamonds. She had cried and nodded enthusiastically, her whole body shaking and jumping for joy.

Birthdays were not always so bad, after all.

This thought brought me back to reality with a painful bump. Engagement rings, at least elegant ones, were not cheap, although a more comprehensive selection might be readily available to me should I earn a London salary.

I sighed. The faint echo engulfed the room, which made me feel very small.

Still, the truth was I couldn't predict the future, nor the simplicity in which things might be, and my cynicism was almost sure that there would be many more sombre moments against the happiness of which my heart desperately clung.

Thus with somewhat darker acknowledgement, I thought of Andy and his mother, who was terminally ill. Andy never talked about his father, and indeed, when we had been at school together. However, admittedly he was a couple of years below me; I had only seen his mother once or twice, usually redressing him or smudging his cheek with kisses. As her condition worsened, Andy would be spending more time at the hospital than at work or drowning his sorrows at Morses'. It was sad to think of someone who had dreamed so passionately for her son's future, now confined to an impersonal hospital bed. I hoped he would confide in Mia about it rather than revert to his former womanising ways, but grief does funny things to a person's mentality.

There was also an equally troubling scenario where Toni might not get into university. No one could doubt her passion for her subject, although it had left her dispirited before. Her former love interest had thrust her into an artistic frenzy, but would this be enough to propel her to the disciplined rigour of heavily concentrated studies.

And bleakest of all, whilst it scared me to think about it, Mary's ex-husband might try to re-enter her life. The divorce had not been an easy one, and from the little I understood from her, she had married young and pregnant with Willy. I couldn't tell if the man had been abusive, and at this, my stomach churned. But, the double bolted latch she had fastened to her front door echoed unspoken truths.

All these things were equal and tangible possibilities. But for now, all I had was speculation and building blocks of hopes and dreams. Those dreams had still to be built up and now tumbled by an offer for a job I had never hoped or prepared for.

But such new-found fantasies of gleaming red AEC Routemaster London buses or broadened horizons were not for men like me - No, not for a middle-aged and close-minded cynic who sat on the closed toilet seat and blew my nose with cheap, mass-produced toilet paper from the stall, terrified of what might come. That which lay beyond the bus routes and life I knew.

At *FRANC*, we had a collective mentality: *"Just keep swimming,"* no one noticed or even cared if you were drowning. Not when they were barely keeping themselves afloat.

Looking ahead of the cubicle towards the long rectangular mirror, my blotchy red face from sweat and panic, I knew it was probably right. After all, though it had perhaps only been a few moments, no one had rammed into the bathroom seeking me out or thrown their arms around me as I cried. To do so wasn't very manly. Andy had shown me that.

But I had to move forwards.

Not least because the longer I sat, the harder it might be to regain feeling in my legs. They had a habit of cramping at times, though I didn't want to bother the doctor with my paranoia about becoming old; I pondered this for another second before reminding myself that such distractions detracted from the point.

I was better at treading water.

* * *

By the time I stepped out of the bathroom, returning to the central hub of the office, no matter how long I had stayed, I was no further forward in my decision making processes. I could hear unnatural, canned laughter - the kind that always reminds me of terrible, cheesy sitcoms or clip shows of awkwardly timed home videos.

It was one of the receptionists. Her name was Becky. She was young, petite and peroxide blonde with a face full of makeup deliberately contoured and polished for the occasion. Usually, or at least, when I passed her desk, her voice was professionally pitched, but here it was flowery and superimposed with a giggle. No doubt to impress the London reps.

I caught a glimpse of her words as I sauntered back to my desk.

"You must tell me," She had almost choked out an antidote against the backdrop of laughter, "About the time that-"

No one had noticed I had gone.

Not that in that time I wanted them to.

Someone had hastily gone around the office's mainframe, rearranging the desks where necessary to accommodate the greater number of people who would be watching the projected slide-show earlier that day. Thankfully, mine was undisturbed, and I took my seat, looking down at the flashing lights of the switchboard of callers left on hold and resigned to the forgotten abyss of out-of-tune, distorted Vivaldi's *Four Seasons*.

I took a call.

"Hi, you've reached *FRANC; my* name is Frank. How may I help you today?" I said automatically.

Somehow the perceived formalities here felt more bearable - as though distanced from reality by the phone.

"Finally!" came the exasperated reply, an older gentleman who sounded like he had called five minutes before lunch and had been caught in the system. "I'd like to register a complaint."

"Certainly, sir, please bear with me, and I'll just take a few details?" I asked.

As always, other people's problems were seemingly safer or more contained in such a way to tackle than my own. A neatly timed and welcome distraction.

It was then I noticed Alice was working too.

* * *

Alice was tucked away in her own little corner, sat with her feet folded neatly under her on the swivel chair like an owl perching on a branch. This was

246

a habit she had acquired out of convenience as she was somewhat shorter than the rest of us, even though she wore thick heeled rock boots, which I couldn't imagine were very comfortable.

Alice had her headset on, although there were no signs of life from the other side, save for her faint humming, perhaps though she were listening along to a radio station remotely via the computer.

Alice hadn't bothered staying at the meeting, diligent in her attempts to avoid the pomp and circumstance that followed with such gatherings. Largely she kept to herself, although a small paper plate on the side of her desk suggested that she had at least had, or been provided with, a slice of the complimentary pizza.

I gave her a cordial thumbs up as my client scurried around his room for a pen and paper. One Alice returned once she noticed me from the corner of her eye.

Alice had a habit of straying into her own fantasy world. A fact I certainly envied her.

She worked with a smile that radiated around the otherwise clinical space, seemingly undeterred from the world around us.

"How do you do *it?*" I asked her once my call had ended.

Alice blinked at me; she seemed somewhat surprised.

"Do *what?*" she asked shyly.

The others had started to stroll in as it neared 3 pm, Andy swearing under his breath, and I gestured at them vaguely with a raised brow.

She smiled and pressed a finger to her lips. "Check your email."

I obliged, refreshing the page just in time to see her name pop up amongst the sea of unread, unstarted, unfinished conversations.

Inside were a dozen or more pictures of cats that had been collated together for my viewing pleasure. Some were wearing silly costumes or headgear, others lounging in awkwardly unnatural poses. All of them had captions written in a cartoony, bubble font that had been selected for contrast. Something Alice later explained to me as memes. I didn't understand all of them but acknowledged each with a smile.

I made a note to show the less crude ones to Willy later. In particular, a set of cats, squishing themselves into small bowls, vases and boxes thus captioned: *If I fits, I sits.*

It felt good to laugh again. Lord knows when at work I might again.

Especially with an impossible decision looming.

Gratefully I replied to her with a picture of Mol, one I particularly liked for her seemingly relaxed nature as she perched on my shoulder watching disapproval.

But even now, I knew that mindfulness techniques and internet jokes were not enough to save me. My insides grumbled in discomfort, and I sighed again as I forced my thoughts back to the job offer.

If I accepted Fisher's proposition, relocating Mol and I would be the only viable option, but how would it affect Mary? True, I could provide for her better if I went. Still, long-distance relationships all seemed doomed to fail after the novelty wore away - something that seemed unfair when I was finally allowing myself a pocket of happiness.

Thus, the crux of the matter remained: Cocklescanslanky or London.

Home or Away.

Chapter 35: Heart Matters

Willy was colouring as I stepped over the threshold of Mary's flat. She had let me in with a brief and slightly frantic kiss on the side of my mouth before rushing back apologetically toward the kitchen, rushing around in a pair of worn-out kitten heels and a somewhat sauce-splattered apron that covered her dress. *Chaos was the norm here,* and I did not envy Mary; I already knew better than to interfere.

Instead, after laying my coat on the arm of the sofa, I bent down to Willy's level and smiled, forcing the demons of indecision from my mind. "What you drawing there, buddy?"

Willy looked up, holding up his picture proudly, where I could about recognise the vague wobbly outlines of shapes and wiggles made by his thick crayons. It was time to use my imagination.

So pausing like an art critic or one of the judges at the *Guinea Pig Games,* I studied the picture a bit more closely, scrunching my face a little, a tactic sure to amuse the boy. "Hmm," I said, pinching my voice a little, "This is the *finest* drawing of an orange I've ever seen."

Willy shook his head, giggling. "No, silly," he answered boisterously. "It's you, me, Beth and Mummy! *See?*"

The fear of the child's acceptance had always weighed heavily on me, and although I could not tell which squiggle represented each of us, I listened to him eagerly as he explained his masterpiece, which would later be pinned onto the fridge. I nodded along at intervals and offered to help him with his next project, a fire truck, which should be bright blue in his mind.

Beth was already sitting in her high-chair at the table and watched us curiously, burbling away as she entertained herself with a pink and red teething ring. I greeted her as best I could, and she blew a bubble at me with a toothless grin.

A warm, herby smell had begun to fill the room, rich with the taste of roasting meat. On the hob was home-made mash potato, golden and crispy at the edges with melted cheese. It was all very homely, and I breathed it in, my stomach rumbling loudly.

"Mummy, Frank's tummy is talking!" giggled Willy, pointing at me.

Mary smiled. "It's rude to point," she whispered softly with disapproval, but her eyes were light and mirthful.

I determined to be helpful.

"Want to help me set the table, Willy?" I asked, watching Mary for approval.

She smiled, nodding.

"Show Frank where the plates are, please?" she directed; as her son scrambled around the kitchen to one of the lower cupboards.

"In here!" He squealed, tugging at the handle.

I followed him obediently and played along. I recalled roughly where things were from Mary's and my makeshift fish and chips date, but it was reassuring that Willy trusted me and wanted to work together.

Over the next few minutes, we went back and forth to the table with cutlery, plates, bowls and a prized bottle of ketchup - which was the most essential part of the meal, at least to the mind of the toddler. He placed this carefully and proudly next to his plate and grinned, sporting a row of neatly crowned baby teeth.

Mary had prepared a feast. A medley of buttery carrots and spring greens, with roasted chicken wrapped in bacon and stuffed with rosemary, sage and thyme and the aforementioned mash potato. There was also a strawberry trifle in the fridge.

"This looks fabulous!" I told her sincerely, wondering how long she had been hard at work.

Mary beamed broadly as she settled Beth with a small plastic bowl and spoon of peach flavoured baby food before taking a seat opposite me. Willy sat on her left.

"Thank you," she flushed, her cheeks colouring slightly before deflecting. "How was work?"

I buried my frown in my napkin. There was much we would need to discuss, but I would wait until Willy and Beth were in bed, at present uncertain of the emotions that may follow.

"Oh, you know, just *busy*," I said nonchalantly, hoping she might catch my meaning.

Mary nodded, her expression more thoughtful.

Despite this, Willy was more than happy to dissipate any awkwardness, and he led the conversation between large, shovelled mouthfuls.

"Tell Mr Frank about my costume!" he begged somewhat avidly, swinging his tiny legs back and forth with a slight thud against the table.

"Please?" his mother prompted, to which he eagerly bobbed his head, looking over to her with puppy dog eyes, his teeth and lips somewhat red from the sauce.

So between the two of them, mother and son entered a duet of animated and fast-paced dialogue, telling me about the play, describing it as a nativity-like segment with the nursery and reception aged children taking on the role of various baby animals.

Willy, or so he told me, was going to be a chick and had already begun drafting out what I supposed were wing designs on a strip of unfolded cardboard from a cereal box.

"Can we cut them out later?" he asked excitedly.

"Yes, Willy, If Frank wants to!" He seemed too young to use the scissors himself, and I wondered if he had a small dwarf pair, like the ones I had used forty-odd years before. Mary nodded.

It felt comforting not to be thrown in the deep end.

"Let's finish dinner first," I suggested gently.

The youngster was more than obliging; digging deeper into the pile of mash potatoes on his plate, he offered another sincere grin. "Then pudding!"

Beth cooed in approval.

Such proceedings were much-needed light relief and all I would readily appreciate as my boat anchored on the shores of our small corner of Kent, tethered by fantastical whimsy. Jobs came and went, but I was done running. I had chosen *home*.

* * *

We made love for the first time that night.

Basked in a glow of warmth that radiated from Mary's smile and the way her hair tumbled so effortlessly down her shoulders like gold. I preferred it loose and murmured this softly into her ear, nibbling it gently in a way she seemed to like.

Mary had encouraged me to the bedroom, whispering to be silent not to wake the children. But with this motion, our senses heightened, exploring each other on her bed, intimately drawn together. Like two moths propelled towards a flame.

Mary was less experienced than Toni, but I felt closer to her since we had only been with one previous partner. Everything felt safe and new.

Outside, the clouds had gathered in an April storm, and I listened to the thunder as I held Mary closer in the aftermath of our intimacy as she drifted away to sleep. I had no desire to wake her—the turbulence mirroring my reluctant state of mind.

I was resolute in not accepting the job offer, even though I had not discussed such things directly with anyone, save my conflicted mind.

I had intended to, but the timing had not been suitable. While I watched Willy running around eagerly flapping his arms as though to prepare for his role, I concluded: I would always favour the simple promises of our small-town domesticity over the stuffy suit alternative presented by the city.

But while the storm above lingered, seemingly grumbling in discontent, it was in my best interest to sleep. I closed my eyes, clutching Mary closer as I dared so as not to hurt or wake her. She looked so delicate in her sleep, and I longed to protect her. I would hold her close and never let her go.

It would only be a few hours before the world returned to its harsh and sometimes brutal reality — one where all my insecurities and fears were muddled together against the backdrop of others like them.

Before I left the office in the evening, I had somewhat been propositioned with accepting the business card for Clarence Fisher before I went home. Its unwanted presence had burnt a hole in the pocket of my blazer jacket, with its airbrushed, glossy finish.

I imagined that he was back in the city now or at least would be in the morning, depending on whether or not the two regional representatives had decided to go to dinner before taking an early car at dawn to beat the traffic. I was somewhat glad to avoid facing that painfully fake row of sharply polished incisors.

Surprisingly though, this would not make the decision easier. Company loyalty at *FRANC* was somewhat complicated, especially when it came to the painful balance of impressing and rubbing shoulders to show our division's strengths against the submission imposed on individuals' merits and futures.

My choice would be broadcast, somewhat publicly on the phone, under hovering supervision from Mike Sr - something I somewhat dreaded. Not least for the very public manner in which he would serve my execution once he knew their imposing peer pressure would not sway me.

Mary was wearing a lilac flannel cotton pyjama set, the kind that came in a budget pack of two from the supermarket, which had a pretty recurring motif of cartoon sheep printed on the bottoms. I shivered a little, attempting to clear my mind, comforting myself with the smell of Mary's perfume scented deodorant, as I held her in my arms, reminding myself of the here and now. Even in the dark, I was soothed by the warmth of her body curled against me in the crook of my arm. She was a fidgeter, subconsciously wrestling with her own insecurities, yet they didn't quite wake her. So, kissing her on the forehead and stroking her hair away from my cheek, I subconsciously wished her sweeter dreams before drifting off a short time later.

* * *

I woke around 7 am, to the sounds of high-pitched squeals and giggles from the kitchen, and scrambled to the nearby chair to grab my somewhat folded trousers, hastily running my fingers through my thinning hair at the dresser. Mary was already dressed and had braided her hair once more, which was a shame although kept mainly out of practicality. Willy looked up at me as I entered the room, giggling slightly as his mother poured him a bowl of Cheerios.

"Hi Mr Frank," He chorused, waving his spoon from where it had previously sunk deep into the bowl, milk splashing slightly onto the table.

"Good morning," I replied somewhat sheepishly, keeping one eye on the boy's mother.

"Did you sleep well?"

The chance that he had heard us in the throws of passion the night before seemed unlikely, but his small mind was still naturally curious, and he asked.

"Why are you here for breakfast, Mr Frank?" I gulped quietly, grateful as Mary steered the inquisition away from me.

"Now, Willy, it's breakfast time, then we've got to get you to school," she directed firmly. Her eyes retained that sweet sparkle that had easily captured my heart.

I smiled at her comfortingly, forcing myself to resist the temptation to gather her into my arms once more.

Motherhood suited her, a soft matriarchal role that lacked the spite and frustrations I had observed in Marina Jones and my mother. Not that I had any illusions that this was always easy. The first bus ride in which I encountered her family proved that. By and large, her manner was calm and gently spoken, serving as a reminder rather than painful, often rebuked discipline, which Willy predominately obeyed. His acting out, as I had long suspected, had been for attention, the three of them, including the baby content in the bubble of their daily routine.

"What can I get you?" Mary asked, smiling at me.

I looked down at the table and the existing bowls already placed for each member of the Sutton family, quickly finding my place amongst it. "Cereal please?"

* * *

I determined to keep my head down as I entered the office. Somewhat clinging all I could to the positive feelings I had as I left Mary's, her kisses still lingering on my cheek from the sneak farewell she had given me when Willy's back was turned. Whistling was not my default mantra, having previously seen it as smug and conceited, especially when it had come from Andy's lips. However, today I was steadfast in my convictions to remain happy.

To do this, however, I must first address the elephant in the room, and I retrieved the business card from my pocket to find Cuthbert's details, written in cold, clinical, red letters to match the company logo.

It read: 'Cuthbert Cecil Fisher, London Managing Director for *FRANC*' on the front, followed by an email address, LinkedIn and two phone numbers on the reverse. One was mobile and the other I suspected would take me to his personal secretary at the main office.

Double then triple checking the time against my computer, watch and phone, I decided to call his direct line, knowing that it would be less painful to avoid being placed on hold.

Cuthbert Fisher picked up his phone on the second ring, his voice as it had been the previous day, clipped, self-imposed and snooty using a well-polished introduction. "Cuthbert Fisher speaking."

Pausing for a second away from the phone, I forced my voice into a professional smile. "Mr Fisher, it's Frank Davis; we met yesterday?"

"Frank, yes, of course," He deliberated slightly, rolling my name unnaturally on his tongue.

"I've considered your offer," I said, swallowing, resisting the urge to cut to the chase. Such was a vital part of the dance, something my years in customer service had taught me well.

"Yes?" the voice puckered in interest on the other end.

"And I'm afraid I will have to decline,"

Fisher was silent. I sensed he was frowning, and his voice lowered. "May I ask *why?*" he asked darkly.

He was a man who was not used to rejection.

Perhaps he hoped I might crumble under pressure.

I held my nerve, thinking about Mary.

"Mr Fisher, I'm sorry, truly I am but-"

He cut me off, impatiently resorting to a sales pitch. "Mr Davis, Frank, London would provide you with fantastic prospects, progression, growth, the expediential chance to-"

His long words were an obvious ploy.

I could see Mike Sr heading towards me; he had already marched past the reception desk. I needed to put a stop to this.

"*Goodbye*, Mr Fisher," I answered bluntly and placed down the receiver in the cradle.

"Frank, Frank!" Mike called urgently.

I took a breath and smiled once more, resolved.

"Morning, Mike."

His face paled, drenched in sweat and breathlessness, and I could see it in his eyes as though he had just heard everything.

"What did you do?"

Chapter 36: The Language Of Flowers

"I thought Mike was going to pop a blood vessel!" laughed Andy as we recollected the events of the morning. I had accepted the offer of a quick drink with the guys at the close of the day, somewhat keen to rebuild my stamina after my feat of bravery first thing that morning.

My knees knocked together slightly as though preparing for my boss to reprimand me. Something he hadn't done *yet*, though the colour had all but drained from his face as he acknowledged my behaviours, muttering under his breath about the repercussions he might face.

"I suppose," Dave mused thoughtfully, "he admires our Frank's bravery!"

I smiled wearily as my friends raised their bottles to mine with a clink of cheers. "Something *like* that, maybe."

The boys downed the beers relatively quickly whilst I paced myself, munching on the odd bar snack from a bowl of nuts I had bought to restore my equilibrium.

"I'll get another round in!" Andy said undeterred. Dave and I nodded.

A group of loud young lads egging each other on had come in, no doubt readying themselves for the *Curry and Darts* offer that had been scrawled in white chalk on the blackboard outside.

Dave hunched closer. "That wasn't very *you*, though, was it?" he asked pensively.

I blinked, surprised at his unusual display of perception. "What do you mean?"

Dave tapped his nose, careful not to hit it with his wedding ring. Occasionally drinking gifted him with confidence. "It's a girl, isn't it?"

"What?" I stammered. *"No*, you know me and Toni broke up."

"I do," he replied, taking a sip of his drink. "But I also know you fell for someone else."

I frowned a little. "Keep your voice down," I begged. "I don't want the whole town to know!"

Although our most regular drinking spot was the pub, it was also frequented by various other ghosts of the past in town. Ghosts, whose disposition worried me; that they might talk, as too much liquor made for loose lips. One such example was the town's resident drunk, a man named Boris, who regaled us all on occasion about increasingly unrealistic antidotes and shaggy dog stories seemingly without end.

"I like ale, whiskey, gin and a good pint of cider," He had told anyone who would listen as he entered *Morses'* one evening, red-faced and cap in hand, the other clutching a rather bent out of shape guitar.

"What about sherry?" asked another punter cheerfully.

"Can't stand her!" Boris had replied with a laugh, "Always tight with her waistline and her money," The older and more inebriated punters were erupting into good-spirited laughter.

Or there was Dotty, a similarly aged woman, though that could have easily been her glasses, oversized thick bifocals with green rims. She came in for Karaoke and Bingo and was always boasting about her latest catalogue purchases, even though most of us now preferred the simplicity of online shopping or that in the high street.

I also could not entirely discount Billy, Toni's hard-nosed brother. He had already taken a distinct disliking to me before his sister and I had dated. I was positive he was even less included to like me now. Nevertheless, I was grateful that he didn't frequent the bar too often, sure that my nose would not survive another beating so soon after the last.

Into the elapsing silence, Dave continued to wait for my answer expectantly. Recalling how he and Andy had acted the last time I had told them of my love life wasn't a comforting thought, but our friendship had evolved slightly through Dave's marriage dramas and Andy's kerbside confessions about his mother. Aside from Mol, the two of them were the closest I had ever had to friends. Toni had to, of course, for a time, but I doubted she would want to know I had moved on from her so quickly.

My heart burst thinking about Mary, and I smiled a little. It would be tempting to leave right now and return to her side, although I had business to attend at home, not least a guinea pig to feed. "Well?" asked Dave again. "*Who* is she?"

I blushed and looked down.

Andy was coming back with another round of drinks. Now was as good a time as any to speak my mind, even if initially it was into the cheap, mass-produced wooden table.

"Her name is Mary,"

"I knew a Mary once?" reminisced Andy. He had returned and handed out our new pints from the cheap plastic serving tray before placing it down under the table until his food came. "Tidy woman, black hair, big boobs, think she had glasses-"

"We were talking about Frank's," Dave helpfully interjected. Not that he didn't have his own motives for hearing my story to completion.

"Yes, sure," nodded Andy, turning to me. "Go on, what's she like? Where's she from?"

I took a breath. "She's from here," I continued slowly. "And she's wonderful."

Describing Mary out loud was not a simple feat. She could be described as beautiful, intelligent, kind and perfect in every single way, but that would discredit many of her other emerging talents and quirks, one's I was slowly discovering.

It was the way she looked like a goddess when she wore her hair loose, or her fantastic cooking, which quickly put my culinary skills to shame. And as such, it would be a disservice to label her as a newly divorced single mother of two, a statistic I'm sure she had uncomfortably worn since she came to the town. She was shy at first, but once you got to know her, she was bubbly and funny, creative and a breath of fresh air in what for a long time had seemed a stale existence.

Guilt could easily overwhelm me if I purposely sought to compare Toni and Mary.

Both women had caught my attention in entirely different ways. Even if I had somewhat been swept up in the heat of the moment with the former, I reasoned, had been caught in the dust of her waxy red handbag, which hit me so sharply on the head.

Mary's presence helped me to think clearly. Everything I did now was for her. Especially since she had so comfortably found a place in my heart.

Still, I told them what I could; my confidence was growing, and I found myself smiling broadly before lapsing into a comfortable silence.

"So what's you going to do tonight?" asked Andy lazily, popping a peanut into his mouth. His grammar was lacking.

Around us, the pub was more crowded than usual, especially for a week-night and the loud, raucous buzzing of voices drowned over the music from the speakers. Typically, I would have felt claustrophobic and sweaty on such comparable occasions, but somehow, everything seemed much simpler after my confession tonight.

"I'm going to get her some flowers," I suggested warmly.

"The petrol station on Magdalena Road does nice ones," Andy mused. Dave nodded.

I wondered how many times the two of them had visited it, on the need of a hasty apology for a forgotten anniversary or a token gesture of romance.

My efforts, however, were more sincere. "Daisies," I decided. "I'll get Mary some daisies. *Nice* ones!"

"Every else will be shut now, save the supermarket," Dave reasoned.

At nearly 8 pm, I hated to admit he was right. Petrol station flowers and supermarket selections weren't necessarily ugly, but they always seemed staged.

There was one other place I thought to look. When Mum was in her botanical faze, my mother had dragged Dad and me around a local garden centre.

Apparently, she was hoping for several pairs of *strong* arms to help carry the various pots and plants she decided upon back and forth to the car whilst she directed us. It made her *feel* important to see us struggle.

I did a quick check on my phone to search and retrieve their website, searching predominantly for the opening hours, as I suspected they tended to close at 5:30 or four on a Sunday. Perhaps Mary and I could make a trip of it at the weekend with the children. I made a mental note to ask her when I finished here. We could have lunch at the cafe, which promised freshly baked cake and generously filled jacket potatoes.

For now, I still needed to get home and cook for myself and Mol.

"Right," I began, clearing my throat a little, and after downing the last of my pint relatively quickly, I stood up from the booth and looked towards the door. "See you tomorrow."

"See you tomorrow," both men chorused in a slight stupor.

Unlike my peers, I was not a heavy drinker. Nor seeking solace and fortunes in the allure of a tankard.

But I understood.

Everyone has their own coping mechanisms to get them through the day.

Mine was an elegant, wholesome blonde with twinkling periwinkle eyes that reminded me of a clear blue sky: Mary Liza Talbot was my cloud nine angel.

The rest of the evening went by uneventfully; Mol and I spoke a little about the night before and the ins and outs of my latest work drama. She was happy for me, more so once I fed her some parsnip shavings as a treat, and via text, Mary and I made plans for the Saturday.

The only problem was someone else frequented the garden centre, someone whose presence I had determined to forget.

That was the force of Toni's mother - the formidable, argumentative and unbearably snooty: Ms Marina Collins.

Tonight, though I acknowledge now that it was in my temporal ignorance, I would sleep soundly.

* * *

By Saturday morning, I was grateful for the sun, which parted through its blanket of clouds the same way Mol gazed at me through her bed of hay.

261

I had risen around 6, excited to greet the day with some enthusiasm, browsing through my wardrobe to find a suitable shirt. Many of these that I possessed were faded or thick, heavy autumnal colours rather than my original linens, which were now only static, functional pieces for work. Toni had helped to a point in 'refreshing' my style, but casual, short-sleeved, slogan embellished T-shirts were more Andy's thing, and sweet, pastel shades were Dave's.

When I was younger, my father had only worn plain white, starched collar shirts that Mum bleached in a bucket once a week to "best enthuse the chemicals". I could smell it psychologically every time I went over to my parents, particularly in the downstairs cloakroom. The smell had always made me gag even though the product had long been discontinued for their less than Eco-friendly, planet-saving practices.

The other options I had remaining were also wrong. These included my suit from Dave's wedding and a rather tired, winter dressing gown that was not suitable. I wanted something that served as a friendly, semi-casual alternative without it being the Sunday best I wore when Mol and I went to the races.

After a process of elimination, I was wearing a light biscuit colour jacket, one such design I had purchased a long time ago in a summer sale. The label with the washing instructions was faded now, but given the bulk of its shape, I reasoned I would have it dry-cleaned anyway. I paired the coat with a simple pair of chinos and a denim blue shirt, which would be practical outside.

My mood was predominately positive, and I straightened in the mirror as I passed the bathroom, taking the time to loosen the top button of my shirt and adjust my hair. I was determined to make some form of effort and flossed twice, something I usually reserved to the moments before a dentist appointment. Then after feeding Mol and refreshing her water bottle, I headed out to greet the day.

* * *

"Good morning Mr Frank," waved Willy. We had agreed to gather at the bus shelter around 8:30 am. The toddler was wearing a rather large hat, no doubt to protect his fair hair and eyes from the sun, shorts and a lightweight red jumper with cactus green dinosaurs on it. His mother was wearing a sundress, a delicate pale powder blue that brought out her eyes and a string of pearls that tied together at the back, and in her arms, blinking away from her stroller, was a similarly dressed Beth sans pearls. All smiled at my approach; from where they had rested a little on the small strip of the green plastic bench, Willy was eyeing up the sloping flint and brick wall as though toying with the idea of exploring but was held firmly in the grip of his mother's hand. Since we were near the main road, he would need extra supervision and, for now, at least, less adventure for Mary's peace of mind.

"Good Morning, Willy, Mary, Beth," I called, awarding Willy with my attention, scooping down to his level. "You looking forward to the garden centre?"

Willy puffed up his chest importantly. "Yes, I am," he replied before his mother explained.

"We looked it up; they have a petting zoo corner," she said.

"I *want* to see a dragon!" Boasted Willy.

Both his mother and I laughed, and I was more than happy to play along despite her temporal look of concern.

"A dragon?" I replied, feigning panic, "*Wow*, do you think it has been scary teeth and big bulging eyes?"

Willy pulled a face in mock seriousness before giggling at the thought. "No, silly, it's a *wigwana.*"

Mary nodded, explaining. "They've been learning about iguanas and lizards at nursery."

I smiled, understanding. "Ready to go?" I relayed as I stood back at full height to examine the timetable on the shelter wall.

It wasn't long before the familiar sight of the *DONALD'S* bus approached us, the smokey beige and blue design not too dissimilar to my camel styled outfit.

The number *509* operated in two directions from the middle of town. It headed towards the coast toward the North, with its chalky row of cliffs and sand, and one could head onwards to Dover. It stopped once you got past the hustling industrial centre, which was home to the larger, industrial-styled businesses for car maintenance, ferry and shipping companies, cruise liners, and larger fishery chains. We were heading South to the more rural areas, where the grass became greener and more neatly mown, the gardens of larger, more traditional styled houses rather than the crummy, formally council-owned properties people like my parents inhabited.

They say that Kent is the *"Garden of England,"* and as we approached the Garden centre stop, I listened with some amusement to Willy as he leaned against the window to gasp at the prominent topiary figures at the entrance. These were two overly pruned hedges that had been reformed into Dolphins, perhaps to distract visitors from the car park, which bore no responsibility for theft of damages, according to a yellow brick sign hanging on the glossy green lattice fencing nearby.

Linking arms with Mary, I gave her a small squeeze and announced to my small group, "Let's go."

After a week of automated, monosyllabic, monotoned conversations at work, I would embellish and narrate each part to my little group as though we were on an African safari. I was on the lookout for daisies.

Chapter 37: Dragons

The *Earth's Bed Garden Centre* described itself on their website and an abridged version on the tannoy as "the ultimate place for the budding gardener to visit in Kent and the South East," The company had a vast selection of plants, pots, composts, seeds, bulbs, shrubs, gardening and preening tools, trees, gloves and Wellington boots at mid-range and competitive prices. I smiled a little at the intentional puns as we entered the store with its refreshing bursts of cool air and row upon row of perennials, petunias and greenery.

It was primarily undercover, save for a yard at the far end, which housed garden sculptures, water fountains, birdbaths, sheds and decking chairs. Above us, there was a helpful direction guide to the various departments, describing a brief overview of each aisle, the toilets, the cafe and finally, the checkout.

Not that we immediately needed this part.

We walked at a leisurely pace along each section, keeping one eye on Willy to ensure he was within his mother's reach and talking about the various items that caught either of our interests. Mary, rather unsurprisingly, had been very fond of gardening in her old home and told me she was looking forward to placing a few window planters on her window sill when the weather warmed a little further.

As we went around, I became increasingly aware of how many different types of flowers there were, including daisies. There were annual daisies, Corsican daisies, common English daisies, round leaf daisies, and southern daisies and painted daisies, to name a few, not to mention the colour combinations. Since childhood, the staple appearance of white petals and a sunny yellow centre was only one variety on many bright and colourful blooms, including red, purple, and pink. These were very popular with butterflies.

One hour or so later, Mary took Beth for a quick nappy change, and I took advantage of her temporal absence to consult one of the staff members. We had prepared a generous bouquet of rustic wildflowers within a few minutes. Among the bridal white Shasta daisies were a selection of vivid yellow dandelions, daffodils and sprigs of lavender. Willy watched with mild curiosity, more than willing to have something to do, rather than left impatiently waiting for his mother and little sister outside the bathroom door. I let him pick the ribbon to bind the flowers together as he assured me of her favourite colour - blue.

Both he and I watched with some mild fascination as the server carefully bound the flowers together, wrapping them in a layer of brown decorative paper, before being kept at my request behind the counter to match up with a receipt, which I concealed in my wallet for later.

It would remain a surprise for now.

"Can we go see the dragons?" asked Willy, looking up at me with a curious, coy smile.

I chuckled. It was clear that the boy had seemingly an abundance of energy and memory skills.

"Let's wait for Mummy," I promised, looking out across the shop floor in the general direction of the customer loos for the missing half of our quartet.

"'Kay," Willy replied, somewhat sullenly, before scampering over to look at the other ribbons and decorative options on the counter. The matter, temporarily forgotten.

Ten or so minutes went by before Mary and Beth returned. Mary placed her daughter back into the stroller and clipped the front buckle into place. Then plopped down the somewhat large navy blue diaper bag on the back containing the usual formula, nappies, wet wipes, toys for both children and a bottle of water for the bus, offering a small apologetic smile for their extended absence.

"The queue was manic," she explained, looking a little stressed. I had never changed a baby before, but I acknowledged that the single changing stall in the accessible toilets was not necessarily a sensible measure in a shop catered for a predominantly middle-aged and upwards community.

"Mummy," Willy piped out, quickly sensing the opportunity. "Can we go see the dragons?"

"Please?" asked Mary.

Willy screwed up his face into a large, broad smile showing two rows of small white baby teeth. "Pleeease?" he begged.

Mary looked pensive for a moment and then nodded. "Okay, we'll go to the petting zoo and then it'll be time for lunch."

"Yay!" Exclaimed the toddler, dashing forwards excitedly. His smile and laughter, carefree and genuine as he bolted away.

* * *

The so described petting zoo, or 'Animal Corner', featured a maze section of different animals, birds and tropical fish. Willy ran from cage and pen to tank after tank, dividing his attention with the usual childlike enthusiasm, occasionally stopping long enough to comment "Awww," Or "Oh," depending on his curiosity levels. Finally, he stopped at the reasonably large lizard tanks. These were rectangular glass boxes with bulky black plastic frames. Each was lit by a series of round oval-shaped lamps and filled with vast arrays of sand or pebbles, branches and fauna.

A squat, long animal with a long banded tail blinked at him disinterestedly.

"Which one?" Willy chirruped, tilting his head back at his mother and me. Mary looked to the side at the corresponding placard, previously placed by the garden centre staff.

"The bearded dragon," she told him, reciting the information and watching as his eyes widened, realising there was a dragon here.

"Tell me, tell me?" he begged.

Mary nodded.

"Bearded dragons are part of the genus *Pogona* and come from Australia. They grow to 2 feet long and eat lots of insects, such as grasshoppers and worms. They also eat leaves, fruit, vegetables and flowers."

Willy giggled, repeating his version of the Latin, replacing the word *"Pogona"* with *"Ponga,"* which was arguably funnier for a small child. Perhaps he thought this meant the poor lizard smelt funny. Not that we could tell as it was behind the glass.

My stomach rumbled a little. "Shall we have lunch?" I asked, clapping my hands.

"Yes!"

***

The garden centre's cafe was a large open plan room with indoor and outdoor seating separation. Two large French doors separated these, an effect not too dissimilar to a Victorian-style greenhouse.

Chairs and tables in sets of twos, fours and occasionally sixes were strategically placed, each made from a pale, white wood like the inside rings of a tree. We opted on eating outside for some fresh air and looked over the plastic coated menus supplied.

To his delight, Willy's menu was smaller to fit his hands and came with an activity page and a pack of six crayons; I watched as he excitedly tipped them onto the table. Red, Yellow, Blue, Green, Orange and Purple.

"Willy, what would you like to eat?" asked his mother, trying to take the abandoned menu and giving it a once over. All the food came with a portion of chips or potato smiles, baked beans and ketchup. "Fish fingers? Sausages? Chicken Nuggets?"

Her son followed her voice to look up momentarily.

"Burger," He decided, more interested in the prospect of drawing something rather than acknowledge the seemingly fancy words written in front of him.

Mary tried again, repeating the options. "Willy, would you like fish fingers, sausages, or chicken nuggets?"

The child hummed slightly to himself, mulling it over. "Nugs," he said at last.

I smiled, taking a note of this on my phone, "What would you like, Mary?" I queried.

Mary looked at the main menu, browsing the jacket potatoes, pasta, quiches, salads, sandwiches, baguettes, all-day breakfast, a soup of the day, and cakes.

I had already chosen mine, the lasagna, which came with a side of garlic bread and courtesy servings of tossed leaf salad, opting for a beer since it has passed noon.

Mary was more modest. Her eyes scanned the food and the prices, checking things over.

I comfortingly put my hand over hers, somewhat intentionally blocking the prices.

"Pick what you like," I told her. "My treat."

She frowned. "You sure?"

"*My* treat," I repeated, nodding.

"Hmm," She mused. "Jacket Potato?" she asked before looking over the fillings.

"Go on," I persisted encouragingly.

She paused, then smiled. "This is gonna sound weird-" she mused, trailing off a little as though reconsidering.

"What will?" I asked, genuinely curious.

"Could I please have a jacket potato with tuna Mayo and a cheese scone?"

I chuckled at the thought. "Of course, my lady, I'll see what I can do."

Mary scrambled with her words, already trying to justify herself, which wasn't necessary.

"I've just not had a cheese scone in a while, and well-"

I guessed like me; this was a part of her anxious personality.

"And what would you like to drink?"

"Water will be fine, thank you," she blushed, a little embarrassed.

Standing up from the table, I gave her a small kiss on the cheek and a comforting smile before heading indoors to order.

Since it was a weekend and peak serving time, there was a slight queue for those wanting to get to the central counter to order. This main console was at the back of the cafe, wrapping around the wall in an 'L' shape for its staff to safely get in and out of the kitchen space and display a wide range of cool drinks, a medley of cakes, and a large, espresso machine. The wall itself also featured a condensed version of the menu on a chalkboard, revealing today's soup of the day. 'Cream of Asparagus and mushroom,' a fitting choice for a garden centre celebrating fresh produce. Not perhaps my stomach.

This layout made it easier for the indecisive types. There was a number who continued to debate to themselves or a partner. Even though they had gone up together clear about what they wanted, it was easy to get collective amnesia - especially when it came to the cakes. All of them looked equally delicious-even if, in reality, such delicacies had been sat in the display unit since at least 6 am, if not even earlier.

I was bent down examining some of the ones on the bottom shelf when I heard a slightly exaggerated gasp of surprise and turned to find myself face to face with Toni's mother, the formidable Ms Marina Collins.

"Well," she exclaimed, somewhat recovering herself as we locked eyes involuntarily. Marina had a habit of examining people with the same disgust one might have for a piece of excrement on someone's shoe. Not that it would be hers of course. I was nevertheless relieved that Mary was safe at our table, away from the uncomfortable inspection.

"Good afternoon Ms Collins," I answered politely but gingerly as I sighed inwardly, hoping the queue would move again soon and I could escape her.

"Frank Davis, so *nice* to see you," she replied in that horrible, false tone before pushing a man closer to us from behind her in the line. "And this is my husband, Earnest."

"Ernie," The man stuttered slightly before extending a hand.

In contrast to his wife, Earnest "Ernie" Jones seemed a more grounded gentleman and not as well-groomed or airbrushed.

They seemed an odd couple with Marina's skinny cut, white jeans and golden drop-down earrings, which fastened themselves into her dyed hair. Her husband was slightly shorter and wearing a green Parka jacket and a flat cap, which made him seem more his age. I wasn't entirely sure what had brought them together or why they stayed - perhaps money had allowed the man to age comfortably and his wife expectant of ever-abundant luxuries. It was clear, however, why Toni preferred her father.

I shook it awkwardly before turning to discretely look ahead of me at the rest of the queue, where at the front, a woman was accepting her table number, a gold-painted flower pot, which contained cutlery and sauces. Time seemed to be painfully slow.

"I don't believe we've met," said Ernie. His wife pulled a face.

"Frank and Antonia *used* to date."

I wanted the ground to swallow me.

* * *

Although his smile didn't fade, the older gentleman's hand dropped away. Instead, he nodded and fixed his eyes in an intense stare as though he were an entomologist studying a rare insect. I might even have compared him to Bazil, although he lacked the regimented facial hair from a by-gone age, his hair kept short and in small cloud-like tufts at the sides of his head.

"I see," he replied, nodding as much to his wife as himself in affirmation. I worried there would be more to say and offered a small, awkward smile.

"Yes, sir. That's me," My words were meaningless and uncomfortable.

Ernie Jones said nothing.

It was difficult for us to gauge each other even or adequately. Impartially as one might otherwise in one's first impressions. From Ernie's side, he was wearing the rose-tinted glasses of a doting father, considering how I compared in the long line-up of men and boys who had failed his daughter.

Contrasting from his wife's seemingly harsh indifference to her daughter, Mr Jones carried a deep-set fear that should Toni be left alone; she might snap clean in two. Something he had thought since she was a child, even though she had long since proved herself to be perfectly strong-willed with or without her father's intervention for many years. Toni's place, though, still held like a paperweight over his heart, along with the concern he would always keep for loved ones and closest companions.

Whereas I barely knew about him. I had only heard Toni mention her father on the odd occasion. Her choice to distance herself from her parents no doubt meant that the little information that had been discussed was little more than second-hand sniping from Marina. Who I presumed had returned home resentful and bitter about my lack of hospitality during her solitary, unannounced visit.

His wife's reaction to me now was one of spite.

Time seemed to pass uncomfortably slowly, even though it had been barely a few minutes since I had crossed over from my table. It seemed so far away, like an island of tranquillity. Undoubtedly, Mary would be focusing on entertaining her children, Willy waving his coloured crayons proudly around the treasure map activity sheet, missing all the lines.

I wanted to move forwards quickly.

"Do you come to the garden centre often?" asked Marina, her eyes narrowing slightly as she followed my gaze. "I don't recall seeing you."

I attempted a brief smile and kept my words short and non-committal as I dared. "On occasion, yes."

Her reply was terse. "I see."

Thankfully the line ahead was beginning to move.

"It was *nice* seeing you," I finalised. The words escaped me cheerlessly as I moved away from the counter, determined to make no further eye contact, where possible, with my former in-laws.

My heart thudded painfully, desperate for a distraction.

Thankfully the queue had decapitated. The customer who had been in front of me had begun to walk away. I was next.

"What can I getcha?" greeted the smiling ginger cashier, whose red curls peeked through the black meshed hairnet, clashing slightly with her frog-green apron, her hands hovering on the till. Her name badge said, *Amber*.

I returned the smile, pausing for a moment to open the reminder I had scrawled on my phone, placing it in front of me as I recited each item. "One jacket potato with tuna Mayo and cheese, please."

"Side salad?"

"Please," I nodded.

Tap, tap, tap. Amber's long nails keyed the price into the register. A mint LED total flashed up on the screen.

"Anything else?"

I scrolled down on the digital notepad. "One child's chicken nuggets and chips and a lasagne with garlic bread."

"Chips for the lasagne?"

"Please,"

Tap, tap, tap. The same laborious process.

"*Anything else?*"

"One cheese scone,"

Two more taps.

"*Any* drinks?" she continued.

I nodded again. "One water, a pint of Guinness and a Fruit Shoot,"

"Ice?"

"No, thank you,"

One more tap.

"£23.97, please," Amber repeated the price displayed on the screen.

After I had paid, she passed me a large wooden tray, which had been cheaply embossed with the garden centre logo. She then began rummaging around for a set of glasses and a silver flower pot containing several sauces and condiments, a selection of generically wrapped cutlery in paper serviettes and a large wooden spoon that had been painted with black paint with the number 5.

I took them carefully, making sure to put my phone on the vacant space, awaiting further instructions in the same way I had at the cafeteria at school. Thankfully Amber knew her script.

"That'll be with you *shortly*; drinks are in that fridge over there,"

Marina was staring at me, and I shivered, hoping she wasn't eavesdropping. The glasses and flower pot wobbled with a slight clammer against the tray, still pressed awkwardly in my hands.

Quickly as I dared, I moved forwards to the fridge, grabbing a purple bottle of branded fruit squash for Willy, spring water for Mary and my beer. My temporal confrontation with the past had left me somewhat shaken, and I prayed that the liquor might calm my nerves as I returned to the table.

Mary looked up from where she had been playing with her daughter; Beth was comfortably settled in the high-chair was chewing on her teething ring. "Mr Frank!" cried out Willy keenly, wanting to show me what he'd drawn, wiggling disembodiment of lines and shapes in red and blue.

His mother smiled at me and took the bottles from the tray, and passed Willy his drink before pouring herself a glass of water. She had fine lines under her eyes from exhaustion but still looked radiant as ever.

"How long?" She asked.

"About twenty minutes, maybe thirty at most, I guess. They seem *pretty busy* today," I mused.

But it was a good thing.

I wasn't really hungry.

Chapter 38: Clearing the Air

My lasagne was hot, and I was grateful for the wad of steam that came away from the plate if only to conceal us from the prying eyes of other diners, not that the majority cared. Despite the fact, I knew it might be met with some scrutiny and disapproval, committing to Mary was something that came easily. I took her hand in mine, feeling increasingly drawn to her, relishing the sight of her sparkling, mischievous smile as she squeezed my hand gently before cutting into her newly arrived cheese scone, her knife quickly rich with butter.

I dreaded getting up in case Marina swooped in with further questions. So, to pace the meal, I determined to relax and looked over at Willy, who had begun mopping his smiling potato faces into the bean juice, giggling to himself as the golden yellow textures transformed into tomatoey, red-headed creatures. Her sharply manicured nails and eclipsed, narrow eyes reminded me of a hawk.

"You having a good day, Willy?" I asked, taking a bite of garlic bread.

Willy half nodded. He was seemingly content in his own little world. *Ignorance to the judgement of adults was surely bliss.*

"The lizards were impressive, weren't they?" encouraged his mother, nudging her son gently. "*Bigger* than the ones from school."

"And more teeth!" I exclaimed in turn, thinking back to a boy of similar age when I was young who had been passionate about dinosaurs.

I took another big bite of garlic bread and made a roaring sound posing my hands and lifting my upper body up and down like a puppet imitating a T-Rex. The boy grinned broadly, clapping.

"You're silly, Mr Frank," he chirped happily; even Beth seemed amused, letting out a mirthful giggle amongst her bubbles of drool.

This sort of sight might have once repulsed me, but I felt endeared even more to my small party of four. We looked like the secular unit of a conventional nuclear family to those who didn't know us. A thought that propelled me forwards and away from the whirling circus of my previous infatuation and fancies.

I would protect them.

That said, I knew I had to talk to Toni before her parents did because, as Hanny had warned me so ardently when I told her about Mary, "No one likes others airing their dirty laundry!"

And as I felt Marina's gaze continuing to burn into the back of my head, I knew my sister wasn't referring to mismatched socks.

I would tell her tonight, *no one* needed to get hurt.

But as I recalled with painful hindsight later, *ignorance is bliss.*

* * *

The rest of the afternoon was lovely. We continued around the store for a while before strolling out to the outdoor yard, which housed the sculpture section and other pieces of varying definitions of grand or overstated garden furniture. I took advantage of the time to host a small game of hide-and-seek with Willy, who delighted in "disappearing" for a few moments at a time between water fountains, carved wooden toadstools and ceramic gnomes.

Before leaving, I presented Mary with her custom made bouquet, and a warm fuzzy feeling fluttered in my heart as she held them lovingly to her chest and whispered a sincere, "Thank you for today," Her cheeks flushing a delicate shade of pink.

It was about 4 pm, we parted ways at the bus stop, having finished up in the shop early to avoid the last-minute shopper's rush. I had previously observed groups of shoppers, usually young couples and first-time owners, who darted through the shop looking for the reduced price spring bulbs and split bags of manure that gave them meagre savings. It was something I had always been reluctant to consider for fear of getting the boot of the car dirty. Not that I drove beyond my sister's old 1994 Ford, which had formally belonged to my father and now sat slightly rusted and neglected in their joint terraced house drive.

With a kiss on my partner's cheek and a hug to Willy and Beth, I waved the group off before walking down the hill towards the town.

Toni had agreed to meet me at *Morses',* so I grabbed a table at the back, away from the distracting squeals and lights of the slot machines, close to the pool tables. These were largely vacant, save the odd teenager who grabbed at the cues for a laugh with his mates as if to mimic the snooker on the pub's television displays, spurred on by peer pressure and alcohol.

Ordering a drink for us both, I chose Toni's usual and awaited her arrival, praying that the red wine would be seen as a peace gesture rather than end splashed like one of her paintings on my shirt.

She arrived a few minutes later, dressed in lethal-looking seven-inch mod-rock heels and a black and green striped t-shirt dress embossed with the logo of a band I hadn't heard of. Her familiar red handbag was swinging from her shoulder as she strode down the bar, looking around before coming to greet me.

"Hey,"

I nodded awkwardly.

Pleasantries seemed difficult.

My voice clipped.

"Thank you for coming, Toni,"

"Sure," she replied, looking at me seriously. "What's this about?"

It would be easy then and now to tell you I didn't hurt her. But, I apologise, for I cannot write tomes of fiction.

Because truthfully, there were many ways, kinder and more economical ways, I could have done what followed. Perhaps I might have followed the examples set by great military leaders or members of the United Nations navigating a peace treaty after the war. Great men and women who were famed for their rhetoric and diplomacy.

I was not one of them.

I should have remembered the way her heart had crumpled like a discarded paper bag when I had left her.

But again, I blurted it out, rash and unrehearsed, "I'm seeing someone, sorry!" The final word felt like a doomed afterthought from someone who has never known tact.

Toni stared. Her mouth opened before closing as she mulled over her reply like a fish.

My reflexes as a child had never been remarkable, perhaps in part to my solitary, crouched activities spent watching televised documentaries and cartoons about buses whilst playing with my sister and the guinea pig. Or as was often the case at school, where hormones and tensions rose, cowering under the desk away from the fists and tempers of older teenage boys.

Still, I was prepared to duck should the occasion arise both from Toni's brick of a handbag and the glass of wine that had hovered slightly in her hand, hoping that my prior taste of the pub's carpet had been my last.

I swallowed, my throat suddenly felt painfully dry, and I reached for my drink, rambling on. "I just thought you should hear things from me rather than someone else."

Toni, in part, mirrored my actions, sipping her wine in slow, measured sips, seemingly processing everything. I wondered if she would speak to me again.

Finally, she replied, her voice low like a whisper: "I see," Her expression became deadpan like a poorly made waxwork.

Regret and fear paralysed me, but I knew running from her would sour an already bitter meeting. I had done that before, perhaps far too often. I would let her navigate things now and watched as she leant back in her chair against the backdrop of the whirring, soaring cries of the slot machines.

Part of me wondered if her mother had already told her, not that Toni had a habit of answering or acknowledging Marina's calls.

But the silence was killing me.

"Are we *still* friends?" I asked, running my hand against the back of my head, my fingers sticking slightly with nerves and sweat.

No answer.

Then just as suddenly, Toni stood up, grabbing her bag and pulling it up her shoulder. Her eyes looked dead, conflicted with anger, rage and confusion. "I need some space," she mumbled, trying to force a wall of indifference between us the same way an angsty teenager might barricade themselves in their room. "*Okay?*"

"Yes, sure, I'm sorry, though, okay?" I asked, stepping forwards to her also. Toni was fumbling a little with the clasp of her bag to get some cash to pay for the drink.

"Leave it!" she replied, protesting, almost spitting the words and my offer to pay on her behalf away.

I sighed heavily, and Toni's eyes softened temporarily. "I hope you're *happy*, Frank," She finished with almost resolved sincerity before bolting away with freshly dripping mascara.

* * *

Despite the rather chilly encounter, I knew that I needed some air.

I stepped out, heading along the road into town.

This scene was usually picturesque and overlooked the chalky cliffs and flint walls that decorated the raised hilly pathways. There had been many a time I had walked it, subconsciously tracing the bus route from Town Centre to Dover.

I knew better than to be surprised by how Toni had reacted but still felt reluctant to go home, tossing through the turbulence of my town thoughts, and so I kept walking, taking the scenic route for a while.

Above the grey sky of dying sunlight flecked with auburn had burnt in its ashen flames, now replaced with the gradual blanket of night that cropped over the landscape, which in time would be barely recognisable.

At a nearby bus stop, there stood a group of adolescents, who between them both smelt like cough syrup and cigarettes. Neither they nor I paid each other any mind.

It had started to rain now, although I couldn't remember if it had been forecast, not that I had brought an umbrella with me.

Doing the right thing was hard, even if, for now, Toni had seemed so lost. Toni had her path towards art and university, and I had mine of work and Mol and Mary, both sides for a long time balancing precariously on a weighing scale of ever conscious decisions. Neither side would tip entirely in favour, though. I considered looking out for her on my walk but thought better of it and continued on towards home.

Part of me was still consumed by guilt.

Moving on was best for both of us.

Wasn't it?

* * *

For the next few weeks, Toni was silent.

She had not blocked my messages or my number, nor had she been online.

I thought better than to reach out and call.

Comfort and concern both rocked me to sleep, like the Devil's mistress, soothed by the radiant love of Mary.

And yet, with torment, my mind worried about Toni.

"It's only natural to care still," Mol had consoled me. We had sat once again in the twilight hours discussing together something that had, of late, become a form of group therapy. My beloved pet perched on my knee between a patchwork of hay and an old tea towel I used to protect my lap from cleaning out her cage and refreshed her water.

"Do you think she'll *still* go to university?" I asked, remembering the way Toni had laid out the prospectus and paperwork on the coffee table as if they were a Venetian fan. Everything awkwardly reminded me of her, although I reminded myself that I *was* happy.

Mol paused, mulling it over. "Everyone has their dreams."

I nodded and carefully helped her back into her cage.

Though a relatively new experience for me, breaking up with someone, I had expected to be the bad guy. But the pain and discomfort were nevertheless terrible. A brief dark thought wondered how Andy had done it, seemingly immune for many years to the girls he had deserted without a second look. Not that this was fair, especially now he was settled with Mia and focused on his mother.

Being with Mary made me cheerful in a way that made me dare to dream. Every day I spent with her was beautiful, enraptured by her selflessness, sweet kisses and home cooking.

Yet my conscience made my ear twitch. I was 40 something, it reminded me, just a *nobody*, a shabbily dressed every man with thinning, unkempt hair who thought that he would prefer not to be lonely one day.

Just way of the world, right? I asked myself.

So why did the nightmare of Toni's faded pink hair and hollowed purple eyes haunt me?

The answer stamped itself in permanent red marker capitals as an unwanted statistic across my heart.

MID-LIFE CRISIS, CONFIRMED.

Chapter 39: Facing Mortality

But whether it be mid-life or life in general, sometimes it's just not fair.
On Monday morning, I trundled into the office, smiling a little
as I propped up a generous 16 x 9 metallic frame on my desk next
to my computer. Whilst usually inconspicuous about matters of the heart, I
had been very pleased with the glossy printout I had selected at the photo
booth in town on Sunday.

The picture had been taken some time ago at the *Guinea Pig Games* but
had only recently been forwarded to me by the event's organiser. She was an
eccentric but spritely old lady named Gerti Granger who hosted the Games
every year: just as her father and father had before. Similarly, she had asked
her grandson to help her attach the photographer's albums onto the website.
A matter made slightly more complex by his hurried explanations over the
phone. Primarily because he was based in the opposite toe of the country in
Cornwall, and our chairwoman was somewhat or at least selectively deaf.

It featured the five of us, myself and Mary with the two children and Mol,
the latter of us who sat proudly on her winners' podium, preening over her
new rosette.

Willy had looked directly at the camera a few times before this final shot.
Although usually wriggling and squirming or pulling a few goofy faces, his
mother had eventually encouraged him with a reminder of the yummy ice
cream that we had passed in one of the many generously filled confectionery
stalls. His sister sat cooing obediently in her stroller - pacified from her
latest nap.

Lastly, there was Mary and me.

Although we were not a couple then, she had nestled quietly against me, choosing not to pose but enjoy the relative closeness and her quiet, unassuming, natural femininity. I loved her soft blue and daisy dress and the way her wave of golden hair slipped seemingly so effortlessly over her shoulders, complimenting my smartened ensemble of bottle-green and black accents. She had gently taken my arm and looked directly into the camera with a warm, bright smile.

Since I had made the conscious decision to remain in Cocklescanslanky, the air in the office felt decidedly heavy, the same way the smoke and tar might hang around a chain smoker. Mike Sr had taken a few days off to return the courtesy visit to the capital. I suspected he was away playing golf with Cuthbert Fisher to appease Human Relations and his high blood pressure, the fact that his son wouldn't entirely deny, despite it being merely an emailed rumour among colleagues. Albeit, not one of which I voluntarily subscribed.

Thus the order of command had defaulted to another senior staff member, a busty, wide woman named Angela with an even broader Scottish accent who had once come to the town for a holiday and stayed for the chips and ice cream. She was a woman of order and schedule, her accent clipping as she frogmarched around the office in tight-fitting heels, encouraging us to focus on the incoming phone calls and not at the clock.

"Andy's late!" Dave hissed to our small quadrant at quarter to nine, peering round with his receiver on his ear as he gestured to me to the vacant desk opposite mine.

I nodded, wondering quietly to myself whether he was with his mother. Discretely as I could, I unlocked my mobile under my desk as Angela rounded the corner, stalking with superiority and a tartan power suit. She was reciting her mantra, humming it like a doomed nursery rhyme. "Efficient workers and efficient bees make good honey, and all *are* pleased!"

The office groaned with internal despair.

Modern espionage is not entirely an easy mission; I would recall later as I attempted to text Andy discretely without breaking the momentum of office activity. Less than a decade ago, phones had buttons that made it easy to feel what we might be pressing, built into a comfortable rhythm like a typewriter. Today's smartphones, however - including the one my sister had insisted I upgrade to - were as much a guessing game of Auto-corrected code. It made the overall process seem less *intelligent* than the spy games of war.

Somehow I managed to scramble out a 'Are you OK?' before returning my phone to my pocket and resuming the never-ending database of call logs I had been assigned years before.

Half an hour later, and mid-way through a call with a depressed sounding gentleman, my phone vibrated silently in my pocket. Andy had sent a brief, terse reply. *"Fine,"*

Andy had never been a prolific texter, save the women he had previously fawned upon, but still, the message seemed uniquely stoic, as though he needn't have texted back at all.

"You *not* in today?" I wrote.

He replied with another non-committal: "No,"

I would attempt to call him during lunch or the morning break when I inadvertently would need to stretch my legs or grab a cup of lukewarm dispenser tea - whichever came first.

"Excuse me?" came the impatient simpering of my client, returning me to the present, "I have a problem with my account."

"Do you have access to the computer now, sir? I would be happy to talk you through things," I asked, keeping my tone as pleasant as I could.

There was a pause; then, the gentleman called out for his wife or carer to bring over the laptop. It was a routine I had rehearsed many times before.

I only hoped when I was older I would not be like my father, confined to a chair and television set, angry and bitter.

But at least some of us still get the luxury.

* * *

Andy updated us at lunchtime.

"I'm at the hospital," said Andy. Presumably, he had stepped outside into the car park for a smoke or some air. The sound of a passing vehicle somewhat drowned out his voice.

He had picked up after the third ring, his voice gruff but his insides trembling a little as though he had been crying, although he had determined to be tough now.

"Your mum?"

Andy swallowed. "Yeah, she's *not* good."

I thought for a moment, considering my options.

NHS Buckland ran a shuttle bus service every 20 minutes, and I could easily align at Pencester then Lambton Road if I wanted to avoid the traffic. However, the bus would also contain several elderly patrons who made their way to their daily appointments, at least a handful of whom smelt like cabbage.

Lunch was ending soon.

"Do you need me?" I asked directly.

And just like that, his wall broke, and Andy told me everything.

It was cancer, breast cancer. Already too advanced and cruel given his mother's age.

She had found a lump a few weeks ago and done what any mother might do to protect her child, not to tell him, that was until she had been admitted and some higher power had forced her hand. Genetically some people get years; some even enter remission, but others were unlucky, even if their health had previously seemed invincible.

Beyond me, I could hear the horrible, clacking sound of Angela's cheap plastic heels on the cobbled parts of the courtyard. She was raising herself onto tiptoe, attempting to see over the queue of colleagues waiting by the sandwich truck, perhaps surveying the amount of time it would take to eat and return to the endless monotony. "*Come on, come on,*" she called out impatiently. Seemingly angsty for food and time. I bared her little mind. The power had gone to her head.

On the phone, Andy hesitated in unspoken vulnerability. His tone cracked. "Please."

Adrenaline propelled me forwards, and I dashed away from the crowd and into the rain, Angela's high accented shouts of confusion and anarchy following in my wake.

* * *

Buckland Hospital had been opened in 1943, although the current site had only been open a few short years, which meant that the wards all looked the same, an impersonal white colour that cloaked the clinical, sterile room.

Mrs Jacqueline Ross was sat up, propped up by a cluster of pillows and a spindly silver railing on either side of the bed. She had been hooked up to a cannula: this dripped the chemotherapy into her veins out of a bag. It hung from a steel framework like a half-suspended balloon at her wrist.

She looked fatigued, but her eyes glittered with strange alertness. Andy was sitting on a heavy wooden chair at a diagonal angle at the foot of the bed, his head burrowed. "Andrew?" his mother quipped, shuffling her bed jacket uncomfortably over her chest. Despite everything, she was determined to have her dignity still—something I deeply admired.

Andy snapped his head up, somewhat startled, before relaxing again as he saw me.

"Frank," He whispered gratefully.

"Hey," I replied before turning to the patient and attempting a smile. "Hello Mrs Ross, it's Frank Davis."

"From the school?" She muttered listlessly. Some memories were intact. I nodded.

"Good of you to come," She replied, no longer interested. "Unlike my good for nothing husband!"

Andy frowned apologetically.

His parents had been divorced or separated for years. Mrs Ross suppressed this information.

Here Andy showed none of his usual bravado or showmanship; instead, he had dark circles and red streaks on his cheeks; a mixture of insomnia and barely suppressed tears that he furiously scrubbed away.

"Come on," "Let's get you a drink," I urged gently and gestured to the corridor where I had spotted a vending machine, hoping that we might have a chance to talk.

Andy shook his head, but I steered him towards the door, where he mumbled something about pocket change and hot chocolate.

It was important for Andy to have space to talk.

* * *

Strolling down the adjacent hospital corridor, I punched in the code for two hot chocolates, wondering whether the taste would be better or worse than that at *FRANC*. Andy said nothing, sitting somewhat numbly against the wall.

Offering him one of the polystyrene cups, I asked. "How are you holding up?"

Andy sniffed dismissively.

He had almost always shown himself as a strong, determined alpha male, as though the projection of assuredness he clung to would help his mother be strong too. However, the difference between here and the bar was the harsh reality of the situation. The sobering view of seeing her there hooked up to several wires and machines that attempted to make her comfortable, if not entirely pain-free: it was more than a soul could bear.

"Couldn't sleep, just came straight here," Andy answered, his voice low and directed at his shoes, barely acknowledging the plastic cup that I held out to him. His eyes were framed with dark circles like a raccoon, and he had a morning shadow on his chin from where he had forgone his usual morning routines.

"And Mia?" I prompted, trying to distract him from the echoed sounds of the hospital, the squeaky sounds of pattered feet of doctors, nurses, patients and visitors from differing departments, the drips and beeps from machinery. It could easily make someone feel very small. "Have you told her?"

He sighed, reluctantly shaking his head and taking a small, reluctant sip of his drink. "No," He paused, considering, "No, it would only worry her!"

"Isn't that my job?" came a rather shrill female voice, approaching us with louder, quickening footsteps at the other end of the hall.

Andy stared through her in disbelief. "Mia? How? You're here?"

His girlfriend nodded to each question, smiling a little as she reached us. "Yes, Frank *told* me to come."

Andy seemed numb as he processed this news before hastily placing his hot chocolate on the narrow window ledge nearest him and pulling her into a tight-fitting hug.

I didn't remember texting Mia. But I didn't remember much of anything.

The two remained cuddled together for a moment before Mia began a round of quick fire questions.

"Why hadn't he told her exactly what was going on? Had Andy eaten? When was the last time he had? Should she get him something 'nutritious to eat?"

Through all this, Andy mumbled almost incomprehensively.

Now Mia was here, my purpose somewhat diminished.

Peeking through the small circular windows to where Mrs Ross lay shrouded by the cobalt blue medical curtains, I was grateful she had some privacy. The hospital had a strict visitors policy of only two people, which made a lot of sense when the doctors attempted not to overwhelm the wards. Chemotherapy was often painful, especially in advanced cases where it seemed to be serving as a respite to guilty or panicked family members desperate to keep their loved ones alive, close to their former existences.

"Call me if you need anything," I promised to Andy. "I'll come straight over."

He nodded, offering me a small, nervous smile. "Thanks."

"I'll keep an eye on him," Reaffirmed Mia, giving her partner a comforting squeeze.

After all, there was no need for me to stay. I was a nobody.

Just a friend.

With my offer accepted, I picked up my hot chocolate and walked out into the main building, where I could tell it was starting to rain. It would be best to leave now and attempt to avoid the puddles from fast-acting cars and ambulances that had gathered in the adjoining depots and slots of the front-facing car park.

It was just another gloomy Monday and only **3:05 pm**.

Too early to go home.

Too late to return for the working day.

Stuck in existential limbo.

If this was the *Game of Life*, I wasn't entirely sure how to play.

Chapter 40: Uncle Frank

Thankfully the preparation for Willy's play was going well. He stood proudly beaming for his mother in a set of brightly coloured, buttercup yellow wings that fastened to his arms through generously attached loops of Velcro on the underside. They had been adorned with dozens upon dozens of yellow craft feathers and hints of gold glitter, presumably from where his little hands had attempted to help Mary in her work.

Mary had sent the photo to me in a text, thus captioned with:-

Chicken Little.

Her novel use of wordplay warmed my saddened heart, and I knew it would improve my outward journey back to the small insignificant town I called home.

Unbridled joy from my adopted stance of parenthood was not something I had previously believed I could obtain for myself. I had certainly not inherited such traits from either of my parents, who seemed to tolerate each other in their older years with increasing disparity. Beyond the odd occasion I had attended on Hanny when she had worked at the school, errands in hand, I had little direct interaction with children in my advancing years.

I admired the seemingly boundless energy that Willy displayed towards the school play. He was ready to greet the audience with his warm smile and sing- albeit an improvised version of the songs the children had been given with both enthusiasm and determination.

Thus, still half-buried in my phone, as I constructed what I hoped might be a witty reply, I didn't immediately acknowledge the world around me.

But just as I neared the large front doors of the hospital, I felt a soft bump into my chest. A gasp swiftly followed this, and as I looked up to apologise, I was met with the startled and unexpected appearance of a woman—one who looked remarkably like my sister.

"Hanny?" I asked uncertainly.

The woman did not immediately answer and had quickly looked away, but there was little mistaking the shy pink blush on her cheeks that blossomed through her ash brown hair.

"Oh, hi Frank," she murmured awkwardly, giggling a little with nervous energy.

My brow narrowed somewhat thoughtfully, "What are *you* doing at Buckland?" I said curiously. "Is everything alright?"

Instead of replying, however, my sister tugged me towards the exit, seemingly preferring to speak alone. Not that she had never been particularly good at secrets.

Out in the crisp, cool air, with the rain clouds looming, we found a partially sheltered bench and took a seat. I had hoped once here Hanny might begin to explain herself, but instead, my sister sat wringing her hands nervously, seemingly tongue-tied.

Like me, confrontation and nervousness were familial traits.

Even so, she looked uncommonly troubled, losing herself for a moment in her thoughts.

"What's wrong?" I repeated myself, prompting her to snap back to reality with some reluctance.

Thus Hanny paled and finally met my gaze, and in a small voice, she finally replied. "I'm pregnant."

* * *

It turned out that Steve, the milkman was good at delivering *more* than just milk, and my sister placed a hand delicately on her belly, which was still flat save for a small unremarkable bump that hid within the folds of her dress and jumper.

"How long?" I asked quietly as I processed my newfound status as Uncle-to-be.

Hanny smiled awkwardly. "Twelve weeks,"

This explanation was more than enough.

Hanny was at Buckland Hospital for her first ultrasound.

I considered asking her if our parents knew, but given how our mother was almost always in someone else's business, it seemed unlikely - especially since she was absent now.

Had she known, our mother would no doubt have run across the car park like an Olympian forcing apart from anyone who stood in her way to make her daughter the priority. It was probably best she didn't know, and Hanny reasoned it was *too early*. She was only getting used to this new chapter in her life herself.

Was I the first one she'd told?

Nevertheless, something still seemed off, so I directly addressed the elephant in the room.

"Where's Steve?"

My sister's already half-smile faltered. "He's at *work*," she dismissed, somewhat quietly- this was an awkward lie, one which might have seemed more believable to a stranger or a midwife, rather than someone who knew the routine movements of a milkman who delivered door to door between the hours of 4 and 8 am, not now in the afternoon. Despite what Marina Jones might say, we were too small a town for such frivolous luxuries.

Regardless, it would do me no favours to dwell on such negativity. Hanny would do better with my support, and I was not exactly the fighting type. My knuckles and my nose bruised too quickly, and my ear twitched at the thought.

Hanny's lip trembled.

"Want me to come with you?" I asked gently, pulling her slightly into a hug.

She paused, weighing up the options and then nodded, her nerves betraying her.

"Please!"

Once Hanny had composed herself, we walked back into the hospital building and the front desk. "Maternity department please?"

The receptionist smiled.

"Down the hall and to the left,"

* * *

The maternity unit had been painted a soft shade of sky blue, which I assumed was a decorative choice to promote a bubble of calm and tranquillity in the otherwise busy hospital. This space was similar to the local surgery in town, with a row of carefully spaced heavy wooden chairs and a medley of magazines for anxious mothers to be or their partners to wait.

The enormity of the situation was dawning on my sister as she gave her name. The words fumbled, awkward, and formal, which jarred with the slightly girl-like panic she tried to suppress.

But despite her efforts, Hanny was still shaking, so I squeezed her hand reassuringly a little as we took a seat.

She was safe here, I promised, and I was there with her.

Big Brother was stepping up.

We sat, facing the vacant nurses' station, positioned at a skewed angle away from the main examination rooms, for documents, filing systems and occasional cups of coffee.

Much like a community centre, there were additional larger areas for group sessions and activities. Stretching my legs, I looked at some of the classes, noting their names should I find some to help my sister or at least discover ones that Mary might later recommend. These had been listed through the cluster of brightly coloured, pastel flyers and posters on a nearby cork-board on the wall closest to us. There was *Betty's Birthing, Mum's Water Aerobics with Tina, Pregnant Pilates* and Tea and Coffee with some soft play options on a Tuesday or Thursday from 3 till 5.

"Henrietta Davis," Called a nurse in pink coloured scrubs and a cobalt blue apron carrying a clipboard. "Would you like to follow me?" She had a navy blue lanyard attached to the top, with her I.D. and credentials featured a small grainy passport-style photo.

Hanny turned to me expectantly, her large eyes pleading.

"I'm right behind you," I whispered firmly and strode up to her steering my sister up from where she had rooted herself to the floor.

The nurse took the other arm and turned to me, "And you are the father?" she asked pleasantly.

"My brother," Hanny croaked out, her voice heavy.

If the nurse seemed unsettled, she didn't show it. Instead, she guided us into one of the smaller, dimly lit examination rooms with a bed lined with disposable paper towels and a chair - usually for the spouse or birthing partner on one side and the ultrasound station and screen on the other. "My name's Sue," continued the nurse, encouraging us to our retrospective places. "If you'd just like lie on your back and get comfy, then present your stomach, please,"

Hanny nodded dazedly; it was a lot to take in. "Do I need to undress or wear a gown?" She asked.

Sue thankfully understood and was more than willing to appease her fears. "Don't worry!" She reiterated comfortingly, "The sonographer will be through shortly."

Another woman entered a moment later wearing similarly coloured scrubs. "Alright, Miss Davis, my name is Dr Yang," she told us both with a smile, taking a seat on the benched workspace and typing in a few crucial details as Hanny shyly lifted her top. "We're going to just get some ultrasound jelly on here, and then we're going to take a first look at your baby."

Sue passed Dr Yang a metallic tray with a fresh oblong tube, which reminded me a little of toothpaste if it had been invented in the Space Age. She squirted this onto my sister's exposed belly, which had been shrouded by more of the disposable paper towels.

"It's cold!" Hanny breathed, shivering a little and reaching out for me. I let her grip onto my wrist.

Dr Yang smiled. "Sorry, but it is sometimes good to break the ice when meeting for the first time," she reassured as she passed the tube back to Sue, instructing her to dim the lights before finally lifting a probe which she ran over Hanny's stomach. "Right, let's take a little look."

Hanny bit her lip in anticipation as we listened, waiting.

In a few minutes, we would see her child for the first time, something that was both awe-inspiring and terrifying, although I relished the opportunity for practice, should Mary and I be blessed with children of our own further down the line.

The sonographer ran the probe up and down before turning the screen for us both to look.

A monotoned image greeted us of what looked like a deep, dark hole and a single white blob within that looked vaguely baby-like. At around the 12-week mark, the fetus was no bigger than an inch, barely more than the size of a strawberry.

"Congratulations!" Said Dr Yang, "Your baby has completed the most critical portion of the development phase and should now start to fill out of the coming weeks of your first trimester."

Hanny's eyes welled with tears as the reality of motherhood dawned upon her fully.

"Is the baby healthy?" she asked, reaching forward towards the screen as if to stroke the small blob-like head.

Dr Yang smiled, moving the probe to sharpen the image a little. "Certainly seems to be." She promised encouragingly, "Would you both like a printout?"

Hanny beamed with joy. "Please," we said in unison; our smiles obvious as a Cheshire cat at the small, developing miracle which my sister dubbed *jelly bean*.

After a few minutes, I had my copy of the scan and proudly slid my printout of the square Polaroid into my wallet. I had decided to give the ladies some privacy so that my sister might ask any questions she had in confidence. She was learning about her due dates and any additional tests needed. I was glad not to know about the date and manner of conception. I preferred to avoid such over-familiarities with my sister and strolled out towards the waiting hall, whistling joyfully.

But before I could take a seat, seemingly from nowhere, a strong pair of arms steered me into one of the larger community halls. Directly in front of me was a 'round, bloated beach whale of a woman who was cursing loudly and gripping onto her husband's hand, for dear life and screaming. Whilst an overly perfumed, sweetened voice announced, "Welcome to *Betty's Birthing*, my name is Betty Burnose, you're in good hands here!" from a tall, thin lady in a neon pink spandex with matching eye shadow and long beach blonde hair ensemble, who had seemingly brought me here.

Panicked, I whipped my body around, looking for the doors as the woman continued her sales patter, seemingly undeterred.

"Don't be shy!" infused Betty, "All our mothers are *very* happy here, and of course, fathers are *very* welcome!" she gushed, fluttering her eyelids.

"Umm," I stuttered, aware of the grave misunderstanding. The father-to-be on the mat looked at me apologetically. No doubt he felt he too had made a mistake, although his own was a personal matter of skipping contraception. I could offer him little sympathy. "I'm not a-"

"Not sure about the *cost?*" Betty skimmed over my words as she steered me away from the rows of yoga mats where six or so women sat sweatily stretching out. Each with varying degrees of swollen stomachs, activewear and tracksuit bottoms.

"Your training will be once a week, with exercises at home, we encourage the participation of other family members and friends. It makes the baby feel *safe*."

I wasn't sure quite how much of this was true, still processing how I might have unwittingly moved from the quiet sanctuary of the maternity ward into the local zoo.

"Betty!" I pleaded, attempting once more to rectify the situation. Yet Betty had already strolled away to the front of the 'class' and clapped her hands for silence, the room suddenly darkening as a projector screen slid down the middle of the wall in front of them, subjecting everyone to Betty's *Introductory Video*.

"Welcome, I'm Betty Burnoose. You're here because you have made the *right* decision to attend my Birthing classes, providing you all the support and guidance you need to provide you and your partner with the knowledge and confidence you need to give birth and make informed decisions as a well adjusted and independent woman..." Betty's film counterpart thus reaffirmed. She looked a little younger here, as though the video had been filmed in the late 1970's or 1980's, somehow still wearing the same bright blue spandex jumpsuit.

Taking advantage of the distraction of sales brainwashing, I guided myself back towards the exit, almost sure that if I were not careful, I would fall into the trap of paying through the nose for a lucrative birthing plan, step-by-step DVD and consultation guide.

Pushing the doors as quickly as I dared, I was met by my somewhat confused sister; whilst the backdrop of the mother's to be, their nominated friends and spouses stood in a 'circle of trust', their hands joined together, they had begun collectively chanting.

"We are in our circle of trust, all of us friends, family together," A chorus that could still be heard as the doors swung closed.

"Don't go in there, Hanny!" I urged, tugging her gratefully away from their hall and back to the main space.

"It sounds like a *cult!*" my sister replied.

I chuckled at the thought. Hanny wasn't wrong.

"Come on," I confirmed, brightening at my sister's newfound pride, "I'll get you a drink from the vending machine before we go home,"

Chapter 41: A Matter of Unemployment

The following day I lost my job.

It had *not* been because I had been "particularly *bad*" as a call adviser or that I had "failed to meet a set target of calls". If anything, Mike Sr donned the phrase "*double-dip recession* which had reared its ugly head". Instead of ambitious young graduates, the pressure of employing old hands had somehow lost its appeal with the company.

All of these were tailing off as excuses, no doubt due to my decidedly brazen decision to refuse the transfer to London and Mike looking to placate Mr Cuthbert Fisher during their golf meetings.

It didn't *really* come as a surprise.

"It's not that I don't *like* you, Frank," Mike said, leaning forward from his desk, in a dishonest, feigned act of interest, "It's just I feel there's *more* for you to see in the world, and as we get older, or so I'm told, we *like* a challenge."

Angela stood behind him, taking notes of the session, a redundant HR requirement. Her eyes were glittering somewhat smugly like a hawk. The irony was not lost on me.

They were going laboriously through my work record, digging metaphorical holes in my employment history; and my self-confidence.

I had worked at *FRANC* for nearly eleven years, been promoted once, and had taken a holiday only twice in that time. Once, during a bus-spotters rally in the home-counties, arranged, acknowledged and paid for in advance. And the other, during an icy cold winter where I had been laid up in bed with the flu following an ill-advised attempt to avoid picking it up at work, had been bedridden and quarantined to prevent it from spreading around the office.

I had turned up, always on time, always punctual and always well-spoken and respectful to my peers.

"Why not *take up* buses?" Mike continued, primarily to himself. He was glancing somewhat awkwardly at my CV's interests section, a thin crumpled page of double-sided paper that had been presented to the superior before him when I had been initially accepted for my initial role. He had not joined until eight years ago during another company shuffle. *"I've been told you've got the drive."*

Despite the slight guffaw he made afterwards at his personal comedy routine, his bad pun did not amuse me.

I politely sipped from a cup of water and waited for him to get to the point. This meeting was not so much a lay-off of my services, but an ego stroke on his part, such as when the quiz game show host will hold a breathy pause to emphasise his superior knowledge of the correct answers against the contestant's answers. Angela was undoubtedly enjoying herself. We had never warmed to each other.

"Do you understand the terms of *your* dismissal?" she asked, taking over the already one-sided dialogue.

I nodded now and then, ignoring the slight dig in her words as she rallied off severance pay, holiday entitlement, notice periods and future references for employment. I was somewhat grateful that I could serve my notice at my leisure at home rather than continuing to save face in the office.

In the end, everything had come down to boxes.

There was the box cubicle where I had worked within the box-like fish-tank office and the single courtesy cardboard box that contained my desk elements. Here was my new picture frame, a plastic ruler, a company-branded mug, pencils, highlighters and pens, and a half-eaten sandwich I had made earlier that I had intended to consume for lunch and finally, my name tag, which I placed into the box. Everything else was either digital or impersonal, although my heart tinged a little with nostalgia at the now detached set of objects that had so long occupied my life.

No one had left me a card. Not that I suspected the office knew, save for the odd glance and whisper by the colleagues and friends of which I more immediately familiar.

For the last time, I walked through the thick glass doors, nodding to people I vaguely recognised, Andy, pumping his chest in a mock gladiatorial salute, perhaps referring to a show or movie in pop culture that had as usual escaped my attention.

"Thanks, Frank!" Sniped Angela. "We'll send the letter and your pay-check in the post."

Her words were already beginning to blur away.

"*Sure,*" I responded automatically.

I owed her no loyalty.

My mind briefly considered where my career might take me next. The customer care call centre was one of the largest but not the only employer in town, and given my generally strong track record, it was unlikely I would struggle for long. Part of me was even excited in a way to finding new opportunities, and maybe even a position where I might interact more directly with clients, rather than the faceless, droning monotony of phone chatter.

I could even start writing a book.

Heading down the hill towards the bus stop, I took a final parting look at the fish tank, the glass slattered building looming over the otherwise unimpressionable Kent landscape. Like any other building, it was a block of bricks and mortar that had quickly become a prison to young hearts dreams. I wouldn't miss it.

Now- bus routes permitting, I could go anywhere.

* * *

But I was still somewhat at a loss at how to spend the rest of my day. Hoisting the cardboard box of mostly stationery supplies to a more comfortable position, I debated whether to head home or back into town.

Having the better half of a weekday afternoon was a luxury I had somewhat forgotten about in the last ten or so years. Still, it did grant me the luxury of stretching my legs by taking the scenic route. Thus browsing and rediscovering my quaint little town, comprising of its unique blend of boutique and high-street shops, that Dover District Council attempted to use to appeal to the occasional tourist, whether it be the odd camper-van family or the high-expense cruise liner power couple.

Despite the evident variation in such clientele, most of the local stores, save Bazil, of course, weren't fussy. I considered whether or not I might pop in and window shop, although I felt some reluctance to appear with a collection of my personal effects and curios in the slight chance he might wish to confiscate them for his own purposes.

It was too early to go straight to the pub, something Andy and Dave had encouraged me towards in the evening as some form of an impromptu farewell party.

I could go to Hanny's to spend time with my sister but was unsure if she was ready to speak to our parents about her pregnancy, any more than I was prepared to let them know I was job seeking.

Instead, I let my feet carry me down the street past the quaint rows of houses and the sloping flint walls, taking the time to scribble ideas and casual observances into my little leather notebook. I always found joy in the blissfully mundane and used the storage box as a table or seat as my energy allowed me.

Cocklescanslanky was a total of thirty or so miles at the longest point, which made it longer if more forgettable than that of the Isle of Wight, not least because when one compared it to the long boot of Cornwall to the west. It was in many ways unremarkable, a mixture of chalky limestone that made up the slowly eroding landscape. But I had always found it beautiful and before long found myself at the vacant field where the large marques had temporarily brought the town to life not long ago. The ground still held slight sludge marks in the mud from where it had rained the day before and from trucks driving away. I recalled dog walkers sometimes came here in the summer for some social activity, but taking Mol around on a leash seemed cruel.

I could lose myself here with the cool sea air and the bed of cotton wool clouds drenched in grey ink, threatening the onset of rain. It would be best not to damper my belongings in the eventual rain shower, and I moved on.

Further on, I passed by Toni's work studio, which still tucked itself into the community hall. A few new paintings had been left to dry on the fence, each of them in her usual style of flamboyant flippancy and angry neon colours.

While Toni had not blocked me on social media, the likelihood of talking to me now seemed unlikely. Especially - whilst she rightly took time to move on from the brief romance we had had. I peered in through one of the small half windows, considering clearing the air since our last meeting. But the light was off; presumably, Toni wasn't in. My experience knew better than to look for her.

Thus in the elapsing hours, I made my way at a casual pace down to *Morses'* to reserve a booth for the evening, texting confirmation and reassurances from Andy and Dave that it would be a small gathering. I was expecting Poppy and Alice to join us and extended the invitation to Mike Jr, if only out of courtesy. It was not typical for the boy to attend outside functions with either existing or former colleagues. Andy had once told him to *"go out more"*.

"Be right with you!" called Morse, his voice somewhat muffled as though he were under or behind the bar. Presumably, he was changing a barrel or pump and hadn't looked up. I acknowledged this silently and placed my box on the counter as I waited.

The pub was somewhat quieter at this time of day; the music had been temporarily switched off, leaving only the occasional slides and rising inflexions of the slot machines. It was then I heard a giggle.

A distinct female giggle I had heard a few times before, memorising the almost precise way it snorted out the nose in an unladylike fashion.

At the other end of the bar was Toni, her lips locked in the embrace of another girl.

* * *

Toni had once described her sexuality to me as fluid and experimental, preferring a person's personality and moral attributes to their eyebrows. When we had started dating, I had accepted this wholeheartedly as part of her identity, yet now found myself somewhat uncomfortable by the invasion of her private space.

"I'll be back later, Morse," I stuttered out childishly, attempting to mask my voice, as I scolded my brain at the darkened thoughts of how such kisses compared with my own. Both of them looked happy, and seeing as I was contented with Mary, feelings for Toni - temporary though they were were not necessary even petty jealousy.

Somehow though, Toni's eyes met mine.

Dislodging herself sheepishly from her kissing partner, she whispered shyly.

"Hi, Frank."

Her shyness caught me off guard. I had observed both her acidic, sharp tongue and her sweetened demeanour, but here she seemed thoughtful as though considering my response before her own.

Clearing his throat over the temporal bubble of silence, Morse popped his head up from the bar, finally noting my appearance. "You're out of work *early*, Frank," he stated casually, as though nothing had happened.

I turned to him gratefully, nodding as I clutched subconsciously to the box. "Well, yes, about that, *they let me go*."

"What?!" Toni quizzed, frowning. She moved closer, excusing herself from the other woman temporarily as though she were going to order a drink. The unnamed companion nodded passively.

I focused on Morse neutrally, attempting to relax. "Yes, so the guys were wondering if we could have a farewell party here tonight?"

Morse tilted his head, deliberating as he scratched a small red pencil behind his head. "Two parties, hmm, let's see,"

"Two parties?" I queried curiously.

Toni nodded, interjecting. "Yes, I'm off to university in September."

"UC-?" I started, vaguely remembering.

"UCA, Canterbury, yes," she beamed earnestly. "I got in!"

303

The rest of the night blurred into hazy insignificance, fuelled by fledgling memories and alcohol.

Chapter 42: Frank – Just Frank

So here I'm sat drinking a cheap lager with a lesbian from Dover. The two of us are sitting on the cobbled wall made of rambling brick that slopes down at a jagged angle beside the flaking green paint of the bus shelter. She, with a cigarette perched between two tightly pinched fingers, held up to overtly red crimson lips. I, with a bouquet of cheap chips in greasy newspaper, that seemed like a hangover cure, once upon a time.

It is just past half one in the morning, at least that's what my phone says—awkwardly blinking with its dying battery, drained from a night of photos and future memories with loved ones and friends—serenading each other with karaoke and seemingly cheap pints of beer and ciders, that my wallet may well regret later.

If I were to try and ask where the lady was headed, the current short absent-minded bursts of cigarette stream would probably erupt, diluting into vulgar terms. That much I understand, reading between the lines from the tattoo on her upper left shoulder:-

BITE ME.

A tattoo that is covered now by her leopard-print coat and layers of shared experience.

The air is crisp, the chips soggy, and the lady is *drunk*.

Toni has never been able to hold her liquor, and her red handbag swings dangerously from her wrist as she lets out a low laugh whilst our partners scurry around calling for a taxi cab. I would have offered to car-share, but she is going the other way.

We live opposite ends of our lives and differing junctures of town. And soon, she will be gone forever, or at least till her university reading week or the Christmas holidays.

She leans back, hiccuping slightly as she lets out a loud laugh. "Fan-bloody –tastic! Is the bus not comin'?"

"Of course, it isn't," I reply, with a slight smug snort. "Toni, it's gone 1 AM!"

"But Frank," she reprimands me with a tipsy grin. "The buses always *come* in the morning, remember?"

I smile, raising the cheap lager in sentiment in a toast, as my girlfriend quickly crosses the road, waving at me to get my attention.

"Frank, come on, I've got a cab!"

"Coming, Mary," I say, attempting to heave myself upright, my posture not entirely dignified, not that there will always be nights she can call up a babysitter, especially when we have children of our own.

Toni grunts unladylike and carefree. "See ya around **wanker!**" She calls. A term that might once have caused my ear to sweat in panic at her hastily made judgement.

But we are familiar now.

We were lovers in a past life, under a fallen star.

Now friendly acquaintances, ships in the night.

"See ya, Toni," I echo after her. My words are seemingly clumsy and disorganised - the reproduction of a night of partying - glazed farewells and tomorrow's future chapters.

At this present time, I don't entirely know where I'm going, beyond the promise of someone's bed, either Mary's or my place, as we sleep off insobriety.

There are probably better ways we could spend our time, although I no longer remember them, feeling however temporarily as it might be as a teenager, love-struck and dozy.

Tomorrow I will have to start being more responsible and begin the process of job hunting and adulthood. I will put on a tie and head into the job centre as another faceless statistic buried in a sea of paperwork and application forms.

Tomorrow I will be a father figure to a small boy, listening to Willy tell me about monkeys with blue faces. I will be busy decorating a yellow onesie costume for the Easter play and discover how fish fingers taste in custard.

Tomorrow I will engage in a cup of tea and a friendly ear with my sister whilst we try to dissuade our mother from another hap-hazardous hobby.

Tomorrow I will wake up in the toilet bowl, my head pounding and my tongue on fire from a shot I never asked its name.

But *tonight*, I shall watch for a brief moment as a lesbian I once knew attempts a cartwheel on the tarmac of the ground and proudly dances to unheard music in the street as she waves me off to the taxi.

I am an average man of average build and 45 years old. An oblong face and greyish eyes framed by my round cheaply produced prescription glasses and a gradual, receding hairline of strait-laced schoolboy brown hair and no distinguishable job to speak of.

Dover is 5 miles north.

My name is Frank Samuel Davis, and you won't have heard of me.

This is my life.

About the Author

Emmalena L. Ellis lives in Hertfordshire, UK, where she collects vintage dresses and old books. She enjoys people watching from cafes and bookshops or spending time engaging in intelligent conversation with cats. A lifestyle copywriter, Emmalena dedicates the majority of her craft to writing. She was previously published for poetry as a teenager before winning the Chief Poet of *Suffolk Skalds* competition in 2016. 'Ginsterpigs' is her first venture into the world of fiction.

You can connect with me on:
- 🌐 http://www.emmalenalellis.com
- 🐦 https://twitter.com/EmmalenaLEllis
- 📘 https://www.facebook.com/emmalenalellis
- 🔗 https://www.burtonmayersbooks.com